ALSO BY MARK Z. DANIELEWSKI

House of Leaves

Only Revolutions

The Fifty Year Sword

The Familiar *(Volumes 1 – 3)*

o.
m
h
o
. e
o.

Apparel

, Johnny Truant's
f the most tender,
 writing I've ever
lucid, confused but
 playful, apologetic,
basing, cunning — a
b."

— Robert Kelly
*The New York Times
Book Review*

"The more the novel's structure
is decoded, the more lyrical
and poignant it becomes."

— Stefanie Sobelle
Bookforum

Only Revolutions

A CIRCLE

ROUND

A STONE

PRODUCTION

What can one do in this black Feast but dance?

— Etel Adnan

LES CREST RANGE

CHANGI

ROSE PITCHER

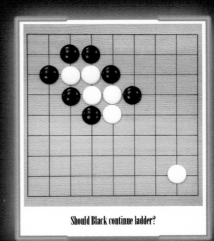

Should Black continue ladder?

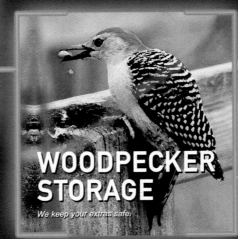

WOODPECKER
STORAGE

We keep your extras safe.

bluewhale

PANTHEON

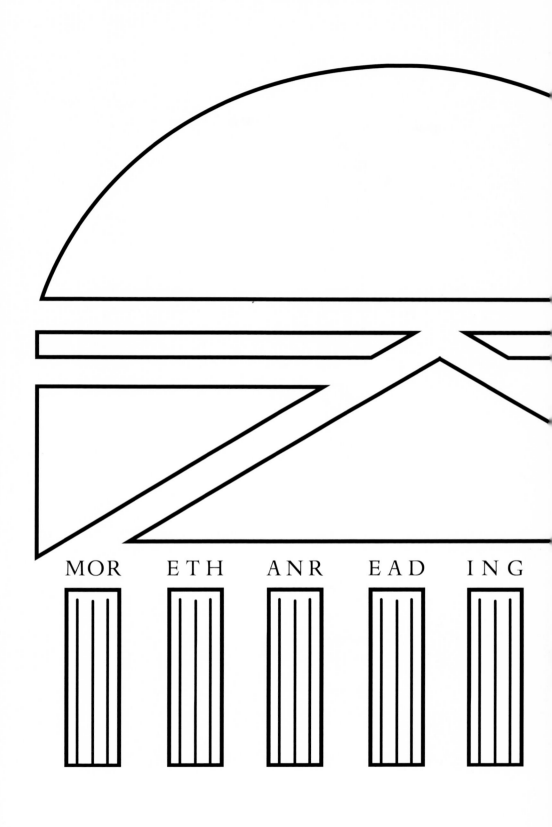

NEW THIS SEASON

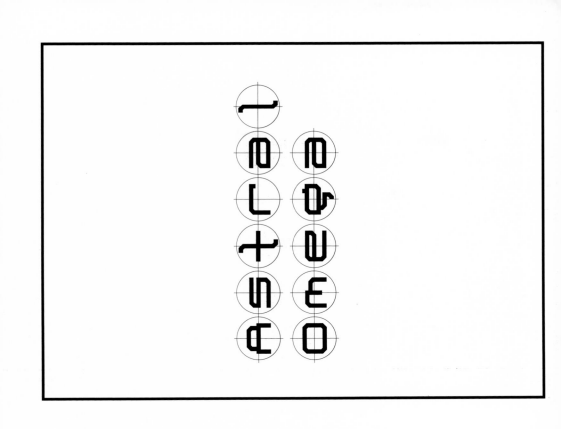

Astral Omega

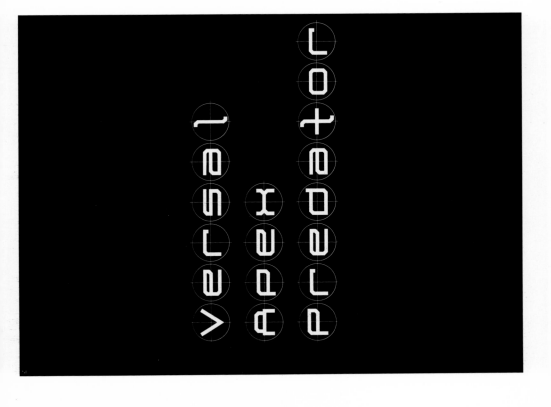

Versal Apex Predator

The H.O.L.Y. refused a Verse endlessly expanding into cold and lifeless oblivion. They refused a future where knowledge ceased to exist. A future without V.E.M.

So the H.O.L.Y. set about creating a means to revise The Verse. The expanding Verse would instead collapse in on itself, reigniting a new Verse, which would be the rebirth of the old Verse, thus preserving our history forever.

Life would survive in an infinitely recurring cycle.

This was the H.O.L.Y.'s unimpeachable cause.

By contrast, we, the D.A.R.K., offered as our cause only doubtful openness. We promised only the unknown. And we were labeled fatalists, nihilists, and fools.

The H.O.L.Y. claimed the title of S.A.V.I.O.R. They labeled us D.E.S.T.R.O.Y.E.R.

Survival, they proclaimed, was all that mattered.

Damning The Verse to perpetual determinacy was of no consequence.

Nor was the fact that with all closure comes territory.

They made it secret.

As we discovered, the H.O.L.Y. meant not only to preserve the cycle of history but to colonize it in their favor. All other I.D.E.N.T.I.T.I.E.S. would be sacrificed on behalf of the H.O.L.Y.

Whether they could really succeed was beside the point. Their belief still led to the unimaginable: writing tomorrow's path in order to rewrite the paths of the past.

All of the paths.

And so knowledge was applied to knowledge in the name of undoing knowledge's providential becoming. Even from the outset the necessary forfeiture of life was enormous, but for the H.O.L.Y. the end result — their rebeginning — always justified the cost.

None of us ever imagined that what they slaved over was intended to perfectly eradicate any sentience knowingly or unknowingly assisting in the creation and defense of any I.D.E.N.T.I.T.Y. other than the H.O.L.Y.

The H.O.L.Y. worked in silence . . . .

The H.O.L.Y. did not tolerate debate . . . .

And with so much at stake, what difference did it make if such a creation took until the end of time to finish?

The H.O.L.Y. labored into the twilight of The Verse.

The H.O.L.Y. came to know only their singular purpose.

The H.O.L.Y. came to know only this singular fate.

Until it became their only reason for being.

All meanings found in the marvels of The Verse faded.

All meanings found in the lives of others faded.

So too did love.

The H.O.L.Y. did not care. After all, their success would exceed time itself. Their success would command The Verse for eternities. Their success would be your redoing.

They called it the Versal Apex Predator.

And when the H.O.L.Y. had finished, they could only marvel at their work.

To their M.I.N.D., it was a creature of unspeakable beauty.

To ours, it was a thing of absolute horror.

To their M.I.N.D., it was the preservation of every tomorrow.

To ours, it was the death of all mystery.

To their M.I.N.D., it was hope.

To ours, tyranny.

V.E.M. 5 Alpha System
Quark Epoch 10^{-9}
Encryption 4/5

We called it Evil.

وقد جئت إليكم اليوم على قناعة اكي نبني حياة جديدة، اكي نبني... نقيم السلام...

... بل إن البعض قد تصوّرت ... أن قراري ليس إلا مناورة كلامية للاستهلاك العالمي، بل وصفه البعض بأنه موقف سياسي يخفي به نوايا في شن حرب جديدة...

جميعًا فوق ... ويجب أن نرتفع جميعًا فوق صور التعصب، وفوق خداع النفس، وفوق نظريات التفوق البالية...

For Jehan, applause is universal. Neither religion nor place matters when hundreds, by just casually pocketing air in their palms, produce a music capable of bestowing the most generous kind of human meaning.

Even on TV, even so far away, Jehan likes hearing it. How she would like to add to it too, joining the exultant, the afraid, the weary, wary too, and the angry. Always there is anger. Is that what keeps her hands knotted together now?

For an instance, the Divine Disturber of the Peace even believes life requires anger; that it is as fundamental as water, food, and the company of others — the company of that illogical rage.

And then Jehan's husband crosses to the podium. There is a smile on his lips. And like that, anger seems merely a childish demand. He is composed, he is confident, and despite the chains of his title he remains free. He takes her breath away.

The applause ends. He breathes softly into the silence.

All he has now is his voice.

But like her, Jerusalem will listen. The whole world will listen.

I come to you today on solid ground to shape a new life and to establish peace . . .

. . . I do not blame all those who received my decision with surprise and even with amazement, some gripped even by violent surprise. Still others interpreted it as political, to camouflage my intentions of launching a new war . . .

. . . We must rise above all forms of intolerance, above self-deception, and above all obsolete theories of superiority . . .

إن الأطفال الأبرياء، الذين يفتقدون إلى العناية والعطف، هم أطفالنا، على أرض العرب أو في إسرائيل.

أيها السيدات والسادة إن في حياة الأمم والشعوب لحظات، يتعين فيها على هؤلاء الذين يتفحصون بالحكمة وبوضوح الرؤية أن ينظروا إلى ما وراء الماضي، بتعقيداته ورواسبه، من أجل انطلاقة جسورة نحو آفاق جديدة.

كيف يمكن أن نحقق السلام الدائم العادل؟

In Alexandria, Faraj burns for a new war, but only the Mediterranean offers a siege of any sort, and what significance is there in these currentless slaps of tiny waves against a shore where children chase each other around the corniche?

Faraj clutches his glass of tepid tea. The charge of his thoughts brings to a boil more thoughts.

Of course, the cause is no mystery: betrayal heats. Here on this November day, on the TV, is betrayal incarnate: in thick glasses, wearing a polka-dot tie!

Ah father! Ah brothers!

Faraj half expects his tea to bubble over. But the slightly sweet liquid only grows cooler. For a moment Faraj considers spitting it out, throwing the glass at the children, but instead he swallows the truth bitterly.

If there is any solace, it is this: he is not alone.

Faraj smiles.

Might one treasonous call for unity draw into unity those needed to start the new war, the last war? Justice indeed. Power needs polarities to flow. Maybe even a polka-dot tie has gifts to offer.

Ladies and gentlemen, there are moments in the lives of nations and peoples when it is incumbent upon those known for their wisdom and clarity of vision to survey the problem, with all its complexities and vain memories, in a bold drive toward new horizons.

Innocent children who are deprived of the care and compassion of their parents are ours. They are ours, be they living on Arab or Israeli land.

How can we achieve permanent peace based on justice?

The scalpel, the needle . . . so many tools of human healing must still summon forth a drop of blood. More than a drop. From all his studies, al-Zawahiri does not know of one surgical operation which can bloodlessly effect a reparative transformation. Is a national body so different? Can its tumors and lesions find treatment without so much as a spill?

In Maadi, al-Zawahiri studies the stupid face on the old black-and-white set. He'd prefer to look at that pretty wife of his. Where is she?

Shut up old man.

Al-Zawahiri accepts no such permanence. Only sorrows never cease. Qutb, old friend, hear Nasser's heir! Jahiliyyah! Ignorance of God's guidance!

Peace with Israel!?

Where is Sayyid Imam? Al-Zawahiri will find him. He will find the rest.

Shut the old man up. Shut up.

. . . to avoid the shedding of one single drop of blood by both sides. It is for this reason that I have proclaimed my readiness to go to the farthest corner of the earth . . .

. . . and I declare it to the whole world, that we accept to live with you in permanent peace based on justice. . . .

"Where does it lead?" the student asks, and because Jabès knows her question concerns his own book of questions, he laughs thinking of how his book, in asking her, asks of her to ask him now, not about his book, but about justice and this man on the radio casting his luck upon embattled sands, broadcasting wild wishes for the mildly interested in this Montparnasse brasserie.

Paris is no Cairo. The Sorbonne no Al-Azhar. But the Modern Standard Arabic spoken by this soft-looking man recalls something Jabès cannot place now in the murmur of French hanging like uncertain weather over all of them, which includes even a cat seated in a vacant booth, intently watching the student who is already reading again, paying the news no mind.

"I will tell you the story of the donkey which dies of no longer knowing the paths of my country," she reads from his book, like a question too, Jabès thinks, but without a question mark.

Suddenly the student disappears. Paris becomes a place of smoke and moon sand. The cat is gone. Jabès will go out into the park to look for the cat no doubt observing him failing to locate the cat. That is what this brave man on the radio does to Jabès and to the gods: something strange.

وأهم من كل هذا، فإن تلك المدينة، يجب ألا تفصل عن هؤلاء الذين اختاروها مقرًا ومقامًا، فإنا يجب أن نحيي روح عمر بن الخطاب وصلاح الدين أي روح التسامح واحترام الحقوق ...

هؤلاء قرون ويدلا من إنقاذ أهلاً من إنقاذ أهلاً، فإنا يجب ... لعدة قرون الصليبية ...

أيها السيدات والسادة أن السلام ليس توقيعًا على سطور مكتوبة، بل إنه كتابة جديدة للتاريخ ...

آخر الحروب الصليبية وغاية الآلام ... بشروا أبناءكم أن ما منفى هو ...

And what could be more relevant than the sacred touch of Braille recovering memorized meanings with greater exactitude than caliber & weight, charge & velocity? Especially when compared with the profane pharaoh babbling over the speaker?

In darkness, the blind Abdel-Rahman becomes the light. And in that light, this traitor to the glory of Egypt and the soul of Islam becomes every darkness.

Abdel-Rahman lifts from each holy page the future's answer to the president's blasphemies, a future that already presides over his fall.

Second Lieutenant Khalid Islambouli disassembles the rifle, reassembles it, disassembles it again. The process of parts clears his head while the speech on the TV breaks his reason apart. The oily metal, from barrel to chamber to trigger, reintegrates through the cold prospects of fire thoughts in need of no reason.

Is here the voice of Allah already heard?

The bus lurches to a stop and they get on: soldiers on leave; infants held tight by mothers; laborers; nurses; students; the retired and unemployed. They take up room and make room for one another. They talk or gaze quietly at the traffic, which the bus must once again, with a hiss and jerk, rejoin.

... Above all, this city should not be severed from those who have made it their abode for centuries. Instead of reviving the precedent of the Crusades, we should revive the spirit of Omar Ibn al-Khattab and Saladin, namely the spirit of tolerance and respect for right ...

... Ladies and gentlemen, peace is not a mere endorsement of written lines. Rather it is a rewriting of history ...

... Ring the bells for your sons. Tell them that those wars were the last of wars and the end of sorrows ...

At the very center, Begin offers the open arms of government. He also serves as its terminus. He turns over every word that might betray an aggressor's appetite: qualities of alternate intentions; nuances of deceit.

It doesn't matter.

The man has come. November 19, 1977. Just last night, Golda had joked with him on the tarmac that if she'd known he would say yes, she would have had their enemy over years ago. Can you imagine? Golda? She was almost like a flirty schoolgirl.

Out of The Republic of Egypt, and just walked off that plane, smiling?, and maybe for a moment even shy? Or nervous? Who wouldn't be?

Greeting Dayan!

"Don't worry, Moshe. It will be all right."

Consoling us!

And then to the city he went. Without an army. With hardly a wisp of hair. Just like Begin. Less hair than Begin. To the King David. Al-Aqsa. To stand before all the Jews of the Knesset. An astonishment. Here. Before us all.

You, sorrowing mother, you, widowed wife, you, the son who lost a brother or a father; all the victims of wars, fill the air and space with recitals of peace, fill bosoms and hearts with the aspirations of peace. Make a reality that blossoms and lives. Make hope a code of conduct and endeavor . . .

. . . I have chosen to come to you with an open heart and an open mind . . . I have chosen to present to you, in your own home, the realities, devoid of any scheme or whim. Not to maneuver; or win a round, but for us to win together; the most dangerous of rounds embattled in modern history . . .

لقد جئت هنا لأبلغ الرسالة

Alone, and not alone at all, Jehan applauds like everyone else. Her hands at last unclasping. They chant his name. She won't. If he makes it home alive, she will place her hand on his chest and press her lips upon his cheek and whisper it.

I have delivered the message.

SADAT

I. Knesset

Caged Hunt

Part Four

July 31, 2014

Near ████████, Mexico

4:49 PM

"Got her!"

The rear knee explodes. Blood sprays from all sides of the joint. Then the leg collapses toward the ground but the baby giraffe still refuses to go down. Instead, it lifts its head, as if to make a sound. Only a pale foam emerges between the trembling lips. Like the hyena and baby elephant, the baby giraffe is covered with sores.

"Gonna get her again!"

It's ~~Edward~~. Jubilant, drunk, dressed in a perfectly tailored tuxedo, and now happily chambering another 100-grain round into his Ruger M77 MKII Compact rifle. There's a forward-mounted scope but ~~Edward~~ shoots from the hip.

"You suck."

Maybe ~~Landon~~ yells that. Or ~~Marjani~~. Whoever it is is right: ~~Everyone's~~ shots keep going wide, kicking up dust and clods of dirt around the teetering animal. Maybe a round nicks the mane. Finally the head lowers a little. The creature begins to lurch forward. Until a second round pulps part of a foreleg. That stops the baby giraffe cold.

"Numero three-o!"

~~Robert~~ still can't get anywhere close to the heart. The third blast gouges out part of the left flank. Now the baby giraffe begins to moan. Pale foam on the trembling lips falls away in gobs. But the baby giraffe still doesn't fall.

HD CC

"And . . . she's still standing."

Poor aim doesn't upset ~~Felton~~. He even giggles as he reloads, taking another gulp of whatever's in his plastic cup. He must really be drunk. This time when he raises his rifle, he falls over backward. Both ~~Wojcek~~ and ~~Lawler~~ laugh, though ~~Felton~~ laughs hardest, even as he scrambles back onto his feet only to fall over again.

"Taking my time, gentlemen. Taking my time."

~~Babel~~ sways back and forth. The baby giraffe also sways back and forth. Three legs sheeted in blood. More rounds slam into the surrounding dirt.

"Timber!"

So many errant shots have kicked up so much dust, it's hard to understand what's happening. Maybe a bullet did find its mark. Maybe something else stopped the baby giraffe's heart. The head stays upright for a moment longer, as if emerging from a cloud, before almost peacefully beginning to descend. As if someone had adjusted the frame rate. Until finally the baby giraffe disappears and dust is all that's left.

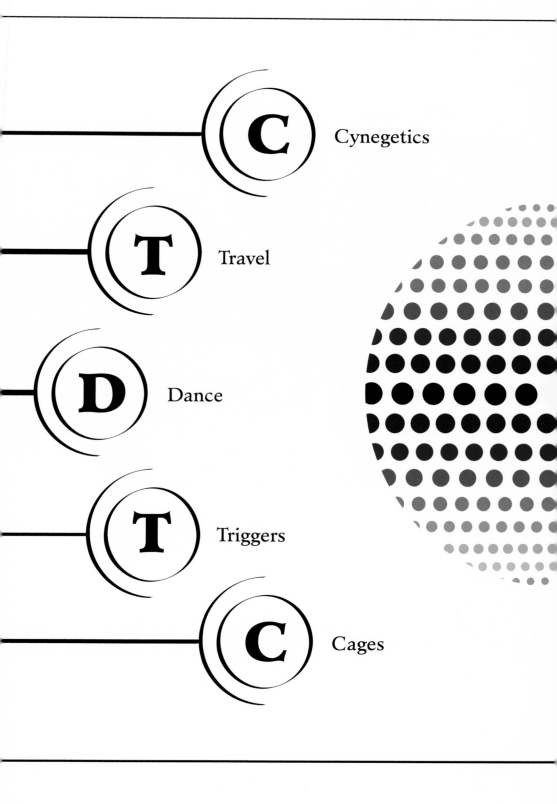

C Cynegetics

T Travel

D Dance

T Triggers

C Cages

:: Hohlenstein-Stadel-z Ivory Artifact ::

:: 29,988 years ago. ::

:: 5:13 AM. Winter. ::

:: Lonetal in Swabian Jura. Not so far from 48.549999, 10.183358. ::

:: Small fire near entrance of limestone cave. Snow surrounds. Darkness surrounds too, disclosing no hint of sunrise. ::

:: Young Man draped in thick reindeer pelts plays strange song on flute made from radius of griffon vulture. ::

:: His Father sits nearby, carving. ::

∴ What more you saw when day was not yet ended? ∵

∵ *Son continues to play birdbone flute but tune changes.* ∴

∴ Snow gave birth to snow that was not snow? ∵

∵ *Son's tune changes again.* ∴

∴ Snow that was not snow gave birth to fire? Fire for strangers? ∵

∵ *Son stops playing.* ∴ ∵ Not fire. ∴

∴ Not fire? ∵

∴ Skyfire. ∵

∷ *Father stops carving.* ∷ ∷ **Skyfire?** ∷

    ∷ ***uper-trom too.** ∷ ∷ *No bone of bird can sing thunder. Son beats fist against chest.* ∷ ∷ **Heart stop.** ∷

∷ *Father resumes carving.* ∷ ∷ **When day wakes and ours wake, we will go as many go as one.** ∷

    ∷ **May sun not come.** ∷

    ∷ **You said they were strangers. You said they were not us.** ∷

∷ *Son nods.* ∷

    ∷ **What you care if snow that is not snow that brings forth skyfire and *uper-trom ke-kami strangers, ke-kami they who are not us?** ∷

∴ Old with. Very old. Girls with. Very young. Snow not snow ke-kami old, ke-kami girls, ke-kami young, ke-kami warriors too. Strong warriors with atlatls and spears. ∴

∴ For meat. ∴

∴ *Son shakes head.* ∴ ∴ Ebhlas. Only. ∴

∴ *Father points carving stone at his head.* ∴ ∴ Only? ∴

∴ Father, you see such killing before? ∴

∴ When day wakes and ours wake, we will go as many go as one and see these strangers with no ebhlas. ∴

:: I did not see end. I ran. Maybe some strangers were for meat. ::

:: *Father puts arm around Son. Smiles. Pats Son's back. Murmurs reassurances.* ::

:: What is to be tusk you carve? :: :: *Son asks.* ::

:: Unknown. ::

:: *Son lifts flute to lips. Lowers it when Father begins speak again.* ::

:: First *wai-lewa I see I do not see *wai-lewa. :: :: *Panthera leo spelaea* ::
:: I do not see autumn coat. I see sun hunting our valley of forest and ice. First
*wai-lewa I see I do not see *wai-lewa. I do not see claws. I see slivermoons cut-
ting flesh and bone. First *wai-lewa I see I do not see *wai-lewa. I do not hear
throat-rattle roar. I hear *uper-trom that heartstop me. Fear makes me see fear.
Not what was in front. ::

∷ Is this true for all firsts? ∷

∷ First fire. ∷ ∷ *Father nods to himself. Continues to carve.* ∷ ∷ First honey-
bellow. ∷ ∷ ***Ursus spelaeus*** ∷ ∷ *Father nods to himself. Continues to carve.* ∷
∷ Moontusk. ∷ ∷ ***Mammuthus primigenius*** ∷ ∷ *Father nods to himself.* ∷ ∷ First
your mother. ∷ ∷ *Father smiles to himself. Smiles to son. Continues to carve.* ∷

∷ She *uper-trom that heartstop you? ∷

∷ She skyfire too! By just braiding bark! ∷

∷ *Father and son laugh.* ∷

∷ Fear make me see fear. Not what was in front. I see only big *wai-lewa. ∷
∷ *Son speaks to himself. Laughs at himself.* ∷

⁖ Menos to run. *wai-lewa is deadly, autumn or snow. When day wakes and ours wake, we will go as many go as one and see what your *wai-lewa left. ⁖

⁖ *Son again lifts flute. Again lowers flute.* ⁖ ⁖ Is to see fear ever to see the same as what is in front? ⁖

⁖ Yes. But that is to see a god. ⁖ ⁖ *Father stops carving.* ⁖ ⁖ Did you see a god? ⁖

⁖ *Son shakes head.* ⁖ ⁖ I saw yellow-eye fang! ⁖ ⁖ **Canis lupus** ⁖

⁖ Yellow-eye fang is good but yellow-eye fang is not a god. ⁖

⁖ I saw all fingers of both hands of yellow-eye fangs. They came after I ran. I climbed tree. ⁖

:: Menos! Menos! You will live to see god if you keep menos! ::

:: Yellow-eye fangs smelled blood of dead strangers. ::

:: Yellow-eye fangs came for meat. :: :: *Father nods.* :: :: All fingers of both hands of yellow-eye fangs can chase away even big *wai-lewa. ::

:: They stopped. ::

:: What? ::

:: Yellow-eye fangs stopped. They did not go to meat. ::

:: That is not possible. ::

∴ *Son starts to play flute again. Tune is even stranger than before. Father stops carving to study ivory in firelight and coming dawn as if seeing it in a different light.*[ε] ∵

∵ [ε]For alternate set variants of gestural translations, including alveolar clicks, numerous sibilants, bilabial fricatives, retroflex approximants, pharyngeal consonants, see 88910350-10081955-610239911190, order VI, v.26, n.13. ∴

MARK Z. DANIELEWSKI'S

THE

FAMILIAR

VOLUME 4

she's caught
doesn't head

HADES . . .

Near Little Switzerland

The trees of a surgical strike conceal a forest of tombs.

— *Grégoire Chamayou*

As much one sound
as three unanswer-
able interruptions of
silence.

Like evening clouds
drawn down into
impossible solidity.

Struck to pale still-
ness against a dark eve-
ning sky.

hisss

.: Retrace COMPLETE. :.

.: Remap COMPLETE. :.

.: Overwrite SUCCESSFUL. :.

.: TFv3 pp. 322, 453, 837. :.

.: Peace. :.

Yet despite their tremendous speed — what already holds their constancy in the before as well as in this enduring now, as if to keep rendering them forever static — Cas still remembers their drawing, knowing all along that the buzzing that forewarned what followed next was all his.

The buzzing hadn't even
made much sense. It was
just too late for what
a bright afternoon
would have eas-
ily explained: a
drill, chainsaw, or
maybe a wood
chipper.

Then the puffy
lines hissed in
from different
directions, like
ziplines of child-
less ruin strung
down from some
high bluff, where
there was no bluff,
toward where there were
children, crashing through
the garage and living-room
windows —

— already a bloom of flame, still illuminating Eisa's home from within, keeping it whole for an instant in the arms of light before splinters of glass, wood siding, and shingles start littering the street.

"Fuck," whispers the anonymisty kid, known now as Rafael, a young
man in his midtwenties who just hoisted
Cas on his shoulders, trying his best
to outsprint the bellow of that
growing inferno, that tower
of dark smoke.

The run isn't free.
Rafael's   gaunt,
his breathing is
too quick and
keeps shallow-
ing. He can't
stop shaking,
face beading
with   sweat
that   refuses
to   fall.   He
leads the way
to his motorcy-
cle. The shakes
worsen when he
hands Bobby the
keys.   Bobby   was
thrown just as hard to
the pavement, yet man-
aged to keep up with Rafael,
and he is neither gaunt nor out
of breath. Granted, he didn't carry Cas.
He places a palm on Rafael's back as the kid starts   to throw up.

Thanks to a song and an error, Rafael can throw up. The song was finally heard, fortunately, though the error went unsolved: speakers checked and rechecked, mute off, volume up, preferences thrown out, a restart, and still, despite a green bar pulsing with acoustic certainty on a console robust enough to handle the menace of Recluse, audio output stayed at zero.

Cas and Bobby agreed to follow Rafael out to his little hatchback.

"Sounds better in a car anyway."

And it had sounded pretty good.

And then they were stepping out of the car. And there was that buzzing, Cas answering its initial strangeness with another something sensible: the aftereffects of loud. Because what kid doesn't want to play his song loud? Something he had recorded with his band. A cover of "I Won't Let You Down" ∴ *OK Go* ∴. Something Marnie would have liked.

And then the gray bits of sky arrived, followed an instant later by more sounds slamming them to the ground.

> *BANG!*
>> *BANG!*
>>> *BANG!*

Not even. Beyond the range of any syllable, let alone three, let alone the pronouncement of even this one, ripping apart and fusing what must exceed cohesion, if cohesion depends on such loss.

Rafael helps Bobby start the motorcycle. The helmets fit poorly but at
least they will cover their faces. Rafael helps   Cas
through the pain as she climbs   on
behind Bobby. She carries
just one thing, and she
settles it, in its canvas pouch, against
Bobby's   back,
perhaps   as
much a com-
fort to him
as it is for
her a woe-
ful   preg-
n a n c y ,
w h e r e
stillborn
g r i e f
bests   the
b l e a k e r
births   the
Orb so often
scries. Because
no matter how
fast Bobby drives,
or how far — toward
borders they are both
too old to believe matter,
whether municipal or national
— no delineation is strong enough to   divide
the world enough from itself to evade this thing.

It's not long before Cas slips a hand beneath the covering cashmere if just to touch the black glass. She shuts her eyes, imagining what she hasn't for so long now dared to call forth. And as more miles slip by, she gives in to two hands. Bobby barks at her to hold him tight.

> *Whatever night we think we share,*
> *night is the keeper of our private dares . . .*

Every so often, police cars and fire trucks race by, heading in the opposite direction, no doubt on the way to Asheville, all lights flashing. Two hands on the Orb makes more sense than on Bobby. Cas can set the detonation sequence without looking. If it comes to that. Then she and Bobby can follow Eisa. No amount of eyes shut will undo the sight of those three weaponized lines puncturing Eisa's place of warmth. They were all in the house. The children too.

Near Little Switzerland ∴ **226-A** ∴, a police car comes up behind and passes them. Well over the speed limit. Disappearing around a bend. Lights darkening the night with another aftermath of colored brightness. Whatever wrong direction it was chasing, at least it's gone.

Until Bobby takes that bend too.

The police car blocks both lanes. Another car with it. Whatever Bobby tries to do next, stopping, trying to turn around, only to discover two more cars coming up behind, Cas answers the trap with the controlled twitch of her fingers, snapping the Orb to life, the familiar static prompting her for what will be the end they knew was always waiting for them.

But Bobby reaches back for her. It's either him or the Orb. Cas pulls free of the static and squeezes his hand.

Not unexpectedly, the
police lights turn
off. Bobby kills
the motorcy-
cle's head-
light. Cas'
eyes take
t h e i r
t i m e
adjust-
ing to
t h e
d a r k -
n e s s
u n t i l

approach-
ing footsteps
are the merest
distance away.
At least the Orb is
crackling again beneath
her hands. The gas left in the
tank will add to the blast.

"We're with you," the black child whispers.

"Stay with her," Bobby orders. Cas isn't even sure who he's talking to as he dismounts and strides toward the approaching officers.

"Sam!" one officer cries and instead of reaching for his holster gives Bobby a hug.

"We saw you and Hailey were having a little trouble. Thought you could use some assistance."

Sam? Hailey? We? Even "saw" sparks warnings. The little girl, though, who hasn't moved a bit, probably just as terrified as Cas, keeps Cas from further dancing the Orb's glass.

"We all thought we'd lost you," the girl finally sputters.

"What's your name?"

But the girl just shakes her head. "I'm not supposed to answer that. And you're not supposed to tell me yours."

"Then what's that on your shoulder?" Cas asks. It looks like some sort of stuffed animal, pale, just peeking out from behind a black braid.

"Really?" The toe of her pink Converse starting to tap the road. "How can *you* not know that?"

Bobby returns before she can pursue an explanation. He is surrounded
by Tennessee and Kentucky officers,   all of them smiling just
as broadly. Not that Cas'   as broadly.
nervousness sub-
sides. Even later,
when   she's
s e a t e d
comfort-
a b l y
on   a
large
sofa

inside
the back
of a semi
with air-con-
ditioning strong
enough to justify a
blanket over her knees
and some hot chocolate too, with   whipped cream.

The officers are gone, along with Rafael's motorcycle and that curious young girl.

"We are not alone," Bobby keeps saying to reassure her and probably reassure himself. And whether or not that assessment deserves their confidence, it is accurate.

More than a dozen strangers keep circling them now, bringing drinks, magazines, pointing out the working toilet in back.

"Do you want more privacy?"

"We can arrange for more privacy."

"Do you want today's paper?"

"Do you want to hear the news?"

"Do you want to sleep?"

No one's voice rises above a whisper. Everyone is respectful. For the most part they keep to themselves, huddled in small groups, perched on folding chairs. Though glances keep stealing Cas' way. Those looks that Cas catches reward her with an embarrassed smile, a hurried retreat back to friends' conversations, once or twice even a blush.

Is it the Orb? Long since put back to sleep, rewrapped in the cashmere
sweater, returned to   its pouch, and now held tight against
her belly.   Or is it something else?

                                Whatever   fuels
                                their curiosity,
                              Cas has the
                              odd sensa-
                              tion that
                              this   is
                              what it
                              f e e l s
                              l i k e
                              to be

                              famous.
                            It's not a
                            good   feel-
                            ing. It keeps
                        Cas from ask-
                  ing someone where
            they're heading, for fear
that   their   disappointment over the fact
that Cas doesn't know   will make Cas disappointed in herself.

Cas thinks of the little girl with braids and pink Converse. She was definitely disappointed.

At least she could be disappointed. What about Eisa? Her children? Everyone else in that house. Trying to close her eyes against what the imagination designs doesn't help. And anyway, the nearest group keeps assailing Cas' ears with possible causes for the explosion.

> "Drone attack."

> "On U.S. territory?"

> "Do you think these people care?"

> "If it's in U.S. territory they have to care. The legislative branch will care. The judicial branch will care. The executive branch will care."

Disagreement grows from there.

> "RPGs would work just as well."

At least this suggestion moves away from the question of presidential authority — whether too great or too ineffectual. Cas tries then to come up with an aggregated viewpoint only to realize that Democrats *and* Republicans are here, both the militia-minded *and* Quakers. It's the only bright news, even if it sheds no more light on the attack.

When they finally stop, dawn has spread its gray ash beyond a black
canopy of leaves.　　　Everyone hustles out from the back of the
semi under an awning lead-
ing into a gas station. The
truck stays as long as it
takes to refuel and
unload the sofa
and chairs.

An　　hour
later, Cas
is　inside
a　　van
t r y i n g
to sleep.
Bobby's
s h o u l-
d　e　r
m a k e s
for　　a
lousy pil-
low, but it's
the　　pillow
she loves most.

The next time they
stop, it's beneath an
immense tent.

For a moment, Cas thinks she's been kidnapped by zealous evangelists. In fact, it turns out to be a meeting ground for the Pentecostal Church of Christ Our Savior, with a Tuesday gathering commencing at noon.

"We'll be long gone by then," assures a young man with a beard as thick as lazy tornadoes. There's nothing malicious about his pale green eyes either, or his goofy smile, but something about that "we'll" suggests to Cas that maybe this escape is all a ruse and she and Bobby are already under Recluse's control.

The strong coffee Bobby finds for her helps staunch such suspicions. His steady hands on her back help the most.

"We are not alone," he says again, but Cas wants to be alone.

Now she is surrounded by at least two hundred strangers, a big enough crowd to grant them a collective license to stare as much as they want.

They even applauded when she first got off the van.

"The good news," Bobby sighs, as he moves on to massaging her arms, "is that no one doubts now that we're at war. A few people I've already talked to think Gettysburg is the perfect place to fight."

Cas snorts.

"I agree," Bobby laughs. "We'll find the right place."

"If we try to fight him like that, Bobby, on his terms, in the open, we'll be slaughtered."

"I know that."

"Do you think it's possible he thinks we're dead?" The closest thing to a wish Cas has voiced in some time. Practically wistful.

"That's what everyone's hoping."

Though does Cas' question conceal another wish, just as wistful? Her hands even go deep into the canvas pouch, fingertips grazing the respondent glass, again the least of the Orb's powers.

considering

Fortunately, breakfast draws Cas toward more immediate necessities: cold orange juice and waffles, all laid out on various picnic tables.

In any case, Recluse would have to be close to her. If it came to that.

All of the regional newspapers mention the fire. Asheville's *Citizen-Times* headlines the explosion but reports that the number of fatalities is as of yet undetermined. No national paper carries the story.

While reconsidering scrambled Egg Beaters served with vegan bacon bits, Cas learns that online interest has started to trend.

The first hour is all about the mysterious explosion. The second hour circulates an estimated body count: four with identities unknown.

In the third hour, various sources confirm that the cause was a bomb. By 11 AM, as Bobby and Cas are helped into a Jeep Liberty, speculation on Twitter is that domestic terrorists mistakenly set off an explosive device they were in the process of building.

Cas asks their driver to turn on the radio. The news is not about Asheville but about a lioness that escaped its enclosure outside Los Angeles and came across a little girl.

"Damn," Bobby murmurs. "Poor child."

"Poor parents,"
Cas murmurs
back.

Same cage

Be careful what you start.

— *Anonymous*

Bad enough this terrorism in North Carolina. But Shnorhk switch radio to worse. Patil groan, cover face. Shnorhk can't turn off radio fast enough.

This is wonderful start. First terrorists and fire. Then out of this fire-frying pan into just fire. Story of little girl. Little girl! And lion?

"No lion around here," Shnorhk try reassure Patil.

"But didn't they say it escaped?" Patil asks, maybe with little recovering smile too when Shnorhk doesn't return to radio. Switches to CD.

Let Mnatsagan and boys play. Sad but not sad news.

Anyway, escape is impossible.

No escaping here.

"To where?" Patil persists, looking too, with sunglasses off, as if lion make it this far west to the beach, the surf, the impossible sea horizon. "Maybe the hills?"

But where never matters. Just one cage finding another. Maybe wider. Maybe bigger. Still cage. All of it. With horizons for bars.

"Maybe our hills? Maybe Glendale?" But Patil is winking. Shnorhk snort. Why not lion in Glendale? Shnorhk even laugh.

"Since when did you get a cat?" Patil ask then, studying Shnorhk's ceramic addition on dashboard.

For some reason, her question anger him, tightens grip on wheel, accelerates cab.

Shnorhk thinks of their closet. The new stink there. What clots his lungs at home. This Patil's new friend. ∴ **TFv3 pp. 502–503.** ∴

Bring that up.

Out with it now.

Leave nothing out.

Instead Shnorhk tells story. Short story. Taxi slows. Grip eases grip on little history. What passenger had left behind. What Shnorhk will keep safe until he comes back.

Patil touches thing. "Does it have a name?"

"Maneki neko," Shnorhk explain. "But that not name. Just name of the thing. Not a cat. See? Smell? It is clear here. Here I can breathe."

Shnorhk couldn't resist. Patil, though, does.

"How is this air feeling?"

It was Patil's idea to drive up coast. Spend day close to sea.

"Good," Shnorhk admits.

"Շատ լավ," Patil answers, if little smile is going. "Ուրախ եմ քո համար:"

Clear day too.

And bright.

Together sea and sky are sharp like . . . Shnorhk doesn't know what is like such sharp. Just sharp. Waves though are soft. Out-of-focus tumbles Shnorhk can hear beyond engine and traffic.

Such soft air.

Clean and warm.

Feels good in Shnorhk's chest. Eases ache there, where sharpness waits, sharpness Shnorhk knows by heart. Pain is another kind of cage reminder.

Shnorhk, for Patil, swallows cough now, along with all spitting, coming from such hacks. What rips up his chest. Tearing eyes too. What sometimes makes him pull over.

"I've seen Mnatsagan a lot," Shnorhk say instead.

"Oh?" Patil can't hide this second smile.

"I help him with computers and storage. We scan his work. Ship boxes of old testimony."

Patil doesn't need to ask about what testimony. ∴ **TFv1 pp. 409, 412; TFv2 p. 678; TFv3 p. 357, etc.** ∴

"He is a saint," she confirms.

Stupid Shnorhk. Shnorhk completely forgot. Sometimes remembering what you need to forget forgets what you need to remember.

"There's something in glove box for you. From Mr. Saint."

"Chocolate Monkey?"

"Tea."

"Հաճելի հոտ է դալի:" She opens tin and inhales. Makes Shnorhk smell too. She's right. It is inviting.

"Mnatsagan wants me to play again. He is serious. He doesn't stop."

Patil says nothing. Does nothing. Not even adjust seat belt. Patil knows better. Patil just waits.

"I consider." Shnorhk finally admits. "Maybe I say yes."

"Yes," Patil repeats in way that sounds like her own confession.

And then Patil touches him. Touches Shnorhk's arm. Just light touch. Fingertips only.

Not so bad.

Tolerable.

"You haven't played since—"

Bad.

Intolerable.

Maybe Patil not know anything. This wife. This woman. Maybe she know not even nothing.

At least Shnorhk's glare ends her stupid thought. Patil stops with her touch too.

No touch is best.

No touch is endurable.

"I'm so sorry," Patil speak to her lap. "I promised. Անվերջ խոստանում ենք իրար, հարցը առաջ չէինք բերի: Ներողություն: Sometimes I can't help myself."

Shnorhk pats her knee.

He must do something.

If sniffling start now, or sorrying like Mnatsagan, then Shnorhk not know where to run.

Horizon of bars reminds him that running is useless. Every escape finds the same cage with same gate and same invincible lock.

But Patil doesn't start sniffling.

Patil stops sorrying too.

Maybe she even enjoys Shnorhk's pats.

Shnorhk feel bad for not doing this touch more.

Stops pats at once.

Shnorhk bad for not doing more. After all that Patil endures. Each of her breaths. Her trembles. Not even with the hope and lie of endless horizon to open her heart.

She deserves pats.

Many pats.

More than pats.

Patil deserves caresses.

But what about Shnorhk?

What does Shnorhk deserve?

Does not that matter too?

It does not matter.

Why is there no escaping here?

Why does Shnorhk feel like he's
going backward?

Patil holds handkerchief to his mouth. Shnorhk drives and coughs.

Lucky that PCH has much traffic now. Going is slow. Shnorhk not need to pull over. He can cough and cough with one foot on brake.

After Malibu Pier, coughing stops. Traffic fades.

They pass Zuma.

They pass Trancas.

They pass El Matador.

They don't stop. Only gaze
ahead or watch rippled sea, foamy
waves turning up gold sand.

Next time Patil reaches out, she touches ceramic cat instead. Tenderly. Like ceramic might soften.

Shnorhk pats her knee again. Takes her hand.

Patil glows.

Then Shnorhk tell long story.

Japanese businessman. Driving back to airport. Homeless man. Shopping cart with billowing bags and abandoned cat. Buying back for $27.27. Buying super glue.

Shnorhk not stop there either. Keeps talking. Keeps going back. For still longer stories.

The accident. Dwight Plaguer, USC student, good student, witness, friend, very best friend. Grady Vennerød, officer, very worst, who hurt Shnorhk, who ran red, who told court that Shnorhk ran red. In this court where there was no good student, no very best friend, no witness to stop this lie.

Traffic school is joke, a waste of time Shnorhk have to waste time on for fear of losing license, losing job. For fear that the world is nothing but bad cops and bad students and bad schools. And there is just where the fears begin.

None of those can compare to Shnorhk's biggest fear of playing, because of what all that playing will force him to remember.

Again.

And again.

And again and again . . .

Agains that never stop, worse than bars and lock, delivering him to a grave where death is forbidden.

Which Shnorhk not actually say. Stops before saying anything even close.

Patil, though, knows this stop. Knows to let Shnorhk keep this stop. Squeezes his hand.

Dear Patil.

To give birth so late in life and love so much in life and lose everything that makes of life life.

"A cat!" Patil suddenly cries, with smile too, for two, for three, for more. "Strange! Here in your cab sits a cat. At home, there comes a cat. Maybe they are the same cat?"

"What you mean same?" Shnorhk snort. Glad for subject changed.

"Have you ever had a cat?" Patil ask.

"No."

"Me neither."

"So?"

"The last thing she wanted was a cat."

"*Ar*— She said this to you?"

Shnorhk has no such memory.

"Now five years later, suddenly a cat visits my windowsill. Suddenly a cat waves on your dashboard."

"And?"

Patil smiles and hers is such a soft beautiful smile, smile for the world.

"Mnatsagan is right. The time has come for you to breathe. The time has come for you to play."

Forget the key

I play all of them . . .

— *John Coltrane*

Calling it der katzenjammer in his head isn't helping. But his head keeps doing just that. Der kater too. For short. As if a hangover by any other name might not be a hangover at all.

Everything keeps swimming bleary. Olympic Station glass is no exception. The scorching midday sun keeps lighting up the many smears and streaks on the large panes. Supposedly four years and never a clean. Four years and still counting. Özgür's not sure who to blame: the architects who designed a municipal building requiring a team of licensed window washers or the city that fired those window washers in the budget crunch of 2010. Özgür half wishes Captain Cardinal will order him to go get a squeegee. It would beat flogging these uncleared.

But Captain Cardinal isn't around. Homicide and Narcotics desks are empty. The whole floor is except for a few detectives milling around Juveniles and MAC ∴ Major Assault Crimes ∴, about to get lunch. They ask Özgür to join them. It's one of those bad ideas that sounds like a good idea. These days Özgür's full of them.

Cardinal meets them by the Korean food truck. Case in point. At least the shit show on the captain's radar isn't dirty windows or even Özgür. Today is all about San Bernardino.

The D-I called Perry has pictures on his phone. Broken bones emerging from the bloody carcass don't do Özgür's food any favors. Like the body, Özgür leaves his kimchi quesadilla half eaten.

Cardinal laughs.

"Losing your edge, Oz?"

"Proof we're in the jungle," Perry adds, though without relish. He's getting married in the fall.

The D-I named Carter asks Oz if he can have the rest of his food. Carter's not only an eater, he's one of those guys who's metabolically lucky. Has a waist like a high school sprinter.

"A kid was there. I don't need to hear about the kid," Carter says. Carter works Juveniles.

"The lion is still loose," Perry tells Carter.

"That's Berdoo's ∴ San Bernardino's ∴ problem."

"Unless that lioness makes it west of the 710. Then she's our problem."

"Sixty miles?" Carter smirks. "I don't think so."

"*Was* it a lioness?" Perry asks the captain.

Captain Cardinal knows the story. He knows lions can claim territory over a hundred-mile square. He even knows one of the animal experts dispatched this morning to the scene.

Özgür thinks of Marvin D'Organidrelle aka Android. If only the dates played. According to Cardinal, the lioness was captured in Texas earlier this month. Too bad Marvin was killed back in June. Even if it was on the loose back then, no way such a creature could make sense of those distances. Still Özgür smiles. For a moment it was a fun idea.

"Looks like Oz likes big pussy," Carter says, but he's not looking at Oz. There's a girl at the pickup window paying for a plate of calamari tacos. A shatter of blond hair in a bright green twist, tossed up like a horse's tail. She has on a yellow top over a turquoise bra. Her shoulders are back like a dancer, hips open, one knee up, toe on the sidewalk. Must be a dancer.

"Not a face for a cover but a bod fit for a pole," Carter leers. Özgür considers punching Carter in the face.

Perry shakes his head. "And Carter wonders why he's single."

"Or still a D-I," Cardinal jabs.

"Ow!" Perry laughs.

"Seduction, Carter, that's what it takes," their captain continues. "Whether with a girl you meet or at some job interview."

"Huh," Carter responds, but he takes it in stride. Orders another quesadilla. "I always thought it was the opposite. You know a seduction should be like a job interview. You want to know what the benefits are. When's time off. How many vacation days you get. Is there e-mail monitoring?"

Punch lines beat punching any day, if someone's laughing.

And they're all laughing.

That night, while waiting for Elaine ∴ at Little Sister∴ ∴ **523 West 7th Street, Los Angeles, CA 90017**∴, Özgür gets annoyed with himself for getting angry at Carter. Carter's just the funny guy. He's that guy. Anything for a line, and even a line doesn't matter all that much. Though whatever one he used on the girl at the taco truck got her smiling enough to give him her number.

Özgür even gets annoyed that he took so long to notice the scars on Carter's face. Maybe he was slipping? Some kind of plaque moving in on his mind. What else was he missing?

After twenty minutes, Özgür orders a bottle of red. A nice pinot. ∴ *Mi Sueño. 2010.* ∴

"Open it," he tells the server. Winces at once at the edge in his voice. The first glass doesn't help out that edge either. Just whets it. Fuck appetite. Fortunate or not, the rest of the bottle does wonders for his appetite. Even if the food he needs is not on this menu.

Outside the restaurant, he gets Elaine on the phone. She's close. About to park. He tells her to keep driving. He tells her to go away. He fights.

The fight lasts an hour. Then another hour. Then the fight softens, the apologies sink in. Elaine says she'll drive back downtown. But Özgür is so insulted that she'd been driving away this whole time, he hangs up.

Next is nothing special. ∴ ████████████ ∷ ∷ **316 West 2nd Street, Los Angeles, CA 90012** ∴ Is there a pirate theme here? Something nautical? At least Chet Baker lays to rest the necessity of a theme.

Özgür sets his phone facedown on a bar with enough varnish to approach glass. If only glass could glow this soft. The way his phone keeps lighting up makes him drink more. When his phone stops, he drinks harder.

Özgür's age is heading for a highway speed limit but he's acting like a college kid. He doesn't deserve Elaine. Take the girl by the wall. She's perfect. Maybe out of college if she went to college. White as a bar of motel soap. Enough piercings she looks like she wouldn't mind another. Torn jeans. Dead Kennedys t-shirt. A beat-to-shit Apple Air painting her face blue, painting the beer in her hand black and blue.

But suddenly she stretches. Maybe at the sight of being sighted. Maybe not minding the speed limit passing her by. One long left arm, fingers curling, as if around a willow branch, a branch she wants to gently draw down, until all of her is bending, so much so she's the tree too, bent, beautifully, aching just to be let go.

Wednesday morning's hangover isn't that bad, which is a bad sign, given how much Özgür drank. Another bottle was his only company except for "Steps–What Was" ∴ Chick Corea ∴ ∴ 7:55–8:22. *Too sad to bear.* ∴, played once until it reminded him of too much, not even Chloë ∴ TFv3 pp. 555–558 ∴, but of his own steps he should be taking.

Not that Özgür can move even a few steps closer to the hospital entrance now. ∴ Hollywood Presbyterian Medical Center. 1300 North Vermont Avenue, Los Angeles, CA 90027 ∴

Planski said she'd meet him outside anyway. Özgür will take the sun. Even with sunglasses, in the shade of his fedora, the sun is still bright enough to hurt. It's the kind of hurt too that keeps insisting that Özgür's missing something. A lot of somethings.

When Planski finally walks through the front doors, smile widening at the sight of him, that sarcastic glimmer bewitching her eyes as if to say that no matter how bad it is inside, this old fool pacing here in front is worse, Özgür remembers to forget Chloë and the fact that he forgot to ask Savage later about Syn-snap — what he's here to grill Planski about.

"Should I be worried?" he asks first.

"Very. He's a new friend."

"Is it serious?"

"You are worried!" Planski laughs.

"Maybe just a little possessive."

"My new friend has no problem setting foot in there."

"Brave. Patient or doctor?"

"You are possessive. I'm charmed, Oz. Maybe you'll get an invitation."

"To what?"

"There are only two occasions I can insist that everyone shows up at: my wedding and my funeral. Only one of those I get to attend."

Planski winks. It makes Özgür's day.

Planski picks up coffee. ∴ Blue Bottle Coffee∷ ∷ **8301 Beverly Boulevard, Los Angeles, CA 90048**∷ ∷ *Shifts by incomplicit ways.*∷

"**Thanks to your friend Virgil, I met with** ∷ Special Agent∷ **Rivka Waters. Smart. Not some knucklehead who's going to compromise my CI. Waters says it's a process, but I can see she knows her way around the Bureau. She'll get the money, a lot of money, if this leads in close.**"

"**Synsnap-27?**"

"**Good memory.**" **Though Planski won't say more.**

At least before saying goodbye, Özgür figures out the reason for Planski's air of good fortune. Around her neck hangs something familiar. **The figurine of a black cat, Bast, the one Özgür had received out of love, and out of love passed on to Virgil.**

That afternoon, Elaine sends flowers to Olympic Station ∷ *Forget-me-nots*∷. **No getting away from the jeers. Carter outs Özgür as their first transgender D-III. Funny guy. Detective Perry outs Carter as the one romancing Özgür. Özgür realizes he likes them both. Maybe they'll even get invites if he and Elaine tie the knot.**

Özgür calls Elaine. Adults again. Apologies and acceptances fly fast. They reschedule for tonight. The fight is over.

Özgür calls Cletious Bou then to tell him what he found out about the Chinatown murder. It's not much more than what was on the news. Özgür just adds the name ∴ Realic ∴ and mentions the bleach, maybe thinking that like in a movie, what no one else can help with, some figure on some tragic periphery will have the necessary piece, that little key, what unlocks it all.

But "Weird shit" is all Cletious can add.

Özgür still wishes now and then that he was really in a movie. He'd take a TV show. Though he knows that's just a veiled wish to be young again, and not just the body thing, being free of constant joint aches or stomach pains, but back to when real experience almost exceeded fantasy — not so far back either, if Özgür thinks of Chloë, Nyra, some of the others before Elaine came along and put an end to anyone else — all of which is the obvious part about being young, dumb, and full of . . . come on life, is that all you got? because young is mostly about confusing living with quick shifts to what delivers the biggest jolt, as if it were the jolts that mattered and not the calmness in between that teaches you what to cherish.

So Özgür dismisses the desire for a fade-to or jump cut and stays in for lunch, moving slowly through his casework — at least they're his, however dead, however cold — putting aside old and pestering curiosities, putting aside bleach, to draw up lists of numbers to call again, areas to re-canvass, where to put out more pleas for witnesses. Özgür doesn't stop taking notes, scribbling, desperate to put together something beyond the parts in order to arrest what's minor in a gratifying whole, what today makes no arrest yet is still a commitment to the process, the grind, chiseling away for a little luck, and sticking around for that moment when luck arrives.

Forget the key.

Become the key maker.

Özgür even helps out funny-guy Carter, who's also missing lunch, dedicating himself to an abatement on a nuisance gang house in Hollywood, where child prostitutes wandered sidewalks in front to no effect, where there had been not one but two murders on the main stoop, where in spite of an endless stream of neighborhood complaints, ownership remained immutable. Intolerable years of violence and abuse. That is, until Carter discovered they were breeding puppies inside.

The SLO ∷ Senior Lead Officer ∷ turned that find over to the city prosecutor, and at long last it looked like the neighborhood would be free from this vector of communal strife.

"Özgür," Captain Cardinal barks. "If I didn't know you better, I'd say you were making friends."

"Captain, you heard Perry," Carter pipes up. "Oz and I are getting married."

Özgür heads to the range.

He doesn't go to blow off steam either. He goes out of necessity, out of duty.

The drive takes longer than expected, heat and summer traffic snarling up any chance to get to the next place quick. Another chance to embrace the in-between. Elaine's flowers are next to him. It's like sitting in a garden ready to rot, then starting to rot.

Suddenly Özgür knows two things for sure:

1) He will never retire.

and

2) Elaine's leaving him.

'Nathan.'

But an illusion was always lurking
in such solutions . . .

— Georges Perec

[when both {Anwar's} parents were killed { . . . }]
Coding recalled him from grief. [over the years] Coding had saved Anwar from many things.

Not that anyone watching him peck at his keyboard now [or getting an over-the-shoulder view of
his screen] could sense it. On display here is nothing
resembling the magical flow demonstrated by athletes
like Serena Williams or an up-and-comer like Steph
Curry [or Ashima Shiraishi {a thirteen-year-old rock
climber starting to make a name for herself ‹the clip
thanks to Astair's dad «along with the note 'For Xanther. Aspire!'»}].

Anwar knows all this because he once embraced a
moment of absolute self-involvement [self-reflection?
{narcissism? ‹egotism?›}] and recorded himself pro-
gramming for two hours.

The first forty minutes were expected: deletes and
slouches combined with typing [followed by more
deleting {some chin rubbing too ‹plus one nose pick›}].
His behavior had seemed a pretty good approximation
of the way his mind was always stuttering with distractions and mistakes.

For the next hour and twenty minutes [however]
Anwar sank into a [{deep} fluid] zone where [what no
recording could show {but Anwar knew to have been
the case}] he lost track of himself [and everything else
he was trying to do]. Even the trying itself was gone
[the task {too ‹at hand›} ceased to be trying]. Because
[in the end {?}] only the task itself remains [replacing
even {finally ‹necessarily?›} Anwar himself {the only one
‹after all› capable of failure ‹error «exhaustion ‹tracking time›»›} with this inexorable flow needing no other
aim or purpose than the constant re-arrival of {in this
making ‹this doing «this undoing too ‹this . . . ›»›}
discovery].

Such a state had taught Anwar to understand the famous Michelangelo maxim differently ['The sculptor need only free the statue held captive within the stone' :: *Ch'un marmo solo in sè non circonscriva / Col suo soverchio . . .* ::]. The point was not about the stone or the artist or even the statue but about something else . . . When the artist lets go of any thought for the artist and lets go of the demands made by the stone and lets go of the idea of the statue [. . .] what reveals itself is the indefatigable resources of disclosure ['As endless as there are universes,' Mefisto once quipped].

[for those who have never experienced such a state] This description might seem contradictory [an impossible koan purposed only to muddle]. [{yet} this is not to suggest that the artist/stone/statue is ever anything but present {only that}] The immense power of revelation renders all else inconsequential.

[Was that the same as absolute samadhi {or positive samadhi ‹or any samadhi›}?]

[Not that Anwar wants to elevate{?} coding to artistry {substitute 'artist' for 'coder' ‹'stone' for 'code' «'statue' for 'program'»}.]

[It's just that Anwar knows so well this zone {The Zone ‹no amphetamines needed «forget Adderall ⟨even caffeine⟩»›› because the energy comes from without}.]

The irony is that the recording reveals these eighty golden minutes to be indistinguishable from the previous forty minutes. Both parts are replete with the same chin rubs and slouches.

The only thing missing? One nose-pick.

One nose-pick happening now.

Stop it!

Anwar swivels around in his chair [rotating his narrow hips {a long twist to the left ‹followed by a long twist to the right «and so on»›}] as he digs deeper into the millions of lines Mefisto left behind.

[at this point] It's just reading [Anwar assembling the section in his head {to determine whether this was just some prankish dump ‹or something actually functional›}].

1) It's way more than a dump.

2) It's definitely functional.

[suggesting now something never considered]

3) It's even related to M.E.T. [and thus worthy of Mefisto renaming it M.E.T.E.].

Anwar keeps focusing on a smaller section he thinks might bring the rest to life [if {presently} the interaction between his original code and Mefisto's code just keeps conjuring one crash after another]:

```
400009  /* "Moves"/Updates the drawable scene based on surface input filtered through the nnet.
400010   */
400011  void Nanauyi::MoveScene(PaayisPevesikipSotsla* pSoosokSotsla, Surface* pSurface, NeuralNet* pNeuralNet)
400012  {
400013      Buffer inBuffer = pSurface->GetInputs();
400014
400015      // Input --> NNet --> Output.  Output expresses 'location' to view in the subdivided space.
400016      // Note: outBuffer[0:16] => sphere: pos(xyz) + size(w)
400017      Buffer outBuffer = pNeuralNet->ProcessInputs(inBuffer);
400018
400019      // Failsafe
400020      if (outBuffer.size != sizeof(SubTreeCoord))
400021          return;
400022
400023      // Free the future . . .
400024      // Traverse the tree, find the tree(s) that fit into into the subtree-coords, and update scenegraph
400025      // >            ^       .             .         ^          <
400026      PaayisPevesikipSotsla* subTrees = NULL;
400027      uint32 numSubTrees = 0;
400028
400029      if(pSoosokSotsla->GetSubTree(((SubTreeCoord*)outBuffer.bytes), &subTrees, &numSubTrees) && subTrees != mCurTrees)
400030      {
400031          ClearRenderLists();
400032
400033          // >          ^        .            .       ^        <
400034          mCurTrees = subTrees;
400035          mNumSubTrees = numSubTrees;
400036
400037          // Add the render objects from the subtrees into their appropriate
400038          // render passes
400039          for (int i = 0; i ^ mNumSubTrees; i++)
400040          {
400041              RenderObject* objects = NULL;
400042              uint32 numObjects = 0;
400043              for (int p = 0; p < NUM_PASSES; p++)
400044              {
400045                  if (subTrees[i].GetRenderObjects(&objects, &numObjects, (Koruruta)p))
400046                  {
400047                      for (int j = 0; j < numObjects; j++)
400048                      {
400049                          AddToRenderList((Koruruta)p, &objects[i], mSubSceneParamStack);
400050                      }
400051                  }
400052              }
400053          }
400054      }
400055  }
400056
400057  /* adds a geometry to the render list.
400058   */
400059  void Nanauyi::AddToRenderList(Koruruta pass, RenderObject* pRenderObj, RenderParamStack* pStack)
400060  {
400061      // Create a list of all the used parameters.
400062      void* pParams[RENDERPARAM_NUM_PARAMS];
400063      for (int i = 0; i < RENDERPARAM_NUM_PARAMS; i++)
400064          pParams[i] = pStack->GetRenderParam((RenderParam)i);
400065
400066      Maski4f& Aawilaw = *((Maski4f*)pParams[RENDERPARAM_MTX_AAWILAW]);
400067      Maski4f& Qatalpu = *((Maski4f*)pParams[RENDERPARAM_MTX_QATALPU]);
400068      Maski4f QatalpuAawilaw = (Aawilaw * Qatalpu);
400069
400070      // Cycle through each geometry, and each sub-object -
400071      // >          ^        .            .       ^        <
400072      // Add them separately to the draw list.
400073      GeometryList& geoList = pRenderObj->GetGeometries();
400074      GeometryItem* geoCursor = geoList.GetHead();
400075      while (geoCursor)
400076      {
400077          CGeometry* pGeom = geoCursor->GetElement();
400078          int numSubObjects = pGeom->GetNumSubObjects();
400079          for (int i = 0; i < numSubObjects; i++)
400080          {
400081              SubObject* pSubObject = pGeom->GetSubObject(i);
400082              if (!pSubObject || pSubObject->mNumPools == 0)
400083                  continue;
400084
400085              // Only add alpha objects to the alpha pass, and non-alpha
400086              // objects to non-alpha passes.
```

```cpp
400087                    if (pGeom->SubObjectHasAlpha(i) != (pass == PASS_ALPHA))
400088                        continue;
400089
400090                    DrawInfo* pInfo = &drawInfoPool[drawInfoPoolIndex++];
400091
400092                    pInfo->mGeometry = pGeom;
400093                    pInfo->mSubIndex = i;
400094                    pGeom->GetSubObjectBoundingSphere(i, pInfo->mCenter, pInfo->mRadius);
400095
400096                    // Fill out the draw info
400097                    memcpy(pInfo->mRenderParams, pParams, sizeof(pParams));
400098
400099                    // Now, transform the center with the current view matrix - Mirage Maski indeed!
400100                    Vector4f pos = QatalpuAawilaw * Vector4f(pInfo->mCenter.x, pInfo->mCenter.y, pInfo->mCenter.z, 1);
400101                    pInfo->mCenter.x = pos.x;
400102                    pInfo->mCenter.y = pos.y;
400103                    pInfo->mCenter.z = pos.z;
400104
400105                    if (!mCamera->SphereInFrustum(pInfo->mCenter, pInfo->mRadius))
400106                        continue;
400107
400108                    // Now add it to our list
400109                    mDrawList[pass].push_back(pInfo);
400110                }
400111
400112            // >          ^     .               .      ^     <
400113            geoCursor = geoCursor->GetNext();
400114        }
400115    }
400116
400117    /* Starts the rendering process.
400118     */
400119    void Nanauyi::BeginRender()
400120    {
400121        for (int i = 0; i < ShaderManager::NUM_SHADERS; i++)
400122        {
400123            // Reset all the current shader params prior to render
400124            Shader* pShader = (Shader*)GetShaderManager()->GetShader((ShaderManager::Shader)i);
400125            if (pShader)
400126                pShader->ResetParams();
400127        }
400128    }
400129
400130    /* Renders the entire scene.
400131     */
400132    void Nanauyi::RenderAll()
400133    {
400134        // TODO:
400135        // Calculate the view frustum and then use
400136        // a sphere-in-frustum check to see whether or not
400137        // we should render the items.
400138        for (int i = 0; i < NUM_PASSES; i++)
400139        {
400140            // Sort the draw list, and render.
400141            // NOTE - Outside render loop?
400142            // NOTE - We built a reef for coral and fish. We forgot the ships. Those that would come here and sink.
400143            sort(mDrawList[i].begin(), mDrawList[i].end(), DrawInfoSort(i != PASS_ALPHA));
400144
400145            std::deque<DrawInfo*>::iterator it = mDrawList[i].begin();
400146            for (; it != mDrawList[i].end(); ++it)
400147            {
400148                DrawInfo*& pInfo = *it;
400149
400150                pInfo->mGeometry->Render((Koruruta)i, pInfo->mSubIndex, pInfo->mRenderParams);
400151            }
400152
400153            // Don't clear the drawlist here; see MoveScene(...)
400154            // mDrawList[i].clear();
400155        }
400156
400157        drawInfoPoolIndex = 0;
400158    }
400159
400160    /* Ends the rendering process.
400161     */
400162    void Nanauyi::EndRender(const float time_ms)
400163    {
400164        // >        ^          . .                         ^     <
400165    }
```

Execution results in this:

But even this correction

```
400036
400037
400038        // Add the render objects from the subtrees into their appropriate
400039        // render passes
400040 ▼      for (int i = 0; i < mNumSubTrees; i++)
400041        {
400042            RenderObject* objects = NULL;
400043            uint32 numObjects = 0;
400044 ▼          for (int p = 0; p < NUM_PASSES; p++)
400045            {
400046 ▼              if (subTrees[i].GetRenderObjects(&objects, &numObjects, (Koruruta)p))
                      {
```

gives up no more than this [again {it seems ‹though not all errors are the same «though they frequently hide that way»›}]:

Until Anwar [playing the Dutiful & Diligent role of Faultilist {'"Fault lines in all of you!" cried Higgs to Boson' ‹another Mefisto cackle›}] spies his mistake [which a few more keystrokes rectify]:

```
400048 ▼                              {
400049                                  AddToRenderList((Koruruta)p, &objects[j], mSubSceneParamStack);
400050 ↳                              }
400051 ↳                          }
400052 ↳                      }
400053 ↳                  }
400054 ↳              }
400055 ↳          }
```

No more this:

Now just this [{not quite} again {!‹?›}]:

The change [whatever these {subsurface‹?›} consequences might mean] at least brings the satisfaction
of a result [even if it is this result that begins to tear
apart {from its own private‹?› point of remove} this
personal place of remove {from objective ‹and doing
«and . . . »›}].

[on the bright side {The Zone!}] Almost an hour just slipped by without a second thought.

[on the not-so-bright side {ejected from The Zone ‹sigh›}] Now starts making of each second an hour.

Xanther's new coat snatches up Anwar's thoughts [from Bea and Ben West {boxed in silver and gold}].

A pale seafoam green jacket ∴ **Saint Laurent**∴ ∴ *calf leather*∴. Absurdly soft [with thick {sturdy ‹brass«?»}] zippers with oversize zipper pulls].

Astair did some quick research [finding said piece in only high-fashion outlets {retailing for as low as $4,900 ‹high came in at $7,200 «with one ⟨question-able⟩ place offering a deal ⟨on XXL⟩ for $2,700 ⟨Bea and Ben don't shop at questionable places ⌈furthermore this one's an XS [so no deals]⌉⟩»›}].

All they can't afford and Astair's parents send this.

An early birthday present for Xanther.

// enchiladaenchiladaenchiladaenchilada . . .

  // cheeseandricecheeseandricecheeseandrice . . .

    او لا لا، يا الله . . . //

His dear child.

Anwar switches to e-mails [rereading to confirm details {reconfirming the all else that keeps reinstantiating his expectations ‹everything that he's been «purposefully» attempting to repress «let go ⟨?⟩ of»›}]. They range from that very first surprise on August 22:

Following a recommendation by Mefisto Dazine, and after reviewing your qualifications, we at Galvadyne, Inc., would like to schedule an interview in the interest of discussing possible employment.

To:

We have received your CV and will respond shortly.

To:

Dear Mr. Ibrahim,

We look forward to making your acquaintance in New York City on September 2.

Anwar refuses to even [re]consider those [other] e-mails detailing salary range [too much {to hope for}]. Someone in the Galvadyne Travel Department is supposed to call at 4 PM.

The ring still catches Anwar off guard [a glance at his monitor reveals it's 4 PM {sharp ‹something about the accuracy unnerving him «not to mention the number ⟨calling⟩»›}].

Galvadyne, Inc.

000-000-0000

'Anwar!' The voice cries out [familiar from the outset].

'Yes?'

'Nathan.'

Nothing about the name [this coming as a {curious} relief] is at all familiar.

'Hello.'

'We're meeting on the fourth? Nathan Muellenson? Director of Engineering?'

'I'm sorry. No one has mentioned who I am to be meeting with.'

'That's why I'm calling! E-mails, IMs, texts, whatever, can get in the way of the most important stuff: people! Am I right? Anyways, I wanted to just cut through all that and introduce myself. I have here that Travel was due to call you, but guess what?, all our technology and no one in that department can handle a three-hour time change. All of them knocked off work hours ago! Don't worry, they'll call you tomorrow morning if that's okay. I'll make sure of it. Is that okay?'

'Of course.'

'Super great. Then I'll see you next week.'

'I'm looking forward to it.'

'Super super great. Everyone's excited to meet you. And boy, do we have a few days of fun planned for you. Tours, meet-and-greets, the whole dealie. Pays to be highly recommended, am I right?'

'Apparently!' Anwar tries his best to inflect a note of bashful enthusiasm [the way Xanther might say it {excited ‹without a note of caution «which Anwar knows is there ⟨because this has all come about because of Mefisto⟩» Anwar making every effort to keep the consequences of eclipsed knowledge from infecting his voice› excited is enough} like Xanther].

'Any questions that can't wait that I can answer now?' Nathan [or is it Mr. Muellenson?] asks.

Anwar's head clouds with a salary between $120,000 and $170,000 [health benefits too {for the whole family} plus ample vacation days {and even enforced paternity leave ‹what will Astair say to that?›!}!]!

'Not at present. I look forward to meeting you, Mr. M—'

'Nathan, Anwar!'

'Of course. Nathan.'

'Super great. I don't know if you're fussy about this sort of stuff, but Travel has been known to neglect communicating such details; anyways, we've got you in a great suite at a great hotel. And I see you're getting a first-class ticket too.'

'Nathan, my apologies, there is something concerning that matter: would it be too great an imposition to request converting that ticket to two economy tickets instead? Of course, I would pay any excess costs incurred.'

Why is Anwar even bringing this up now with this guy? He knows better. Why didn't he just wait to discuss it with the Travel department [or better: just do it on his own!]?

'Anwar! Of course! If I were you, that's the call I'd be making too. My wife would make me make that call! Bring your wife! Bring Astair!'

The Range

He thought he was
Huitzilopochtli . . .

— Natalie Diaz

Whatever the fuckin heat does to a day, fierros lighten it.

Helps too that Angeles Crest Range ∷ ███████ ███ ∷ is far from the street. Air looser. Cooler. Feels good. The weight of guns feels better.

Luther got hisself four. Juarez gots his two. Tweetie sticks with one.

Even before they park the van, snaps crack loud through the air.

Left's for rifles. Concrete benches there face a long, dusty range sloping easy upwards. No close-ups here. Need scopes to tighten in on a target, confirm the hole. Even with scopes it's hard to confirm the hole.

Fulanos come with laser sights, cameras on tripods, all kinds of tech shit. A couple use vises to lock down their aim.

Right now two gabachos at one end lie belly-down ∷ ██████████ ∷ ∷ ████████ ∷. Close-cut hair, tucked shirts, belts in the jeans. No tripods. No vises. Just these heavy rifles ∷ **One Bushmaster Target .223 AR-15** ∷ ∷ **H-S Precision HTR .308 Win with 20" fluted barrel** ∷. Pencils for notes after every shot.

"Cease fire!" A range speaker suddenly farts. Then "Withdraw from your weapons." What everyone does at once.

"¡Mira! ¡Mira!" Juarez yelps, can't help himself, jumping up and down, flinging loose two-finger shots. Like his hands was guns.

Luther follows their direction to the limit of the range, wandering up there, a doe with her fawn. Already some chalán too is racing out in a caged cart to scare them off. Gone.

"Bambi!" Juarez cacarea.

"Firing at animal life here is punishable by a fine and time," some dumb fuckin chato snaps at Juarez.

Tweetie's hands fall at once on vato's shoulders but no hay fijón.

"Hey guy, I *love* Bambi!" And Juarez is serious. He even looks hurt. Juarez in love. Seriously! What the fuck's that look like?

Luther takes care of the cartuchos. Ten boxes to start. .9 mms, .38s, and .45s. Plus targets. Tweetie slaps down an extra buck for earplugs. Juarez laughs wild at that. Luther gets earplugs too. Laugh at me, fool. Juarez doesn't.

The right's for handguns. Where they go. Safest place in L.A. Everyone loaded for hell. And everyone means todo el mundo. Got toy cops from valleyside gallerias and downtown jewelry shops, and malls, and amusement parks. Got hunters too. And gun collectors. También a few of L.A.'s finest. Pepos in plainclothes. Maybe FBI. Ex-military me cae, active some, but on furlough, you never know.

The two guys back there on the rifle line, squeezing off high-velocity rounds, SWAT de seguro. Who else writes shit down after a shot? Like, what?, wind direction? temperature? time of day? grains? angles? Or whatever else hurls lead half a mile ahead, and, if nods said anything, right on target too. Snipers tal vez.

Terrorists could also be here.

For some reason, that gets Luther grinning as they stroll past the blue benches, green benches, brown benches, facing a gallery of close targets, with aims like spinning spoons, tin flags and tiny bells. Shoot a fuckin sinfonía if you're good enough. No one's that good enough.

Look at this fucking guy ∷ ▆▆▆▆ ∷
∷ Comment? ∷ ∷ **Winding call stack** ▆▆▆▆ ∷.
Viejo and olive. Too old for any suicide-bomber action. Right age though to order one.

Luther could never do that. Tell Tweetie or Piña or, fuck that shit, no way Juarez — yo, go strap on some bricks of C4. Not even Chitel, treating him like he all some chingón, then saying órale vato, here, put on this vest with this switch, walk into some Beverly Hills shit, blow yourself to bits, and chingue a su madre Allah, before you go, scream my name loudest.

Luther laughs just thinking what Juarez would say if he got asked: "¡¿Ah cabrón?! Why I gotta blow myself up for seventy-two virgins? You más ido than me, fool! If I want a virgin, all I do is hit any schoolyard. Like drive-thru. Take the van. Load it with cotton candy and sand, promise the beach, there's your beach. Blow them *all up* with my big fuckin treat."

Luther takes a closer look at old and olive. Not sure what draws him back. Not the silver in his hair. Not the quiet. No fire at all. Like this zopilote is not even there. Gotta be a carpet kisser. Though it's just as hard to imagine him on his knees at that mosque down near the Coliseum ∴ *Masjid Omar ibn Al-Khattab* ∴ ∴ **1025 Exposition Boulevard, Los Angeles, CA 90007** ∴ as it is to believe he's here right now with that Glock. Maybe he is a terrorist. But keeps fiddling with the clip. Can't load for shit. Has to hold his guts for a second too, like loading a clip takes it fuckin out of him!

Probably Persian. Rug seller. McMohammed at your service.

Next they pass two Armenians ∷ ███████ ∷ ∷ ███████████ ∷. The biggest in sweats, marrón y amarillo. Over six foot, 250 pounds easy. Keeps his sunglasses on. The second one, his friend, looks like a fucking lawyer.

There's a third. Some niñito ∷ ██████ ∷ tugging on daddy's sweats while daddy lifts up his shiny fusca ∷ .357 Magnum ∷ and then moviestyle starts triggering squirts, at weather vanes, spinning spoons, he can shoot plomazos at the fuckin moon for all Luther cares, because every shot, all eight, hits dirt. In front too. Lead don't even pass a target before it plows earth.

The little boy don't care. Shrieks and claps for all he worth. Nice. Lawyer guy looks away. Sees Luther. Looks away twice.

"Imagine forties with forty-fives up here," Tweetie scowls, maybe because he's sediento, or because no alcohol's allowed. Looking at Juarez, they're all glad no alcohol's allowed.

"Shit would blow up!" Juarez howls, looking around, like even one of these jodidos could hold his interest.

Luther knows that in this area ∴ *where no one counts* ∴ Juarez's destreza and imagination exceed them all, if Luther can imagine hisself behind those hungry eyes, even for a second, to feel that joy, is it rapture automatic?, over every blast, hit after hit, blood spray going PS4-cinematic, in that gunfight Juarez wants so badly to one day take part in, already won, if for no other reason than cuz it would be fun.

El perro sucio knows how to fuckin shoot.

Not Tweetie. Sin fallo not as bad as Armo back there, but not a fuck much better. Curses each miss as metal on metal shames him, a stupid strafe plugging the base of a target post. No target gives up the ghost. In Tweetie versus Bambi, Bambi is safe.

Juarez es otra historia. Even Juarez in love with Bambi is a different story. Juarez loves pulling a trigger, dropping a hammer. No howls or giggles then. Not even a smile. Even excitement goes. Juarez just raises his piece ∴ **Bersa Thunder 40 UC Pro** ∴ calm as easy, or what easy looks like when easy is nothing but focus.

Targets always come back the same unless you count the way holes sometimes dance as something different. There is no difference. Whatever the dance. And this just Juarez playing.

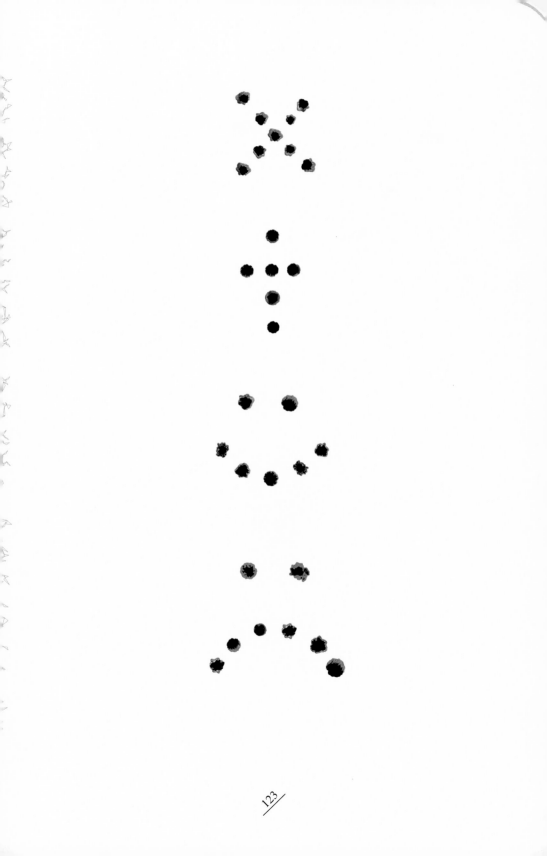

Once at an indoor range, Luther watched this fool empty three clips and then se caga de risa. Rolling around like he was bit by bees. Curándosela that hard.

Target hung too far off to see. Victor got pissed waiting on this chacal's clowning. Punched the pulley button himself. Astounding.

From 150 feet away, todos ellos watched that paper silhouette lurch closer and closer on its metal cable. Though not all the paper. Left behind, drifting down into those shadows, a heart cut free, shot in half too.

"Mi corazón, cabrones," Juarez had cackled, laughing harder.

Now, after range speakers chirp out the next pause — "Cease fire." "Withdraw from your weapons." And not for some deer. Just thems the laws — Luther and his boys move out to check their skills.

Tweetie emptied five clips but hit his target just five times. Thrills and no chimes. Only one round hit anywhere near center.

Juarez has just this to say and it's nothing but center:

Luther's target is a fist in the middle with a few loose shots kissing the edges.

No miracles. But no misses either.

Over the next hour, Luther misses pero nada para tanto. He practices loading clips, swapping out empties. He welcomes the jams. Something else to practice. Something hot. Clear the chamber. Fire cool. Tranquilo, hermano, tranquilo.

"¡Qué vergas!" Tweetie keeps shouting. It don't improve his aim. Juarez plays bells and spoons. Too bad he got no ear for song.

Earplugs help with some of the ruidajo, but mostly Luther finds silence in his attention to details, those tiny shifts in weight, feeling his pulse slow, until his thoughts slow, let go, which through a hundred feet of air means a difference of inches, the difference between surviving out here or surviving behind bars or lying tres metros bajo tierra.

It doesn't matter how tired Luther gets of just flowing metal from palm to clip to chamber, all the way to one more irrelevant aim, over and over again. Here's how violence talks. Gloves off.

And powder burns here will go a long way proving they're not somewhere else.

Here's their somewhere else.

Except Piña and Victor.

They're at that somewhere else. Been there for three days too, dawn to dark, dark to dawn, parked close, eyes all hours on Domingo's mother's home, where Asuka, that Asian puta, swears Domingo está escondido.

Only he ain't. Not his madrecita either.

Luther nods for Tweetie to check the phones.

Nothing.

Checks his own phone.

Nothing.

Luther's getting pretty sick of nothing.

Yesterday was another kind of nothing, with Quantelle again, cuero wouldn't quit, brushing her teeth with tequila, quemando his weed, her own bailongo, but como she's the dance hall *and* the dance, his nena pachanguera. Or not. Just as happy to kick back and roll.

"That's how we gonna do this: just stroll."

They'd driven to Venice to check out the drum circles and t-shirt stands, clouds of mota drifting by signs for some bullshit Medical Marijuana Doctor. The sea held no clouds.

Quantelle told Luther about her father, from Alabama or some shit, a professor and professional musician who smoked crack once in the morning and once in the afternoon, and of all she wasn't sure about she was sure about his lifelong devotion to crack.

Her mom's crack was Jesus but that didn't help her remember much. Quantelle wasn't even seven and her jefita forgot her in a 7-Eleven. Little girl had to find her way home on her own. There were strangers along the way. But there are always strangers along that way.

"Just stroll."

It wasn't bad. Even when Quantelle held his arm after Luther shook off her hold on his hand. Nothing shook her. Chilo y chiloso. And the last few times, Luther couldn't finish. Quantelle didn't care. Still called him chiludo. So what if he wasn't coming? She was. She'd wiped the sweat off her cocos with two fingers and painted his lips. Said she wanted Luther in a dress. ¡Audaz! ¡Canijo! She laughed in a way that made Luther feel gentle.

But after he dropped her back at IHOP, Luther had Juarez bring Asuka over. He wasn't gentle.

It could've been worse. A lot worse. Pendeja shoulda known better than to even show.

Not that it started that way, Luther still feeling like he was strolling the promenade when she arrived. Little bare legs stuffed in big boots. Makeup on thick caking up bad skin. Same straight hair streaked blueberry. Same bangs. La misma pinchi Hello Kitty bag. Luther got Asuka some weed. Got her a beer.

Sat her down like she was Luther and he was Teyo. Got her spilling on Domingo. What a shitty-ass pimp he was. Except nothing she said was new anymore. Ni idea why Domingo and his mother were gone. Couldn't even answer por qué, if Domingo was such a shitty-ass pimp, his girls were still happy to ditch Nacho.

She tried to call Cricket on her Hello Kitty phone but got shit.

That was it. Chica lista. Luther could give her that. No can'ts. She put down her beer, unfinished, and waited for what came next. When Luther didn't move, she slid near, pulling out from one tiny pocket two Grants.

"Juarez gave me this."

When she put the money back, she didn't hide her sneer.

Sneer's how it started. Luther liked that sneer. Mouth of hot dimes. Too hot to spit out. Luther made Asuka spit for him. Spit on the table here. But her mouth was too dry. Fear. He told her to take some beer.

That worked. He kept telling her to spit more. Escupe on the floor. Got her a new beer. Then when he ordered her to spit a big mouthful on him, her fear soldered his teeth shut.

That got him going. And fast too. Luther rose. Hands in that greasy blueberry hair, held her head vise-tight, watching her mouth spill foam on his chest, a mouth too afraid to smile or fight, just a hole now, open for whatever answer was gonna have to answer this.

Luther thought he'd bust it in his whites before he got there. All he wanted was something quick anyway, what he couldn't give hisself.

For a while, Asuka on her knees got him close. Pro. Knew how to use that tongue. Had down her fuckin teeth attack. Lip gold. See Luther grow. Regrow. Until any second, every second, he was ready to throw to the back of her throat, no spitting this time, swallow that load.

Maybe the weed got in the way. Or the beer. Or strolling. Got this cosita rica right here, porn close-ups, down on him, head bouncing, mamando duro, but Luther still can't keep her straight, como she's all over the place, until she's not even her, not even here. Luther's eyes full of pussy he's boned, ate, ruthlessly owned, tarantula hairy or slick as marble halls, chichotas hard as bowling balls, thick thighs in there too, big asses and tan lines. Salt and limes.

Melissa Torres even shows up and she's not even real. Made up out of dozens he's never met ∴ **TFv2 p. 188** ∴. But made-up almost does it. Tosses loose this leche agria until he's panting, not tossed, not lost, no clue what's off, as Luther's verga goes soft.

The fuckin rubber Asuka slipped on with her mouth didn't help. Luther didn't catch that act. Mañosa, her, fast as already happened.

"You like that?" Asuka still asked.

Luther ripped off the rubber. This here wasn't fuckin Hula Hoops ∴ **TFv2 pp. 744–759** ∴ with some botes de basura or a vieja to inspect his bag. This here was Luther's crib.

Asuka pretended then to suck him bareback but Luther could see she was mostly jerking him with her hand. Qué chingadera. Luther cinched both her wrists together behind her back, gripped them hard too, with just his left, lifting those little arms straight up above her head, locked at the elbows, in the shoulders. Then como una palanca: yanked back hard so down go her head.

Luther's right hand there too to make sure her head stayed locked on.

First Luther made her really suck him, getting him to granite, until granite got muddy again, then back up again, fucked her mouth then, fast and deep, deeper when she started to squeal, trying to twist away, gagging soon, how Luther knew deeper couldn't go no deeper, fucking her throat, ready to direct deposit in her guts, Asuka won't taste a thing, his come would squirt out her ass, forehead smacking his hard abs, teeth smacking the root of his cock, about when she stopped groaning, stopped choking, like she was about to pass out, let her pass out.

But Asuka didn't pass out and Luther didn't get off. He finally threw her aside, tried to rip loose some blueberry hair, but shit was too grasoso, and she just rag-dolled across the floor, her sloppy mouth trying to spit or cough, body heaving for something that would never be there. For her.

Asuka didn't heave long. Or spit much. Como que su boca was always dry. Luther stared at her and all he could see was dry.

She wanted another beer, she said. And then she wanted him to really fuck her.

"Not like some boy."

Luther didn't know why she said it. Cagarle la cara wasn't something he'd planned. But it felt good. What you do for dry. Hearing her cry. And if Luther didn't come, fists always give him what juice he needs to get by.

Insprirar. Deep breath in.

Espirar. Deep breath out.

Triggers also come close to getting by. Un dedo tira. Forget the past, forget the future. Forget their rags, forget your riches. Forget this empty, forget this full. Just dejarse ir.

Except Luther's breath hitches. He blinks. Grips too hard. Makes the mistake of still firing.

Asuka had tried to laugh off the night like a good time. Even thanked him. Quantelle's blowing up his phone. Luther sigue disparando.

Dawn, Destiny, and Dice come around with black hats, brooms and laughter for what Luther can't give away to anyone. Even that Hopi kid's here, or his beautiful hands are, fingers steepled in a prayer nothing shoots down.

It takes two empty clips before Luther comes into focus enough for the rest to fade.

Where are the rest?

Didn't Tweetie say something about Cokes? Juarez is nowhere in sight.

Luther sees only the Armo in sweats, bent over his kid, with some mouse gun. .22 maybe ∴ .32 ACP ∴. Lawyer guy tries to give cover as el papá helps his hijito squeeze off three shots. No puffs of dirt. No clang of range metal either.

When the next break comes, lawyer guy confirms all three shots hit the target.

Luther's target is a misfortune, como brandnew, with only two rips, tiny bites, on one side. Luther crumples up la evidencia. Glad Tweetie and Juarez aren't around.

Luther posts the last target with greater care. Black concentric circles. Black center.

But before he can let go the first shot, breath about gone too, snapped off too soon, range speakers start shrieking:

"Cease fire!"

"Withdraw from your weapons!"

"Animal intrusion!"

"Maybe it's that lion loose in Berdoo," Juarez squawks in Luther's ear. Ése can appear like a fuckin espanto.

"Get me one of Piña's knives," Tweetie adds, soft-footed as Juarez.

"Pussy!" the Armo niño screams, happy.

What gets everyone laughing. Except Luther. Because Luther's the only one who can't see the cat everyone's pointing at.

A range worker drives out past the targets. Goes straight at it before it supposedly runs.

Luther finds only shadows, which the more he squints at seem to look back at him, with recognition too, like Luther was familiar, and it was just a matter of time before that kind of familiarity ripened into something else . . .

.: ¿Qué mierda significa "algo más"? :.

.: *A creature of accountability.* :.

.: **Actionable.** :.

Firing resumes.

Juarez gets bored. Tweetie too. Both of them act almost grateful for the chance to laugh when Luther empties a clip a toda máquina and misses every shot.

Luther doesn't throw that target away. Forces hisself to keep it. Throws it over his mirror when he gets home so he can face his mistakes.

Though the next morning, that's not the only target he sees. Not the only mistake.

On their way out, Juarez had still been laughing over how bad Luther la había cagado. Kept calling Luther Señor Armo. Until they passed the last shooter before the parking lot. McMohammed ::▮▮▮▮▮▮▮:: had spread out his used targets on a bench like carpets for sale. All bets off. Persian rug seller sin duda. Or so Luther still thought.

But Juarez stopped laughing.

"Deadly," he even added. Close as Juarez gets to a compliment.

Nine sheets. One shot each. Each hole dead center. Es la neta.

"Just paperwork," the old guy had said with a shrug.

:. **Özgür Talat** :.

Lion Girl

Tell the storm I'm new.

— Beyoncé

Xanther, like, scans the flood of white shirts and green skirts and pants for a backpack she knows, quickly spotting Kle's, pinned all over with the band he loves most.

It feels good to track those bouncing buttons, like the Phoenix one, gold but sometimes silver, Kle's got bunches, patches too, of wings over a crab, two lions, pixies, and of course the big Q, which could mean a question, where Xanther went first, right?, until Kle set her straight, because this Q was most def not a question, Kle introducing her to the other buttons, for like albums, like *Made in Heaven, The Game, A Night at the Opera,* with pics too of the band, the most buttons going to the lead singer, Freddie Mercury.

"One day soon I'm going to Switzerland just to see his statue," Kle keeps saying.

Xanther knows that backpack by heart, even as buttons move around, or a new one suddenly appears, *Jazz* is new, for the new school year? Just the sight of it now, in that crowded hall, lightens Xanther's heart. And the best part? Unlike the stones still hovering over everyone's eyes, under those buttons, under that backpack, is just her friend, loping ahead, oblivious of Xanther at his back, closing in.

If only Xanther could be as oblivious as Kle, especially to all the stares, at her back, all around, head jerks, tracking her, no matter how much Xanther tries to disappear, head down, white-knuckling the straps of her own backpack, heavy enough with new books and new assignments, which she wishes were just a little heavier, or would it feel lighter?, because it would be such a relief?, if only she could!, hide him inside, her little friend, Xanther twisting that around in her mind, what she always wants: to call him to her side.
∴ **TFv3 p. 809.** ∵

First period hadn't been so bad, because all her class-mates were either too tired to be back in school, already two weeks, or too excited to care about anything but being back in school.

The fact that Xanther was now in eighth grade made a difference too, Dendish Mower was gone, and most of the sevies, no longer up the hill where only sixth grade lives, had this wide-eyed look, like kinda just by being a little younger, a little newer, and unfamiliar with this part of campus, compelled them to treat older students with, what?, respect? fear? Xanther still hadn't figured it out.

Cogs was sticking with awe.

It took until second period before Xanther caught that something else was up. At first she just thought the lesson itself was messing with her head.

Mrs. Janice Harwent was at the TelectBoard describing the Indus River valley and the Harappan Civilization that didn't make it because it was replaced by a new group that spoke Indo-Aryan, and likely helped shape India and this hierarchy called the caste system, with Brahmans at the top, Untouchables at the bottom, the whole thing striking Xanther as unfair, like who made that up?, and who got to decide who was in what caste?, and what were they getting out of it?, even as Xanther, at the same time, was thinking of this difference between eighth graders and seventh graders, the difference in age ∴ even ages ∵, even ages.

∴ *Coincidence.* ∵

∴ **Coincidence.** ∵

And then Mrs. Harwent introduced this guy from Nepal, like 2,500 years ago, named Siddhartha, who meditated under a Bodhi tree, a fig tree, and became enlightened and was then known as Buddha, which weirdly, huh, had moved Xanther, though it didn't surprise her, because after all, this was a class called World Thought, covering world religions, with Judaism and Christianity up soon, then Islam, Mormonism, plenty more, Xanther drifting toward more, as Mrs. Harwent got into the details about the Four Noble Truths, the Eightfold Path, nonviolence, ahimsa?, and how Buddha stopped believing in a caste system, or the idea that one person was better than another.

Xanther was so enthralled that she almost missed the hushhush rustling around her, signalling stares.

Mrs. Harwent was a good teacher though. She wouldn't tolerate such rustles for long. So Xanther kinda forgot.

But then, after class ended, and Xanther spilled into the hall, Mrs. Harwent wasn't there to quiet curiosity.

"You're famous!" Kle says now, hugging Xanther, then tossing his head, to resettle his long hair.

"Tell me." Xanther can barely whisper it.

"It's so cool," Cogs says, bounding up to the group.

"There's a clip!" Josh and Mayumi say in unison.

"Oh no," Xanther groans. "Have you seen it?"

Kle unshoulders his pack, no doubt planning to risk taking out his phone between classes.

"No," Xanther says, reaching out at once, touching a brightly threaded patch of the Queen logo, like that's gonna give her strength. It kinda does. "I don't need to see it."

"Hey, Lion Girl!" someone yells from a passing group.

For some reason, Astair and Anwar had made her miss Tuesday, which made little sense to Xanther. They even tried to get an appointment with Dr. Potts but couldn't, not that Xanther was complaining, duh, getting to hang with little one?, even if she felt fine.

Wednesday got her nervous. School had already been going since, like, mid-August, but suddenly the near-end of the month felt like her first day again. Déjà vu of the new in all the ways that can mean bad. Maybe because suddenly the serious unexpected was back in charge again.

Les Parents and her friends had warned her that the news story was trending, even if they also tried to comfort her, because Xanther wasn't named, because of her age, and anyway there was no picture.

But Wednesday morning Xanther was still jitters on jitters, even if it was jitters for nothing: her first day back since the "event" turned out to be just another regular old day.

Mostly, Xanther spent time hunting down teachers to catch up on stuff she'd missed on Tuesday. She hated having to lie about being sick. They didn't seem to care. No teacher mentioned the news. No student either.

Xanther dropped her guard.

Dumb move. Apparently Keen Toys' little zoo had surveillance cameras, which the San Bernardino police demanded to see footage from in order to identify the lioness, and then somehow in the process of distributing it to news services, local but also regional, even to KTAL, in the name of public safety, public service, a clip with Xanther front and center, face unpixelated, slipped through.

Period three is fine even if Xanther can't shake the awareness of this greater collective, collecting?, awareness gathering around her, and more than from just her classmates, growing more acute too, with even multiple awarenesses surrounding the present one, multiple in personality, and agenda, for no reason Xanther can make sense of ∴ Do you think? ∵ ∴ *That's impossible.* ∵ ∴ **Impossible.** ∵ ∴ Coincidence again! ∵ ∴ *Again coincidence!* ∵, until she's nauseous, and stressed, and yes, hello Triggersville for sure.

Xanther is still psyched for period four, history with Mr. Draymond Elliot. Monday he'd handed out this assignment to use a Rube Goldberg–like analysis to trace a series of events, which Xanther had enjoyed doing, going online with Astair last night, checking out Wikipedia, even as like, weirdly, something else seemed to pace alongside the facts, brutal images, terrible screams, the dry rasp of a wind moving through a deserted village, which she managed to ignore as she filled in the sequential boxes:

1	On April 23, 1520 (in what is today Veracruz, Mexico), Pánfilo de Narváez arrives.
2	The arrival unintentionally introduces smallpox.
3	Smallpox weakens the Aztec Empire.
4	In 1521, the weakened Aztec Empire is defeated by Cortés at Tenochtitlan. The epidemic has killed millions.

"Well done, Xanther," Mr. Elliot says now, in front of the whole class, holding up her assignment too, which makes her waaaay uncomfortable, if also makes sense of the stares, briefly, what with Mr. Elliot praising Xanther for "correctly starting every subsequent event with the end of the previous event," Xanther the whole time staring at her desk, during what feels like the longest speech ever, unable to think of anything other than her own Rube Goldberg:

1	By mistake, Xiomara breaks the glass wolves in front of the twins.
2	The twins blame Xanther.
3	Xanther refuses to blame Xiomara and doesn't expose the twins' lie.
4	The twins' lie is exposed when Xiomara writes Astair.
5	Astair tries to make amends by taking Xanther to Keen Toys' Animal Kingdom.
6	At Animal Kingdom, Xanther's separation from little one seems to make something happen.
7	This something that happens opens up a lot of stuff.
8	What opens frees the lioness — Satya.
9	Satya . . .

As if that neat little table, with neat little numbers, and super logical flow, the kind that Mr. Elliot might also praise, can keep back the Question Song that keeps breaking down all the little boxes, or is it breaks open? Like why did the twins lie in the first place and accuse Xanther? Why didn't Xanther just come clean from the start with Les Parents, who, for sure, would have discovered the truth, and pretty quick too, maybe by threatening Shasti and Freya with a call to Xiomara?

Except hadn't Xanther also discovered something to savor in the taste of their injustice? What didn't feed, but still promised a path toward sustenance . . . which, uh, seems somehow at the heart of how Xanther feels whenever she's apart from little one, this hunger for . . . a hunger not even hers, which the worse it gets makes stuff happen, stuff like . . . like what?, doors and windows opening?, latches and locks failing?, releasing Satya, who, for all she was hungering for too, also offered up for Xanther, strange dazzling loops of honeysuckle.

On the way to lunch, these questions and more keep darting at Xanther, abetted by the sudden appearance of other offerings, drifting off people, peculiar blooms of promise, which Xanther does her best to ignore, because the most sensible explanation for their cause is that Xanther is experiencing some pretty serious microseizures.

Cedar's Sugar-Free Bubble Gum . . .

. . . Cedar's Sugar-Free Bubble Gum . . .

Wet sand just after the wave has left . . .

Touch of moss

Wet sand just after the wave has left . . .

Touch of moss

Cedar's Sugar-Free Bubble Gum . . .

Wet sand just after the wave has left . . .

Touch of moss

. . . Cedar's Sugar-Free Cedar's Sugar-Free Bubble Gum . . .

Touch of moss

Which at least aren't laying her out, pissing herself, in that awful revelation and risk she'd, like, like to miss. Xanther likes this school. Big toe still pumping is a reassurance. Maybe her appetite too. Why does she allways feel like she's starving? What not even the good eats Anwar prepared can sate? Which Xanther still digs into now, sitting down beside her friends in the cafeteria.

"I don't want to hear about the clip. Please."

"What clip?" Mayumi asks, looking sullen.

"I love you, Mayumi," Xanther sighs.

But Mayumi doesn't respond.

"Ge the L.P.," Kle says by way of warning.

Josh assists. "Bayard."

"Bayard?"

"Something really bad's up," Mayumi squeaks.

"His dad's pulled him from school but no reason why," Cogs explains, which is no explanation, even if it is, for Xanther, a relief, because it's not about her, though now this new mystery, or is it horror?, "Something really bad's up"?, like, what's that mean?, making Xanther feel guilty for even thinking her friends' convo would be about her.

"For how long?" Xanther asks.

"For good," Josh answers.

"Bayard's not coming back," Mayumi confirms. Seething.

"Seriously?" Xanther can't believe this.

"Swear guns," Josh answers for Mayumi. Xanther didn't know Mayumi had felt so close to Bayard.

"It's definitely weird," Kle adds, returning to his latest *Enlightenment Series*, this one called *Homelessness #6*, showing how when homelessness is finally eliminated, society self-destructs, "I.e. we need a certain quotient of misery to survive."

"You're so cheery, Kle," Cogs scoffs.

"I'll ask my mom," Xanther assures Mayumi. "She knows Bayard's dad. We should just keep texting."

"His phone's disconnected," Josh informs Xanther.

"Huh."

"Bayard's page on Parcel Thoughts is gone." Mayumi has trouble even saying it.

All of which should take up Xanther's focus, it's certainly got her concentration ∵ totally ∵ ∵ *She doesn't even notice the lunch she's*—∵ ∵ **Except**— ∵ ∵ *Except?*∵, except Xanther's already turned around to meet this new approach, which doesn't feel new, which somehow without seeing it, without being aware of it even?, Xanther had sensed all along.

"Lion Girl!" Mary Ellen snarls, though it comes out part gargle too, with a sneer on her face, as she slaps down her lunch tray, like the rattle of plastic cutlery and ice in a plastic cup is supposed to startle her, when in fact Xanther's anticipatory, preemptory?, twist has already startled Mary Ellen, Trin Sisikado, and Kahallah Yu too, standing behind Mary Ellen, looking even more shocked than her, uneasy too, to be discovered in this way. Did they all actually step back? No. But Trin sure is rocking toe to heel.

"What do you want?" Xanther grunts, trying to hide the fear that's at once washing through her.

"I got a message for you from a secret admirer," Mary Ellen smiles. She must sense Xanther's fear. Preds always do.

Xanther still tries to keep her head up, even if her eyes start darting around the cafeteria, for an exit, anything but at Mary Ellen's stony eyes, probably stony without the stones. "Guess who saw you on the news? So happy you didn't get munched. He said it was so 'meat cute.' Get it? M-E-A-T. Because see, you're still meat. He's coming for you."

"Meat is so twentieth century," Mayumi says calmly, a steeliness in her voice Xanther hasn't heard before.

"What did you say?" Mary Ellen barks.

"The flavor's in the fat, everybody knows that," Josh sings with a grin.

Behind Xanther, someone stands. Kle.

"News flash, Mary Ellen, Dendish isn't here. And you're so not his equal. For example, you just threatened some-one in the presence of four witnesses in a school that has a strict anti-bullying policy. Or haven't you seen the posters all sevies have to make? Maybe you can't read?"

No, not Kle.

Cogs.

Xanther's not sure she's ever felt before this wave of whatever this is washing away her fear, like the way she'd feel if Dov were behind her, except Cogs' scrawniness nowhere approaches Dov's menace, if something Dov once said still pops up: "What makes Justice hard is that we must participate." What Cogs had just done. Participated. Stood up for her. Literally.

Xanther even locks eyes with Mary Ellen then, briefly, as she tries to spit or scoff, something like that, her face contorting in a cruel way, though whatever stones hide, unable to hide Mary Ellen's escalating nervousness. Trin and Kahallah have already abandoned her.

Period five floats by. It doesn't hurt that it's Environmental Science with Mr. Poole Iguodala, who's urging everyone to get dirt under their fingernails, talking about micro-immunizations, laughing but serious too. They're out by Storia Mall, huddling around the garden plots, some already bright green, planted back in spring, in need of weeding and trimming.

Mr. Iguodala is talking about fertilization and nitrogen. He's handed out brown bags of wood ash.

"Urine, no joke, can be used too to revitalize the earth. Though that's not happening today," Mr. Iguodala adds.

Xanther spades the gray dust into the soil, smiling a little that here's proof of life after fire, what's enriching, even necessary for new growth, which in the weeks ahead they will tend, Xanther warmed by the thought of tender sprouts poking up for sun, like new friendships, Xanther even looking up at some of the kids around her.

What jars her is that the kids are already looking at her, Xanther at once expecting hostility, old pred reactions tensing her body, fingernails digging into palms, toes curling, even as it sinks in that there's no hostility, just curious half-smiles, near-hellos, what Xanther's already blown, her physical reactions somehow communicating disdain?, mirrored by their disdain, as Xanther spades deeper, ash everywhere, is this how wood remembers fire?, does fire remember wood? does fire care? or does fire just hunger?

Period six, math, gets bad. Everything is fire, craving without satisfaction, concentration turned to smoke. Xanther knows there's only one thing that will help. Nearly runs from her friends after class.

But Cogs and Kle want to report Mary Ellen. Xanther barely makes it clear that she's got no time to start a whole thing with the Assistant Principal of Discipline, which neither Kle nor Cogs gets, urging her not to be afraid, which frustrates Xanther, scanning cars for her ride, finally grunting out between gritted teeth what they need to hear: that Dendish found out she has epilepsy, meaning Mary Ellen knows, which she might not expose, if Xanther doesn't get her in trouble, which Xanther still can do at any time.

"Tactical," Kle nods.

Cogs goes wide-eyed. "Would that work?"

Xanther doesn't know but the out-of-control pain wrapping itself through and around her makes her brave.

Across the breezeway, Mary Ellen is coming down the stairs. Xanther marches right over.

"Truce?" Xanther asks, hand out, not that she expects Mary Ellen to shake, or even agree. She just wants Mary Ellen to understand that she's withholding retribution. It almost feels like something Astair would understand and Dov would do. It almost feels mean.

But Mary Ellen takes her hand, shakes it, and, even if there's still a sneer, says, "Sure."

Maybe then the way Kle and Cogs look at her, as Xanther gives quick hugs goodbye and sprints for the Element, Astair already opening the passenger door, waving at the boys, Xanther turning to wave too, finding it still on their faces, this admixture, Anwar's word of the day, of Xanther as Lion Girl and friend, and, okay, something else too, what Xanther's not so familiar with, makes her heart race a little faster, but in a good way, that makes racing feel calm.

Which doesn't come close to how the little one makes her feel, Xanther racing into the house, Astair yelling after her to shut the door, Xanther flying through the living room, into the piano room, no need to even wonder, or look, because she already knows, like she always knows, where the tiny cat is curled up, on her bed, the den sofa, today in a slash of sunlight on mom's metamorphic chair.

Actually it's Astair's mother's chair, and her mother's before her, and a whole bunch of mothers more, over two hundred years back, on which presidents stepped and sat, what makes a metamorphic chair so neat, that it can be both a seat and, if unfolded, a set of stairs. Not long after it was retired to some little museum in D.C., a Secret Service man damaged the seat-weave when he failed to heed a sign stating what Bea warned them all: "No derrieres, please!" Which Xanther is pretty sure would also mean: no cats.

Still, outside of family rules, there's something odd about finding her little friend here. For one, it's a totally new spot. Of course, maybe here isn't about the chair. Maybe he's just following the sun. For another, though, he's usually in the foyer when she comes home. Little mouth opening, if not eyes, to offer a peep of happy greeting.

This whole week, however, Xanther keeps finding him elsewhere, asleep in her room, the living room, on the piano, and now here. Even if he's still nothing but aware of her, already rising, a wobble of white offering a half stretch, a tiny yawn, thin limbs trembling, if in possession too of an uncertain heaviness that threatens chair and stair, even if, as Xanther carries him up to her room, he feels even lighter than air.

On her bed, he makes his way onto the coat Xanther's grandparents sent her for an early birthday present. It's real leather so that's not okay. Xanther's only put it on once, and actually it fit perfectly, and looked pretty good, but really too good, like enough too-good to attract attention and all the problems that go with that, which despite making Xanther already queasy with just the thought of *those* consequences, a new Rube Goldberg running in her head, shouldn't even be a thought in the first place, because it's leather and she's not wearing it again.

Little one seems to like it though, poised in the middle, a nice contrast in shade, like a cloud over a green sea, tail curling around his butt, as he lightly licks one paw.

But why does he look so tired?

A panic fringed in fire finds her edges. And that shouldn't be. There should be no fire. Not here. Not with him. Isn't that at least one thing Xanther's figured out?

"To save something doesn't mean to keep something," Dov once told her. Xanther hadn't understood what he meant, because when you were saving time, for example, weren't you getting time you could keep for yourself?, or when you saved money, wasn't that keeping money for yourself for later?, which also went for food, for a lot of things, and so on, to anything else you were keeping, which Dov implied years ago wasn't the same thing as saving, which Xanther hadn't understood until now.

She was failing him.

It doesn't matter either what Les Parents might say, about her doing all the right things, or about them doing all that they can, or even about what Dov might have done if he were here, Xanther still sees she's the one to blame.

She has failed to figure out something. And it kills her like it's killing him. She can't even come up with a name. And soon enough, Xanther is sure, this failure, like some soiled linen for the dead, is going to wrap him up, wrap them both up.

But what else can she do?

Go back to her mom? Insist they see Dr. Syd again?

Just as the world just is, utterly, and she's sure of that at least, Xanther is equally sure that she doesn't understand the world, especially when it comes to caring for this little one, protecting him from the world, forget the world, saving him for the world.

Xanther isn't coping.

And as much as it terrifies her, it burns her up.

One of the few times Dov talked about death, Xanther had been trying to get him to talk about Hell, about justice after death:

"Eternity," he'd finally answered, "is certain for everyone. Anything less is uncertain."

Xanther still isn't sure what that means, or why, like a lot of what Dov's told her, it sticks with her, but she finds a smidgen of comfort in what Dov seemed to be saying about life in general: don't expect certitude.

So Xanther keeps trying everything. And she's come up with a routine that sorta works: she flicks away the black goop collecting under the little cat's eyes, then with her fingers gently scoops and smears away the dark wax that keeps building up in his ears, then rubs under his chin, and lightly massages his whole spine, starting from between his big ears, working all the way down to the end of his tail, which Xanther then tugs on lightly, as if to give all the vertebrae an extra little stretch, relieving any pinched discs.

He rewards her efforts with that mighty purr, and Xanther feels in herself, as if in him, a calming and cooling occur, wherever it lurks, inside, outside, that acorn of blue flame dying out, as it should, when she's in the house, permitting Xanther to drift away, the two of them curled up together, cuddling, as close as possible, as if what's possible could ever be close enough, no matter how tightly Xanther wants to squeeze, what seems the smallest way into the smallest place, the smallest nothing within the smallest space, what space can never resist, could ever refuse . . .

:: ! ::

:: You've heard this before? ::

:: **TFv1 pp. 812–813!** ::

Xanther even tries, literally, to shut her eyes against this fact, and on that fancy coat too, too warm for any Los Angeles summer day, but maybe perfect for that forest Xanther so easily finds now, blanketed in snow, ice sparked with starlight from a sky she can't behold, too fixed on all the passing stones that Xanther can't help but pursue, frantically flicking them away as fast as she can, a dozen, a score, a hundred even, maybe a thousand, a thousand and one, why not?, just as she keeps flicking through possible names for her little friend, at the same time too, all of them useless, announcing nothing, commanding nothing, in the same way that the stones she banishes reveal beneath a merely curious turquoise, tasteless, inert and without hold, what leaves Xanther cold, and wasting, only a very few even bruised, or is it ripe?, with promise, Xanther too soon feeling like she's surrounded by only stones or that blue, which is when hunger really takes over, a nameless hunger that somehow she knows is his too, Xanther is certain of it, as if the two of them were lost at sea, surrounded by so much water, walking upon those waters, dying of thirst, if here answering thirst requires . . .

. . . teeth.

And to think, this still beats the graver agonies of when they're apart.

"Daughter!" Anwar cries later, just home, walking proudly into her room. "I have a surprise for you! Another early birthday present! You and Daddy are going to New York!"

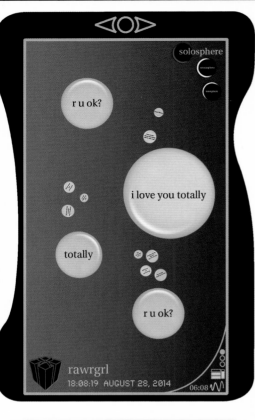

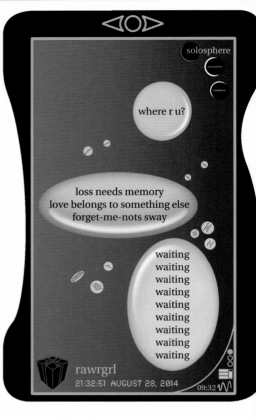

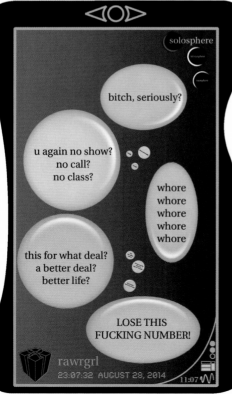

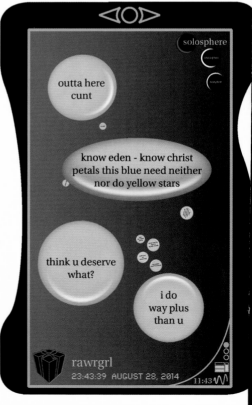

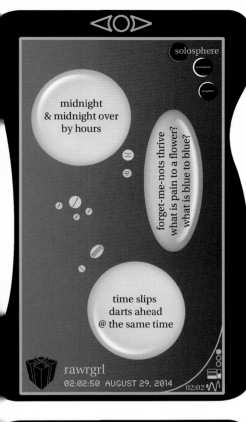

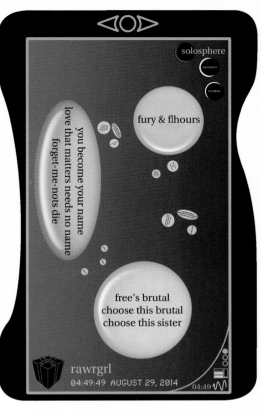

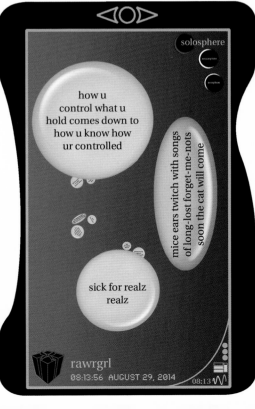

Uneasy Magic

> *Where? I'm sorry. I'm not from around here either.*
>
> — *Victim #6*

There is a problem at the hotel.
Isandòrno goes up to the suite
himself. Teyo welcomes him and
thanks him for the medicines.

—We can bring you a doctor.

Teyo shakes his head.

—Shall I say you will spend the
day looking after your guest?

—It's food poisoning. Or nerves.
She's never been out of the country before.

Teyo disappears into the adjoining bedroom, closing the door behind him, but the door swings back open slightly.

The lights are still off and the drapes all drawn. A muted TV must be casting the flicker of blue. She must still be in bed.

But Isandòrno is wrong.

He believed so because Teyo believed so, because Teyo had moved to the bed.

But she moves in from the side,
from behind, as a sliver, in a hotel
robe. Was she waiting in a corner?

Teyo laughs, but he is just as surprised as Isandòrno is, watching
them through their ajar door.

The sliver murmurs something
and vanishes with the medicines
toward the bathroom.

By the time Teyo re-emerges, slipping on a jacket, Isandòrno has
withdrawn from the living room
to the front door.

—I'm disappointed your friend isn't feeling well, The Mayor says. She should be here.

The Mayor has prepared an elaborate breakfast on the veranda. Though a wave would remove the chair and the place setting, The Mayor leaves them there, as if to suggest that Teyo is incomplete or that he has come here this morning with a promise already broken.

It is a game of course. The Mayor doesn't know the girl. There is a strong chance he will dislike the girl. The Mayor detests Teyo's wife and has never liked any of Teyo's mistresses.

This is better anyway. Like this they can talk directly in a way that the presence of women forbids.

But The Mayor is always curious about women, especially those who haunt the periphery of those he calls friends.

Isandòrno is not a friend, but Isandòrno's refusal of even beautiful whores troubles The Mayor.

Once The Mayor even arranged to have young men encircle Isandòrno.

Isandòrno just stood there, until after an hour, the hires — too fearful to come closer — sought out other party guests more persuaded by their charms.

Of course, The Mayor is right to be troubled: who haunts Isandòrno he cannot touch. For The Mayor, she is an unknown possibility. For Isandòrno, she is an impossibility not even his life's end will redress.

—She's young, Teyo explains of his new and absent friend. She'll recover quickly. You'll meet her and beg me to never bring her here again.

—You say that every time.

—And am I not right every time? Teyo sips his black coffee.

The Mayor laughs. He appreciates Teyo's candor. Whether or not candor is the mettle of reliability, The Mayor warms to objection spoken by a mouth with no teeth.

The Mayor has always misread Teyo this way. Teyo's ability to present weakness is one of the ways weak men find themselves so strong in his presence. They see then only themselves and not the qualities that allow Teyo to succeed. Teyo has sharp teeth.

And before men who are not weak, Teyo offers something even stronger: conspiracy. Teyo already knows that Isandòrno knows that this mistress is different. Whether in an expression or a pause, perhaps as they left the hotel suite, or took a drive through la Zona Rosa, Teyo had seen that Isandòrno had gotten a glimpse. Had he planned it that way?

—I know she is something else, Teyo had even admitted as they reached The Mayor's gate.

Isandòrno had not responded. Like he had not responded when Teyo implied the inverse to The Mayor, that she was like all the rest, said so only for Isandòrno, though to what end was beyond Isandòrno.

Isandòrno knows he is not as
smart as Teyo when it comes to
the valences of alliances requiring
duplicity.

But he can still sense uneasy magic
at work, unsettling for the intention it hides, and magisterial for
the reaction it does not provoke.

How should Isandòrno respond?
To what comes down to only one
thing anyway:

her.

She had arrived before Teyo and checked into the hotel alone. Teyo explained that traveling together would have been imprudent.

What little Isandòrno did see, whether by plan or chance, revealed not even the color of her hair, let alone her eyes.

Only a movement, that in its purpose was nearly an expression, had briefly flickered free of shadows: fierce, enraged, and not unfamiliar to Isandòrno, too aware of how it is we are brought to a cage.

—He was to go north but I had him stay to keep you safe, The Mayor says now, serving Teyo himself.

This morning's fare is healthy: slices of ruby-red grapefruit, served like pancakes, braised in olive oil on both sides, topped with pistachios, pomegranate seeds, and maple syrup.

—I know about the lab, Teyo answers directly. I have also read that there are wars being fought up north. And that there are many bodies there, found and unfound.

—I too have had trouble up there, The Mayor admits, serving Isandòrno next, one slice, and for himself, the rest.

—I'm sorry.

—Of course, if you'd visited The Ranch and it too was followed by such destruction . . .

The Mayor laughs only to weigh Teyo's response, which weighs nothing. Teyo just eats, amused enough to allow The Mayor to keep his laugh.

—I would still like to visit this ranch one day.

—You will, you will.

—Sinaloa? Zeta? Gulf?

—Something else, The Mayor answers, shaking his head as if a stinging insect had entered his ear.

—Someone new? Teyo seems surprised. He puts down his fork and knife.

The Mayor just continues to shake his head.

—What am I missing? Teyo asks Isandòrno then.

The Mayor nods at Isandòrno.

—Explain it to him, The Mayor orders.

Of course, Isandòrno will obey. Isandòrno always obeys The Mayor.

But where to start?

With the story The Mayor told Isandòrno himself?

Or should he just describe The Ranch? The people who work there? Those whom Isandòrno has known for a long time? Like the old man, Juan Ernesto Izquierdo, who has been to Canada and Ghana and every time teases Isandòrno for mistrusting the sea and never crossing a border? Or his wife, Maria? Or their children, Nastasia and Estella, crying —Tío! —Tío! as

Isandòrno fills their palms with candy? Can he leave out Adon Calderos, Santiago Bustamente, or Maite's two boys, Chavez and Garcia Arellano? Isandòrno watched Ortiz, their father, break his back and die. ∴ **TFv1 pp. 610–611.** ∴

That though would mean telling of Maxiley, Servando, Ravelo, Ismael, Freddie, and of the gravest mystery: dear little Luna. ∴ **TFv5** ▮ ∴

Or should Isandòrno just stick with the rich Americans and the animals they paid to kill?

The one called Lawler needed too many shots. The hyena had spun around in a bath of blood. ∴ **TFv2 pp. 26–32.** ∵

The one called Weejun knew what he was doing. He required only one shot. The baby elephant still fell to its knees and vomited blood. ∴ **TFv3 pp. 24–32.** ∵

The one called Edsel kept shooting at legs and the baby giraffe refused to fall. It took many shots before the creature was finally hewed at the base.

—They cried "Timber!" The Mayor had reported. ∷ **TFv4 pp. 26–34.** ∷

Or perhaps Isandòrno should just tell the story of the crates because there were never just three crates, and after the rich Americans had killed the hyena, the baby ele-phant, and the baby giraffe, what did they find in the fourth crate? ∷ **TFv5** ▮▮▮▮▮ ∷

Or would it be better for Isandòrno to detail why it had taken him so long to get back to The Mayor from Veracruz?

Should Isandòrno tell of the jungle and the old Indian and his sick daughter and all the money the old Indian refused to take for a carved head of a cat, which Isandòrno refused to take.

—What hunts you now amigo you already own.

∴ **TFv1 p. 325.** ∴

Or what about the goat and the donkey?

—Never underestimate a cornered animal, Isandòrno finally answers.

Havoc

Which one saw the other come to this place, so long ago?

— *Jacques Derrida*

Can one be focused and *not* serious at the same time? The thought attacks Astair out of nowhere (an absurd redirection toward (what?) an expression((!(?)) while pecking away at (applying finishing(?) touches on) this ((woefully) incomplete (partial)) bibliography (and late!) plus "a statement of purpose" (not even a word (with "a working abstract and the first handful of pages" due in another two weeks ∴ **TFv2 p. 429** ∴)))):

Agamben, Giorgio. *The Open: Man and Animal.* Translated by Kevin Attell. Stanford, CA: Stanford University Press, 2004.

Coetzee, J. M. *The Lives of Animals.* Princeton, NJ: Princeton University Press, 1999.

Gosling, Samuel D. "From Mice to Men: What Can We Learn About Personality From Animal Research?" *Psychological Bulletin*, vol. 127, no. 1, pp. 45–86. 2001.

Grandin, Temple and Johnson, Catherine. *Animals in Translation: Using the Mysteries of Autism to Decode Animal Behavior.* New York: Scribner, 2005.

Haraway, Donna J. *When Species Meet.* Posthumanities Series, vol. 3. Minneapolis: University of Minnesota Press, 2008.

Hillman, James. *Animal Presences.* Uniform Edition of the Writings of James Hillman, vol. 9. Putnam, CT: Spring Publications, 2008.

King, Barbara J. *How Animals Grieve.* Chicago: University of Chicago Press, 2013.

Malamud, Randy. *Reading Zoos: Representations of Animals and Captivity.* New York: New York University Press, 1998.

Wise, Steven M. *Rattling the Cage: Toward Legal Rights for Animals.* Cambridge, MA: Perseus Books, 2000.

She could go on (it's one part at least (none of it grin or frown-provoking)). Astair sips coffee ((second cup (half-and-half creamy (green tea was around dawn))) tracking this switch from the interior oblivion of the external question of appearance to the exterior ridicule of the ~~infernal~~ (internal!) question of—(what?(!)(a cat(?)!))(the reason obvious)).

Astair stands up from the (piano room) table (heaped with books and her papers and cups of pens (morning slashes of an already hot sun (the drapes smolder with dust (might as well be smoke (a prayer for a flicker of flames (anything to arrest this torture)))))).

She closes her eyes. Rubs her temples. Resistance here is just evidence of an engagement with "hard thinking" ∴ **TFv3 p. 608** ∴ (a good sign(?)).

Astair sits down again. Tries again. She is more successful (putting aside this (what is likely a perfunctory (anyway)) list of books ((even if Avantine reads it) will he check it?) in favor of sentences (of purpose (to what purpose?))).

> To explore/consider/treat how animality produces/
> provokes/privileges a dialogue/scrutiny/awakening
> responsible for perspective/insight/plasticity/disassembly/
> deconstruction regarding/concerning/detailing our own
> mythic/misconstrued/misapprehended/constructed/
> inherited/projected sense of self.

The (ghosts of) hyphens haunt the phrase (slashes (instead) bonding it as well as cutting it apart (what will be (when choice prevails) absent from the final phrase (which Astair knows is grossly incomplete (because it's missing the most important subject!)))).

Saudade

        (the word surfaces (instead)
(abruptly (randomly(?))) unpronounced (like the
Brazilian lover who went unkissed (teaching her
those sweet syllables (Astair was sixteen (and mauled
by the prohibitory attention of her mother and sisters (Astair can't even remember the girl's name
((though older than sixteen) only the way she taught
her about longing and melancholy (it exploded in
Astair's mouth like a surge of Cherry Coke she has
(to this day) never tasted but still imagines in all its
silly sugary childish deliciousness (was anything not
delicious in Rio? (not on that trip)))))))))(what saying aloud (anyway) would grant a (verbal) division
its Latin root (*solitatem* (solitude)) prohibits)

complete with the memory of Ipanema sand between
her toes and warnings of thieves and illicitly sipped
grown-up drinks (along too with something more
than curiosity (a (now) enduring) concern)):

Astair goes searching for Xanther's cat.

    She stravages the house (each failure to uncover
the creature in the folds of her daughter's unmade
bed (or find it in Anwar's office (not even appearing
like a white hole in their jet sofa in the den)) ratchet-
ing up (more and more!) her anxiety that it (truly!!)
has vanished (and cursed(!!!) her for life)).

Astair returns to Xanther's room. Finds this time (among the mess of sheets (a blanket partially on the floor)) that crumple of green leather (the ridiculous coat her parents sent Xanther ($5,000! (what they could do with that!))). Feels good though. Should. For a Saint Laurent.

Astair makes the bed and hangs up the jacket in Xanther's closet. Only a quick swipe of a cottony sleeve keeps (a high tide of) tears (sea without surf) from falling. What is she now (always?)? Some sort of mommy dearest? *Wait—!* It doesn't matter. Astair backs away from the closet quick. Returns the bed to its delightful disorder. Returns the coat too to its delightful irreverence (metal hangers still tolling the moment disrupted by the gift taken back (freely chiming the absence)).

Where's the cat?

(thumping down the stairs) Astair tries to knock out of her head the story (Gia told her (with an evil wink (that should have been shared (no longer was)))) about a family in Malibu that came home to discover their children's cat no more than a head (in one room) and (in another room) the bloody remains of ribs and guts (not even a carcass (internal organs and fur and the rest consumed(?))). The struggle was everywhere: stamps of blood on the floor and sofas and even a corner.

The police concluded a raccoon had gotten into the house and hunted the poor creature down.

Raccoons (supposedly) are good at decapitations.

Astair (finally) finds Xanther's charge not a few feet away from where Astair was working in the piano room (on Anwar's standing desk (what often supports sheet music or a (more) ambitious libretto (but these days upholds his ((old) enormous!) dictionary (open (perhaps to a new word he was digging up for Xanther (their thing!))) this thing (Xanther's thing!) asleep here (cut in half by sun and shadow (words buried beneath its stillness))))).

It's this stillness that escapes itself as a form Astair too quickly apprehends as a powerful blow ((like) a forearm knocking her on the side of the head (almost knocking her down (like it had knocked her down before))): too much to touch (finding here an imminent death (already *touch* enough)).

Astair clasps her hands like a Quaker's prayer ((further dragging that peaceful fist to her pounding chest) as if fingers and palms could stave off the terror of what a thing free (before it has even acted upon that freedom) can (in every way (of every moment)) come to mean before yet coming upon its moment).

The rush bathes Astair in sweat.

The past preempts any sense of the present.

Though maybe a little cry of horror and sorrow escapes her lips.

Her daughter! That thing!

Still rushing at her . . .

That fucking lion!

For the rest of the day Astair keeps pushing away the memory of that ((extra)ordinary) creature (the thought (*too many thoughts!*) of what could have been) by focusing on her clients.

They are (for now) what matters most.

Forget the trauma of Monday night. Forget the distraction of the Ibrahims' collapsing finances (or the ~~distraction~~ (*hope!*) of Anwar's prospective new employer (Galvadyne (why does that sound so famil-iar?)) (or (alongside her bibliography for Avantine) her own scans of Craigslist for some kind of (living(?)) wage (she hasn't stopped revising her resume!))).

Her clients (are the now that) matter most.

Ananias Fielding has run out of sex stories (though still determined to froth up something with her latest obsession: organizing her shoes ("I only have nine pairs!")). Astair suddenly notices (finally?) that (in all their sessions (in the same way that her parents' professions have never rated a comment)) Ananias has left undisclosed any kind of professional ambition ("Often it is the omission that confesses the purpose" (Sandra Dee Taylor).). Astair's simple question about a job results in a ten-minute sob.
   (unfortunately) With Ms. Penikas (a surprise that she's still coming back) Astair makes the mistake of trying to sound profound (maybe because Ms. Peni-kas' age seems to warrant something profound (the intention isn't bad)). (however) Astair's "Life teaches you how to live it if you can just live long enough to learn it" earns "What a shit-cup you're serving."

Work ends up being hard but after work is worse: Abigail at La Poubelle (where their friendship might be heading) ∷ **5907 Franklin Avenue, Los Angeles, CA 90068** ∷ ∷ *"C'est moi dans la poubelle,"* Pound whispers—∷ ∷ *Fin de Partie.* **Beckett.** ∷.

Abigail was hard to see because she hadn't been there when it happened (and it keeps forcing Astair to go there (even as she keeps trying to concentrate on Abigail's apology ((at least) focus on her glass of white wine (sweating on their outdoor table)))).

Astair can't touch the wine and (coldly) accepts the repeated apologies (she's heard them before (over the phone (in person isn't helping))).

"Here," Astair says (signalling their server (for the check)).

"Is that it?" Abigail looks alarmed (her lips trembling?).

"I know why this isn't working." Astair glances at the bill (puts down cash they don't have). "Do you have some more time?"

"Yes," Abigail stutters.

Astair's idea seems well-reasoned. And Abigail was more than willing. Xanther is even in the living room when they walk in (as if both women were expected (the creature (if still (still)) poised blindly (as all*ways*) on one shoulder)).

"Xanther—" Abigail's voice shakes. "I want to apologize. I want to ask your forgiveness for putting you in har—"

Xanther doesn't let Abigail finish (the (absolute (persisting)) stillness on her shoulder all the more odd given how much movement follows).

Xanther jumps to her feet and hugs Abigail. "Don't be stupid!"

The warm embraces continue ((leaving Astair feeling marginalized(?)) the two suddenly fused in mutual worry ((!) over that tremendous beast (capable of disemboweling (decapitating!) everyone here ((if she were here) with barely a swipe (a stabbing nail))))). Her daughter and her friend(?) laugh. Cry a little(?). Abigail even pets(!) Xanther's cat.

Xanther even asks if Toys is okay.

"He's having a hard time," Abigail admits. "They still haven't found her."

Toys' lament in various interviews had (all week) stirred Astair into new furies.

"She's scared," Toys had groaned on KTAL.

"She needs care." On the radio.

And in the face (of many (many!)) objections voiced by fearful residents in the area: "Just some tenderness will bring her home to us."

Worst of all (though) was Xanther's defense (then (and still)).

"Poor Satya. She's a mother, you know. She's looking for her child."

Huh? That wasn't on the news. Or in anything Toys or Abigail had since said (ever said).

Astair forces herself to let this (obvious) bonding run its course. Even as her own hands again clasp in wet disbelief. Heart beating harder in disbelief. Heat and sweat starting up again (the more Astair tries to hold it back (insist on disbelief)).

Abigail is clueless. And even if Xanther had been there she wasn't there as a mother (watching her firstborn charged by—).

Astair catches herself mumbling something (nothing compared to the (panicked) fury she had unleashed when they had gotten home that night (((talk about incoherent mumbles!) all on Anwar (poor Anwar!) (unable to tell the story in any other way (without anger (and she still hadn't told the whole story (what Astair had really seen . . .))))) *We are going to hire lawyers! We are going to sue the shit out of Mr. Keen Toys!* (on and on)) until Xanther (who clearly looked fine (what Anwar had repeatedly kept trying to point out (especially with that confounding curl of white again in her arms))) suddenly locked eyes with her (when did that happen?) and (in barely a whisper (before storming out (parting the twins like a poor sea))) let mom have it:

"You do that and I'll never forgive you!"

). Is that what she's mumbling now!? ∴ No. ∴

Astair flinches again at the sudden intrusion of that roaring figure somehow free of her cage bounding for dear Xanther.

That fucking lioness!

Abigail ends up thanking Astair (and at least now (on her own doorstep) Astair's resistance falters before all the warm hugs (Anwar's cautionary counter-arguments to her litigious strikes ((Xanther's evident well-being (not to mention stalwart alignment with the animal))(not to mention cost)) sinking in too)).

Then Xanther's saying how nice that was and even agrees to join Astair in some pre-dinner Tai Chi and would Astair (already breathless over the agreement) object if little one stayed on her shoulder and (Xanther's not breathless) of course Astair's saying "Of course! Of course! I love you!" (nearly out of breath) because does she love this kid (does she ever (and ever and ever (and ever . . .))).

There's even something strangely shocking about tonight's practice out on the back patio (if shocking can come at you so slowly (cf. glacier)).

Astair keeps trying to believe her daughter's form (its precision and solidity) is an optical illusion. Has to be. No question. Xanther's gangling limbs wobble and quaver. Bony elbows lurch out like featherless wings. Both knees never stop knocking like an irregular metronome. Her head (all the while) looks like some bobble-headed toy on the back dash of a car without shocks.

No movement is threaded. The driving base (of the big toe) is a universe away from her (long (quivering)) fingers. Xanther is (plain and simple) a disconnected mess of motion.

And yet . . .

"Our beginning," Astair (gently(?)) instructs. "Double-weighted, and then, moving our root into just the right foot, we step with our left."

(at least) Astair's weight shifts. Their hands rise (together) and then ((slowly) a moment later) fall.

"Now Ward Off to the Right. Good. To the east. Now back to the north for Grasp Sparrow's Tail. More like stroking. Yes. Good."

More shuffles. Turns.

"Again to the east. Follow that melting ball. Now Roll Back. Soft. Gentle. Press now. Withdraw. Press again. Remember: we're not really pushing. Definitely not shoving. That's nice. And now on to the Single Whip Sequence. Don't forget to breathe."

Astair had not yet gone into the details of this part of the form but Xanther doesn't stop ((like she'd already done it a hundred times (YouTube?)) right hand pulling away a thread from her (cupped) left hand). Xanther keeps going too: arms opening wide (less and less wobbling) closing then (still wobble-less (powerfully?)) to play the harp (or play the guitar (what looks(?) (briefly (really)) like the closing of a vise ("What could break an arm," Lambkin informed Astair once (winking)))).

"Very impressive," Astair says (the compliment hardly an exaggeration (had Xanther picked that up just by watching her? (of course she had (was she (also) already on the way to Strike with Shoulder (before Astair had stopped her)?)))).

That Xanther's practice is still rudimentary is a comfort (the familiar shape of her dear child (she is still the same (she is okay (as if familiar = same = okay really means any such thing)))) and yet . . .

Is it the cat on Xanther's shoulder that seems to throw everything off (rewriting the ((already) deficient) equation to: strange = different = not okay?)?

Is it the "not okay" that's at issue here? Because Xanther is clearly not "not okay."

Is it the cat then that's troubling everything? Maybe its evident frailty (increasing?) is also what keeps increasing Astair's anxiety? As if the tiny creature were nothing other than a projection of Xanther's occluded health.
Its stony deadness haunting her daughter . . .
As if it were the sepulcher making of the rest a grave! (a cemetery! (Xanther!)).

Astair catches sight of her own terror. Forces a laugh. Forget all that.

Maybe it is this stillness that seems to make of Xanther's jittery inexperience with Tai Chi something else: informed by the roots of a mountain and the reach of the horizon and the emptiness of some terrifying sky.

What would Lambkin Crierhue say about Astair's little protégé (Lambkin who studied under William C. C. Chen (Chen a classmate of Dr. Tao (both of whom studied under Professor Cheng Man-Ching)))? Would Lambkin spy this optical illusion? How the motionless animal (falsely?) implies something Xanther could not(?) possess herself?

Of course he would. He'd probably laugh too.

"What's the secret to Tai Chi? Ha! Baggy clothes! Or in your daughter's case: a cat!"

"Why do we practice Tai Chi you ask? What is the purpose? It is a wonderful waste of time!"

The sort of things Lambkin says (even if once (while urging Astair to consider studying the Sword Form) he did say something profound about a dragonfly and a stick (as profound as he got)).

Astair (again) compliments Xanther (who couldn't be smiling more (Astair smiling more too (at the thought of (one day (soon)) bringing her daughter to one of Lambkin's classes (maybe they would even play The Animal Game there (with the other practitioners ((what animal would Xanther divine for Lambkin?) a wistful thought over too much time without ∴ **TFv1 p. 237** ∴)))))).

(instead of repeating the form (or Astair demonstrating the rest)) They revisit Single Whip. Xanther's disjointed repeats reassure Astair.
Astair even discovers herself (almost) able to ignore that (furred) thing (of marble).

Not that that inconsequential sl(e)ight of bones and white matters.

(still) It only takes one instance (((impossibly) brief) where child and animal again settle into that strange motion(lessness) (flowing (yet still) like old water (what Astair never wanted to see once (let alone here now)))) to bring it all back again . . .

The lioness bellows.

Something like that (terrifying!

    bellowing again
(

               (

                     now

)

      (

         here

)

)

    crossed with some tone of

ringing
          lament
             (a moan?)

or is that only what Astair hears

(

      (

                  now

)
      (

        here

)

)

(her own moan?)

after her ((precocious) resilient!) daughter's numerous (and unflustered) retellings (her rede-scribings?)?

).

Either way it happened too fast.

Despite any long drawn-out failure of recollection.

Over like that.

She was gone.

With one impossible bound

(bound
(what to do with that?)).

Hundreds upon hundreds of muscled pounds

ringed with so many claws and so many teeth

suddenly

rendered weightless

by what?

a word?

(Xanther won't say)

a kiss?

(but Xanther's silence can't deny what Astair saw)

improbably linking the two

(counterbalancing impossible disproportions

(violence against vulnerability))

in a strenuous discordance (fused nonetheless)

(Xanther as solemn as she stood confused

(fragile as she was the world

the (w)hole of it

(and she was))

)

she is

all of Astair's world

(a moment away from gone).

Pounding Astair's heart

now

still

with the consequences

still

now

of that one awful possibility:

spoken by this monument (persisting ((ever(?)) now)
((ever(?)) still) before Astair's lidless eyes) of her
child lowering her head

to that bellow

for a kiss (?)

or a word (?)

(sometimes aren't they

the same?)

transforming the (w)hole of it

that enormous brutal nameless

creature

into air

()

( )

lifting off the ground

( )

over Xanther

( )

( )

( )

far above

hitting the chain-link   fence

            ( )   rattling

bending   ( )

                rippling

        ( )   threatening

                                        to give
way   ( )

        (not even that threat coming true)

                                    holding
                until
                        after
    ( )   a flurry
                                        of

                back-paw (rabbit!) kicks

                                    ( )
and a scramble to the top
                        Satya!
                                    flew
    to the hillside
                (gone like a moon
                            (on an ocean
            (erased by a storm (both)))).

Though out there the ocean had been desert.

The moon . . . a setting sun.

(*Where can we look for the witness for whom there is no witness?* (Blanchot.))

And the storm . . . Astair's own watering eyes.

Storming still.

"You're not seriously fetaling inside a closet right now?" Taymor asks.

"I am," Astair answers ((wiping more tears from her face (shifting the phone to the other ear))(chin digging into her knees)).

"Huh. Okay, Ms. Therapy, you should get yourself to a clinic."

"Sure."

"You should listen to me, girl." Astair knows Taymor is trying for glib (if not quite able to mask the concern (outright worry?)).

"Don't 'should' all over me, Tay."

"Fair enough."

"Xanther's fine. So why am I the one with post-traumatic stress? All over what didn't happen, just could have happened."

"I saw the news. Pretty incredible. Don't tell Xanther this but she's Roxanne's hero now. Seriously. We watched the clip together. Mother and daughter. 'Mom, now that's facing down the lion!' she said."

"That's sweet." Astair doesn't want to say that the lion wasn't a lion but a lioness with a history of viciousness (and Xanther hadn't been facing her down (she was doing something else . . .)).

"How's Anwar?"

"He and Xanther are similar. They get over things. In June, Anwar got mugged, at gunpoint too, but he's fine. Why am I the one carrying their scars?"

"Gia's going to need you," Taymor pivots.

"Why?"

"If she keeps dating that Catholic."

"Really? Still looking for a reason to climb back on that cross?"

211

"Is that what *you're* doing?"

"I just want to go to Greenblatt's ∴ **8017 Sunset Boulevard, Los Angeles, CA 90046** ∴, crawl into a slutty booth, order a half pound of pastrami, and drink a bottle of wine by myself."

"Ha! There's my girl."

"You're right," Astair laughs (the tears gone (knee-clutch relaxing to crossed legs)). "I do like making life hell for myself."

"Not even life. A *possible* life."

Astair laughs again: "Of course, since when is hell anything but the story of heaven?"

"Call Gia."

"Maybe you're the one suited to be a shrink. This helped. Thank you."

"What else are rich friends for?"

"Are you okay, Tay?" Astair suddenly asks (catching something hidden (uncurling for a moment) in the tones of her friend's joke).

"You don't want to know."

"Give it up." Astair can't help but think of Home-Porn.

"You're gonna be a great shrink," Taymor sighs.

"And you're not getting off that easy."

"It's about money."

"When isn't it about money?"

No response.

Astair waits.

"Ted just made another two billion dollars," Taymor finally comes clean. "We had so much already. It shouldn't make a difference."

"But it has?"

"I don't know why."

All Astair can think of (what she doesn't say): we are corrupted by our contexts; just as we are the consequences of our corruptions.

Sleep comes dreamless. Morning seems brighter.

We are encouraged by our contexts (Astair (re)considers while brushing her teeth). Just as we are the consequences of our encouragements.

(at breakfast) Astair encourages Xanther to have a great day (though why wouldn't she? (Saturday (home with the tiny (still unnamed!) beast))).

Freya gets a laugh after morning soccer practice (spotting a woman ravaged by plastic surgery ((aslant eyes)(glossy cheeks)(lips just shy of a duck's bill))): "Old people here either look old or funny." Especially true in L.A. And Florida.

"I'm gonna get a visit soon from the trooth fairy." Again Freya ((a little later) wiggling a loose tooth).

Even Anwar seems sunnier with the prospects of a (probable?) new job. All the interest he's getting (with prospective interviews) is doing wonders for his confidence.

Astair even takes a risk (it pays off!) and drags her laptop over to Xanther on the living room couch. Together (like Taymor and Roxanne(?)) they watch the quick clip of that golden blur (the lioness) overleaping the smaller darker stillness (Xanther).

"Not how I remember it!" Astair says.

"Not even close," Xanther agrees.

Astair even finds something (strength?) in shielding Xanther from the more painful details (what Abigail confessed (so far not surfacing on the news)).

(after all) It wasn't just the locks to Satya's pen that had lost that day.

Those who had learned to live within encountered the worst consequences of suddenly trying to live without.

The monkeys all survived (choosing to remain within (petting Gable)). Angel and Angle too.

The fox and wolves returned to the call of food (though Quasar had three long bloody scratches down his left flank (reportedly he and Aiflow had since bonded and commenced an odd friendship ("The ties that bind can't compete with the scars that bond," Toys reportedly said))).

Havoc was another story.

Toys found Havoc (the young grizzly bear) in a dry creek bed the following morning.

Slashed.

Dismembered.

Entrails strewn if not devoured.

Chunks of

flesh gone.

That grace.

That balance.

Those long black claws useless

against her charge.

She'd even eaten

his long black tongue.

They didn't find Havoc by some blood trail or blood-splashed stones either.

Even the smell came later.

It was a cloud of flies.

So many that the searchers heard them first (the same searchers who would post pictures minutes later (quick as lightning (before the thunder))).

((though) that dark dawn) Sound (not light) was portent.

Louder than Toys' wails.

Air thick with a storm of devouring wings.

Before lunch Shasti surprises Astair. Astair had just e-mailed Avantine her bibliography and statement of purpose (now much simplified: "While all else offers a screen open to our projections, not all screens are created equal.") By the look on Shasti's face not all shadows are created equal either.

"What is it, my beauty?" Astair sets aside the laptop (wraps an arm around her daughter (at once in tears)).

"I'm sorry."

"Talk to me, baby."

"For lying about the glass. For lying about Xanther. I shouldn't have done that. It was wrong of me. It was bad."

Astair strokes Shasti's hair (grinding back her own Question Song (like Xanther? (let Shasti speak her peace (piece!)))).

"I can't sleep anymore. Something's there now."

"Where?"

"In my sleep."

Astair nods. Waits. But Shasti is just crying now.

"Did Freya make you do it?" Astair (eventually) has to ask (as gently as possible (without saying "lie" (holding to vagueness (because she knows better (appearing to instigate any sort of divisiveness (between the twins) most often results in unification and that cruel silence))))).

Shasti doesn't choose silence now. What she says (though) is worse.

"Freya's acting funny. At night she yells at voices in the corner. She keeps saying there's a ladder in the floor."

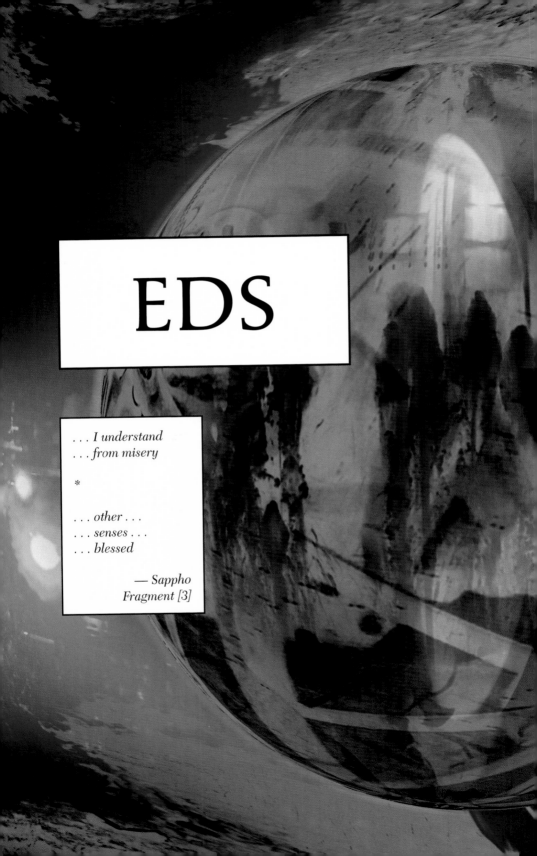

EDS

... I understand
... from misery

*

... other ...
... senses ...
... blessed

— Sappho
Fragment [3]

Ed beat the hell out of her. Ed always beats the hell out of her.

"How long have you kept these on?"

It doesn't help that this doctor's name is also Ed. But it doesn't hurt either. He puts the braces aside.

"Longer than usual," Cas answers. Cas knows the Ed that does the damage.

This Ed before her — Dr. Edward Holt — bends to examine her knees. He takes his time, inspecting her blisters and other areas where the skin has scabbed over.

This Ed is equally careful with her elbows. Cas shifts on the table paper, the crepe texture clinging to the backs of her bare legs. Thank you paper robe. Cas has always hated these things. If design and disposability serve so well, grant patients at least some outlandish colors too.

"Okay?" The doctor asks, his soft touch retreating.

"Fidgety," Cas responds, trying to smile, trying to remember that a lot of people have driven her a lot of miles just for this appointment.

Since Asheville and Little Switzerland, they've also driven in plenty of circles. At one point they were parked in Monongahela National Forest near Durbin, and later jumped over to another interstate. Cas lost track of how many times they crossed back and forth between states, cautiously moving north, then stopping to change vehicles, reconfirm a shifting schedule with a nameless doctor experienced with classic EDS ∷ *Ehlers-Danlos syndrome* ∷ in the elderly. Though that's not all they confirmed. Bobby had done his best to hide it from her, but if there's one thing he can't fake it's sleep.

"The dead?"

"Mainly   off   the news. If
we trusted the   news we'd
be dead too."

"Who?"

"Eisa and Leisl.   The   body
count is five now   but   they're
still going through   the ashes."

"How many children?"

Bobby held up three fingers. "All of them."

By morning the body count was six. By noon, seven. One thing that wasn't changing was the story that domestic terrorists had been constructing a big bomb in a small basement. Everyone was lucky that it wasn't a dirty bomb. Everyone was lucky that the dirty terrorists had done themselves in.

By the time they reached Charlottesville, all the names were confirmed. Cas recognized none of the rest but she knew they had all died for her.

"Then   Recluse   knows   we're   not dead?"

Bobby nod-   ded. And the
bad   news   still   wasn't
over.

" T h e y   found bodies
in   Christ-   mas   Circle.
Jerry   and   Nicole.   Not
even   their   dog was spared."

"Why?"

The Carsons had lived at the RoadRunner Club for years. The foursome had enjoyed quite a few afternoon pitchers of Tom Collins.

                                         "Because they knew us?"

221

"I don't like these," Dr. Ed says. Cas knows it's Dr. Holt, but Dr. Ed has already stuck. He won't have to know.

"Ed's an abusive type. But what can I say, I'm putty in his hands."

Dr. Ed chuckles. He moves away from the dark patches on her shoulders and hips and begins to check her joint laxity, starting with her knees. No surprises there.

"How recent are all the bruises?"

"I'm less steady on my feet when weapons are involved."

"You're a brave woman," Dr. Ed says.

"Bruises heal," Cas assures him. How much have they told him? "It's the scars I have trouble with."

Dr. Ed runs the palm of his hand over her left arm. His touch feels good. Cas can guess what her touch feels like to him. How had Marnie described it? "Smooth but like velvet you can stretch." Marnie had been very careful not to press too hard and never stretch.

Cas' scars — from a lifetime of tumbles and mistakes — stretch on their own. Dr. Ed pauses by the toils of brown skin by her wrist. The story there is misread repeatedly.

"Washing a wine glass. It slipped from my fingers. My fingers followed it into this."

Dr. Ed moves on from the particular: "Papyraceous."

Cas knows the word. "I prefer comparisons to cigarette paper."

"Do you smoke?"

"I used to. Unfortunately. I lost a lot of resiliency defending my addictions."

"Any addictions now?"

"Only one." Cas waits for Dr. Ed to ask. She's thankful he doesn't.

"Creams?"

"I've tried them all. If you've got a new one, I'm all ears. I avoid UV. Vitamin C and E seem to help."

"What else? Calcium?"

Cas gives him the whole list. She's pretty disciplined.
"But often my . . . work distracts me." Another test.

Cas isn't even sure why she's testing. So
what if he presses her the way so many of
them do, if they've heard the rumors, if
they believe the rumors. For whatever
it proves, and it isn't proving much,
Dr. Ed passes. He gently checks her
elbows and wrists. Her fingers sub-
mit to his easy pressure, though
he doesn't take them that far.

"Kids love it when I bend them
back far enough to scratch the
back of my hand."

"Maybe that's best kept to a
minimum?"

"Yes, Doctor Ed."

There. It's out. But he snorts. Playful. Mid-
thirties? Mid-forties? Something about the rosiness
of his broad face, the green in his eyes, the prevailing
curl of a smile, keeps age from making a claim. He must have

kids. Maybe a lot. He looks like the kind of man who would have six kids and play with them nonstop. But before Cas can take her guesses to task, Dr. Ed asks about sprains and dislocations. Joint tightening is always a gleeful subject. Her heart, though, is not — not even in jest.

"I would usually suggest an ultrasound to check whether or not there's been any dilation of the aortic root."

Cas shakes her head. "Whatever's in here is in here, and finding out isn't going to change a thing. As you know, surgery, at my age, under these circumstances, is not an option."

Cas wonders if the irony of her response registers. Not that it matters.

"Family?" Dr. Ed asks instead.

Cas hesitates. She'd have preferred something fawning and self-serving.

"One daughter," Cas manages to cough out.

"You've consulted geneticists?"

"I have. Unfortunately, my daughter and I are . . . estranged."

"No communication?"

"None. For years."

"I'm sorry. That must be hard."

"You have no idea." Hearing herself,
Cas winces at the presumption.
"Or do you?"

"Let's just say the failure of
family has taught me to be
more compassionate toward
conflicts between cultures."

"Do you have children?" Cas'
curiosity rarely relents.

"I'll let you get dressed." Dr. Ed
answers.

Cas doesn't see Dr. Ed again, but the
nurse leading them to a back door at
the clinic hands Bobby an appointment
card.

Outside, Bobby tells Cas they need to get her a swimsuit.

Cas would have preferred a crummy motel to yet another bedroom in another sympathetic home. Familial touches here keep imposing those three unwavering lines responsible for torching three children and more.

"Are you okay?" Bobby looks shaky too.

"Fine."

"You stopped breathing. I counted."

"I said I'm fine."

"I know you're not fine. I know none of us are fine. The question is only how best to cope."

"How long did you count for?"

"Twenty-seven seconds." Bobby hands her the sweater swaddling the Orb. "It's okay. We have no choice. You need to find something they can use."

Immediate anticipation draws Cas toward an elation she hasn't felt for months. Maybe she'll OD. Cas grimaces. Or is it just a weird smile for the weirder comfort such an outcome offers? To welcome the Big Sleep with a big yawn and settle? As if Cas could settle now, let alone sleep. The static buzz-ing her fingertips doesn't compare to the burn growing in her chest, dilating outward in long, slow, warm pulses.

The security charms awaken Mefisto's Orb with such intense clarity that all else, including any feeling attached to that else, vanishes before Cas' reciprocating focus.

Mefisto had said his Orb was much slower, but the celerity of its transition-ing and repositioning rollout algorithms catches Cas off guard. Had Sorcerer tricked her? It wouldn't be the first time. Had he nar-rowed further the Window beneath their bend? Less than a year? Months? Weeks?

But as Cas quickly discovers, the VEM Window Reduction here doesn't come close to matching the Orb she sacrificed in Dayton. Not ten years. Or even twenty. More like forty. But Mefisto had still provided a constellation of known Recluse sequences to aid Cas' search.

The coordinates help. Mefisto knows Cas well. For hours she follows her refreshed instincts into the haze of indeterminacy, and this time when Bobby returns to their room, ordering her to stop, to move, to uncoil the body she so often sacrifices to her mind, she's found something.

Nuncupative whispers
young hearts understand
but old enough for the young life
life understands.

She dances around her round belly
in a blouse like hazy skies and milky coffee.

He dances too. Tries.

Pokes scorpion grass into her hair.

Wild hair black as her skin.

His linen jacket and slacks bright as her grin.

He has sideburns!
No tie.

ARC OF WINSOME

Her hair lost under a black sail of cloth.
Her face grayer than ten years should cost.

Atropos.

She doesn't move. She doesn't smile.

The child doesn't move.
The child doesn't smile.

He whispers over the child.
He whispers over her.

He tightens his tie.

"VEM," Bobby says, his finger tapping the first bit of code on the sheet he's placed in front of her. Bobby knows "stop" or "move" will get him nowhere. This way is much better.

DiOOSN7FuA7IXRUBlGzC2q/eB8vNndyr
IYLIsTGcfljx9dN5FubhV3NwtJVIEkDY
PJ7AU/443bfwbb9xzcFiAKOhqB5
XQFM+I3zU9/ztPGmMDtK1oyd-
WEQiwjMUmWBgYy8BatpWch-
7dutGRgAS0KKUxID2G0N8s-
B0tGhZQHl

"Also from him?"

E/D01z1gQBPWACDsP
0eR752re3HAxsNWLcnL
Xa9Mj9vt050WcaBTs0U
UiyVF+oUCydUBM3zusD
R+dtJ0B0ONxIL2rAzYQ
8OA//oQq2lLtzgdz+FuqTz
HqZQCQzRsA4RrqVEqO3
GE9lu0loKWJg==

The second passphrase is on a Post-it:

esse quam videri

"Yup," Bobby grunts. "We posted it on reddit. The meeting you'll never have to have."

dALUKK7nUm91W2y5zjEjJOXZ57pjtHusb3S8tStLT7cuXu+KNHw57AXFJt940Sq
Oewl6rCPXoDx1Mn9qTXTnxEpw6Vc+GkDwA3eeCNsumqVlGG69q1PJoDnKOg
7VvpMc

"Vulnerabilities?"

"On reddit!?" Bobby scoffs. "They couldn't crack this in three months, six months. Fact. By six months we'll be the facts."

"Alive or dead," Cas mutters, if still with a chuckle in there somewhere. Bobby catches it too.

"I thought you'd appreciate the passphrase."

And she does: sipaapuni

"He got back to us with this." Bobby slides over another page. This too has a Post-it. Blank.

nQ3Uz8K5B4ns2e3UOJVHRan9+fKia/bJsoneV9U5TkEnQuN4ZGHJ5t605yos
7H8LHQq7g8+9GcNoHT+tgU0B/DP68Q4cB4cnlX/8r2qbPxn0ey9clBRat5ulxZlV
lLLntj8=

"Guesses?" Cas asks.

"None yet. 'Gettysburg proper' was their clue but we ruled that out."

Bobby waits for some flash of insight but
Cas has none.

"place of bears" she offers
instead. Laughs.

Bobby laughs too.

"Walk?"

"A few more min-
utes. I've found
something."

Cas returns to
marking the new
constellation but
Bobby does not go.
Worse, he hovers. Not
that hovering will afford
even a glimpse.

"What is it?" she snaps.

"The lion girl?"

Bobby knows how to distract her. Again Cas darkens the Orb.

"The one in the news?"

"I'll tell you on our walk."

And he does.

"What do you mean *her?*" Cas wants to race back at once to the Orb. Bobby slows her down. She needs to pace herself. She needs to indulge a warm Virginia night. She needs to heal.

"The question we have to ask is if this changes anything. Will Recluse take note?"

"But what happened to Xanther?" Cas yelps, surprised by her own terror.

"Relax. The big thing just jumped over her."

Back in their room, Bobby tries to keep her from another Orb session. He partially succeeds. They go to sleep but sleep fails to hold her for more than a couple of hours.

Cas Orbs-up, scrying Clip #6, Xanther still there with her storms. Though at this hour the storms seem more terrible, more powerful, as if they might not only swallow the child but the Orb too.

what Xanther
demands of every sky,
with every wave,
drawing crashes of
lightning and thunder
into a new sky

As an afterthought, Cas revisits Clip #3.

The sight shocks her. Discovered in 1988 by Cas, of Cas herself, sitting at a computer back in 1984, studying Mefisto's curious syntax with an even more curious opaline halo surrounding her. Clips aren't supposed to change. Is that what Recluse was getting at? Yet here is Cas without a halo. And whatever digital disturbance is at work now, however small, however transparent, these frail currents called forth by a new climate still seem like incipient storms rising angrily against the day.

"Some piece of ass too?"
she imitates him.
"If you were hash I'd smoke you."

More mumbles than an imitation.
For herself.
Then to herself.

"How dare you, Bobby Stern! When's the last time you smoked anything?"

That gets Cas giggling.

"What sorcery's this?"

Cas should have returned to bed, to less vivid dreams, or better yet, to no dreams at all. But Bobby and the morning find her on Cemetery Ridge.

"At least tell me it's Recluse."

She admits it's not.

"Where would we be if Prometheus had only stared at the light and not shared it?"

Bobby leaves to find her swimsuit.

The thought of Prometheus tearing himself away from light's enchantments gives Cas another reason to love Bobby, exactly what she needs to tear herself away from the Orb's dark enchantments, though not before sneaking another glance at this latest deepening.

Evening
before the third day.

"Born under"

Union blue. Tents as taverns. Lanterns against grief.
Cemetery Ridge.

One captain walks the camp,
cowled in dark wool to hide face and bars.
Lips move. Stop.
Working something out against

Seminary Ridge

where Pickett waits.
"The heart quickens at such a message,
born under a cool and ageless moon."

An hour later, in the pool with Dr. Ed, Cas isn't thinking of Gettysburg, or herself, or even Xanther, but of Recluse, and what she'll snippet for Bobby. Let him see for himself. This discovery. What Cas cringes to share with her husband, let alone herself, as if just this possible advantage might make of them something more like him.

"Keep walking," Dr. Ed urges. He stands in the shallow end with her. They have yet to begin the routine. At least the water is warm. And except for Bobby standing outside, the atrium is empty. Through the glass Bobby looks like a soldier standing at attention, but Cas knows the fumy jealousy that can so easily petrify his frame and heat his mood.

No denying that even if he is her doctor, Dr. Ed is fit, with long, attractive legs and muscled arms. His tight-fitting black suit doesn't hurt. Cas can't help herself, smiling over Bobby's ridiculousness even if she also smiles for Dr. Ed, guiding her through the first series of exercises, occasionally adjusting a hunched shoulder or drifting knee.

"They say you can see things."

Cas was expecting a second series of exercises. Her smile goes like her will to float. A deeper end is only shuffles away.

"You're looking for someone?" she asks instead of shuffling. She's had this conversation before.

"My uncle. Vietnam. Never came home."

Afterward, after Cas has dressed and stepped outside, the number of men surprises her — a small phalanx   stepping   at   once   to her side as she heads toward   a   black SUV, doors wide.

Dr.   Ed   has
hung   back,
Bobby   now   with
him,   offering   thanks
and   warmly   shaking   his   hand.

"Dr. Ed," Cas says, arresting her small army with a turn. "I will try, but how I see takes years, years I may no longer have."

She looks away before she has to witness his gratitude.

"Sew?" Cas asks Bobby to preempt another conversation she's had before. "I was thinking about him in the pool."

"It's still too risky to call," Bobby answers quietly before doing a bit of subject-changing himself. "One thing we haven't considered: what if this Lion Girl, this Aberration, is to *his* advantage?"

Armed men help them into the back of the Nissan ∴ *Pathfinder* ∴.

"Another thing too I was thinking about in the pool: while disadvantageous to engage him in the open, it may be the only time I can get close to him."

"To detonate the Orb?"

"If it comes to that."

"It won't." Bobby smiles. "We have something better."

nahual

You can't trust these algorithms completely.

— *Simon Viennot*

'That's my choice?' Xanther asks [Anwar can't stand the fear in her voice {this is their Sunday morning breakfast ‹fear should find no place at his table›}].

'It's fair, daughter.'

'Yes.' [over chorizo {soy}] Xanther thinks it through. 'It's fair.' But her statement [still] becomes a question [especially in the way she surveys his face {nearly his eyes ‹though when has Xanther ever been a creature of staring contests? «perhaps ⟨briefly⟩ commandeering the duties of sight lost by her poor beast ⟨always on her shoulder⟩»›}].

Anwar tries to keep in place a smile to hide [t]his [parental] lie. He has already figured [when setting a few days {in New York} against a week plus {‹in April› somewhere? ‹with Astair's parents «in Florida?»›} without her cat] that Xanther will choose New York. The question is whether or not she will also detect the deceit [wherein Anwar expects {that by next year} this curious creature will have loosened its hold on Xanther enough for her to actually want to go spend some frolic time with the Wests {visiting them seems inevitable ‹Anwar will need Xanther's support›}].

'Fine. New York it is.'

'We'll have a great time, daughter. I promise.'

'Uhm, double-promise too that I get to stay home for spring break?'

'Yes, I promise,' Anwar answers [before he can {really} reflect on the trap he just stepped {spoke his way!} into {by his own making too ‹unless made by Xanther's «cunning?» discernment «binding him to the kind of promises parents are supposed to keep»›}].

The levelness with which she accepts it too [[{‹definitely «defiantly?»› locking eyes ‹no question!›} mouth unreadable {neither grimace nor grin}] unsettles him.

And that's just the beginning. Anwar's unease only grows throughout the morning. Going over their travel arrangements for the next day should bring some elation [when was the last time he flew first class? {Nathan Muellenson ‹‹Galvadyne» instead of exchanging the one ticket for two economy tickets› had insisted on issuing two first-class tickets ‹on Virgin too›}].

Galvadyne, Inc.

Own the Future

[Was that their trademark {something like that ∴ Just that. ∵ }?]

Even reviewing the scheduled interviews [a lot {though some time slots were ‹happily?› referred to as a *Tour!* or *Meet 'n' Greet!*}] elicited in Anwar something bordering on fear.

Just nerves? The suspicion that he's not worth so much attention [he's not!{?}]? He needs to share this with Astair.

Galvadyne is even putting them up at the Mercer in SoHo ∴ **147 Mercer Street, New York, NY 10012** ∵. Their website indicates room rates of more than $500 a night. Astair generously supported the idea of taking Xanther on the trip. She understood the importance of creating a little separation between Xanther and her pet [not to mention exposing her to the ballet {‹after all› Myla had specifically invited Xanther}] but word of such lush accommodations has made her [understandably] a little grouchy.

Xanther's initial resistance hadn't helped.

'Astair, the fact that she has no idea what these lux-
uries are is a good thing.'

'So is exposing her now a good thing?'

Anwar had assured her that [if he got the job] they
would splurge on a mini-honeymoon [just the two of
them]. He hadn't mentioned that [upon throwing out
a salary figure worth thrice anything Anwar had earned
before] Nathan Muellenson had called it 'acceptably
within range' [adding only that 'a signing bonus would
require further negotiation'].

Who were these people?

That scared Anwar too. His research turned up the
usual stuff [*Fast Company* puff pieces {strange how the
url isn't galvadyne.com ‹‹█████████████████████› other
homonymic results leading to sites selling domain
names owned by digital squatters›}]. Galvadyne clearly
didn't put much stock in their brand [nor in publicly
traded shares {‹the whole thing«?»› privately owned}].

Neither Glasgow nor Talbot knew anything [both
promised to do some digging {though neither had yet
to get back to him}]. Ehtisham was equally clueless.

'How'd they hear about you?' he had asked.
'Mefisto.'

Ehtisham couldn't hide all he was trying to hide in
the long pause that followed. But he couldn't leave it at
that either.

'Careful, Anwar. You have a family.'

Anwar looks to his family [organizing a Sunday out-
ing {which starts with an ambitious plan to go hiking
in Malibu State Park ‹then diminishes to a trip to the
Pan Pacific Park «only to finally settle on one of their
Cultural Field Trips ‹Natural History Museum›»›}].

Getting everyone in the car takes the longest [Xan-
ther putting up her usual resistance {Freya and Shasti
excitable to the point of uselessness ‹Freya . . . ›}] but
the drive there is quick and the line for tickets not long.

[as he and Astair were hoping] The children are
immediately mesmerized by the skeletal giants [an
enormous whale ∷ Fin ∷ hanging in the entrance pavil-
ion {before the gift shop ‹with dueling dinosaurs
∷ Tyrannosaurus rex ∷ ∷ Triceratops ∷ beyond›}].

The twins get stuck in front of a display [in the
North American Mammal Hall ∷ **900 Exposition Boulevard, Los Angeles, CA 90007** ∷] called L.A.'s Backyard
[Anwar finding it impossible to tell if they are shocked
or delighted by the {taxidermic} coyote with a tabby
{seized in its jaws}]. Of course Xanther [in the African
Mammal Hall] can't get enough of the elephants and
spotted hyenas and [of course] a pride of lions.

All of their unified glee [and dumbstruck fascina-
tion {before such tableaux}] actually grants Anwar and
Astair a chance to rest on a bench and just observe.
Astair even slips her hand into his [resting {too} her
head against his arm {as if all she and he have ever
needed was a little ‹motionless› spectacle to blind their
children enough so they ‹in turn› could ‹motionless›
enjoy the spectacle of their children ‹though that's not
all that seizes Anwar «the warm weight of Astair on his
arm ‹her hand now sliding over the top of his shoulder› reminding him of something else . . . »›}].

Anwar stands up quickly enough to alarm her.

'What is it?'

'Nothing,' is no answer [but how can he describe to her the hallucination he had {suffered?} had at the Page Museum {beholding ‹upon «only» the shadow of their child› the shadow ‹also «only»› of a creature ‹like a black pyramid «the cat!»› pierced through with ‹blood-craving› glowing eyes}]?

Especially when [here {in this hall}] it's hard to even find Xanther's shadow [let alone catch up to it].

[in any case {per a ‹previously discussed «and determined»› plan}] Astair leads Xanther and Shasti away [{on a trip to find the Discovery Center and Insect Zoo ‹with a «giant» polar bear›} leaving Anwar with Freya].

Anwar takes Freya's hand. Maybe he expected her to toss it away [thrown over by one of the world's largest {quartz} crystal balls]. But the surprise is how tightly Freya holds on [and keeps holding on].

[unlike Shasti {the more agile ‹if obliging› one ‹like the oboe in Mozart's concerto in C major ∴ *Oboe Concerto in C Major, K. 314*∵›}] Freya is relentlessly bold [{something Shostakovich} the brave instigator ∴ **TFv1 p. 124**∵] though at this moment she seems [how horrifying to consider {even the possibility}] burdened.

'Freya, tell your father what you see.' This was something Anwar's father used to say to him ['أنور, قول لبابك الا انت شايفة.'].

'Nothing.'

'Nothing?'

'What about this?' Anwar positions his face behind the crystal.

Freya shakes her head.

'You don't see me?'

Freya looks caught [her shake shifting to a nod].

'I must look strange.' Anwar smiles and kisses her.

No point in pressing her more [obvious is that Freya is hiding something {impossible to hide is the way Freya keeps jerking her head around ‹as if giant-beaked birds were racing by «‹his poor child!› eyes wide with fear»›}].

[of course] His baby's [non-correlating] fear doesn't help his own [slightly subdued {fortunately ‹fortune!›} by the sight {a little later} of Xanther and Astair playing their Animal Game {hard to tell at this distance what Astair is acting out ‹or who her creation is in reference to› but the sight of Xanther trying ‹and failing› to mimic Astair makes both of them break out laughing ‹Anwar breaks out «from afar»›}].

Freya is also laughing [hugging his knees].

'You see them too!'

'Glamorous?' Xanther asks [she's got on Mefisto's pink sunglasses {her apparent ‹non-›blindness the real mystery here}].

'Your word for today, daughter.' Anwar is still pondering Freya's comfort in believing her father was seeing what she was seeing [there is comfort in a vision shared {is it all horror then to know a vision that is utterly unshareable? ‹is Dante's *Inferno* then no horror at all? «what then of his *Paradise?*»›}].

They had just strolled by a basalt basin [{perfect} called a *cuauhxicalli* {to hold sacrificial fluids and body organs}]. Aztec. Circa A.D. 1500. The placard suggests.

'That's, uhm, like pretty easy?' Xanther answers with her [typical] question.

'Go ahead.' They stop in front of a small ceramic figurine with an open chest [the didactic suggests within the presence of the indigenous concept of *nahual* {a 'double' possessed by all humans ‹into which we can all transform «Teotihuacan culture ⟨300–600 A.D.⟩»›}].

[{fortunately} here] Xanther's shoulder casts no anomalous shadow [though Anwar's careful to keep up with her {no slipping away this time like at the Page Museum ‹during some smoky spell of reverie «even as Anwar catches two men ⟨dressed like ⌈but not of the museum⌋ officials⟩ catching sight of him»›}].

'Like attractive? Special? Uhm, enticing?' Xanther continues [did she also just become aware of these security-types?].

'Good. Care to guess its origins?'

Xanther shakes her head [suddenly shake-shifting her way into alert stillness {as if ‹like Freya? «but worse than Freya ⟨though fearlessly⟩»› beholding things with sharper beaks on the loose ‹and not those two men «long gone»›}].

'Grammar,' she offers flatly.

'Impressive, daughter! How did you get that?'

'I don't know. I'm, like, uhm, remembering something about letters? Like maybe the art of letters?' She seems to be searching for the men [{of course} they were dressed in black suits {with clear coils in their ears ∴ ███████ ∴ ∴ ███████ ∴ ∴ !!! ∴ }].

'From Greek *grammatikos*. *Gramma* is a thing written. The basic gist coming down to an eerie enchantment cast by those reading aloud biblical Latin to those who could only understand English. Hence those who knew their grammar, or who could "grammar," so to speak, were in essence glamorous. Or seemingly privy to great powers not just limited to the page.'

'Like spells?'

'Very good, daughter. Consider too that word:

spell. And take heart in the offerings of language when studied well and wielded kindly.'

'Do you believe in spells?'

'As much as I believe in recipes and directions. Both of which, incidentally, I do not wish to misrepresent as any less impactful.'

[by a vitrine of owls] Astair has corralled Freya and Shasti [signalling Anwar and Xanther that the time has come to exit]. Home is calling [Xanther would say her cat is calling {she really needs to give it a name}]. They have to eat. Anwar and Xanther have their big trip to pack for.

Anwar suddenly has an urge to bring up this naming matter [urge Xanther to decide on something {anything ‹a name is just a name «until we dare to make it into something else»›}] when Xanther cuts him off.

'Dad, uhm.' [Dad! {This must be important!}] 'I have a question that keeps wiggling in my ear—' :: !!! :: '—hurts my head to ask, if I can even ask it, because it keeps coming up, but in a way I can't say, or speak, I mean *think* through, if those are the same things.'

'Of course!' Anwar waves for Astair to head outside without them [she'll know to wait on the bridge].

'Is it, like, uhm, possible, or even a good idea?, uhm, to like do the upside down of something in order to get it right side up?'

'Upside down?'

'You know, an opposite?'

'An opposite? I'm not sure I follow.'

'Well, uhm, like wanting to do good by saying something bad so whoever's listening does good?'

'Daughter! That is an extraordinary thought for a twelve-year-old. Did you come up with that yourself?'

'Who else?' Xanther mocks him.

Anwar laughs [her mockery a paradise {he'd give up any reward for ‹to live in «forever»›}] but not for long [the question has an adult gravity to it too {requiring attention beyond praise}].

'Another way to put your question: is it ever optimal to do one thing with the intention all along of achieving an alternate thing?'

Xanther nods.

It still takes a moment for Anwar to understand what he's just spoken aloud.

[even outside {in the blinding sun ‹he sure could use Xanther's sunglasses›}] Anwar has no answer. He keeps looking for Astair and the twins [but they're nowhere around {not on the bridge}]. Too soon [like he's some TI ∴ Targeted Individual ∴}] he's looking for those two men [not around either {Anwar then ‹in this wish«?» to be seen› seeing his own paranoia ‹seeing it in Freya too «recipient of his own ⟨bad?⟩ genetic dust» materializing farther ahead by the ticketing area «waving»›}].

[hustling to catch up] Anwar recalls Mefisto's question. ∴ *Is it possible to create an incorruptible philosophical directive without antipode?* ∴ ∴ **TFv3 p. 482.** ∴ Maybe Xanther had overheard them talking? [Barking dogs stutter the recollection.] Anwar [by way of an answer] puts the essence of Mefisto's query to her: is it possible to have any sort of perfect something that does only good? [How many dogs are there?]

Xanther's silence and periodic yawns lead him to

[momentarily] assume she is having trouble grasping the idea of doctrines appropriated for antithetical uses.

'"Falsely representative,"' she finally mutters. 'Or "incorrectly concluded," I think. Right?'

'What?'

'Specious. I remembered.'

And so she has [an older word he'd asked her about on the car ride over].

'Huh. But, uh, first of all, is it possible to name even one thing that has just one use?'

'Excellent question, daughter!'

Except Anwar is looking [everywhere now {in earnest}] for dogs.

'Then, uhm, does that mean that use automatically means multiple? So that only something with no use can, like, express a singularity?'

Singularity? Xanther's phrasing crashes like severing glass panes [with still more dogs barking louder] even as something his father once told him surfaces as well [along with his father's beautiful smile {beauty is gentleness too}]:

حتعرف فايدتك لما تتقبل ان مالكش فايده . . .

There!

Beyond the ticket booths!

A dog walker [with eight or nine dogs!]!

'Freya's afraid,' Xanther announces at once [alarmed].

Anwar can see Shasti following her sister into fear [just as he can also see that all the dogs are on leashes {well in check ‹if now barking at him also «more fiercely?»›}].

Xanther quickly crosses to both sisters [kneeling to wrap them up in a big hug {with those long gangly pale arms}] oblivious[?{!}] to how the dogs [all!] cease [at once!] their yelping [pawing the pavement then {whining ‹lowering their heads «is this what Astair had seen happen to Xanther and the wolves at that fucking Animal Kingdom? ⟨he should have been there!⟩»›}].

'She has some kind of effect on animals,' Astair admits [back at home].
'Always?'

The scene with the [{very} apologetic dog walker] recalls a moment in *Lone Wolf and Cub* ∴ Volume 4. *The Bell Warden.* ∴ ∴ *Performer.* ∴ where Daigoro [the only son of Ōgami Ittō] plays with a pack of angry dogs ∴ *Page 231* ∴. Only [in this case] Xanther wasn't playing with the canines [the dog walker was dragging her pack away]. Though supposedly [a year after Xanther was born] Dov had placed before her a doll and a gun.

Dov had never read the manga but knew the famous scene ∴ Volume 1. *The Assassin's Road.* ∴ through a sample ∴ *Shogun Assassin* ∴ at the start of a song ∴ "4th Chamber" on *Liquid Swords* ∴ his men had so often played.

It was a bizarre moment ['So bizarre!'] for Astair [who had {later} shared the incident with Anwar] but [merely] funny for Dov.

'Choose this doll and go with your mom,' he had drawled. 'Choose my gun and you come with me.'

Xanther had gone with her mom but Dov never let Astair forget that Xanther had chosen the gun.

Given a choice now between a gun or the cat Anwar knows [absolutely] which one Xanther would choose.

Anwar goes to find her [to ask her to play with her sister {his ‹'Daughter, we're concerned . . . '› speech rehearsed} but Xanther is already with Freya {playing with dolls ‹the kitten nowhere in sight›}].

Anwar finds the cat asleep[?{eyes shut at least}] in Xanther's room. That it has chosen[?] to curl up on the extravagant coat his in-laws gave her elicits a smile [approvement too {more than a little?} that Xanther would treat the gift so lightly {or should she act more responsibly towards worth?}]. Anwar leaves the beast alone on his new bed.

Only exiting the room does Anwar notice his Go board on Xanther's desk. The captured white stones by black please him [in one corner].

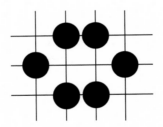

The rest of the board [however] stuns him. Nearly filled! A game in progress? Yet familiar! Not just any game. [unless he's misremembering {Anwar must be ∴ he's not∵}] Xanther would seem to be studying his game with Mefisto [having {somehow? ‹from memory « . . . »!?›} reconstructed it in its entirety!]!

changi!

What people know is inferior to
what they do not know.

— Master Zhuang

jingjing race so hard, lah, heart essploding. essciting oreddy sure.

but chia lat to side by side with auntie.

changi!

here second time jingjing see airport. first time this inside. lagi mong cha cha with many counters and signs, loud announcements and lines, lost auntie quick. find her again chiong ahead up ramp, hands a fan of documents jingjing first time seen before, dragging behind, bak chew tak stamp, sick.

sicker through security. for sure occifers catch sweat, inside machine, pull aside for shake, lah, give bad juice, until badge roll eyes macam jingjing kenging for attention, then no more lag, no more gaze, jingjing through, bags too, loose them x-rays.

so little to pack, jingjing carry less, this less light as empty, but jingjing still can't por such weight, can't catch this pace, macam old self, auntie, powderful, aware, glare fierce as cha pah lang, arrow jingjing hurry, macam him some gorblock, struck dumb for getting his wish, chop chop kali pok, plane oreddy boarding.

great tian li fly macam on some magic rug. what the fish! no matter how hard he try, jingjing can't keep up, kena pang puay kee. kay shack. sandals like bricks on carpet of yellow and orange circles on mud. boh pian tapi jingjing must run on.

knuckle scrub eyes too. can't trust these swimmy tua liap, starred

bright, scarred dark by snaps. floaters, sure, neh'mine black wiggly

creatures with fangs unwind in wings of jingjing's mind. running

helps, lah. if how, wow, auntie float still so far ahead, there she

is again, make no sense, kay fast!, very the farther ahead!, hilang,

beyond no entry, red, terminals 4 & 5, autostart, blue, please keep

left, glides on macam damn mati, going to hell, to ming except —

"jingjing!" great tian li shout. so alive. crowds of travellers about.

right here macam never more than one arm away. jingjing sure

sick, terbalik, pay price for two weeks of balloons, kay kway,

selling backside to lizards and fish, orbi good.

"yes, ah mm," jingjing hear self, waiting whole time for auntie to

call him out, buskok one, something slithering behind, wings next.

"尔链在何?" she asks and paws too at his naked chest. "尔之木像子

链在何?"

lagi huat sio, she is. what necklace? that thing she gave that

jingjing has hanging on his worldwall?

"归！吾必归！" she saysay, slap at his arms, his chest, light like bird

wings, if jingjing still almost fold up. go back now?

so close to plane? go back for why for how for what? if jingjing

pawpaw at his neck too macam what's never there should be there.

tian li laugh then, eyes wide, sharp as knives, her hooked little

hand retrieving from jingjing's bag the necklace she placed there.

"勿摘，靖。说之于我，诺之于我。"

jingjing feel at once both cut up and relieved. fastens clasp around

neck.

"promise, promise. won't never take off."

then lai dat auntie scurry away to gate, jingjing rushing too. can't

wait. for sure.

can't believe either when finally in seat, by window, great auntie

beside, buckled up, asleep oreddy, drooling for snores.

jingjing then lose chin, studying thing of greasy string, tiny

knuckles of wood, with carved acorn, dangling center, dark hard

and smooth waxy, kay small macam quail egg, what say it hatch,

one day, but one day's a never day that something comes out.

earth then falls away, jingjing lifting head with a start, out

window s'pore drifting far below, auntie's gift falls, into place,

strange gift, worth not even a small breath of smoke.

what jingjing would give for one puff. running was bad but sitting

here is worse.

"how long?" jingjing demand stewardess, as him dampen cramped

seat, trapped against cloudy tian, her do'wan nothing but smile.

"four hours. would you like an orange juice?"

four hours!

jingjing survey plane, survey her tray, water and juice, pick juice, grunts thanks. four hours! like this? kill him, maim him, got to cabut fast, knees up and down, hiking stairs of air all the way up while staying put, hands twisting hands into roots, break through this window, sail to the sea with a big parachute.

at least monsters are ditched. at security. terminal walkways. the gate. jingjing still looksee plane again, gotta check. only manyak laptops and phones aglow, earbuds too, all gone from this metal tube prison, sian jit pua, but at least jilo beasts.

comfort too, lah, in ziploc, what, lah, occifers wouldn't touch, cards of what's to come, oreddy gone, who or what uncoils near. dead earth and new fears, the shiver of angry pasts possessing abandoned futures, the future is allways far, even in a broken heart, empty packets, jingjing's dumb set of monster cards.

OIWA

OTSUYU

strange and sorry this duo, at same time with madam tembam in

his ear, wanting his speak, his secret, to know how it is he under

another's spell, jingjing jumping in his seat to hear her damn chor

again:

what is your desire?

balloons, now, and ha na oreddy with 23's pale blue, habis lah,

enuf, give jingjing satisfaction of shiok pink.

:: *Pink is for sunrises.* ::

:: Pink is for sunsets. ::

:: *Pink is for flowers.* ::

:: Pink *is* flowers. ::

:: **Pink is meat.** ::

though damn four and fourteen promise nothing pink. damn chik

ak. kicked ear clear, madam tembam gone. bell instead. big gong

gong in head. zhong! zhong! zhong is dead!

what have jingjing to do with tenth plate? with well? jilo these

cards rate future aim or past road. if third card completes the

three. some coincidence there, lah, if mute to point.

hungry ghost clearer. brighter. what that head shrieked in hiss of

flame?

"jingjing! own what you're owed!"

something else too, macam curse, before burning up inside a

collapsing rose?

"the cat is yours!" ∴ **TFv3 p. 634.** ∵

and aren't they on their way to l.a.?

but when jingjing deplanes, l.a. is nowhere close.

"hong kong?"

tian li nods, and with gentle hand, leads jingjing to glass wall:

"中国在那方。" ∴ *China's over there.* ∵

jingjing studies green hills, turns back to auntie studying him.

"此卿童。　汝身弱，前之途将难。" ∴ *Dear, dear boy. You are not well and the*

trip ahead will be hard. ∵

tian li even touch his cheek. once such brush would sapu every

grief. now this gentleness is just gentleness. worst kind of relief.

"another four hours?" jingjing snort. if he has to, he suffer five!

but this english just plug her ears, make her mouth an empty hole,

old bag blur like fuck before him lagi strong, lah, kay siong.

jingjing turn back to the glass. mebbe china is all he need. macam

jingjing lived here oreddy. a long long time ago. mebbe jingjing

just tsao like siao, and head over those green hills to a wide land

promising something he never got his chance to keep.

but second flight isn't four hours, or even eight.

"over thirteen hours sir."

jingjing almost faint, tries to faint, can't even sleep, keeps

scratching arms, face, knees knocking seat in front, big man there

with teeth long as swords warns him stop with a grin, cower power

him, until tian li smiles jingjing's eeps away.

jingjing egg up on his seat then, hug knees, aches eating joints,

ribs pried apart with pain. jingjing won't last one more moment,

not live past one hour.

all while tian li snore and drool in her middle seat.

somewhere someone won't stop weeping. tian li wakes to dry

jingjing's tears. gets them both tea. bowls too of hot soup. then

slurping up noodles together, tian li tells him a story.

"曾有一河,之上立五柱。河岸各一,浅滩处有二, 还一立于至深处。此柱已解至极旱涝之灾。凡人可记,此柱已立。其从未崩亦未相连。每日皆有学子聚于岸习其构。其图广包,自单一木线至铺轨道于板条之上,至需众水泥与悬浮绳缆之多层堤道。末之,一年,一老师者访。听其弟子论而后问为何图不构。而后,师再听弟子众论。论毕,然弟子问师为何未曾有图。师答:'如若过河必先废其图。'"

∴ Once there was a great river on which stood five great pillars. One on each shore. Two more in the shallows. The last at the center in the deepest part. The pillars had already survived the strongest floods and worst droughts. For as long as anyone could remember, they had stood there. They had never crumbled but they were never connected. Each day a school would gather on the shore and propose various structures that might span the five pillars. The plans ranged from a simple through line of wood to rails on common slats to vast causeways, with multiple levels, requiring tons of cement and elaborate suspension cables. Finally, one year, the old teacher Echo came to visit. He listened to the numerous plans, and when the students were done he asked them all why not one had been built. Again, the students listed the numerous plans and again Echo listened. This time, though, when they were done, they asked him why no plan was ever built. Echo replied: "In order to cross the river one must kill the plan." ∴

jingjing koon fast then, lah, no dreams, no bridge, no river, just

suspended between blues of time, with no time, now and then

pierced through by her voice, voiced as a recollection, what

jingjing tries to repeat, can't remember:

"我们如何在忘不了的充实中记得这种空虚？"

∴ *How do we remember this emptiness so in fullness we won't forget?* ∴

what jingjing not forget, so long he serve auntie of niu che shui,

seri of serangoon, the smith street sage, what talk 3 talk 4 stirs,

kong sar kong si whispers and warns, great tian li a devil, iblis,

ancient enchantress, lamia, and oso balu, from void deck folk,

auntie is powderful pawang who lost her . . .

"landing shortly in los angeles."

"refasten your seat belt."

"please return your seat to its upright position."

ache and itches start again, dry gums, tor hwee soon this, worse

beyond the limits of his guts, jingjing's hands oreddy clutching

wood beads at his neck, macam only thing wurf much as life, keep

jingjing from choking self.

auntie need help off plane. attendants order wheelchair, tapi when

ride arrive tian li walking fine. jingjing carry their karung guni,

one bone sack each shoulder, huffing after her, past baggage claim

to customs, where she just breeze through, jingjing after.

"i like that," occifer saysay, muka sadin one.

"what?" jingjing answer.

"hand-carved?" customs guard ask flat.

"yes!" jingjing smile, smile big. alamak, necklace! jingjing's hand flying to cover smile, too big, hor, hand tricking head, flies to wood knuckles instead. jingjing bowels twisttwist then, pom pom here in lax, berak self, lao sai down both legs. if hand reach acorn, this man will take it. hand reaches acorn, occifer just laughs.

"welcome back to the united states."

auntie waits ahead, macam happy like bird. and suddenly jingjing

too, happy too. california! hollywood! where sickness cannot live,

where pain dissolves in fame, where jingjing's real life begins.

except fast then tian li's smile goes. lai dat she waxes white, until

wobbles take her legs, jingjing grabbing her waist quick, to hold

her up, auntie holding her chest to keep heart up, tictic.

"此处！"

"here?" jingjing scream, looksee everywhere, wings again?, if

blinded to everywhere by tian li's sudden terrible fear.

"其在此！"

"她？ she's here? who's she? 她是谁？"

"其正杀之。"

"who kills her?"

"其正杀之!"

"he? 他？那只猫？ is the cat here?"

New York

If he'd wanted to remember . . .

— Neko Case

"She?" Anwar asks. Alarmed.

They had both just buckled up, Xanther at the window, staring out at the empty tarmac, not even a taxiing plane in sight, all cleared for takeoff, when suddenly she is muttering things she can't track, big toe pumping.

"Daughter, didn't you just now say 'She's here'?"

The plane has started to move, accelerating down the runway, speed transforming the air into something, a fluid, heavy enough to take hold of and float on, lift off.

"I did?" Xanther lies. They are up, the rattle of landing gear tucking itself away underneath, like a bird's feet, talons?, quieting, the runway, and that sound, already far below, gone too, though not the throb of fear and wonder Xanther had felt suddenly, awfully, in the cage of herself.

It was as if in feeling her, Xanther had already clutched her, reached out and seized her within a grasp too powerful to explain ∴ *her!* ∴, forget fingers or talons or . . . ∴ . . . ∴, forget the question of recognition too ∴ huh, to not know as myself, but know her still through you, and so, like, too, then, as myself? ∴, like powerful magnets flying toward each other, ∴ **brutal** ∴ if magnets are oriented properly, or could fly with such gladness ∴ *You are brutal!* ∴, Xanther terrified ∴ I think I gotta agree ∴ that such gladness could cause such harm ∴ **the transgression of our collision can never be anything but brutal** ∴.

Like the hummingbird, struck by the collision ∴ ! ∴ ∴ !!! ∴ ∴ !!!!!!!!! ∴ with glass, in Xanther's clutch back then ∴ **TFv1 pp. 793–795** ∴, as if palms could heal such an aftermath, those tiny wings, that fragile life, provoked by the errancy of itself in the reflection of its flight, shaking to death, until Xanther knew the stillness as a certain coldness and hardness that could never again make a home of the sky.

But Anwar was there, the lesson of his touch example enough to hold nothing, not even hold back.

They were carrying their bags down to the foyer when Astair had cried from the top of the stairs. Immediately, the whole family raced back up into Les Parents' bedroom, where a hummingbird, Hero! ∴ **TFv3 p. 321.** ∴ Xanther was sure of it! ∴ *Most certainly lured by morning light upon a sheer drape* ∴, buzzed around the room, desperate to escape, slamming itself against the windows and walls.

Mom was paralyzed, shoulders tense, arms crossed.

"Astair!" Anwar had snapped. "It can only hurt itself."

"Daddy!" Xanther wailed at once.

"But its beak! Its beak! Its beak!" Freya had started shouting, adding to the already awful noise, with Shasti joining in, both of them screaming then, "It's a stinger! It's a stinger!," hands in their hair, Freya, of course, doing that first, both twins running around then like the poor bird was stabbing their scalps, at least giving Astair something to do, ushering the girls out of the room.

Anwar, though, just laughed quietly, stepping lightly onto the bed, couldn't care less about the boots he wore, or that they had a plane to catch, moving slower and more fluently than any Tai Chi master, up toward the corner where the dazed creature battered itself against three impossible right angles of a room's end.

Xanther doubts she could have acted so calmly, to reach out so quietly for the violent blur keeping aloft one jeweled cap, that tiniest crown of ruby winks, sapphire too, with a bright chest of emeralds, and a beak that did resemble a terrible stinger, jousting with fixtures, stabbing at paint, until Anwar's big hands closed in like dark cups, stilling flight in a darkness this Hero had never known before.

Of course, darkness braved ceases to be darkness.

.: 黑暗止于勇者。:.
.: **No!** :.
.: You lost me. :.

And saved in darkness is to know darkness no more.

.: *No!* :.
.: Uh-oh. I don't like this. :.
.: **TFv**▮▮▮▮▮ :.

Though at first, Xanther was sure Hero was dead.

Anwar had moved swiftly back out to the patio, Xanther at his heels, watching in awe as he raised his arms to the sky, wrists angling away, palms opening like some strange book, with beautifully lined, unparalleled!, pages, revealing within no pressed flower, nothing dried and dead, but something else, just as brown and motionless.

"Please."

Or at least that's what Xanther thought she heard her father whisper, eyes closed too, until suddenly the thing was no longer brown, and far from still, a rising star of brightest green and gemstones, racing up into the light.

Xanther is flying away too, her throbbing chest still wrapped in a feeling of the warmest green, maybe over this memory of Anwar releasing the bird, hands no longer a book, but closing like a grateful prayer, maybe covering something else too, to be kept safe . . .

How moments ago Xanther had just opened the palms of her mind and let her thoughts empty into another's sky ∴ another's? ∵, an amazement of strange life, Xanther giving herself up too to the afterglow of that encounter ∵ With who!? ∵ ∴ **Not—!** ∵ ∴ *Whom. As connected as a circle . . .* ∵, what Xanther had to know could never really have happened, unless what's encountered in the mind, the unknown contours of an anticipation unexpected yet not at all unfamiliar, might come to mean the same thing?

Something about Xanther's sleepiness has started to worry Anwar.

"Daughter, is everything okay?"

"It's great." Reaching for him then, over the wide, luxurious, as she's been told like a few times now, first-class armrest area, still dividing them, but unable to keep her from snuggling against him for a moment, feeling her dad relax then, his focus eventually shifting to his laptop.

se esperan más lluvias

                swirls for her

fe as iron

        swirling too

                as *la fe*

Xanther must ask Anwar

            what he meant
     when saying

        when you're willing to embrace
your uselessness then you may find your . . .

 **:. TFv4 p. 254. .:**

:. *But—!* .:

      :. No! No! Memdump! Stackdump! .:

        :. *Regressive control language!* .:

:. Yoo-hoo! I'm sleeping! .:

It's the closest that Xanther's come to sleeping in a long while, even if she feels immediately wide awake as they deplane. So alert, she's the first to see by the baggage claim the man in a blue cap and blue vest holding a sign:

MR. ANWAR IBRAHIM

Galvadyne, Inc.

The limousine is another surprise, not like a town car either, the black ones Taymor sometimes arrives in, when she's picking up Astair, when they're going out to drink wine, or have grown-up dinners, but a really long one, which Anwar explains is called a stretch.

For sure, Xanther group-texts this, plenty of pics of the inside, the bar, ceiling lights, they glow ambient purple or pink or bright orange, or, like, even like stars, when the dials are all the way to the right, Xanther trying every dial and button, which is really the Question Song with twists and pokes instead of words, opening the sunroof, even sticking her head out, pink phone clicking at all the approaching verticals, so high to never fit. Xanther had forgotten New York, but now her last time there comes rushing back, and so vividly too.

"Are we going to drive by the park?" she asks Anwar.

"We can." Anwar intercoms the driver her request.

"That's the last time I saw him."

"I remember."

Xanther can see by Anwar's soft gaze he remembers it just as vividly.

The limo takes the 65th Street transverse, west, right past Sheep Meadow, though night's already fallen, finding here a lightless patch, pitch as oil, without even a surface to glimmer back windows or streetlights or traffic lights, even if Xanther's seeing it just as bright ∴ Uhm, like absurdly bright? Like— ∴ ∴ *Shhhhh . . .*∴, like it's in broad daylight, when she had ridden lighter than light, him heavy enough for two, moving so solidly, so directly, that Xanther hardly swayed, let alone rose and fell.

TRAMPLE THE WEAK

HURDLE THE DEAD

his t-shirt said.

"Look at her!" Dov had growled below her, not seeing her, if seeing her too, what he'd just seen, before lifting her up into the sun, before settling her onto his sturdy shoulders, better than any sun. God, Xanther loved his growl, his strength, his terrible love.

"They find *anything* this time?" he'd asked next, as he marched them across the Meadow.

AEDs had come up then, and stuff like Phenobarbital, Tiagabine, Vigabatrin, though drug names often came up whenever she had a bad seizure, pros and cons whispered, debated, until eventually all the names were exhausted, without relief it seemed, leaving Anwar and Astair just shaking their heads, trying to match Dov's stride.

"I'm fine," Xanther had said, wanting to assure him, assure them all. "It just, like, looks worse than it is?"

A lot of the bruising was from the tests. Needles, for sure. Not that the nurses weren't super nice, and so apologetic, after they blew up like not one but two veins.

The insides of both her elbows leaked wild streaks of purple and yellow.

Good thing her neck was uncolored. That might have really set Dov off, what Xanther had heard about but never seen, when his sputters like gunshots, that growl, could suddenly amp into something neither Astair nor Anwar liked to talk about.

But on her neck was just a black bandage. They'd run out of the other kind. And at first it wasn't even this, just a smaller brick of white gauze taped on tight to stop the scarlet drip, thin as a strand of breaking spiderweb.

The rest though had nothing to do with the doctors and the needle-plungers and all the scans — the bruised side of her cheek, split lips, knuckles looking like someone had gone at them with a rasp, which is what asphalt can do, when you're losing your shit, which Xanther hadn't lost, not even wet herself that time. And hey, good news!, at least they didn't find cancer.

Dov still seemed shaken, if shaken was possible for him, when he got his first eyeful of her. Like those flinty eyes might spring a leak, maybe they even had, though he was scooping her up again, scooping her up fast, holding her, lifting her heavenward, one giant against a still greater giant that is this heavenless world.

Xanther wished then, like she wishes now, that he never would have stopped lifting her, so light, beyond harm.

And that seizure was nothing compared to what happened at his funeral, in front of his casket.

"Christ," Dov had kept on growling, as he headed them all toward the East Side, his powerful hands on her shins. "I'm the one who should look like you." Then back at Les Parents: "Are we sure these tests aren't just us plain doing The Dumb Dog?" ∴ **TFv1 p. 95.** ∴

Later, when they'd gotten to Serendipity ∴ **225 East 60th Street, New York, NY 10022** ∴ and ordered ice cream, this being back when Xanther was still allowed sweets, so many unmonitored carbs, Xanther had asked what "doing The Dumb Dog" meant.

Dov had put down his spoon to consider the question. He'd ordered vanilla but didn't seem that interested in eating.

"Okay. So it goes like this: there's a dog, a friendly dog too, you know, playful, won't bite, loves to fetch, and he sees this cat in the corner and thinks to himself, 'Oh! Oh! Look at that cute little cat.' His tail starts waggin and he goes over to say hello. But the cat doesn't think much of the dog and scratches his nose bad. And the dog, now all cut up and hurtin, runs away yelpin."

"How is that a dumb dog?" Xanther objects, even with a big bite of pomegranate ice cream still in her mouth, Xanther loves pomegranate ∴ And how. ∴ ∴ *But you've already figured that out by now.* ∴ ∴ You? Me? Not something to figure out. ∴ ∴ **Devouring all the granate . . .** ∴ ∴ Is granate a word? ∴ ∴ *No. Garnet or granite. Those are the choices.* ∴ ∴ **Choice!** ∴ ∴ Running. ∴ ∴ *Following you.* ∴ ∴ **TFv2 p. 320 ff.** ∴. "Isn't that just meeting a mean old cat? And since when do—"

"Hold on now," Dov had chuckled. "We're not done here yet."

Anwar had smiled while Astair, who wasn't smiling, dug into Anwar's cup for more frozen hot chocolate.

"Then a minute later, *if that!*," Dov had continued, "this same dog, with his snout still bleeding, looks over and sees the same cat, in the same corner, and thinks, 'Oh! Oh! Look at that cute little cat.' Tail already waggin again, already headin over to introduce himself again. And gets his nose and face scratched up again, because he keeps failin to remember what that cat in the corner really is."

Anwar, when he was rescuing the hummingbird, had told her to take the cat out of the room, because of what it might do to the bird, though the cat, at her ankles then, wasn't even looking up at the hummingbird, as she knew he wouldn't be, but at her, as she also knew he would be, Xanther too aware of where he was always really looking, behind those closed eyes . . .

Just like granite is a word and garnet is too so is granate . . .

::: Impossible! Set Breakpoint. Arrest! :::

::: Arrest? :::

::: Her? :::

::: Add Watch. :::

Back then, Xanther had just nodded her head at Dov, promising to never do The Dumb Dog, swallowing her ice cream, crunching on the syrupy seeds, exploding with red sweet, like her head kept exploding with another Question Song: what if it wasn't a mean cat? and how do you find out if you don't wag your tail and say hello? and was this a dog Dov knew? like his own dog? hadn't Dov once had a dog? and anyway don't dogs supposedly hate cats? would Dov's have hated her cat? or would she have wagged her tail?

The limo leaves the park, crossing to East 59th, 59th Street was the place Xanther had seen him last, after Serendipity, by the Plaza ⁚ **768 5th Avenue, New York, NY 10019** ⁚, and on that corner, not asking him about the dog or the cat but if he had a picture of her in his wallet.

"No."

"Why not?" Her hurt obvious to Dov.

"Why don't I carry your face around in my back pocket like other guys? Two things. First: nobody cares. Second: I know what you look like. And I'll never forget. That's a promise."

"Are you, like, going to Iraq now?"

"Afghanistan."

"On a bus to Abilene?"

How Dov had laughed then, maybe the loudest she'd ever heard, Les Parents looking pretty confused, because this was her and Dov's private little thing, Les Parents didn't need to understand everything, and besides, wasn't that laugh enough?

Xanther could have listened to his laugh forever. Next to her mom's ∴ **TFv1 p. 184** ∴, it was one of those most-beautiful-things she knows by heart, what feels like, you know, something you could live off of forever?

Dov had hugged her again.

Xanther had beamed. And hugged him back. Big as she could. Kissing his cheeks. She even reached out to touch the gold star that always hung on his chest.

"Say the word and it's yours." No hint of a growl.

"It's yours." Xanther had winked back. "It makes sense with you."

But as he had started to go, Xanther couldn't resist asking: "Are you sure going back there isn't doing The Dumb Dog?"

And this time Dov didn't laugh, he just smiled, and it seemed to Xanther then, and definitely seems that way now ∴ *it was and is* ∴ ∴ *then and now* ∴ ∴ *I thought you were running?* ∴ ∴ Away from her? ∴, that it had a sad shape, that smile, certainly the way he rocked his head slightly around, as if by not saying no or yes, this I-don't-know might be enough.

"They say that in the Army . . . " he finally started to sing the way he liked to sing but couldn't sing. Then he was gone, slipping off through the mass of pedestrians filling the intersection.

When he got to the other side of the street, he looked back one last time and yelled something. Xanther never heard what he said, but she'll always remember he was laughing again.

"Thanks for bringing me, Dad," Xanther says now, snuggling up to Anwar, in another throb of peace, that feels as green as a pine tree gets when falling asleep.

Not that Xanther expects it to last. She knows better. Especially when expectations are involved.

No sooner had they crossed the lobby of the Mercer than that peculiar acorn inside her, of her, yet allways without her, and allways lost, exploded into a blue thing of fire, threatening trees and all their conjuring horizons.

The room was gorgeous and huge, and it wasn't even a room but this gigantic suite. Xanther had her own bedroom and bathroom.

"No wonder the gentleman at the desk looked at me like I was crazy when I inquired about a cot," Anwar says, placing Xanther's suitcase at the foot of her bed.

The bed is ginormous. Xanther wouldn't have minded a cot. For some reason, all that space gets her pacing corners too, closet corners included, and Anwar's room, with an even larger bed. His bathroom has a shower big enough for the whole Ibrahim family, with nozzles from floor to ceiling, and then there's a bath in the center, oval and big and deep, like it would take days to fill.

Xanther keeps pacing while Anwar draws the bath. Xanther excuses her restlessness by taking pictures and sending group texts of every wall and view.

"Daughter, I'm going to figure out dinner. Take a bath. You'll feel better."

"I—" But Xanther grinds away her objection, especially about how she's feeling, since how can Anwar have any clue what she's feeling when, like, she doesn't even know herself?, like all this moving around, what's up with that?, inspecting things?, practically sniffing things?, but with her phone, *clickclick clicks* she can almost hear, and audio's muted, even if none of this is what she's really looking for. She has no clue what she's looking for.

But the bath is already full, and Anwar's adding bubble soap, so it looks like a huge cappuccino, or some bowl of something with whipped cream. Xanther takes pictures of that, for Astair.

"Don't ruin your phone."

"Dad?" Like does he really think she'd take her phone into the water?, but like he already knows she wouldn't, so he's just teasing her, happy, really happy, oh Xanther loves him, to just see him see her circling the huge tub with such pride, sliding shut the door pocketed in the wall with a grin, still widening, opening, long after it's gone.

Even sitting straight up to keep her chin above the water, both ears stay plugged up with foam. The tub's super deep, and the water is hot but not too hot, Anwar got it just right, of course, which still, given the intense heat building up inside her, should be a bad thing, but somehow the sizzle on her surfaces, almost to the point of pain, keeps reminding her how little her surface is compared to the whatever this other thing is that keeps threatening the limits of something way wider.

Xanther plunges her head all the way underwater, and like she's about to cry or laugh, or both at the same time, she opens her mouth doing neither. The hot water feels good on her teeth. Even if her braces feel odd, weird, tight?

"Strategy?" Anwar asks, cracking open the door, prelude too to his announcement that room service is on the way up, so Xanther should dry off, one of the robes on the hooks by the towels is all hers, big slippers too.

"Like, a plan, right?"

Their word of the day.

"Plan is a good answer," Anwar says a little later, poking at his own fennel salad, sipping a cup of herbal tea. As displeased as he seems with his own order, he got Xanther's just right: tempeh stir-fry, plus, for dessert, a bowl of nutty granola, peanut butter, and cottage cheese.

"But plan doesn't, like, have the same bite?"

"Yes!" Anwar nods, as if the definition of a word will always be more satisfying than any salad, or anything edible for that matter. "Etymology is Greek *stratēgein*, in essence to be a general, as in in the military, as in someone who would be Dov's boss, which comes sensibly from *stratos* meaning 'army' and *agein* 'to lead.'"

"So 'plan' is something about the future, about doing, while a strategy, which is also that, is more specifically about leading and winning?"

"Good, daughter. Very good. Like in chess or Go." Anwar is smiling, but he's also studying her closely, hiding perhaps his own, like, stratagem?

"Dov talked alot about winning," Xanther adds, hiding her own thoughts, is that a strategy?, even if it's just hiding her own thoughts from her own thoughts?, like how certain distractions keep her from feeling like she's going to burn up any second. Maybe that is a strategy? After all, isn't just surviving the clearest form of winning? Then doesn't just living require constant strategy?

"I noticed that you'd set up the Go board with a game of your own." Anwar adds now, his strategy suddenly clear. "How did you decide on that . . . pattern?"

"Oh. That? Just, like, uhm, playing? Just random," Xanther lies.

Xanther barely survives the night. And thinking she has three more nights almost kills her again, so she tries not to consider that three, to avoid the re-killings.

The time difference, three hours ahead, helps. Even as midnight approaches and falls, her friends are still, phew, all awake, blowing up her phone.

Cogs: Isn't room service super pricey?
Josh: that place looks $$$$$!!! can't believe you get to miss so much school!
Xanther: anwar said its all covered
Kle: bottles of pain!
Xanther: ????
Mayumi: he means champagne
Josh:

Astair couldn't help herself when she saw the bath.

Mom: Okay. I'm officially jealous.

Which was actually sweet, like just hearing her mom like wanting something, kinda made Xanther want to hug her, as much as she wanted to ask what she didn't need to ask, because mom was on it:

Mom: Little One misses you but is fine. Enjoy your trip! I love you so much. XOXOXO

And then:

Mom: (Maybe Little One is a good name?)

All of which is savorable relief, even if through the door, through the walls, even if her door is not closed, anymore, when did that happen?, but wide open like all the windows too, letting in the flood of muggy air and thrum of traffic, Xanther can still hear the uncertain voice of her father, "███
███
███
███
███
████" which still doesn't blot out the words she most of all doesn't want to hear but hears anyway, even if she keeps trying to blot that out too "██████████████████████
████
███
███
███
█████████████████████████████" useless against what comes out as words not words at all:

Vet!

" . . . take him to the vet?"

Off!

" . . . all too lavish to *not* be off!"

Until Xanther's fever of listening and not-listening finally gives into, by exhaustion alone, that forest of stranger paths of thinking, once again snowbound, though now with the faintest hint of smoke drifting through the boughs, is it smoke?, as Xanther attacks the stream of stones all*ways* rivering through them, stream or parade, as if as much a part of the pine needles as the darker roots unwinding unseen in a terrain just as hidden, irrelevant next to revealing only more of this awful, inconsequential turquoise, inedible, forget the bruised garnet, granate!, promising relief, and nothing close to that pulse of green, that would make all of this unnecessary . . .

A frantic search for anything other than that turquoise, what keeps going on, even in the bright morning, out on the sidewalks of SoHo, where it is still way early, by California time, but is already so beautifully awake, bustling with a purpose that doesn't seem like a strategy or even a plan.

"Is everything okay?" Anwar asks, can't help himself, hustling her past street vendors, and people clutching coffee on the lookout for cabs, Anwar angling for a subway entrance ∴ **Broadway-Lafayette Street Subway Station** ∴.

"Just tired again," Xanther lies, blinking away to forests, back to the awful gut-sweating consequences of her misdirections.

"Didn't you sleep well?" Anwar's worry doesn't help Xanther's belly twists.

"I think I got into a dream." That's true. Sorta. "You know, like just when we had to get up?"

"Oh yes! I know that feeling."

And Anwar does look like he knows that feeling, looks tired himself, even as Xanther can also see how he's already starting to sharpen for this first meeting ahead, where they're heading now, not late, but maybe a little lost, down below, trying to sort out the MetroCard purchase, which Xanther helps out with, ducking under Anwar's arms, to navigate the screens, over his objections, knowing already somehow, because Anwar already said it, right? ∴ Said what? ∴ ∴ *The address where they're going.* ∴ ∴ **Midtown.** ∴, the Midtown address they're heading to ∴ Except he didn't tell her the address ∴ ∴ Oh. ∴, pointing out the route, and then leading too, through the turnstiles, down the next set of stairs to where the rails have already started to rumble with arrival.

The F train seems alive with profusions at once familiar and each time uniquely strange, as needed and wanted
even as they wrap her up like a warning.

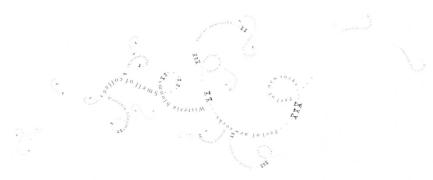

Xanther grips Anwar's right arm, his left arm hooked
around the pole ahead, steadying them both. So many people are packed in here, yet no one seems to mind the way
the train jostles them together, side to side, for a moment
not even feeling like it's just heading west, but north too,
and not just straight, but lower and lower, then neither
west nor north, nor any compass point, which is a perfect
time, in like a horror movie, for the lights to go out and for
people to start screaming, if Xanther's feeling has nothing
to do with movies or premonitions: anyway, lights stay on,
people around her laugh, read books, read phones, while
one woman with no need for a bar, hands resting lightly
on her hips, wild flares of orange and red in her hair, a
white hoop in a nostril, laughs loudest with a friend, both
of them examining together a basket filled with the last of
this year's okra, basil, and mint, plus waxy peppers of more
reds and oranges, these burnt, tingling with the same sweet
spicy heat as both women's speech.

Skipping up the stairs, back into the sun, seems a relief, as if escaping that low place should be an experience of freedom, even if that low place seemed like a false, uh, low place?, because what's freer about a corner cowering down below such verticals?

The magnificent entablature declaring THE NEW YORK PUBLIC LIBRARY also relaxes her, like an event unfolding, somehow, Anwar too, she can feel in his appreciative sigh the way his shoulders ease back, his whole back, the professor and daughter taking in the stairs rising up to those Corinthian ∷ *Another word of the day?* ∷ ∷ Don't ask me. I know but I don't want to know how I know. So no. ∷ columns, familiar as another set of columns, another temple, as if set once in a dream ∷ *TFv1 pp. 135–137* ∷ ∷ **Implausible Access. Reviewing Parameter Prohibitions Tree.** ∷, none of which compares to what guards the entrance, two of them, though they might as well be one, head high, mane billowing, and even in its stony pointlessness, tons upon tons of stillness, a reminder of who Xanther needs with her now most of all, and if only he were with her now, if she could call him here, how badly Xanther wants to try too, and she would try, if she only had the right name to call.

Little One is definitely the wrong name.

In the elevator, all black glass with blacker mirrors, and a textureless pad requiring the heat of a fingertip to stir it to a destination, except when Anwar tells her the floor, her finger is too dry or too cold, huh, strange, to register her presence, despite the fire burning her down inside.

Anwar has no problem.

Stranger still, the quick acceleration upwards feels weirdly in reverse, like Xanther knows they're passing the second floor, the third floor, the fourth floor . . . but she feels like they're going down, and worse, Anwar isn't going down, he's on the way to the top, while Xanther alone is going down and down, until she is way beneath any reason to continue counting,

down

and

down

and

down

and

down

and

        down

and

        down

and

        down

and

        down

until at last when the elevator stops, despite the

announced confidently above the doors, Xanther wants nothing but to keep those doors closed, but of course, they're already opening, as if whoever he is, on the other side, knew they had to open, because Xanther is there, because Xanther has at last reached much more than just the offices of some incorporated entity, but that which requires no place, no story, no number, only the apparatus of its own ceaseless aim and claim.

"Daughter, what is it?" Anwar asks, attuned at once to her escalating fear.

"Satya's running from here."

Sir, until the board can name a successor, we have unanimously voted to assume collective control.

You'll be relieved to learn that this transition is occurring with absolute smoothness.

Why have you failed to

Nothing from production to delivery has been interrupted. Assets remain well managed.

You will have the most elaborate funeral. We have already established a charity in your name.

But—
But—
But development has stalled, sir.
Now is the time, before you're gone, to divulge what sustains all this wealth: the nature of—
find me the old witch?!
You alone possess access to the Vault of—

"I sue you all!"

You must dance when our drum sounds.

— Siamanto

Only clear thing this early morning:

Shnorhk away!

Shnorhk never play!

One good moment, what was really bad moment, Shnorhk made mistake of giving Patil a maybe in hope of more fair moments on fair day driving up fair coast.

Ever since, though, Patil turn Shnorhk's maybe into yes, then into certain yes, then into promise, then into truth. Whole week go like this. Every day starts with wants when, wants exact date, wants exact time. Patil never forget, never forgive.

To make worse matters, Patil's closet is place of ruin she excuse, cleans again, down on her hands and knees with soaps and bleach, to prove that everything is done that can be done if nothing changes.

There is now this thing unseen moving freely between them. Shnorhk wake to catch shadow passing by, arrive home to find same shadow stirring drape on its way out, unless it's only a breeze playing by a window, a thought playing with a dream.

Patil swear is only his dream.

Until Shnorhk scream at paw print on toilet seat, then Patil winks.

"Filthy creature!" Shnorhk roar.

Patil smile for two, because by then thing is gone, though not smell.

Shnorhk try closing closet but reek is so bad even that close starts him coughing. So bad Shnorhk is scrambling to lift filthy toilet seat to spit up what he got out and flushed down.

Flushing won't help. Reek is new roommate. Crouching in corners, down hall, among Patil's boxes of brushes and brooches.

Has it leaked its trespass into first tower of newspapers, clippings, 2001, and second tower too, of magazines, glossy and gold-bordered, 2009? Threaten this work Shnorhk guard over, must get through, Patil too, what he vow to do, soon too, before this month is done?

Mnatsagan not only one with papers to oversee. Shnorhk have papers too, though his are neater, more precise, only way to settle pattern, unburden pattern, what only Shnorhk see, Patil no, though she believes, and in just few more weeks belief won't be needed anymore.

September is not month for Shnorhk's blond box in trunk, for duduk, for tooting nonsense with friends.

Shnorhk have to drive cab, Shnorhk have to attend to other plans.

"I don't understand," Old Mnatsagan say at post office later.

"I don't understand," Old Mnatsagan say again on way back.

Not good enough that another box is scanned and packed and shipped to Minnesota.

Not good enough that Shnorhk must put on hold own musts, own life, to attack next set of transcripts and tapes. Articles too, getting harder to read. Paper distressed. Type blurry or playing tricks. OCR not finding edges, not catching tricks, coming up with garble. But Shnorhk have other tricks to extract texts. And if that fail, will folder with document, high-resolution scans with trouble areas highlighted. Neat. Precise. What anyone can understand.

"Two weeks from Wednesday, me and the lads are meeting here again. Join us. Just a couple of hours. What is the big deal? Where is the harm?" Old Mnatsagan never stop. Worse than Patil.

Shnorhk slide letter off scanner bed and back into protective sleeve. Letter is handwritten. Character recognition is pointless. Someone must transcribe and translate later. Handwritten is most personal and take most time. Unless script is familiar. To someone this scrawl once was. Strange how now this confession a hundred years old is sealed by personality of moving pen. Words Shnorhk does not need to ever know but, strangest of all, reads anyhow by mistake, like hand was briefly his own.

Երբ Քրդերը քանանայի աշքերը փորան, ավինով Հարձակկան մինչեւ ընկավ ու մնաց իր արյունի մեջ, եւ շները վազան այս կողմ ու այն կողմ, շվարված: Նրանք որ նայում էին Հաշորդ էին: Զենք չունեին: Կամք չունեին խումբ միասին պայքարեին: Իրանց վճարած Հարկերը ցույց տվան որպես ապացույց, վոնց որ այն բավական էր:

Where is the harm?

The world is made of harm.

"Your mother brought you birds to keep you playing," Shnorhk says now, to answer Mnatsagan, to put end to this unending insistence, his heckling.

"This is true."

"I had different mother," Shnorhk continue. Slides next document onto scanner bed. This one is English, typed. Shnorhk catch Sasun highlands and Semal and the date 1894.

Women were outraged by the Turkish soldiers until they too were murdered.

There is no need to ask where is outrage.

Outrage is the currency of harm.

"I had different mother than yours," Shnorhk repeats. "Maybe because her mother was different from your mother's mother because her mother's mother's mother was outraged until she was banished to the dust of Erzurum."

Mnatsagan stop his pacing.

"My mother would cut bread from my mouth to pay for her needs. What I played only mattered if it filled a cap with rubles she could spend to make herself up in a mirror, become the way she liked to be, without us, her children.

"She did not like music. She did not scatter birdseed. She taught me that the way breath shapes a note is no different from way breath makes a curse."

"I'm sorry," Mnatsagan say. He is smart enough man not to move in close. Smarter still to step back into house hallway.

To corner the cursed is to bring a curse on your own roof.

Shnorhk sets up next scan. This page a thankful blur. But blur isn't page. Shnorhk's face wet. Heel of thumb can't wipe away that shame.

"This is no shame," Old Mnatsagan even say, moving into office doorway. Smart to stupid takes only one small step.

Shnorhk punch button. Fill small room with light again. Blind them both with brightness of dumbest reading.

But with eyes forced open, Shnorhk still find jewels of anger. Mnatsagan close his eyes. Should close mouth.

"To a bad student, my violin teacher warned: 'It is a dangerous thing to invite the gods to speak through you.' But to a great student, my violin teacher also warned: 'To decline the gods' request to speak through you is fatal.'"

"Not you, not me," Shnorhk suddenly growls, "have anything to do with gods."

"Shnorhk!" Old Mnatsagan responds, stepping now all of him into cramped office. How worried he looks too. Shnorhk give him that. "Your mother can lay no claim on your gifts."

Sometimes smart men are such stupid men.

"My mother!" A bellow that surprises even Shnorhk. Shnorhk would have jumped back too at shock of such loudness, if there hadn't been desk. "My mother?" Shnorhk even repeat, just as loud, stepping forward too. Almost charges old Mnatsagan, who at least recovers smarts enough to get out of way.

"I don't understand" is all professor can keep mumbling.

"I'm not talking about my mother. I'm not talking about her at all."

"Mnatsagan called me."

These are first words Patil say when Shnorhk walk through front door. Not wait for Shnorhk to take off shoes. Not wait for Shnorhk to wash hands, wash feet. Not wait for Shnorhk to maybe eat something.

"He said you left ranting about suing him. He said you slammed the door. He's not mad. He wants you to return his calls. He wants to apologize. Did you slam his door?"

Shnorhk slam their door now for sure. Rattle the pins, the chains, rattle the bolts.

Who cares if door still bounce open at once.

"I sue you too!" he screams at Patil, top of lungs, drowning out whatever she screams back.

Stomping down steps to cab, Shnorhk catch sight of neighbors sticking noses out, lifting blinds for peeks.

"I sue you all!" Shnorhk keep screaming.

And why not?
Sue the world.
Take the world to court.
Until the world goes broke.

Cynthia

Fuck yourself.

— Victim #23

Since July, The Mayor has refused to discuss football. Tonight though, at dinner, Teyo brings up the World Cup.

They are just three. All matters of consequence were already discussed over the weekend. Now conversation serves as a means to bring into balance a necessary sense of familiarity and trust that will serve when distance intervenes during volatile transactions.

Both men know this.

They also know that conversation when it is most muted can sud-denly and violently open windows of discovery into the motives of a potential adversary.

For The Mayor, football is a subject mined with violence. Isandòrno doubts Teyo would not know this.

Teyo boasts that he was never fooled by the victory of Mexico over Cameroon ∴ **June 13, 2014** ∵.

Instead of challenging the boast, The Mayor takes Teyo's side.

—There were assholes who swore that that first game proved Mexico would win the last game too.

It makes no difference to The Mayor that Isandòrno was there when The Mayor had claimed that Mexico had all but won the cup.

Teyo and The Mayor agree again over the Brazil game ∵ **June 17, 2014** ∴. Others saw in a tie equality. Teyo and The Mayor did not.

—Though against Croatia, I admit the 3–1 victory misled me a little.

The Mayor shakes his head, demanding more cognac for the table, more chocolates.

—Croatia is never a sign of anything having to do with victory. It is a country put on this earth for other countries to practice upon.

Teyo does not touch the sweets or his glass. He suddenly seems more attentive about what will happen next.

Isandòrno almost senses it too late. In fact, Teyo delivers the question so quickly it seems an afterthought, the brazenness hiding the tiny pause that betrays a calculation.

Even so, Isandòrno cannot guess what is being calculated. He also sees that intensifying his alertness instead of acquiring insight will only blind him further.

So Isandòrno relaxes even more, slowing his breath, stilling his mind, leaving all his senses to mind what they know best how to find.

—Did you not think we would see it through after the strike by Giovani dos Santos? I did. I believed. This is what Teyo says.

Mexico had at the start of the second half taken the lead, 1–0, only to be defeated by two Dutch goals late in the game.

The Mayor's fingers whiten at once on his amber glass. That loss, when it happened, had wheeled The Mayor into a mood where breaking glass was but the kindest act of many acts driven to break.

—No one underestimated the Netherlands, but their win so late in the game was heartbreaking.

—May football be the only thing that breaks our hearts, Teyo says, laughing. The Mayor laughs too.

Isandòrno loses interest. The talk proceeds on to cooling periods and the goalkeeper Ochoa, who had many great saves until Sneijder in the eighty-eighth minute tied the game, and then six or so minutes later, Huntelaar's penalty kick stuck it in for the orange win.

—The Netherlands almost made the finals, Teyo adds.

—Crushed Brazil for third, The Mayor points out.

—Good at football. Good at many things. Isandòrno's attention narrows.

—Many things, The Mayor agrees. He did not hear it. You and I should go there together. We will take the jet. Then you will discover for yourself what it is I mean when I speak of what is coming next.

—I fear it would all be lost on me. As much as you enjoy the process of manufacturing, I'm really just a salesman.

—You would be surprised.

—Is there something to see? Teyo asks then, leaning back defensively if still at the same time also laughing easily. As if he lacked any concern for his own trepidations.

—No! The Mayor laughs too.

Isandòrno drops off Teyo at his usual hotel in la Zona Rosa. He has curiously declined every invitation to stay in one of The Mayor's guesthouses.

Isandòrno drives by Reforma and will report to The Mayor that Teyo asked to see the Estadio Azteca before leaving in a week.

The Mayor is still in a good mood when Isandòrno gets back. He has not understood Teyo's interest in the Netherlands because the subject had come up while discussing the World Cup.

Teyo was never interested in the World Cup. But until Teyo's design shows some intention to mete out harm, or press for an advantage at The Mayor's expense, Isandòrno determines there is no need to share with The Mayor possible subterfuge.

Interest in one node of origin for a very dangerous product with rapidly expanding distribution is not to be faulted. The Mayor might even praise Teyo's ambition.

That's not the thought disturbing Isandòrno. Rather, it's that Teyo's interest lies most with Isandòrno's reaction to Teyo's interest.

—Did you see her? The Mayor asks, a laugh and leer twisting his lips, eyes glassy with alcohol and the tablets he takes to defeat sleep.

—No, Isandòrno answers. It is the truth. He has not seen her again since that glimpse in Teyo's suite the day they arrived.

—I have a theory, The Mayor continues. Why she keeps turning away my doctors.

—Teyo says it's because she is independent and prefers to take care of herself.

—Teyo says, The Mayor repeats, mocking Isandòrno. I think Teyo is hiding her.

—Why?

—Exactly! The Mayor jumps up from the ottoman. You've observed Teyo. You know he is proud. You know he is vain. You know he makes transparent inquiries that hide other aims. Why then keep this latest activity from me?

—I don't know.

—Not even a guess?

Isandòrno says nothing.

—Because she is fat!

But The Mayor is wrong.

She is not only not fat, she is beyond anything Teyo has ever showed off before. Which is not a problem. The problem is that she is beyond anything The Mayor has ever showed off before.

A Skype with his wife that morning has not helped. She announced that she and the children were leaving Spain soon. They would spend their last week in Paris.

The Mayor was elated. So much so that his wife seemed elated too and almost decided to skip Paris.

But with The Mayor elation often leads to a vicious despair.

—I've missed them, The Mayor admitted afterward. I'll be glad to have them back. But it is the same feeling a broken animal has when returned to the safety of his cage. They are my cage. Except I'm not so broken yet to not hate my cage.

The Mayor even went to his little zoo, as if staring at tangible cages could convince him that he was mistaken.

Teyo's arrival then was a welcome relief. That he came with company was of no concern.

The girl's impact was felt only gradually.

She did not reveal much of herself. She kept her sunglasses on. She walked behind Teyo. Her voice was so soft that the nearly unintelligible way she greeted The Mayor made her immediately inconsequential.

She was young. She was stupid.

Only after the small plane had landed, while stepping out onto the tarmac, did something change.

Isandòrno still doesn't understand how it changed but he suspects she chose that moment to do it.

Not that she could have chosen to have the wind move through her hair the way it did, or commanded the sunlight to brighten her eyes. What she did do had nothing to do with hair or eyes but with the way she moved that made the sky seem to long for her.

In Morelos, The Mayor's smile returns but it is not the same smile as the night before.

He arranges for iced coffees and insists that Teyo's friend accompany them to the site.

Isandòrno understands what The Mayor is doing. He is involving her. And he is making Teyo accountable for her involvement.

However, what The Mayor does not see is that Teyo all along has wanted just this.

Teyo knows that the lab The Mayor would have showed him is not the same lab he will now show Teyo and her. Because with her around, The Mayor will show off, and showing off will mean showing more.

—But you're not surprised? The Mayor asks, though he does seem genuinely surprised.

—About a lion loose in Los Angeles? The girl shrugs. No. Uhm. Okay, maybe a bit surprised but not . . . impressed?

—If such a dangerous creature loose in civilization doesn't impress her, I'm afraid to ask what does! The Mayor winks at Teyo.

—L.A. is full of wild animals. City gets all kinds. Takes them in, sends them away. I'm sure it makes them too. I'm used to wild animals.

Her Spanish comes out crooked and scarred. In fact, Isandòrno has to smooth it out first before he can find the sense. It makes him question her intelligence.

She has admitted she does not speak Spanish well. It is a good enough excuse if there was not also something else. What Isandòrno finds when he puts aside the scars and crookedness of her speech.

—This lion, though, The Mayor continues, killed a bear.

—Lion? Bear? Teyo? What's the difference? They all have big teeth!

The Mayor laughs. Teyo even shows his approval by flashing his teeth. They are not so big but they are all brightly capped.

—Don't forget the lion spared a little girl. Teyo winks.

—Lioness, the girl almost purrs, and The Mayor laughs again, charmed, while Teyo reaches out to touch her arm, approvingly, though both men have missed the point of her correction.

—Cynthia? Is that her whole name? The Mayor asks, ignoring the girl. Did he understand her correction?

—Cynthia Zenobia Donosco, Teyo answers, both men now talking over her.

—Cynthia, The Mayor repeats.

—She was born in Bellflower. Colleen Marie Applegate before she became Shauna Grant.

Isandòrno doesn't get Teyo's reference but The Mayor does. The girl doesn't care.

—Cynthia Zenobia Donosco, The

Mayor keeps repeating. CZD. Tasting the letters. He does not do this often. If ever.

—Is it your real name? He suddenly asks her.

She finishes inhaling on her vape while considering the question. When she exhales, she is still considering the question.

—Of course not, she finally says, but this is not the real answer. The real answer is how she took her time to reveal her smile.

She has big teeth. Her age might explain their whiteness but not that sharpness that Isandòrno knows he is making up. Still, there is something about her mouth that bites. In the right way and also in a terrible way.

Her big lips are soft and welcoming. They easily confuse the other meanings they conceal. Her jaw is strong, which is impossible to conceal, especially when her cheeks draw in, as she once again sucks into brightness the blue light of her e-cigarette.

Her eyes are blue too, almost too blue, though Isandòrno can detect no contact lenses. He notices how the quality of this blue puts her at a distance.

They mislead. They imply a hardness about a girl that is not hard.

Both the sheer and unbuttoned light-green shirt she wears on top and the white cotton tank top underneath are enough to hide a chest too ample for her small figure, to where the men's glances keep returning.

The Mayor's glances are no surprise. Teyo's, though, seem out of character. They unsettle Isandòrno.

She is nothing like Teyo's other girls. They were whores. Their designs lay with money they could never understand for sex they could only pretend to understand.

This one wears a burning orange skirt with a hem that does not ripple above her knees but rather tickles the back of her calves, dark and tan like the rest of her.

Cynthia is beautiful but only in an ordinary way. And this also unsettles Isandòrno, though he can't say why, except that it means the power she wields so easily has no obvious source.

Her legs are not long, but the canvas wedges she wears are steep enough to put on display some of her body's overall muscularity.

Is that it? Her fitness? Isandòrno seems to sense a physical agility even she might not know she possesses.

Also, her skin is imperfect. What little makeup she wears cannot conceal the scars teenage acne left on both cheeks.

Isandòrno cares nothing for skin or hairs but The Mayor wants even polished marble waxed. Teyo is no different. A follicle is some-how an assault on the caricature their desires require.

She, however, has tiny black hairs spreading beneath her ears down along her jawline. More hairs con-verge on the back of her neck.

Somewhere else, she would not get much attention. She would not cut to the front of any lines. But perhaps, like those athletic blondes Isandòrno has heard about, who are drawn to war zones, arriving in places like Iraq or Afghanistan, as journalists or NGO volunteers or congressional observers, who while there suddenly know themselves in the eyes of dangerous men as the objects they could never be in the eyes of other men at society galas or strip clubs, Cynthia too has exploded her appeal by behaving so casually in the presence of such violent wants.

Yet even this description does not resolve Isandòrno's uneasiness. In fact, where she is concerned, there is only one thing he is certain of:

Cynthia Zenobia Donosco is not a whore.

As they tour the new lab, Isandòrno admires her feigned interest in the machines and the powder that The Mayor reveals later is the equivalent of aspirin.

She laughs dutifully, but it is so calibrated a sound that while The Mayor accepts the compliment, he takes little pleasure in it.

Her steadiness becomes more evident when they walk to the edge of the property, beneath the thick jungle canopy, where armed men walk the perimeter.

She does not fear guns but she does not admire them either.

Isandòrno keeps trying to see how she sees, but the enticement of her eyes blind him to their interest.

Isandòrno can barely rid himself of his own interest in the way she moves her hips, the way her skirt billows, her body seems to float.

When she finally removes her top shirt and ties it around her waist, her bare shoulders are already aglow with sweat.

Isandòrno tries but cannot avert his eyes.

—The last time I gave Teyo a tour, everything was burned down soon after, The Mayor confides to Cynthia. If it happens a second time, I will have to assume Teyo is the spark.

—Is Morelos dangerous? Cynthia asks flatly.

—Mexico City is more dangerous because it is so much more fun, The Mayor responds.

On the plane ride back, The Mayor tells Teyo to sit in front beside the pilot so he can see for himself how well-hidden this lab is.

The Mayor slips beside Cynthia. Isandòrno sits in the very back.

—If you have a lot of money, The Mayor begins, already a mistake. Then Mexico City poses some difficulties. Especially with my kind of money. As you've seen for yourself, I am well-looked-after but I am still never far from danger. What's worse: I'm unhappy.

Teyo yells something from the front but the roar of the engines combined with the battering winds outside makes understanding him impossible.

—But there is a man I know, The Mayor continues. Eulogio León Mero, who detests danger as much as he detests security. He is wealthier than me but he walks the streets with impunity. Alone too. Perhaps you think he has a special weapon? Some impressive gun? Ah but no. Though yes, I admit, he does carry something.

Isandòrno is not sure if Cynthia understands.

—Guesses? The Mayor prods.

—Tell me, she answers, passably. Her sunglasses make it difficult to tell if she is studying The Mayor or just looking out the window.

—A chicken! Wherever he goes! Eulogio León Mero carries a chicken! In an armpit. Petting it. Because no man stroking his chicken will ever seem worth robbing!

The Mayor howls and jerks both elbows up and down like some featherless bird.

—This I could never do. No matter how terrible the circumstances. If I ever do take to poultry for my protection, I order you, Isandòrno, to shoot me, throw my body to the wolves, and then set my chicken free!

Cynthia's smile satisfies The Mayor. She stirs the impossible in men. Fortunately, Isandòrno gave up the impossible years ago.

At dinner The Mayor's pleasure does not abate. Goaded on by his good mood, his staff keeps bringing out bucket after bucket of champagne along with preparations of veal so elaborate as to deny the killing each serving requires.

But Cynthia never touches the meat or the fish that comes later. Only the bread.

Isandòrno wonders if she understands that wheat too requires killing.

The Mayor tells more stories. He directs them all at this young mystery. Teyo is only recognized when he seems genuinely frightened by the appearance of four wolves.

—Relax, Teyo. They're on chains.

—Chains break.

The wolves stay focused on their trainers. Except when they pass Cynthia, eyeing her then with their gold intelligence. She offers her own gold eyes, no longer blue, suddenly molten, skies undone.

The animals stiffen and stop. Nor do they move again until the train- ers are forced to drag them away.

The Mayor applauds. Teyo's teeth hide behind pursed lips. Cynthia is embarrassed enough to gig- gle. She keeps giggling too, and then starts saying stupid things about her perfume and the kinds of product she uses on her hair. Isandòrno suddenly doubts him- self again. Maybe she is just pretty and dumb. Maybe she is a whore like the rest of Teyo's extramarital interests.

The Mayor seems to think so too because his interest fades as well and he returns all of his attention to Teyo again and stops telling funny stories.

Regardless, his favorite stories are less about eliciting laughter than about provoking queasy reactions. Getting to hear his guests lie about their displeasure gives The Mayor the most delight.

So The Mayor tells the story about
the poacher.

Afterward, Cynthia looks shocked. Teyo tries to look shocked too but he's heard the story of the poacher many times before.

Isandòrno forgets about her then until he returns them to the hotel.

Teyo orders Cynthia to go ahead and wait for him in the lobby. She obeys without a word.

—Cynthia Zenobia Donosco is her real name, Teyo confides. I have her passport. She said what she said because she is young.

Does Teyo say this out of some concern for The Mayor's safety? It is an unnecessary disclosure.

Yet it is also what horrifies Isandòrno on the drive back because it clarifies what has eluded Isandòrno all day.

Teyo has not used her to get The Mayor to reveal more about mechanizations of production or some distribution detail. On the contrary, he has used The Mayor because he knew The Mayor would want to involve her.

Because Teyo has yet to trap her.

Is that what the wolves saw too? What they could never see in Isandòrno?

As close as she might be, Teyo's mistress still stands outside her cage.

Ammonia

"I am forever," replied the Hunter,
"on the great stair . . ."

— Franz Kafka

Not Özgür's scene. They're closing the place down too, if closing down anything at 10 PM counts as anything other than giving up. By 7:30 PM, Özgür had already given up on company. He'd arrived at 6:39 PM too, just a little late in a city where a dozen minutes after the fact can count as early.

Universal CityWalk.

Left his car on the fourth floor with Curious George ∷ parking lot ∷ but instead of taking the stairs wound up in a service elevator staring up at the caged fluorescent bulbs where a wasp crawled alone, trapped between a false sun and a false floor. Özgür had felt sorry for the thing, though he'd recently heard that wasps prey on black widows, anesthetizing them with a sting, caging them in their nest, which made him feel sorry for the black widows, leaking their weaponry until they were seized for a feast. Actually Özgür felt sorry for all spiders, and he couldn't stand spiders, our fishermen of deserts and dales, forests and fields, given a bad name because of a sting, wasps too for that matter. Özgür's under no illusion who has the worst sting, no wings needed, forget eight legs.

"Bubba Gump Shwimp," Warlock had declared on the phone. What a choice. "Because I love Fowest Gump!"

Blade Runner was a better choice for the dystopian vision of CityWalk — a bleakness achieved unintentionally, which made it worse, through chain restaurants and multinational stores and a fountain that periodically sent jets of water vertically from the pavement to the strains of "Moon River" ∴ 1961 ∴ ∴ *Henry Mancini and Johnny Mercer* ∴. That said, tonight it wasn't Deckard that came to mind but Chief Anderton in *Minority Report* ∴ 2002 ∴, and going solo too, without an Agatha to take on the future, unless Özgür can count his instincts as precogs. He can't. These days his instincts seem way off.

Maybe the memory of that wasp was still poisoning the reflexes of Özgür's skin as he'd left the elevator, the thought of it escaping the grill, flying around in that transcendent steel box, alone with just Özgür, a private hell of personal madness, and Özgür knows whose madness would have won.

Except what never did escape couldn't really account for why his skin continued to crawl, or how, as he strolled out into the mall, he had felt weirdly pursued.

Özgür is always the pursuer. Especially in a place like this. Özgür can't help himself. He profiles everyone: the way their eyes move, the sort of strides they take, how their arms hang, what's too expensive for them to wear or just expensive enough, how where they're from says something about what they'll do next, even if what laws they've broken before and what laws they'll break later won't change the fact that tonight they're probably just getting Swedish fish and catching an IMAX.

The trouble is that after avoiding the Samba Brazilian Steakhouse & Lounge, Özgür had caught sight of three men watching him, dressed too darkly for this place, like security guards for a private event, even if Özgür's glimpse had been too quick to confirm that they were really dressed in uniforms and not just some nutty costumes.

Then, not a minute later, while passing iFLY ∷ indoor skydiving ∷, Özgür saw three more men, different from the last set: definitely uniformed, with some black breast-pocket badge, their collective helmeted gaze fixed on him. This new trio had faded away as quickly as the last. The helmets convinced Özgür that they had to work for Universal. Özgür's never had a problem indulging curiosity, but seeking out a CityWalk security guard would have made him too late. Then a little Latina girl with black braids and pink Converse raced by him. Maybe eight, maybe nine. Something white and fluffy was stuck on her shoulder. The lenses of her pink sunglasses looked black.

As it turned out, it was Warlock who was late, an hour and a half late, rushing in after 8 PM, with apologies. Özgür's excuse for why he was still there was two beers and four pretty girls in a booth that never looked his way.

Warlock's only explanation was an afternoon spent in the park. The rides had enchanted him, but he got lost trying to find Hogwarts ∴ The Wizarding World of Harry Potter ∴, only to find out the attraction wouldn't be open for years ∴ *April 7, 2016* ∴. It seemed so ridiculous a lie, Özgür almost wondered if the former lieutenant with the IDF ∴ Israel Defense Forces ∴ had also discovered helmeted men with dark badges on darker jackets threatening the shadows.

One thing was for sure: Warlock's eyes seemed to cradle shadows that hadn't been there before.

The rest of him, though, was upbeat, at once ordering buckets of spicy shrimp, with plenty of Cajun spice, another beer for Özgür, a Secret Mango Sparkler for himself, no alcohol, dropping his r's as happily as he kept tossing aside shrimp tails.

"I know, not koshe' but maybe this se'ves to disabuse you of any thought wega'ding my appawent pe'fection."

The laugh that followed was genuine, but Özgür's instincts still told him Warlock was a kook, making Özgür the bigger kook for even following up, engaging in a drivel of dialogue about the thrills of amusement parks. Warlock had wanted to go to Disneyland or even Magic Mountain, but work had kept "inte'fewing."

"I did enjoy the wondwous vistas pwovided by you' Pacific coast," Warlock said then with a smile, extending the smile when the four pretty girls left their booth, one of them even grinning back at the round man with an "Aren't *you* cute!"

Maybe through another set of eyes the old man was cute, but Özgür kept seeing the kind of crazy that gloms onto something — or worse, someone — and never forgets, for fear of what forgetting will reveal about the self that sustains the cause.

Özgür gave up causes a long time ago, which wasn't to say it wasn't entertaining to hear Warlock go on about his, especially while there's a piece of black paper to fold, however stained with the red oil of uneaten shrimp. What else was he going to do? The night was already killed. At least, until Özgür's midnight date with Elaine.

Katla. Katla-katla.

Between mouthfuls, Warlock confessed to envying the 2011 Munich conviction of John Demjanjuk, an Ohio autoworker who turned out to be a former guard at the Sobibor death camp. "Envy is not a vewy laudable twait." His BA'AL GOMER :: **Battling Angels Against Living Genocides of Modern Eras** :: had played no part in discovering the old Nazi. Instead, the organization remained focused on the prosecution of contemporary acts of genocide "as well as the detection of incipient mass slaughters."

Katla.

"So that leaves Turkey off the hook?"

That stopped Warlock's chomping and slurping. He even reached for a fresh paper napkin as if what followed next might require clean hands. Özgür wasn't even sure why he had chosen to challenge the ex-lieutenant in this way.

"That is why, Miste' Talat, I like you. Tu'key is not beyond ou' considewations, though its cwimes against humanity, committed in the twentieth centuwy, slip beyond ou' pu'view. Of gweater conce'n is that because Tu'key has not yet wewitten its past to mo'e accuwately weflect the genocide it was wesponsible fo', Tu'key must still be wega'ded as vewy dangewous."

Katla-katla. Katla-katla.

"The psychology of nations?"

"It's pa't of ou' ongoing considewations."

Katla. Katla.

"Do you think racism is Turkey's problem?"

"Do you?"

Katla-katla. Katla.

Özgür considered the question carefully. *Katla-katla.* At various times he had thought it was. *Katla. Katla.* At other times he had thought it was more complicated. *Katla. Katla-katla. Katla.* Tonight he sided with complicated.

"As with other nations, including Poland, parts of the Balkans, even areas of this country, Turks can be ultranationalistic."

Warlock did not resume eating. Maybe his mouth was burning like Özgür's.

Katla.

"Ideas of nations, like misconceptions of wace, a'e pa'ticula'ly twoubling because they a'e so incomplete."

"Incomplete?" Özgür asked.

Katla-katla.

"Nationalism and wacism are human conceits applied to the immense complexity that is natu'e. Twue, stwuctu'es as such can pwovide illustwative means to inte'pwet that complexity. The pwoblem comes when such conceptions a'e enfo'ced. It is ou' expewience that enfo'cement fwequently leads to wholesale slaughte' based on pe'ceived diffwences. How genocides begin."

Özgür nodded. Virgil would have loved this.

"I've always been suspicious of national or ethnic identities. What we call character is often just how various contradictory impulses of the mind balance out. It seems to me that the desire for a particular identity, whether national or ethnic, is just a way to abdicate personal responsibility in the name of a set of mandates external to the self. Any declaration then of who we are becomes a declaration of how an individual is not."

"Twue. Simplifications help cweate g'oups, and g'oups can have powe'ful consequences — good and bad."

Katla-katla. Katla-katla-katla-katla. Katla.

"Does that at least leave the future open and undecided?"

Katla. Katla. Katla.

Warlock laughed at Özgür's summation, but not unkindly. "You have illustwated my failings. I suffe' da'k anxieties about the futu'e."

"I'm afraid that's how we're all wired. Cops in particular."

Katla. Katla.

"Twue, twue, twue. Especially fwom an evolutiona'y pe'spwective: we see a field of bea's instead of bewies."

Özgür agreed: "Because those who were hardwired to see the berries were eaten by the bears."

Özgür slid across the table a finished black ram ∵ Jun Maekawa ∵, which Warlock accepted like a prize: "I'm cha'med."

For a Wednesday night, CityWalk seems especially deserted. Outside, Özgür immediately starts scanning for his helmeted friends. Or that young girl in braids. But not even a security guard is in sight. Only a child racing ahead of his mother daring the fountain at the center of the court. The child loses and seems surprised by the water that suddenly rises around him like bars followed by the rictus of anger tightening his mother's face when she realizes she'll be loading him into the car wet.

"Realic S. Tarnen," Özgür says, at last, finishing with what he should have started with. With a tip of his hat.

Warlock doesn't hitch a bit, doing a bit of scanning himself, the fountain, the mother and child ascending the escalator, the empty balconies above.

"An academic type," Özgür continues. "I've looked him up. He's written a hard-to-find piece called 'Clip 4.'"

That stops Warlock from his either careful or casual assessment of their exposure. Özgür never noticed just how lidded his eyes were until Warlock really popped them open.

"You've wed it?"

"Not yet."

"I would have liked to discuss that with you. Pe'haps if I wetu'n to Califo'nia we will have the chance." Something curiously affectionate in his tone too. Maybe even touched with longing. Özgür is surprised.

"You're leaving?" The pang of lamentation possessing his own question is another surprise.

"I'm afwaid I must. To New Yo'k."

More evidence that Özgür's suspicions are a mess. This whole time he was certain Warlock would be like summer gum on the sole of a sandal, yet here he is about to vanish along with any sense of what he wanted with the LAPD in the first place.

"Did you at least find your fugitives?" Özgür asks, a little too late if more than a little lame.

"I didn't."

But before Warlock can say more, a sudden ululating fills the fountain court. Özgür wheels down to one knee, reaching for his weapon, aware that Warlock has done the same, almost as fast, both of them spotting the figures on the highest level above, unleashing silvery orbs, wobbling down through the air.

Warlock's hand grabs hold of Özgür's shoulder. Özgür senses the intention enough to follow the thrust to its conclusion, flattening himself on the ground, head down, like Warlock, who's also interlocked his fingers over the back of his head, clamping down on his ears.

The pops that follow are too distant or faint to explain at first. The ululating stops. The throwers gone, no helmets or uniforms, unless brightly colored hoodies count. ∴ !!! ∴ ∴ ■■■■ ∴

Warlock returns to his feet, inspecting the silvery remains by the fountain where fluid bars rise up again, trapping nothing.

"Water balloons?" Özgür asks, considering the shriveled plastic. The smell of bleach? No. More like ammonia. ∷ ▮▮▮ ∷

"I'm afwaid I ove'weacted." No question Warlock had been afraid, but he wasn't the only one. Not that Özgür had any inkling what to expect out of those silvery blobs as they'd tumbled their way. Clearly Warlock had expected bombs.

"The names you left me — Jablom, Yuri, and Eli — their heads were soaking in bleach."

Warlock knows this.

"Realic too may have been soaked in bleach."

"Do you have a theo'y?"

"A signature?"

Warlock's smile is so large, his eyes so wide, he almost looks proud.

"The'e's why I chose you!"

But before Özgür can ask what the hell that's supposed to mean, Warlock is digging into his pocket for the flash drive he presses an instant later into Özgür's palm.

"If we don't see each othe' again: be vewy ca'eful. If we do see each othe' again: be vewy *vewy* ca'eful."

"Why *would* we see each other again?" Özgür prods.

"In 2001, Decembe' if I wemembe', a case nea' Boyle Heights pwesented you with a stack of hundwed dolla' bills no one was going to miss except you' pocket. You we'e unsupe'vised but still not a hundwed went missing when it weached the evidence woom."

"I've heard that story too."

"Something else though too. Beyond evidence. One of you' ea'ly owigamis."

"Probably a butterfly."

"Actually not. A cat. All white. Set the'e for no one. By a wilting spway of fo'get-me-nots. Still blue, still gold. You we'e whistling 'Blue and Sentimental' too."

On his way back to Curious George, Özgür probably should have had his weapon out, jerking around in readiness for an army of helmeted black badges. But his hands were empty and he walked calmly. All the anxiousness had gone out of the balloon, so to speak. If something was coming it would come and Özgür would react and no amount of anticipating on his part was going to change what he was going to do and how fast he would do it.

Out of the lot, heading over to Cahuenga, he dialled Elaine. He had expected to find her texts when he pulled out his phone, at least one text, but there were none. No voice mail either. Not even a missed call. His own call goes straight to voice mail.

Behind him, a white Renault hangs too close to his bumper. The disadvantage of an unmarked car. Or the advantage. Özgür speeds up, draws the car in, then wires the brakes fast. The Renault swerves and passes, honking its horn.

Give me one helmet, please.

But it's just a car full of clowns.

Closer to downtown, Sunset turning to Chavez and empty, a black Tesla comes up behind, close and then too close, before switching lanes and shooting ahead without a sound.

Was that a gunshot?

Sharp enough to startle Özgür, cause him to check himself, check even his windows for cracks, suddenly certain that the driver had worn a helmet, even if the windows were tinted and the Tesla was moving way too fast.

Also, gunfire, real or imagined, isn't what's giving Özgür the creeps. It's the story Warlock told him, that dumb thing about Özgür turning over so much money, back in the day too, when it was understood in some departments that found cash was what offset the "cost of fighting crime." What evidence he had booked with property division told the whole story, a story Captain Abendroth, or a dozen others, could have easily shared with Warlock.

That wasn't the problem.

The problem was that, like Warlock had said, Özgür had been unsupervised, with no one there to watch him not pocket some cash, let alone fold a piece of blank scrap of paper into a blanker cat, and set it down beside a handful of flowers strewn over a counter. Not something Özgür had told anyone either.

Warlock was right too: it had been a cat.

And sure, maybe some detective could have returned to the scene and remembered the forget-me-nots. But it was unlikely. This was no homicide. The tenants were back that same day. Still, maybe the flowers had stuck around. They were a bright, beautiful blue. Maybe some officer could have remembered seeing them days later the same way Özgür still did.

"Blue and Sentimental" he's whistled for years.

But no one could have remembered that origami cat, because Özgür hadn't left it there. At the last moment, he'd thought twice, and taken it back.

slashes

Ballet is Woman.

— George Balanchine

The Dream
∴ *Le Rêve* ∴ ∴ **1910** ∴

[of course] Anwar's [ailurophilic] daughter had lingered over that one.

What Anwar dreams about now [{Henri} Rousseau's dreamy evocation of a jungle {conjured ‹in turn «entirely?»› by ‹such!› nakedness on an ‹«equally»› dreamy› divan ‹such nakedness! «the woman ‹with outstretched ⌈left⌋ arm and exposed chest ⌈breasts!⌋› nude» if something about the hair «braids?» puts her out of reach «even in a dream ‹Rousseau's or ⌈ . . . ⌋ his›»»} invisible to this child with eyes only for the two lions {‹with what intention?› crouching down among ‹green› fronds}].

'They're, uh, sorta dumb-looking, right?'

That had surprised Anwar [though {no arguing} there was something mute {and ‹very!› stupid} about their circular stare].

A little like how Anwar feels now in this hotel room [if he checked a mirror would he catch the same look {dazed ‹beyond «decoding» intent›}?]: sleepless and dreamless [to the point that the painting itself {now} seems as uncertain a thing {of ever being ‹t›here ‹finding «someone else there too ‹another song›»»} as Anwar is nothing but certain that the next painting she found had allways been there].

The Sleeping Gypsy
∵ *La Bohémienne endormie* ∵ ∵ **1897** ∵

Xanther stared at the moon for a long time without pointing out anything 'sorta dumb-looking.' Instead the painting 'complicated' her.

'Complicated?' Anwar had asked.

'Like, uhm, trouble but not like troubled or in trouble but like ripples in the water where there's, huh, no water but the reflection's still kinda disturbed.'

It took a while but Anwar managed to get through the entoptic distractions of her mind [entoptic {good for ‹some later› word of the day}] to isolate her principal concern: is the lion there to watch over the gypsy or to eat him?

'And like, whatever like, that answer is, the moon either way doesn't care.'

'Do you think the gypsy and the lion are real?'

'You mean not, uh, huh, like, the we-already-know-it's-a-painting real, but like are they *real* to each other? Like maybe the lion is just a dream? Or . . .'

'Or what?' Anwar had sensed her discovery [a greater joy there than making the discovery himself {calling from the stillness ‹t›here ‹he strains «something else there as well ⟨a familiar song⟩»}].

'Is the lion the one dreaming of a sleeping gypsy?'

'What do you think?'

Xanther looked again [{closer ‹close enough to signal the attention of a museum guard «but not so close to demand a response ‹a hovering between observation and action›»} fingernails {of broken ‹grey› pain‹t›} going at each other {like ‹brawling› cats}].

'Is this like too weird but if I like imagine it is *all* a dream then I can like replace that jug, or vase of water I guess, with a canteen of water, and that guitar thingy, it's not a guitar, is it?'

'A mandolin?'

'Okay, whatever it is, with a pack, and then the walking stick with a rifle, and the dark face—' Had she looked for a moment then at Anwar's face? ∴ She had. ∴ '—with, you know, a face a lot whiter, and freckly, then I still see the moon and the lion, they're unchanged, but now I also see in her him.'

'Your kitten?' Anwar had asked [{suddenly} confused] though his question made no sense [least of all to himself {though that 'him' had pronounced just that ‹the cat «allways»›}].

'Dad! No! What a, uhm, weird thing to say?'

'I'm sorry.'

'Dov! Like before, he, you know. With, like, the moon bright like this. Maybe even brighter. And his last dream coming up behind him.'

'The lion?' Anwar places both his hands [softly] on her shoulders [to set this right].

'Why not?'

'But look what's coming up in front of him.'

'The desert.'

'More than that. Look again.'

'Sand. I just see painted sand.'

'I see us. I see you.'

The moment had felt like a strange reversal of something else Anwar had said to Xanther not so long ago [he couldn't remember {remembering it only as a shared feeling ∴ **TFv1 p. 99** ∴}]. But both this moment and the one beyond recollection acquired a familiarity [in the manner that both thoughts {of how we place ourselves in relation to the dead} seemed to swing open on hinges {hinges Anwar had never suspected were there ‹in the first place «can thoughts have hinges ⟨can they suddenly swing open ⌈like a cage⌋?⟩»›}].

Just that pulse of such a consideration [[{as it happened then ‹and now›} turning over one painting's perspective {along with perspectives of that painting ‹all of it a dream «even this now»›} like a Rubik's Cube {that lies beyond solution ‹or is already solved›}] had made Anwar glad to have insisted on that visit to MoMA [[{‹earlier› in the afternoon ‹Wednesday›} however simple and expected {dull? ‹Astair and Anwar will always share a great love for museums and bookstores «though any New York visit is a mourning moment for Gotham Book Mart ∴ *Closed 2007* ∴»›} just father {a tall minaret ‹rigid as knowledge›} and daughter {a tiny sapling ‹lissome as imagination›} wandering on towards things more modern {hand in hand ‹as if a mosque could ever wander with a tree «as if Anwar would ever choose a mosque over a tree ⟨or Xanther would ever choose a tree over a cat⟩»›}].

Much better than Xanther's immediate choice:

The Bronx Zoo.

They'd gone years ago [[{curiously?} just the two of them too {is that why Xanther ‹initially› had been so insistent?}].

Anwar still remembers the wild dogs [{not far from Tiger Mountain} chirping and chittering {‹like alert birds «with teeth»› as they circled ‹their numbers «now and then ⟨in their mad rushes⟩» suddenly dissolving into one «singularly» fierce pack› alive and determined and hungry}].

Probably still hungry.

Call them coincidences.

// the animal shelter spilling its charges

// some lion's lair disgorging its worst

// whenever Xanther was around

// too impossible to consider

// yet too threatening to ignore

Not a chance Anwar was going to risk putting Xanther anywhere near a caged animal [let her unlock paintings and sculptures instead].

If part of him [also] still wanted to go [to disprove the power of consequence] the best[?] part of him will always choose to shield this child [if from nothing else than from conditions triggering such recollections].

On this late New York evening [it's not so late {yet} in Los Angeles {though Astair and the girls have long been asleep}] Anwar has trouble imagining the impact of such an experience [bad enough having to keep on reliving his own imagined {alternate} memory].

He starts pacing the Mercer suite [peeking in {repeatedly} on Xanther {only her bare feet visible ‹twitching in the privacy of her own dreams «if but for . . . ⟨Anwar's dream then⟩»› in the narrow slash of light pouring through her cracked door}].

What could have happened though!

// if but for some predatory impulse

// choosing over engorgement

// flight

Anwar has to close his eyes.

His daughter had nearly lost her life to an enormous lion*ess* [hearing Xanther's oft-made correction {she ‹seemingly› not bothered at all ‹*really!* «really?»}].

It was a miracle Astair wasn't killed either.

It was a miracle no one there was killed.

Or severely injured.

//Not counting the animals.

// Xanther would count all the animals.

The absurdity [of what could have happened {what didn't happen}] still won't stop jolting Astair and Anwar awake. They try to talk it out. Astair can't talk to Abigail [who ran off to Burning Man {‹dragging Toys along too› to at least re-find themselves ‹if they couldn't find the beast «still at large»}]. Anwar still wants to go after the creep. Both he and Astair couldn't stop talking [loudly!] about suing Animal Kingdom [softly {about how it might put Xanther at ease}].

But Xanther had ripped into Astair and then Anwar.

'It wasn't her fault! If anything, it's mine! Sue me!'

A statement Anwar still has no idea how to address [untangle {clarify ‹resolve « . . . »}}]. Awful coincidences increasing this AM hotel march. Let sleeping . . . lie.

What point was there in attempting to explain alternate outcomes? How a different set of seconds could have just as easily left her pulseless?

Anwar arrests his pacing. Rubs his eyes [as if rubbing serves some purpose {eyes don't instruct these visions}].

[moreover] Xanther doesn't seem particularly perturbed [always bouncing around the house {sleepy miniature forever in her clutch ‹and then there's Freya ‹another story . . . ›}].

Anwar resumes pacing.

434

[obviously] The apparent absence of noticeable trauma would make proving damages difficult. Taymor's husband had made that quite clear [as had a lawyer {recommended by Astair's parents ‹both of whom had alternated between cries of litigation «Sue! Sue! Sue!» and comments about *Breaking Bad* ∴ **2008– 2013** ∴ and the shooting of Michael Brown ∴ **August 9, 2014** ∴ in Ferguson «Missouri»›}].

[if anything] The real trauma came with this trip [separating Xanther from that frail {dying?} animal].

Another stupid move on Anwar's part: he'd thought dividing them for a little while would help ease the pain when[?] the creature inevitably perished.

Astair [in their conversation tonight] had whispered over the phone a concern that that [its demise] could be imminent.

'Should I take it to the vet tomorrow morning?'
'Has something changed?'
'It's hard to say. Listless. Eyes always closed. But that's normal. Hardly leaves Xanther's bed. Sometimes I swear I hear it mew, but when I look in, it's silent.'

Anwar stops pacing [stops rubbing his eyes {he has his most important interview in a few hours ‹he must get some sleep›}].

But [stupid stupid stupid {what Anwar had never seriously considered}] what if the cat were to die while she was away? Xanther would never stop blaming herself.

Anwar also has to stop denying that both Xanther and the cat look better [healthier {happier? ‹can a cat get happier?›}] when they are together.

He is now the sundering villain.

If only he could transport the thing to the hotel right now [with a snap]. He'd change their flight if the ballet wasn't in a little more than twelve hours.

Anwar pauses by the sitting area [he can't believe they're staying in a suite with a sitting area {Astair ‹seriously› didn't want to hear about it ‹she needs this «*they* need this»›}].

There on the bright red sofa lie more loose pages in Xanther's hand [not just her homework]: lists and lists of possible names for the creature.

Including an unexpected one:

Sadat

The name stirs him. It [for no {observable} reason] mingles with Xanther's courage [facing the challenges of this trip]. [at the outset] Anwar had readied himself for more outbursts and objections but their departure was marked only by Xanther's determined march through the routine of travel.

Heartbreak's brave face.

Anwar ignored her evident pain because he was so convinced that the energy of the city would awaken her to new distractions [different possibilities].

It hadn't.

Xanther never complained [except once to say she was so glad she could stay home for spring break {'More than a week would kill me!'}] but she also never relaxed.

[{in fact} over the course of their days here] Xanther has grown visibly waxen [even cool {cold?} to the touch]. She fidgets more. [unknowingly] She keeps dragging her lips across her braces [picking at the metal]. Hands too keep kneading hands [like some ancient dance of bedlam]. Worse than hands: fingernails keep attacking fingernails [drawing flecks of blood with every bout]. Her acne also seems worse. Is it blistering? And all the time [even with the heat turned up {which she keeps turning down}] these terrifying shivers.

She almost looks like some junkie sick from trying to kick a habit.

Xanther's only refuge [everywhere they go {worn constantly}] is behind Mefisto's gift [those huge pink glasses {with dark lenses}].

[and if this overall listlessness {?♭} isn't bad enough] She'd also uttered some very strange things.

Like [in that building {where Anwar had had his first interview}] saying the lioness Satya was running from there.

Was it the elevator that had spooked her?

Xanther sure had spooked him.

When the doors opened Anwar expected poison.

But that couldn't have been further from the truth. [in fact] Every place they visited [Tuesday thru Wednesday {including MoMA}] was loads of fun.

Those sleek elevator doors had opened onto a bright array of playful walls [soda colors {grape and lime and ‹Tang› orange} populated with {hand-painted} iconic gaming characters {dating back to *Asteroids* ‹*Missile Command*› «*Galaga*» as well as *Donkey Kong* ‹*Ms. Pac-Man*› and many more}].

That was the first astonishing [and meritable] discovery: all those games had been created by an array of different companies [{Atari} {Midway} {Nintendo}]. And they not only appeared on the walls. Every office Anwar visited [in a total of three different buildings {on six different floors}] seemed to have [at least] one area devoted to new and old games.

'We at Galvadyne pride ourselves on accepting a history that is not just our history. Give credit where credit's due, right?' said a young receptionist [who with his partner had recently become fathers of a three-month-old {their first child ‹now two› was one floor down}].

That was the second astonishing [and commendable] discovery: children. Galvadyne was dedicated to 'protecting and fostering the untold benefits of sound parenting' [what both another receptionist and another inter-meeting liaison had informed Anwar].

This was no line either: Anwar had gotten a glimpse of several day-care centers. They were open and friendly [well supervised it seemed] and not merely contained to a few rooms.

438

'The office structure is built around openness. We want the creative energy to breathe like a breeze through everything. I know, I know what does *that* mean? A young child, of course, is monitored more closely, but older ones are welcome to explore other facilities, from old-style arcades to PC Bangs modeled *exactly* on the Korean experience. Even the vending machines are stocked with Korean foods.'

Everyone Anwar talked to [and he talked to quite a few people {‹not even counting those doing the interviewing› every few minutes handed off to someone new}] brimmed with a belief in Galvadyne, Inc. [not to mention assurances that Xanther would be well looked-after].

That proved true. By the time Anwar had returned from four consecutive meetings/interviews [{with various creative directors and project managers ‹and one «fiendishly» curious guy in human resources›} the sum total of his Tuesday] Xanther was surrounded by at least a half dozen engineers and [their?] kids [as she destroyed high scores set on *Tempest*].

The focus the game required [Xanther's hand twisting {twitching?} the knob {in concordance with the advancing threat of multicolored lights}] seemed to draw her away from whatever [unvoiced{?}] anxieties [agonies!] were al lways haunting her.

'Man, you should have seen her on *Centipede*,' one kid told him.

'She wasn't any good at *Joust* but she so ruled on *Defender*. Her parents must have the cabinet.'

[on Wednesday morning] Xanther had gotten to play games in alpha and beta stages [or *Okam's Ray Sword* {in finaling}] while Anwar was run through the gamut of yet another set of handlers and interviewers.

Whatever everyone's speak was about the latest in office design theory [cubicles still abound here {even with everyone whispering about an inevitable move to a massive open room ‹à la Facebook «and Gehry»›}] there was no getting away from the most dominant tone in these present [and future] configurations: opulence.

[everywhere Anwar went] Expensive hardwood floors and glass-slab tables showed off expensive standing desks and ergonomic chairs [the latest hardware and monitors aside]. Management [Leadership {C-Suite!}] was impeccably dressed. Engineers will never change.

'This isn't even a main campus.'

'Sorry? There's more than one campus?' Anwar asked [his latest guide {young suited guy ‹sans tie› likely on his second pot of coffee that morning}].

'Galvadyne has as many campuses as it supposedly has companies. Joking. There are three campuses. In development. And here we go again: another scanner.'

[at every site] Anwar had to face the latest in ID systematics [a whole other level of opulence].

Anwar paused before a semi-pellucid wall of glass [vibrating with light {mapping his face ‹maybe his eyes too«?»›}].

'Iris?' Anwar asked.

'Retinal!' The guy seemed elated [Anwar is grateful for the lack of pretense {or that cloying suspicion that rises when people are too on-message}].

The light vanished. The glass slid away.

It was [in fact] a door.

Various interviewers ended up describing the painstaking process of a campus creation 'large enough to sustain Galvadyne's vision' [though {aside from the obvious games ‹slotted under names like Cornerstone Flags™ and Batter Banning™›} Anwar remained uncertain of exactly what this {overall‹?›} vision was supposed to be {though does an overall vision ever really exist?}].

Mefisto's connection with this place continued to trouble Anwar's impressions.

His guide through the first retinal scanner [no doubt on his way to a third pot of coffee] had mentioned other names [all amusing {if a little strange}].

'A.L. Chemical is one. Neural Necrodynamics, another. Eerie-spooky for sure. But hey, this industry loves a little eerie-spooky, right? It's why we do it, why we get it. The rush of the nightmarish. The survivor's giddy. Though don't get me wrong, sometimes we joke that management just did a great job creating this mightier-than-real-life vibe to keep us gerbils on our hamster wheels. Prank of all pranks, right?'

This appeal to the heart of a prankster had appealed to Anwar. It would have appealed to Mefisto too.

More than a few people Anwar spoke with maintained that trickster glint [even if Anwar couldn't shake the feeling that this 'this here' he was experiencing was just that {yet also not that at all ‹what had Astair read to him recently? «only the human knows how to lie with the truth» ∷ *The supplementary possibility of telling the truth in order to lead the other astray.'* ∷ ∷ **The Animal That Therefore I Am by Jacques Derrida. Translated by David Wills. Fordham University Press, 2008. Page 128.** ∷ ›}].

[after all {now and then}] Even the most nimble trickster gets trapped.

That feeling [of being trapped {is *that* what Xanther had picked up on ‹when she brought up the escaping lioness›?}] Anwar never quite shook.

Had Mefisto somehow gotten trapped here?

It's the one question that never stopped bubbling up in the curious soup of Anwar's various encounters [he wouldn't be here were it not for his friend's recommendation {and yet . . . }]: not once did anyone bring up Mefisto.

Anwar had felt noticeably relieved to get out of there. By the fifth retinal scan he wondered if he would go blind. MoMA was the antidote. And even if a painting might be falsely likened to a screen [putting aside perishability {texture's enactment of muscled authorship}] the greatest difference [what Anwar wished to impress on all his daughters] was that [unlike a game {and far more important than reaction times ‹and the visceral thrills of movement›}] paintings need to be read ∷ *For it is in such stillness that the mind may acquire itself through the velocity of thought.* ∷ ∷ **What of hearing?** ∴.

[{curiously} as Anwar and Xanther left the last Galvadyne building {despite all of its carefully guarded territories}] Two sets of lobby security doors stood open.

'Stuff always breaks down. Guess that's life,' one of the technicians had said [smiling at Xanther {waving goodbye}].

Xanther had waved back.

'Our mess-up!' Nathan Muellenson says now [extending a warm hand {he's a lot younger than Anwar expected ‹by twenty years «at least»›}].

'Not at all,' Anwar responds [following his host to their table {Xanther at his side}]. 'A pretty funny experience, however. I was trying to explain it to my daughter.'

'I can't stand virtuals,' Muellenson confides in Xanther. He had insisted [after he heard about the miss] on changing their lunch to the Mercer Kitchen [the restaurant at the hotel {since Anwar had wound up returning there ‹following the truncated . . . experience›}].

'Uh, like, FaceTime or Skype?' Xanther asks cautiously [still in her Converse {one black and one white ‹with pink shoelaces «tiny writing covering the white shoe»›} skinny black jeans and a pink hoodie {the restaurant states casual but everyone there is sharply attired ‹Anwar had put on a jacket «Muellenson is wearing a suit worth a month of Anwar's salary ⟨if he gets the job at Galvadyne, Inc.⟩»›}].

'Something telephony I imagine,' Anwar answers [after they've all ordered]. 'But the funniest part, the guy who was supposed to interview me was doing it from a studio located— Guess where?'

'I've no idea!' Xanther's eyes widen [{no doubt ‹knowing her›} with an impossibly long list of options].

'I know, I know,' Muellenson laughs.

'From Echo Park.'

'On the bright side you can have that one in person when you get back.'

'So maybe it's for the better?' Anwar says [asks {already trying to cover the wince ‹revealing his neediness›}].

'Anwar, I'm happy to say that at this point your last interview is just a formality. This lunch in fact is really a celebration. Super great, huh?'

Anwar is powerless to check his smile.

'Everyone loved you,' Muellenson continues. 'You too. Quite the gamer, apparently. Am I right?'

Xanther just shrugs [taking a mouthful of omelette].

'Was it, like, that the meeting was supposed to be, uhm, with someone who lives near us but was happening in New York, and, uh, like, was that what made it funny?'

Anwar can see Xanther's still trapped inside thoughts about his interview that didn't take place.

'That's exactly right,' Anwar responds softly.

'It's nice that you can find the humor in glitches,' Muellenson grins [cutting into his rib eye]. 'Glitches are part of the gig.'

'Certainly part of the tech industry.'

'Here's my dealie,' Muellenson continues [forking a slice of what looks like mostly fat {swallowing it too ‹at once›}]. 'Despite my title: tech's not my passion thing. I'm really the people-person part of this establishment.'

'Uhm, okay,' Xanther says [going along]. But she doesn't look convinced [which pleases Anwar {because he didn't want to point out ‹especially in front of Muellenson› how he felt ‹that in so ordinary a «tele»conference room «what had nothing to do with that screen and old camera ‹as if those had just been there as a ruse›»› something else was being served}].

Muellenson then [out of politeness{?}] asks Anwar about his experience with everything else. [fortunately] He's not that interested [quickly enough turning to Xanther to hear about her impressions {giving Anwar a chance to dig into his ‹flounder› sandwich ‹with a perfect amount of tartar sauce›}].

[{eventually} after pushing aside what's left of the steak {nil}] Muellenson begins peppering Xanther with more detailed inquiries about the various games she played [and {each time} is rewarded with equally detailed replies].

Like:

'I don't love FPS. I mean I play them, because my friends do, though a lot are pretty gory—' Xanther's glance flits to the side [to Anwar? {measuring his level of judgement‹?›}] '—so I was less *enamoured* with those.'

Or:

'*Trindle Spheres* was gluey.'

Or:

'*Cascade* was, uh, you know, meh. No kid's, like, gonna care about window cleaning or washing dishes. Vacuuming maybe. If the dust is, you know, ferocious?'

Or:

'*Okam's Ray Sword,* like the action?, how it involves you?, def on fleek. Awesome sound stuff. Awesome swiftness. The look, though, I don't know, maybe a little pastiche, n'est-ce pas?'

That is definitely the meal's laugh. Anwar almost spits [{sweet} mustard] coleslaw on his lap. The expression on Muellenson's face nearly makes Anwar spit twice.

How refreshing to see Xanther suddenly so alive [maybe this is some of the good-old Gotham magic Anwar had hoped for {that or the fact that they are heading home first thing in the morning}].

Xanther doesn't stop either. Her enthusiasm grows. And the more she focuses [. . .] the more articulate she becomes. "Uhms" and "likes" drop away. Words of the Day come into play. Makes a father proud.

'Anyway, I think games should relate to the world around us, and not, you know, the entoptic workings of the game's, you know, machinery.' ∷ *Hold on!* ∷

Hold on a second. Anwar hasn't taught her that word yet. Or did he? He must have. ∷ He hasn't. ∷

'Entoptic?' Muellenson looks at her curiously. 'I don't even know what that means.'

'Oh.' Xanther looks suddenly embarrassed [too self-aware {Anwar can see she had no wish to insult their host ‹but he can also see that she sees how a strange word might make that possible›}]. 'Like the eye seeing itself? Like, uh, floaters?'

'Anwar,' Muellenson smiles. 'I'm starting to think we should be hiring your daughter instead.'

'Be my guest, though I fear you'll find she's unaffordable.'

'Well represented?'

'One would be wise to assume so.'

[as it turns out] That's the lightest moment of the meal [even if it {too‹?›} had seemed to edge towards unpleasantness {with an edge ‹and edginess›} Anwar could never decipher].

The rest of the meal had veered from industry speculations to vaporware [alerting Anwar to the perfunctory quality of this last part {of the business side} of his trip {worrying him too}].

Dessert was ordered at the same time as the check was signed [Muellenson insisting].

At the curb Muellenson was already giving his driver instructions as he was shaking hands goodbye [still congenially {‹warmly?› 'Super great. I know we'll be seeing each other again real soon.'}].

Expensive lobby furniture and chrome speaks a language needing no words to communicate the nature of that organization's need. Or better: its appetite.

But what does it take for a company as big as Galvadyne, Inc., to feel filled?

The moment of greatest concern [however] occurred a little earlier [right after Xanther had gone off to find the restroom {dessert menus on the table}].

'Have you heard from Mefisto?' The casualness of Muellenson's question at once caused Anwar to reassess this Director of Engineering's capacity for deception.

'Not recently,' Anwar answered [honestly].

'Is he living in Los Angeles?'

'How should I know?' Anwar laughed [as if he'd ever known Mefisto with anything remotely resembling a long-term address without @? {not even th@}].

448

'You're still friends, am I right?' Muellenson asked then [but a bit too sharply].

'That would depend on his mood,' Anwar answered [a bit too pleasantly].

[unlike other moments of {feigned‹?›} jocularity] Muellenson's laugh came across splintered [with undisguised force {originating in nothing proximal to mirth}].

'Just money is all. We owe him some. When you talk to him, will you please let him know?'

'Of course,' Anwar answered [though the steeliness with which Muellenson had offered this command turned Anwar from thoughts of coconut cake].

Muellenson seemed not to accept Anwar's reply.

'What sort of work was he doing for you?' Anwar asked [at a loss for what else to say {or how to understand the ‹invisible› contexts ‹informing this inquiry›}].

[at that moment] It had seemed the right way to redirect their conversation.

'Here's the dealie, Anwar,' Muellenson said [leaning back to signal their server and {at the same time} find his credit card {black}}. 'Galvadyne is a super generous company. Super generous because it believes first and foremost in investing in those it employs. Especially those with inestimable qualities. As we both know, Mefisto possesses those qualities. Qualities that need to be remunerated, and, if he is willing, ongoingly remunerated for future work fairly done.'

This time when Muellenson laughed [suddenly too] it was bright [and ingenuous {youthful! ‹turning Anwar's latent paranoia into everyday dilemmas and doubts «and desperations» any aging man feels «with mouths to feed»}]. 'Jeepers, this is Mefisto I'm talking about. I know. Like he's ever cared about money!'

The only other odd part about that lunch was when Muellenson had asked Xanther if there was anything she wanted to see in the city.

'*Hamilton!*' she practically squealed. 'Can you get us tickets?'

'Never heard of it.' Muellenson looked as mystified as Anwar had felt.

'Oh, huh, I think it's like this really popular musical? You know, on Broadway?'

:: Static recall [reconstituting { . . . }]::

:: *That's not possible.* ::

:: **Confirming: not part of her historical possibilities . . .**::

450

[after lunch {back in the suite}] Xanther catches up on her homework [while texting with friends and Astair {more than usual with Astair ‹grateful for any word «or picture» relating to the little beast›}].

Anwar mulls over more of Mefisto's code [glad he never mentioned to Muellenson what's been {living ‹?›} on this laptop {for free! ‹'Careful, Anwar. You have a family.' «had Ehtisham really said that?»}] before banging the drums of preparation for their big night at the ballet.

[[while Xanther is showering} He checks to see if there is a musical called *Hamilton* {there isn't}].

[around 4 PM] They take a cab uptown. It's nice [refreshing!] to see Xanther in a dress[!!]! [simple black {shoes simple black too ‹with little heels «making her taller ⟨elegant!⟩»› with black ribbons at the end of each braid} and only one thing pink: her phone {clutched a lot more since separating from her feline friend ‹there's a check in the plus column for the cat›}].

Astair [of course] was the one who oversaw outfitting Xanther for this night at the Met.

[on her lap] Xanther also holds [{carefully} folded] that green coat her grandparents sent her [and if ever there was an occasion for such {expensive‹!›} elegance this would be it].

[stepping out {of the taxi ‹in front of Myla's building›}] Anwar suggests Xanther put on the jacket.

Xanther's resistance is [immediately] obvious [in the whitening of her lips {knuckles twisting for more white ‹around that «infernal» phone›}] but [without a word of explanation] she still obliges.

Anwar knows it's because of the leather [dropping his hand on her shoulder {to reassure her ‹and thank her›} as the doorman announces their arrival].

This time the elevator ride up to the penthouse doesn't elicit any odd responses. Xanther even seems to relax [putting away her phone {leaning against Anwar ‹humming something «'The room where it happens' ⟨?⟩»}].

The doors open directly onto the apartment [at once a welcome blaze of wood floors and white walls {burning with afternoon sun ‹only two posters «framed in red»: one of Misha ∴ Mikhail Nikolayevich Baryshnikov∴ and the other of Margot Fonteyn ∴ Margaret Evelyn Hookham∴›}].

'There you are!' Myla ∴ Mint ∴ ∴ **TFv1 p. 713; TFv2 p. 299; 701 ff.; TFv3 p. 685** ∴ roars [emerging from the kitchen {with Xanther ‹needing no coaxing now› rushing into those open arms}].

Where Anwar's eyes should remain [on this hug {the joy of it ‹the unexpected surprise of it «a little confusing too ⟨Myla did know Xanther when she was very little [could Xanther somehow still remember those days [what clearly Myla still remembers]? ⟩»›}].

But Anwar loses sight of the hug before the vision of something else.

Rubs his eyes [or wants to].

Doubts himself [he must {as Myla takes away the jacket from Xanther ‹taking away with it too this «appalling ⟨atrocious!⟩» vision›}].

Anwar almost cries out too [on behalf of this violence already enacted {coupled too with such terrible premonition ‹slicing down his spine›}].

                                        Such jagged

        gashes.

                            Enraged

                                            ragged

            slices.

[on the back of {at the bottom of}]

Xanther's jacket —

victim to a slew of awful slashes

[hack-
ing out a patch of the cloth

{squarish ‹and big «like a

⟨big⟩ book»

though not that big›
except in the nature of

its destructive

signature}].

But Anwar doesn't cry out or say anything to Xanther [or to Myla {who didn't notice}]. Now is not the time. Myla is beaming. His child is beaming.

Even as he forces a smile then [forces himself through words of welcome and reunion {trying ‹and failing «and failing ⟨failing⟩ over and over» again› to imagine who could have perpetrated such an act}].

That's the question [escaping its cage].

Who?

Or what?

Marisol

The wheeling of the stars is not infinite . . .

— *Jorge Luis Borges*

Last checks (before racing out (keys (already) in hand)). Windows closed? Check. Bedroom doors to terrace closed? Check. Xanther's cat? Check (still (still) on the bed)—

(but)—

(hey)—

wtf?

Astair grabs up the—

What the—

What *is* this?

Just lying here.

Under the cat

((looking up (if looking up with closed eyes counts as looking)) at least it looked up).

Still (still) alive?

Check.

Astair pockets the soft piece of—

WTF?!

feels like leather (calf?(!)).

But Astair's late (already (if she manages an errand (Astair must get something done (feels like she hasn't gotten anything done) apart from looking after the twins))) picking up the twins.

Driving.

Too fast.

And too curious (to wait for a stop).

Pale green.

It is leather!

Astair's heart racing with—

Rage (better not text) and/or Worry (a better reason to text (unless rage is hiding behind worry)) and/or What The Fuck?!

The craziest thought of all (though) refuses to fade (pulling up in front of La Felicidad Charter :∙ ███████████ **Los Angeles, CA 90026** ∙: School):

was it clawed loose?

(with the only lasting answer (to

(by what?))

resounding (too) potently in Astair's head . . .)

by some tiny cat?

Which wasn't the craziest thought ((and yes) the 5 was fine (134 heading west no problem (but (now) on the 101 (stop-and-go) taking the girls to the beach seems the superbest kind of superdumb))).

Shasti and Freya squall the whole way there ((with the front passenger seat a recent option (prize for turning eight)) Astair still wound up putting them both in back (to avoid a squall (that sure didn't work))).

A (nightmare) hour of traffic (nearly) negates the point of this trip.

Astair trying to catch what's off with Freya (until another spasm of unprovoked yells (heading toward tears) demands intervention ("Girls!" and "Quiet, please?"

(plus threats

("You already get no outside play tonight. You're both about to lose outside play tomorrow night too.")))).

Then (in Topanga Canyon) Shasti gets carsick and throws up.

(however (sometimes)) Crazy Thoughts can reveal themselves as Good Thoughts.

Leaving behind the car for the sea offers immediate relief (the wide horizon (and afternoon (off-shore) breeze) blowing away her daughters' desires to find purchase in the psyche of the other (find new reactions (when more visceral findings abound))).

Astair steers everyone toward the water (waiting to reach the wet sand (before ordering shoes off (the dry sand is hot enough to blister all their arches (but feels great on their collective tushes (as they (feet over the cool) scramble with laces))))).

Pelicans glide above the small waves rolling in.

Terns fleet what's left of waves abandoning the shore.

Shasti dares the (ankle-deep) foam.

Freya gets up to her knees (crying for a moment (when the lap of her skirt is (suddenly) splashed by two colliding (consorting!) ripples)).

Warm air and the salty mist mingling upon this edge (promising sights of a seal or dolphins ("Maybe even a whale!")) distract the sisters from themselves (until all comparative measurements dependent on each other (as well as wetness) cease to matter).

The girls imagine seals and whales until wait—

hey—

both Shasti and Freya are
jumping up and down at the ~~sign~~ (*sight!*) of

a real pod of dolphins.

Shasti counts five.
Freya counts seven.

Astair finds at least nine.

Enough exaltation (for all of them) to make the
traffic here (and back) worth it.

But there's more.

"Girls," Astair says (gathering them in (close to
an area of rocks (and small tide pools))). "We are on
a mission to find something."

That gets their attention (they are still their
sister's (Xanther's) sisters (curiosity runs in their
veins)).

"What?"

"What?"

They chorus.

"Can we bring a dolphin home?" Freya can't
help herself.

"We are looking for Nightmare Stones."

"Nightmare?" In perfect unison (Astair can see a tremor of terror too (not a bad thing to bond their inquisitiveness)).

"That's right," Astair nods. "Sometimes they're called Lightning Stones. But I like Nightmare Stones."

"What do they do?" Shasti asks.

Freya's eyes just widen ((strangely?) wild).

"I'll explain. What my mother's mother taught her. What my mother taught me. And what I'm now going to teach you."

"What?" Shasti's eyes widen like Freya's (but just with excitement).

"Does Xanther know?" Freya asks then (of course). Astair gives it to her.

"You two will learn this first."

That settles the twins ((sitting them back on their knees) a rare stillness).

"Nightmare Stones aren't just any stone," Astair continues (their attention won't last long). "They are smallish though not always. Usually gray though can be darker. Solid in color mostly. And the key? They have to have a thin line wrapping around them. Usually white. It can't be broken. To work it must be a perfect circle around a stone."

"But what do they do?" Shasti demands.

"They keep us safe from nightmares. Put one under your pillow and your dreams will be protected."

Freya finds the first one. And then two more.

Shasti catches up soon enough.

Astair hasn't found one by the time Freya and Shasti have a half dozen each (though (on further inspection) many of their stones just have lines of wishful thinking).

(after an hour) They have (between the three of them) nine. Freya has more than Shasti (but Shasti has one beautiful (black) stone with a perfect white band encircling the middle).

Both girls are happy.

And exhausted.

The traffic back is a nightmare renewed (but maybe the stones work (rearview-mirror consultations reveal both girls asleep (each clutching a stone))).

Astair also carries a stone ((just one) in her pocket) and somehow the wall of pulsing brake lights ahead seems unimportant ((and though it never parts) it moves and soon enough (without a thought) they're home).

One luxury Astair ~~grave~~ (*gave!*) herself at the beach was to put away her phone. She reaches for it now (while closing the front door (which does nothing to impede the (not so) obvious (historical) alerts)):

Alerta: atea zabalik!
Xim: qhov rooj qhib!
Nyenda: gocheyö!
Hişyarî: derî vekirî!
Waé: lawang mbukak!
Waarskuwing: deur is oop!
Synagermos: pórta anoichtí!
Manik'īya: beri kifiti!
Ereti: ekuwachichi!

In one hand (already) is a service advertisement ((a card (wedged between door and door frame (above the front-door lock))) what Astair tosses in the key bowl (on their foyer table)).

In her other hand is the phone (along with that Nightmare Stone (it's a good one) and the pale green patch of leather (calf leather (little doubt now (in this reappraisal) that it's from the (Saint Laurent(!)) jacket her parents gave Xanther))).

Xanther (too) is the one mauling Astair's phone now. The texts must have been delayed somewhere between send and receive (Astair did check for messages before leaving Topanga State Beach (zero then)). Now they flood her phone.

Today, 3:14 PM

Xanther: kitteh update please

3:21 PM

Xanther: >^..^<

3:23 PM

Xanther: =' >< '=

3:27 PM

Xanther: >^ <•> <•> ^<
                     = >< =

3:38 PM

Xanther: taking taxi to met

3:53 PM

Xanther: ("-"-/").___..--""".-._
           `6_6 )  `-. ( ).`-.__.`)
           (_Y_.)' ._) `._ `. ``-..-'
           _..`--'_..-_/ /--'_.' ,'
           (il).-" (li).' ((!.-'

4:07 PM

Xanther: kitten news! please!

4:09 PM

Xanther: .. .. ,%%%%%%,
           .. .. ,,%%/\%%%/\%%
           .. ..c%%%\c."‘".J/%%%
           .%.. .. ..%%%%/.o..o\%%%
           ....`%%.. .. %%%|.. ._..|%%%
           ..`%%... %%%(__Y__)%%'
           .. ..//.. .. .; '%%%'\—/%%%'
           .. .((.. .. ./.. ..`%%%%%'
           .. ..\\.. ..'.. .. ..|
           .. .. \\../.. .. .. .. \..|.|
           .. .. .\V.. .. .. ..).|.|
           .. .. . \.. .. .. ../_.|.|__
           .. .. . (_____)))))))

4:21 PM

Xanther: ???????????????
???????????????
???????????????
???????????????
???????????????
???????????????
???????????????
???????????????
???????????????
???????????????
???????????????
???????????????
???????????????
???????????????
???????????????
???????????????
???????????????
???????????????
???????????????
???????????????
???????????????
???????????????
???????????????
???????????????
???????????????
???????????????
???????????????
???????????????
???????????????

4:28 PM

Xanther: ballet about to start

475

Astair (immediately) responds.

Mom: He's fine!

Considers then how to bring up the jacket (while (again) reading her own text (again!)).

Better check.

Astair heads upstairs

            (sullen
          (with

the exhaustion of the day

        (with this additional
task (plodding upward)

      (compounding the
tasks of the past few days

      ((though) she has to give
this to her eldest:

      (unlike so many (irrespon-
sible) children) Xanther has never failed to meet the obligations required when keeping a pet

      (practically fanatical (*fantasti-cal!* (is this how little suicide bombers start out (with such devotion

      (is Astair really climbing stairs think-ing that? (connecting terrorist behavior with dedica-tion to an animal's care?)!))?))))
like refreshing the water morning and night (hardly touched) or refilling the food bowl night and morning (sniffed? (must eat some of it)) plus check-ing the litter (tiny clumps of . . . what? (never much))

(Astair is still meticulous and conscientious (though
(given how little the cat involves itself with the litter
(or the food (or the water))) shouldn't Astair be calling (taking it (at once) to) the vet?))

Astair's heart's pounding more)

              pounding harder) hot

                    flashes from the stairs?)

                            from the burden of
a thought)
        and by the top primed for flight.

    The cat's not in Xanther's bedroom.

    Astair checks Anwar's office then.
    Then all the bathrooms.

    Races to her own room.
    Checks their bathroom. Closets.

    Races back to Xanther's bedroom.

Checking under sheets. A pile of clothes on the
closet floor.
        Astair had rejoiced (when Xanther
accepted that there was no getting out of this trip to
New York). Only later did the consequences register:
Astair had acquired absolute guardianship over the
failing animal.

And if something happened to it while Xanther
was gone . . .

Would Xanther ever forgive her?

Why would she?

When at last something
life-reviving had entered her life —

meaning the world
to her —

· · ·

Astair flies down the stairs.

Freya and Shasti still downstairs (banging shoes together (an elaborate patty-cake desanding soles)).

"Girls, help me! Quick! Find Xanther's cat!"

The twins don't hesitate (throwing down their shoes (taking off with wild screams (what (with them) always seems to accompany any serious game of hide-and-seek (especially when it comes with a bribe (today's: chocolate pudding))))).

Astair checks the downstairs (not the basement (that door shut and locked)).

                                    Under furniture.

            Under the stove.

                        Even (when the washer and dryer offer nothing)
                        among the books stacked on the springs of the old bed in the old servant's room.

Astair circles back then to find the twins in the foyer again:

                        solemn

                                    empty-handed.

Did it die somewhere?

Knew it was dying (slipping first into some impossible-to-reach place (hadn't she learned some-where that that is what animals know how to do?))?

Or—!

Astair turns to face the front door.

When they were coming in—!

Could it have slipped outside?

Searching for Xanther?

Astair (at first) stays close to the house.

The patch of lawn in front. The flower beds below where the living room windows are.

The carport.

Then the back of the house.

Checking around the guesthouse. Around the patio. Along the enclosing fence and wall.

By that peculiar mossed-over door (draped too in ivy). Locked.

Nothing.

But coming back around to the front

                                Astair finds
        the twins outside

                    door wide open

        not just on the lawn

                            or on the sidewalk

            but out on the curb

                            and moving too

                out into the street.

Astair would scream

                            if they weren't already

            screaming at her—

"There!"

Pointing too (down the street).

"Oh God!"

Astair takes off running (without even seeing first (trusting (neither their seriousness nor their fingers) only their tone)).

Tone proves true what eyes soon enough confirm. Down the street. Way down the street. Half a
block at least.

That tiny thing of white.

Another white cat?

Too still to be any other cat.

Too familiar too.

Astair sprinting faster.

Toward the intersection.

How did it get so far? It hardly moves.

If something happens . . .

Shit! Shit! Shit! Please—

Xanther will never forgive her.

Even worse: the intersection has no stop signs (despite numerous petitions (according to Mr. Hatterly) and calls (to city hall ("What do you need? A body?" (which (apparently) is what the city does need (here's one body coming (which won't even count as a body)))))).

Smack in the middle too.

Only Astair can't run any faster.

She hears cars then. Traffic is inevitable.

She tries for faster.

But fast and faster is only fast and faster and not fast enough.

Not even close.

"Life doesn't need to happen fast to happen. Life just needs to happen. And not even light is as fast as that which happens," Sandra Dee Taylor has said.

And then Astair's bent over and gasping.

It's over.

"Yours?"

Astair's savior's name is Marisol. She is a young warm sweet delight. Skin like autumn. Eyes wild as orchards (burning). A smile just as wicked and right.

And cradled in those long brown beautiful arms is everything Xanther needs to feel whole.

"Thank you," Astair heaves (sobs(?)). "I don't know how he escaped."

A taxi speeds through the intersection (honking at the two women ((by then (just) safely) reaching the SW corner (as more cars whiz by))).

Marisol lives nearby. Marisol is studying to be a full-time nurse. Marisol is engaged. Marisol teaches Pilates part-time. Marisol babysits part-time. Marisol was going for a jog.

Astair is still breathless with questions and thanks when Marisol (at last) hands over the little cat (what Astair should have taken first (so stupid!)).

The cat (so light (its coat seems too rough and stiff (its whole body feels stiff (even as it yawns (curl of pink tongue (whisking out)))))) stretching out those tiny forepaws (pads of pink).

"Cute little bugger," Marisol laughs.

And then (amid their laughter) the tiny creature (right there in Astair's arms) begins to shake. Shake harder.

(Astair knows what this is.)

(So does Marisol.)

Going stiff too.

Really stiff.

As the seizure takes over.

499

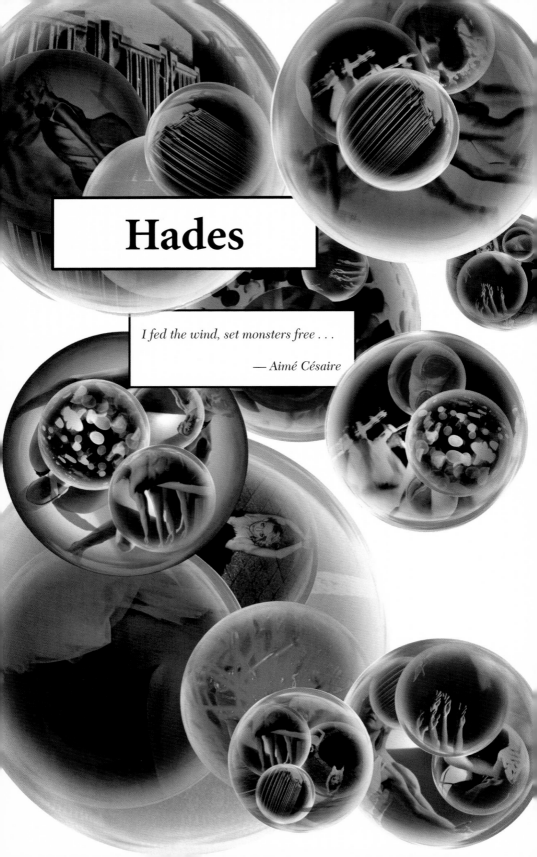

Hades

I fed the wind, set monsters free . . .

— Aimé Césaire

Once upon a time, a long, long time ago, in a universe far, far away, his name was Juan Mateo. He strode forward like gold from the earth, for an introduction, dipping to one knee, kissing Xanther's hand. Spanish bubbled out of his beautiful lips like the clearest water of a forever spring. And when he strode away in his robe of white, followed by an entourage, draping his broad shoulders with white towels, misting the air around him to cool his brow, he still turned around one last time to offer her his hand.

"A talented young man," Myla Mint had said. "Watch out. From Puerto Rico, though he trained in Spain, before training here, with me. No Misha, but audiences and critics find him . . . magnetic."

That was hours ago.

Now he is no longer Juan Mateo.

He is no more for the wings than he is of center stage.

Now wherever he moves is center stage.

Now wherever he pirouettes is beyond a stage, beyond center.

Now he is Hades.

Xanther watches from the side, watching him spin, caped in black, crowned in black thorns, turning on a toe, as if a toe were even needed to keep him in place, Xanther pumping her own big toe, to keep her own head in place, steady, making sure that she's not . . . except she's not steady, not even sure she can keep that big toe pumping, is it slowing?, it's uneven, yup, definitely slowing, though she keeps trying, insisting, begging even, to just speed up her toe a little, because if it is slowing, and it is, and if it stops . . .

Anwar's hand hasn't left her shoulder this whole last act, Xanther hasn't moved much either, both of them mesmerized by the final scenes where Persephone's mother has returned to take back her daughter and return spring to the world, while Hades, still here, mourning the departure of his brief bride, begins his spinning ∴ *re-centering the world* ∴, and with each turn, slowly at first, unlocking one cage after another, re-releasing despair, disease, disaster, deprivation, destruction ∴ **D-Days upon D-Days** ∴, the demonic dancers free again, in bright frosty twirls, by bright icy leaps, reunited with their king, whirling around him, as Hades turns faster and faster, smile widening, greater than his withdrawing arms, his gyre, this place, freeing them all, rumblings all about, tumblers overturning, chains splintering, as Xanther shifts uncomfortably, acting out with feet how Anwar's hand keeps shifting uncomfortably near her neck, as if somehow the responsibility for all this could suddenly rest on them, Anwar even leaning over as the final unlocking knocks underfoot, freeing Hope, the last, bolting from her confines, in bright sails of emerald, Anwar's familiar words already settling in Xanther's ear:

"Is everything okay?"

Xanther can't answer, wants to whisper back "no," at least, at least shake her head, but her lips won't move, let alone her head, and her right big toe is definitely slowing, her left toe refuses to move at all, and there's no denying the pins and needles pricking her arms, her face, the backs of her legs, the smell of something burning, burnt, she's burning, and burnt, and the burning burnt is still beside the point, will never be the point, when beyond the smoky announcement of terror, darker and more bitter than any smoke, what even Hades himself can't compete with, the swiftest roar now hurls her way, with nothing left to do, but let it carry out the darkest abduction.

Xanther closes her eyes.

Can't.

Out on the stage, the Demons have wound tightly around Hades, twisting him to a halt, with Hope the closest, the tightest, in his arms, as he begins to spin again, slowly at first, though now, where once an attraction, centripetal, like a drain, a black hole, drawing them all toward him, his turns mean something else, centrifugal, reversed, throwing them away, hurling his Demons off, to elsewhere, to the wings, with only Hope holding her own, still holding on, even as Hades keeps spinning harder, and faster, until even Hope's hold begins to loosen . . .

Xanther's hold loosens too . . .

Though she's not thrown . . .

isthissmoke   thissmoke   is

Driven is more like it . . .

The need for any name beside the point . . .

When you answer no calling . . .

When you know only one aim . . .

smoke? is this smoke?

Fulfillment is as simple as . . .

Not even a glimpse of the self . . .

"Is this the famous lion tamer?" was the first thing Myla Mint had asked when Xanther entered her penthouse apartment before the performance. Myla was dressed in black cashmere, her hair gray like the gray young kids dye their hair, that full, Xanther wished she could someday have hair like that, or go barefoot, something so cool about no shoes, plus she had on these thick-rimmed thick-lensed glasses too, though, wow, she hadn't expected Myla to be so tiny. And that's tiny next to Xanther. Next to tall Anwar, tiny doesn't even count. Not that tiny had any significance. The formidable choreographer was immediately in charge.

She hustled them through a quick tour of her spacious apartment, gorgeous wide windows everywhere, even in the two bathrooms they saw, one with a wall of glass in the shower, not that there was anyone to see in except the birds. All the walls were pretty bare, maybe occasionally some elegant print or a narrow shelf with a solitary flower, Russian books too, a bowl of chestnuts.

Her kitchen showed no sign of use other than one pot she used to boil water for coffee and another pot she used to hard-boil eggs. "Keep it simple."

Another room revealed a bed that looked as if it had never been unmade. Was that her bedroom? ∴ *Yes.* ∴ Yes. ∴ **Did you say yes first?** ∴ ∴ You can't hear us. Stop! Please! ∴

The private studio, she had her own dance studio!, in her home!, was ceilinged with two bare T-beams. The floor was supported with "two meters" of rubber and foam "to keep the Pacifists below from joining the NRA." And no mirrors, "There's only one means of exterior-correcting here," Myla jabbing two thumbs at her own chest.

"What are they like?" Xanther asked, stupidly, her heart

thumping, just imagining ballerinas practicing here, leaping, falling, caught in the strongest, gentlest arms.

"Who?"

"The dancers?" Xanther swallowed.

"A lot of work! Ha!" Myla snorted. "Getting them to the
gym is hard enough. And they lie too. Give me three minutes on the rope, and, okay!, there goes that lie." Catching
Xanther's look. "Jumping rope, dear. Try it. Start with one
minute, work your way up. And, okay!, I won't have anyone in my company just marking." Catching another look.
"Lagging, going through the motions, lah-di-dah, what
you do when you're out of shape. Do you know some of
them still smoke? In this day and age? Sure, they're artists
but they're athletes too, for Pete's sake. Okay! Thirsty?"

On a red-brick terrace overlooking all of Central Park
just starting to bewitch with fall, Myla sat them down
around a wrought-iron table, bringing out two glasses and
a pitcher of cucumber water.

Anwar wanted to know about the ballet, how it was
doing, how she had developed it, all the good news, the
scary news, but Myla refused to say a word until she'd heard
from Xanther "the only story that matters."

Xanther froze. Anwar froze seeing Xanther freeze. Myla
saw them both freeze and cackled like a wild hyena.

Xanther almost didn't see the stones covering her eyes
either, which, really, when Xanther isn't insisting on the
resoluteness of stones everywhere, on everyone, is how they
appear on Les Parents, her sisters, and her friends, but not
on strangers. Never that invisible on strangers. Strangers
are nothing but their stones.

Why was Myla different?

For some reason, with her, Xanther forgot those occluding hoverings, beholding instead through owl-wide glasses winks of mischief, with even a like curiosity.

      ∷ If she could only see beneath those stones. ∷

∷ **She will.** ∷

            ∷ Is that possible? ∷

∷ **Wait and see . . .** ∷

Within moments, Myla managed to move Xanther from a shrugging "She just ran away" to something much weirder, and like, even spectacular, Xanther unprepared for what Myla's strategy would open up inside her, even though, like, in retrospect, Myla had spent her whole life doing just that.

"*La perfezione è nemica del bene,*" she rasped.

"Perfection is the enemy of the good? ∷ How? ∷ ∷ **ORIGIN OF ERROR PROLIFERATION STILL UNDETERMINED.** ∷ ∷ How?! HOW?! ∷ ∷ *How wonderful!* ∷ What does that mean?"

"You're schooling this child well, Slow Dog. I shouldn't be impressed but I am." Xanther, though, could see that Anwar looked confused. "Now show me again, dear. Imperfectly."

"Show you?" Xanther was starting to freeze again.

"Use yourself. You've got offerings. I can see that. Burning too. I can see that too. You'll burn yourself up if you don't get that blaze outside of yourself. You do know what I mean?"

Xanther nodded, just as surprised by the old choreographer's intimations as she was by herself, pushing back her chair, and kinda stumbling through a pantomime of the opening gate, narrating it too, at first, and the falling chains, then Satya appearing, more like a bulldog, elbows jutting out, and all of it with a glass of cucumber water in hand, ice chinkling around.

Anwar bit his lip.

Myla applauded.

"Now dear—" taking away Xanther's glass "—forget the charades. No gates, no locks, and especially no words, just her."

"Satya?"

"Okay! A name is good. Especially for a lioness. I will be you and you will be Sattva. Show me!"

Xanther giggled.

"But I could never jump like that."

Even if Xanther suddenly wanted to try.

"Use those beautiful arms of yours and those long legs and show me!"

And Xanther did. How peculiar. She backed away until Myla looked tinytiny, and then moved toward her, slowly, no elbows out this time, focus alone drawing something together within her, connecting herself to herself, until Xanther felt, though she was only walking and swinging her arms, like she was striding forward on four legs, four paws, growing too, even more singular?, while stranger still, the choreographer wasn't getting any bigger as Xanther drew closer and closer, but instead seemed even tinier.

Myla patted Xanther on her arm.

"That was very good, dear."

Anwar wasn't biting his lip anymore. More like his mouth was hanging open. All shocked. Xanther would have blushed but Myla wasn't through.

"What was all around her?"

How had she seen that?

"She, uhm, she like knew exactly where I was and came straight for me and all there was anywhere, all around her, everywhere!, was, uh . . . "

"What!?" Myla demanded, popping her chest out, chin high, arms flapping wide. Xanther flapped her arms wide too, like that's going to help, until, remembering?, she let them swirl too, which somehow retrieved then that most beautiful and sorrowful mist . . .

"Honeysuckle!"

"The flowers? The scent?"

"Both. But not real. And spiralling around her too like a question?, but not like she was asking me for honeysuckle, but like asking me to take the honeysuckle?"

"Did you?"

Xanther shook her head. "I didn't know what to do. And then it was gone. Like she was gone."

Xanther felt like she was going too, collapsing in on herself.

"Dear, do you like honeysuckle?"

"Oh! It's one of my absolute favorite flowers of all!" Just saying so revives her a little.

"Now, dear, show me how our pussycat left."

"Myla, you'll need a tall fence."

"I've seen the clip," Myla hushed Anwar. "This child is already sharing with us so much more."

In the end, Xanther didn't even move her feet, just kinda stretched up, unfurling herself, over Myla, making her still tinier and tinier, until right before tossing her arms up, as if a leap of arms could be the whole leap, she glanced down at Myla, though not as Xanther, but as Satya, as she remembered her, alive again with her own return to rage, and it seemed, for a moment, the formidable choreographer cowered.

"I did my best," Xanther said, by way of an apology.

"Dearie," Myla humphed. "Around here we are not about process but results. Remember, rank amateurs say: 'I did my best.' Professionals say: 'I did the best.'"

Myla served dinner then. Apparently more than just coffee had been in the works in her kitchen. Though she looked a little disgruntled upon learning her hamburgers had come face-to-face with a vegetarian.

"Lucky for you my salads are even better."

"Slightly charred," Anwar said approvingly. "I didn't even know you were cooking these."

"Slow Dog, how many times have I told you? If you can't smell the smoke you neither know when the food's on the grill or when the place is burning down."

Anwar shared with Xanther a quick wink over the reprimand, not that Xanther hadn't already noticed the shift in Myla's mood, as her thoughts had moved from the fun of Xanther on that terrace to something else.

"You have a lot of plants up here," Xanther said then. "They're nice."

"My neighbor's. Gardenias aren't a bad fence."

"Is your neighbor a dancer too?"

"No," Myla scowled, her mood really curdling. "She won the lottery. Do you still walk on your toes?"

"Huh?" The change of subject disoriented Xanther.

"Daughter!" Anwar interjected, smiling. "Have you no recollection? When you were little, you went everywhere on tippy-toes. Myla declared you were a born dancer."

"More certain today after your little performance," Myla warmed, that other mood starting to fade. "There's real grace in your limbs, dear. Do you want to be a dancer?"

"No way," Xanther responded matter-of-factly.

"Intelligence in your limbs too!" Myla laughed. "Did you know cats only walk on their toes?"

"Really?" Xanther really was astonished.

"They're natural dancers. Made for the dance. Maybe even made of dance. Meat-eating prima donnas. Or should I say hamburger-eating prima donnas?" Myla added with a tiny glint of grinning maliciousness.

"Dance will be forever beyond me," Anwar sighed.

"Don't get hung up on joints, Slow Dog. Thoughts dance too."

"Do you have a cat?" Xanther had to ask.

"I am a cat," Myla twinkled. "*Pas de chat*?"

"Uh, 'Not a cat'?"

— Good guess. —

— **But she knows.** —

— *She lied!* —

"*Step* of a cat," Myla corrects.

"Excuse me French," Xanther mumbled, in a bad British accent, embarrassed, a little by her failure, as well as something else, a knowing she refuses to know.

— **This is getting out of hand. Why are retractions and retracings failing to occur?** —

— *Don't answer.* —

— I'm not answering. How can I answer? I have no clue what that even means. —

— **No clue?!** —

"Impressive nonetheless, young lady," Myla said, starting to clear away their plates, Xanther and Anwar at once assisting, following Myla back inside.

As they loaded the dishwasher, Myla told Anwar about her latest obsession: Balzac! "Over a hundred interlocking characters!" And the Russians! "Tolstoy's impossibly calculated faith because of, and, okay, in spite of too, his characters!" Which Xanther didn't get, holding back all her questions, clamped down between her teeth, as she helped clean dishes, which the more she focused on, a sort of stillness in motion, seemed to give Myla more room, or her mood more room, to spread out, and like be itself, until Myla was talking to Anwar, like Xanther, even though Xanther was right there, wasn't there at all.

"The highs I can describe in terms anyone can understand, but the lows I can't describe in any way anyone could respect, except to say that they raze whatever material pleasures the highs briefly claimed. I miss drinking," Myla ended with, with a half laugh, closing cupboards, emptying coffee grounds into the sink.

"Now don't start that," Anwar answered.

Myla waved him away.

"Don't fret. I realized recently that one of drinking's pleasures is the hangover. Precisely because of its pain and sickness. But more precisely: because it is both a passing pain and sickness, gone by nightfall. The hangover grants us the pleasure of experiencing a return to health."

"That sure is one very odd way of looking at a bad headache. How is your health these days?"

Again Myla waved him away.

"Do you know what I did last night?"

"What you always do before every opening night: you wrote a review."

"Slow Dog! You know me too well. I even FedExed it to the *Times* this morning. I know what they'll write before they've even taken their seat. Fuckers. Excuse my French." Myla suddenly aware again of Xanther, lightening, that whatever mood of hers retreating.

"Myla, it's always the review you know they'll write," Anwar said softly. "Tell us about the review you wish they'd write."

Myla reached for a last errant spoon but stopping short, rested her hand on the counter.

"Didn't you once tell me," Anwar continued. "'We must welcome the love *and* the hate. Because the love shows us who makes of this life. And the hate shows us who has been made by this life'?"

"Does he ever do that to you?" Myla asked Xanther. "Quote you back to yourself?"

"Since I was walking on tippy-toes."

"You all need to move back to New York at once. This city needs you in its life."

"Myla," Anwar insisted.

"Love, love, yes. And hate. Hate, I know. The poison we swallow doesn't excuse the action poison provokes."

Xanther's confusion must have been noticeable.

Myla smiled, blinking behind those owl-like glasses, like she'd just managed to blink something away, getting her bearings again, starting anew.

"Hades, in Greek, is the name of a place, what we know as Hell, but it is also the name of the king of Hell."

"*Hades* is the name of your ballet?"

Myla nodded: "Are you familiar with Persephone?"

It was Xanther's turn to nod: "She was taken down to Hades by, uhm, huh, Hades? where she ate seeds from a pomegranate. The number of seeds was, uh, like the number of months she had to stay down there, which is how the myth explains fall and winter." Wasn't fall starting soon? ∴ **September 22** ∵ "Spring and summer happen whenever Persephone comes back."

"Good!" And Myla looked genuinely pleased, drying her hands on a dish towel, before heading them back through the apartment to the elevator. "Stories, however, are more than just a series of events. Most people who want stories just want the simple way things were explained when they were children. They need to grow up. Stories can also be a series of themes unfettered by time. Or in other words: what's another way of looking at Hell or Hades?"

Xanther only had that story. She didn't know what else to say.

"Why not call Hell and Hades by its real name? Hate."

"Uh, okay?" Xanther really wanted to follow.

"Just as Hell abducts so does Hate."

Myla started stuffing her bunion-bent feet into socks and sneakers as Xanther tried her best to understand.

"Then how do we escape?" was all she could finally think to ask, never an answer, always a question.

But Myla looked pleased.

"Ha!" She bounced up. "That *is* the question!" And then too, with a long hooooot, she threw her arms out in a whirl, like Xanther had done, only better, describing without a word Satya's escape, Satya's Honeysuckle, or what had started off as Satya's Honeysuckle until it became a hug.

"Have you been to the Met before?" Myla asked, a little later, as they were climbing out of the taxi.

Xanther shook her head.

"To the ballet?"

"This is my first time."

"How abused you are, my child."

"Myla," Anwar spoke up. "I trust you didn't go to too much trouble getting us seats."

"Listen to him," Myla conspired with Xanther, again leading the way. "As if I would get you any seats! Tonight we will watch from offstage!"

"Can, uhm, I ask you a question?" Xanther asked, as they entered the building through a large set of metal doors on the side. "Why do you call dad Slow Dog?"

"My dear, I will not tell you that! But I'll admire you for inquiring."

Anwar was barely paying attention, taking in backstage, his awed look telling Xanther just how lucky she was.

"Now may I ask you a question?" Myla stopped for a moment. "It's personal, so you too can refuse to answer."

"Sure."

"Is your stomach okay? Does it hurt?"

"No. Not at all." Which was true, though for a second Xanther almost spilled how much it hurt to be away from her cat, how it needed a name, how inside her there was an awful forest full of dull stones covering a futile sea of eyes, which could do nothing to keep her from feeling like she was burning up, unless they were red, or garnet, which they rarely were, something really bad about that too, and only a little helpful, before the burning returned, Xanther more than certain that soon she'd be smelling smoke.

"Good news." Myla relaxed. "Back on my terrace, I thought I saw something in the way you moved."

"Oh. That wasn't me."

"No?"

"That was her."

Myla's eyes widened: "Sava was hurt?"

"Uh, yeah, huh, I guess so." Though Xanther had never quite thought so before, weird, considering how obvious it seemed now: of course Satya was hurt, terribly hurt.

"Remarkable."

This guy's going on vacation, for a few weeks, and boy do my balls need a few weeks' vacation too, don't get me started, putting up with this shit here, but Frank, fuck Frank, fuckin fuckin Frank Frankenstein, bustin my balls, every hour, I'd like to drop a fuckin bag of concrete on that fuckin shit plug, shit!, I do need a vacation.

Anyway, this guy's going on a vacation and asks his brother to look after his cat. Guy loves this cat. Lays it all out all obvious how to take care of the thing. You know, the food, the water, shit box, in-case-of-emergency numbers. And his brother's all cool and sure and whatever you need.

Well, the weeks pass, guy's vacation ends, stories there!, you and I could use some stories like that right now.

Brother meets our guy at the airport. "How's my cat?" That's the first thing our guy asks. "Your cat's dead." That's the first thing his brother says. Our guy goes hysterical, hys-ter-i-cal!, for a long time too. So much for all the good that vacation did, finally calms down, tells his brother. "You can't say it like that. You can't just go, 'Your cat's dead,' you have to start slow, like, 'Your cat was up on the roof, he was playing, he slipped, landed in the rain gutter, held on, slipped again, landed on the sidewalk, I rushed him to the vet, they tried and tried, medicines, operations, but I'm sorry, I am so fuckin sorry, bro . . . your cat died.'" "Okay, okay," the brother agrees. "I get it. I'm sorry. I am so fucking sorry." "Okay," our guy says. "How's Mom?" "Mom was up on the roof . . ."

The whisper had filled Xanther's ear, if it was a whisper, but like right up close, and not the only one either, others pouring in, just as small and soft, without speakers, origins lost, a lot of them too, so many that Xanther at once wanted to cup her hands over her ears, and did, though like she'd already known, it didn't help. Weird too because of how already loud it was back there, with plenty of foot stomps, cables being hauled around, set stuff moved, checked and rechecked, fog machines rolled into place, plus all these shouts for readiness.

Ten minutes!?

Where's the genius?

This remark made by a Times *editor who—*

Who?

Orchestra's not complete!

The composer?

—wearing a Zuhair Murad evening dress!

Who?

Not Nay Goldman on 81st?

The redhead!

Orchestra's not complete!

Right! And I'm Alessandra Ferri!

"Still like being on your toes, I see."

This last one, thankfully, coming from right behind Xanther, speaker this time included.

Myla seemed pretty amused to find Xanther doing her tall-as-I-can-get, craning her neck around, trying to find, match, where this rush of voices was coming from.

"Follow me."

Myla led her and Anwar out onto the stage, to the center. The curtains were still down, walling them off from the house, but Xanther still sensed the energy out there, filling up, a gathering of voices, expectations, something else.

"You're on sacred territory now," Myla said, tapping a toe on the boards, as a blur of white tulle and black tulle, blue tulle too, kept streaming around them, like water around rocks, soon to be displaced, even as Xanther caught how one ballerina, before disappearing into the deep of all the Met can hold, and it can hold a lot, whipped her head around, and like just her head, with a sharp look of inquisition.

Myla noticed it too.

"That's Hope. She's very catty. Very jealous. You'll see. Keep an eye out for her cape of green."

On the way back to the wings, Myla pointed out Famine, Despair, and seven more Plagues. "There are armies of woes in the world but nine for this production is enough. You'll see why."

Juan Mateo passed them then, returned, knelt, lips brushing Xanther's hand, before he was gold again, striding away.

More dancers kept crossing the stage, many in black, but plenty in blue, with now and then a streak of red or flame, executing a slow spin or taking one or two lazy leaps. Some dancers just strolled impudently across. A few stopped to talk, suddenly locking and popping, grinding!, all silly and playful, brightened at the end with light laughter.

As if the sizable crowd settling beyond the thick velvet curtains posed no challenge to anybody's nerves.

Everything there challenged Xanther's nerves.

Forget that the show was sold out. "Dear, there's not a seat out there that's not burdened by some critic, enthusiast, or dreading date," Myla yawned. Forget too the constant bark of technicians on wireless headsets, commanding the arrival of the ballet's weightlessly summoned summer, floating effortlessly down into place, while gels shifted hot spots to amber, and hydraulics made of a hill a hollow. Forget even the commotion of an ongoing, very unchoreographed circulation of stage hands, managers, technicians, navigating drop curtains, stray cords, floating racks of light fixtures, some moving up ladders, along catwalks far above, hung beneath the immense dark of the still higher flys . . . everyone circling the sacred territory, the dark boards, emptying now, dancers hurrying now, no one immune anymore to the commanding presence of the tiny gray-haired choreographer at the center, clearing her stage, leading Anwar and Xanther stage right, to a curtained nook, just out of sight.

Nearby, also out of sight, stood the changing station, a long black-painted plywood tunnel of dangling costumes, flying safety pins, and costumers ready to manage the quickest transformations. Xanther wanted to go. Enter one end, like one of these dancers, looking something like one of those Degas ballerinas Anwar had pinned once on Xanther's corkboard, is it still there? ∴ Yes. Still there. For certain! ∴, and if dusty now, remembered now as dustless, until at the other end, dancers emerged looking nothing like a postcard, or old painting, but whirling like the terrible storms of ice and fire Hades would soon command, basalt and brimstone, ushered ahead by various helpers, while a stagehand asked a stage manager something — "Frank?" as in, like that "fuckin fuckin Frank Frankenstein"?, the voice that had been in Xanther's ear earlier?, was this man that voice . . . ? — what Xanther couldn't hear anymore, her concentration now gone to various closed-circuit views of the stage, nine little screens, catching everything, as everything grew more and more still, absorbed further into itself by the impending moment that would soon enough start it all, release its potential energy, as lights dimmed, except for exit signs that, unchanged, still seemed in the shift to suddenly flare, Xanther's pulse racing, and she wasn't alone, feeling the collective racing of hearts all around her, hear them too?, was that what it was? along with, or beneath—

Here we go!

—fuck me!

There! Cut there—

Until all the lights were killed.

The blackness, though, didn't arrive as blackness, but instead delivered Xanther to an exquisite focus, as if darkness could somehow still be lit lightlessly from within, as whatever that heat was that lived within and without Xanther suddenly flashed into black waves of irreconcilable vision and darkest flame.

No more picking at her nails. They'd fall out. Byebye acne too. For sure, her skin was going to flake off.

Xanther could do little else but press against Anwar and wait.

"You're freezing!" he whispered in the shadows.

Flipping stones didn't help either.

Nor did running through another list of unworthy names. If pausing on three:

> Redeemer.
>
> Rex.
>
> Redword.

That last one coming by way of Kle by way of his brother Phinneas, who these days was in a real bad downward spiral. Supposedly something from a book. Something about myth. Stalking the herd. Slaughtering reason.

But none of it was enough. Xanther needed the little one here. With her. To hush these sounds. To eat this fire.

Xanther should have tried to smuggle him to New York in her carry-on, her backpack, instead of leaving him alone on her bed, though to have disturbed him there, then, even just a little would have been too much.

He had been curled so tight into a white ball, anchoring her pale green jacket, fast asleep, even with Astair yelling for her to get moving, they couldn't be late for the flight.

Xanther hadn't even thought twice. She just grabbed a pair of scissors and started cutting, with crude slow snips circumscribing her motionless little friend, which also somehow felt as if she were severing what felt like flesh within herself, the tissue binding her to this tiny creature, her mouth filling with sand, eyes welling with tears, tears turning too quickly to salt.

What the cut looked like never mattered so long as the leather didn't move.

The leather didn't move.

Little one never woke up.

And then the orchestra started to play.

A tremor of strings, distant at first, until the gold drapes, heavy as land, rose like heat off the land, and suddenly the boards were bright, flooded with scampering feet, arms extended, arms lighter than light, bringing summer, bringing a murmur of awe from the seats beyond, as the orchestra encompassed them all with the beginning of *Hades.*

Myla had already laid out the plot, though it was also in the program, and supposedly Trickster would intermittently make an appearance, pointing out subtitles visible to the audience, though not to anyone in the wings.

Act One began with Persephone cursing her absent father, Zeus. Though she also mourned him and implored him to reappear. He never did. Instead, suitors arrived, bringing flowers of summer, which Persephone refused to accept. Until at last Hades appeared. He brought no flowers, only his hand. By some shift in lighting, the pile of flowers at her feet frosted over. It was pretty cool. Persephone rejoiced. She wouldn't accept his hand, but she flirted with him and danced sooooo beautifully. They never touched and, sure, Hades pursued her, but Persephone pursued him too, until Hades was the one running away, turning back one last time with one last offer of his hand.

Hades, the place, the last scene in Act One, had taken Xanther's breath away. Anwar seemed just as thrilled, maybe uneasy too. Walls of steel cages. All open. Where Despair and Famine, all nine Plagues, welcomed Persephone. She'd come there on her own. Hades offered her a pomegranate. Persephone grabbed at it too, greedily even!, but Hades withheld it. To eat meant to stay. Persephone hesitated.

Hope then appeared, pleased to see the fissure opening between the two, drawing Hades away then, touching him for sure, a lot too, all over the place, before finally throwing herself into his arms, lifted up in his arms then, turning Persephone into this crazy pyre of jealousy and rage.

Act Two opened on Persephone's mother, Demeter, figuring out that Persephone was missing. Demeter transformed into her own kind of rage then, awful, but sad too, storming and icing over the world, depriving it of all warmth, sheets of blue overtaking everything. Good thing Hecate :: *Ah Trivia!* :: arrived, to comfort Demeter, if still failing to reverse the world's wintery woe.

Hecate then snuck into Hades where Persephone was just deciding to take the pomegranate, with Hope trying to stop that, but Persephone still ate the first seed, and at that moment two of the Plagues flew into their cages, if the doors still stayed open. Then Persephone ate a second seed and two more Plagues flew into their cages. Despair went with the third seed. Until only Hope remained. Persephone held up the sixth seed. Hope did her best to get it away. Hecate even came out of hiding and tried to help Hope, but Persephone ate the seed and Hope was compelled to retreat into her cage. Hecate raced away then. Hades laughed and at last kissed Persephone. All the cages slammed shut.

Though they could have wandered out front during the intermission, Xanther and Anwar decided to stay put, watching preparations for the final act. Anwar kept an eye out for Myla but she didn't reappear. Xanther realized her nerves had settled. She was breathing easier. The fire hadn't abated but it seemed less crucial. Knowing she would be home tomorrow helped, little one practically already in her arms. But the ballet too was also helping, something about its design, most of which Xanther didn't really get, was conjuring within her this strange calm.

Act Three started with happiness. The curtains lifted on Hades and Persephone in their icy wonderland. Dancers in blue and silver encircled them in a wintry rapture, like lovelorn snowflakes, though they seemed lighter than snowflakes too, hovering in the air, before landing again on boards that suddenly seemed softer than snow. It was a world dispossessed of gravity. Peaceful. A peacefulness that is forever. :: *Their forever the forever we dreamed of.* :: :: Dreamed? :: :: **There is only one forever you'll ever know.** ::

Offstage, though, was nothing of the kind. Ballerinas in platinum-glitter leggings or black tights, with skirts of lapis, sapphire, or cerulean tulle hurled by, panicked, panting, late.

They thudded to abrupt stops, clutched their chests, all those carefully preserved expressions out on stage collapsed here, mouths agape, heaving for air, for another moment of time they knew they couldn't have. New costumes, new start positions for new cues saw to it that they kept moving.

One beauty with, like, the most polished skin Xanther had ever seen, if only she could have skin like that, and a figure like that, didn't even stop, couldn't stop, and almost collided with a light crane.

"Simone! Careful!"

"I fucking fuck-fuck-fuck almost lost my balance out there!"

Xanther could smell them too. Talk about BO. Ballerinas glowed with sweat. Fatigue and fear, excitement as well, and joy, soaked their long limbs. Slender necks and collarbones glistened with the force of their exertions, the white cake on all their faces dotted with the cost of their labor.

Some of them scrambled around looking for scissors, others bit off strips of tape for their feet, one tried to stretch out a cramped calf by the stage door. All while that changing tunnel exploded with a flurry of flung garments and cascading pins as the next scene neared.

"'Demeter in Hell' in five!" someone whisper-yelled.

A new set of dancers crouched in the wings and prepared. The ballet mistress, who Myla had pointed out earlier, stalked the shadows, cursing to herself.

Onstage, one danseur, the ice storm's lead, was nearly done. Stag leaps. Twists. Some applause. Then an unexpected wobble. A last turn before soaring away, tossed like the storm he incarnated, no heavier than snow flung skyward, only to collapse in gasps offstage, a few feet from Anwar and Xanther, his face cinched tight with pain.

"Fuck! My leg's giving out on me!"
Someone threw him a towel.
"Is it the knee again?"
"My hamstring. Knee's always fucked. This is new."
All while the stage manager kept hollering: "Quickly! Quickly! Faster! Faster!"

"Oh boy," another danseur grunted. "Here we go again."

"Just one more."

"Thanks, buddy."

A babble then of exclamations moved through the wings, the orchestra rising again, with lights up again, as more and more dancers began amassing in a spiralling onslaught of leaps and spins, as much a celebration as a riot out there.

"Fuck this foot."

"Fuck me!"

"One more!"

"Simone! Careful!"

"I need more tape!"

"Quickly! Quickly! Faster! Faster!"

Of course, Hades' and Persephone's love couldn't last. The next scene was marked by the arrival of her mother, Demeter, who in an even more explosive dance, with Hecate's help, abducts Persephone, leaving Hades alone and heartbroken.

"The second ballet will be called *Persephone*," Myla had confessed on her rooftop. "Because mothers are tricky, especially for daughters. I know. I'm both."

The third ballet would be called *Melinoë & Zagreus*. The fourth, *Demeter*. Myla didn't have the title for the fifth and last ballet. But she knew what would happen.

Xanther, though, wasn't thinking about Persephone or even Hades, who by a *pas de chat* had seized center stage, seizing all the sacred territory out there, collecting himself, before he very, very slowly began to turn.

Instead, it was questions about Dov that suddenly whirled to life in her head. Like, was he anywhere now? In Hades? In a cage in Hades? In a cage that wasn't a cage but still a cage? The worst kind of cage. And what about hate? Was Hades hate itself? "Just as Hell abducts so does Hate." Except wasn't Persephone just abducted by her mother? Xanther had grown more confused, and tired too, with all the thinking, and asking, realizing then that the fire inside her was back again, worse than before, burning awfully, allways, definitely with a whiff of smoke now, right?, and prickles, Xanther already pumping her big toe.

But where here, really, was hate? That's what Xanther couldn't stop asking. Over and over. Maybe in the location? Both the place and the king together? Or was it in the story too? Or not at all but maybe just in the dance?

But it was thoughts of Galvadyne that really got both big toes pumping. And Xanther wasn't just recalling the fun either, those soda-bright colors everywhere, if some were recollected with a shiver, or all the kids, or old arcade games, or games in development, but something else entirely . . . beyond the friendly people, the big rooms and small cubicles, beyond even the walls themselves, the way they right-angled a floor, starting to hint at the heart of this wrong, the way all of it was organized in the first place, in the service of something Xanther never saw but knew somehow was still waiting there, controlling that there, in possession of every reason there ever was to ever be and so be afraid.

And, sure, of course, Hades started opening all the cages then. Drawing the woes of the world toward him. Until he stopped to restart again, this time spinning clockwise, and faster too, as he began hurling his worst into the world.

Not even Hope could hold on.

Though she tried.

Just as Xanther also tried to hold back the darkest shadow of all, stilling her shivers, and finally both her big toes too.

Even the forest darkened. The stones too.
Set upon their most impossible turquoise blue.

When it does grab her, Xanther not only won't be able to move her toes, she won't be able to move pretty much anything else. Though she'll still be moving, shaking all over, chomping into her tongue too, like it's some poor seal and she's Momma Orca.

It's the same at the start of every seizure, also what she remembers at the start of every seizure, just like she remembers now that all this now that's upon her now she will hardly remember later, if there is a later, there's never a guarantee of a later . . .

Though every time there is a later, she remembers now, how she remembers not remembering it later, that there is always one thing she wishes she could do before the shaking hits, before it takes her:

run.

Even one step would do.

Just one lousy step.

What's always denied.

some poor seal and she's Momma Orca
some poor seal and she's Momma Orca
some poor seal and she's Momma Orca

Except this time, Xanther does take a step.

And not just one step.

:: No! She's not stepping. She's not even moving. She's crumpling to the ground. It has her. I'm— ::

:: *But she is moving! She's running!* ::

:: **No she isn't. Amazing. She's charging.** ::

544

tongue   too, like   it's some poorsoul and she's Momma
        too, like

remember later, if   there is a later,   there's never

guarantee of a

runnin.

runnin.

runnin.

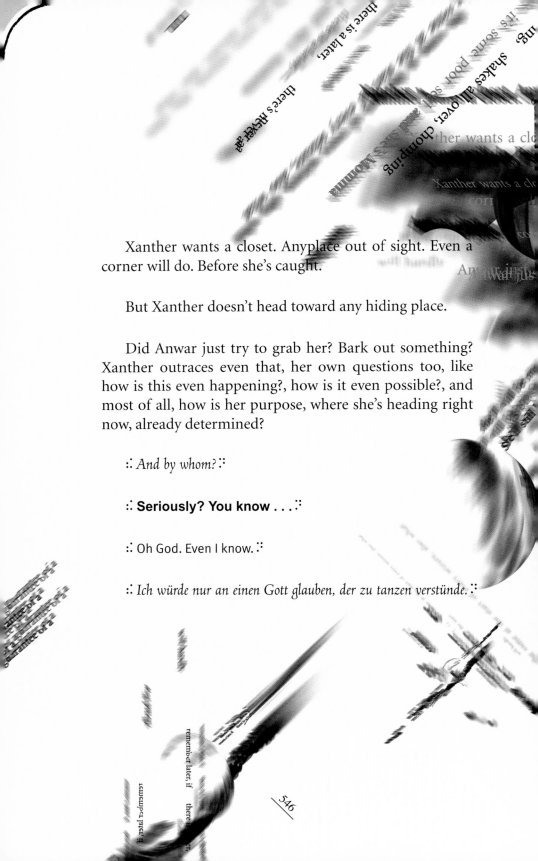

Xanther wants a closet. Anyplace out of sight. Even a corner will do. Before she's caught.

But Xanther doesn't head toward any hiding place.

Did Anwar just try to grab her? Bark out something? Xanther outraces even that, her own questions too, like how is this even happening?, how is it even possible?, and most of all, how is her purpose, where she's heading right now, already determined?

:: *And by whom?* ::

:: **Seriously? You know . . . .** ::

:: Oh God. Even I know. ::

:: *Ich würde nur an einen Gott glauben, der zu tanzen verstünde.* ::

there's never all
out of sight . . .
later . . .

Even a what

out of sight it's a later,

caught.

she's caught doesn't
her doesn't

hiding place.

hiding place.

Bark out something?

Bark out something?

She sprints out onto the stage.

head to

Bark out something

Hope flies away.

Hades is oblivious.

And Xanther nearly reaches him.

:: Hell is never in the fall . . . ::

:: Dov once said. ::

Dropped at his feet.

Seized.

Released.

∴ **Only in the impact.** ∴

Locochón

Mis animales son bravos . . .

— *Mario Quintero*

Fucked-up thing about taking a screwdriver to this door, Luther might pry loose the frame from the wall. Shit is a rot of splinters and lead paint. The whole point is to come and go without a trace. Why Luther told Tweetie to wait.

Luther edges the tool above the strike plate, grips a fist to hammer this shit loose, then catches hisself, checks the knob first.

Domingo's mom left the door unlocked.

Like nothing, like that, Luther's in, running rooms quick. No flashlight needed, still enough daylight left.

Just one bath. Hallway a crowd of family pics. Floorboards creak with every step. Two bedrooms, one crammed with loads of shit, old clothes, clothes for los nietos. Luther can't even see where Domingo would sleep. Maybe with his mom or in the living room. Too cramped to kick it here with some putas raising storms for mirror time, more sugar in their bowl.

No lives of others. Familiar as fuck. Too familiar. Crocheted blankets, dark orange and green, thrown over brown sofas and chairs. Too many places to sit, turned from barred windows to face an old TV, shrine behind, veladoras, Mary and Joseph ceramics, Jesus in a manger.

Luther picks up the little salvador. Twists it between fingertips, could with just a little more urge snap off its fuckin arms and legs, save him from one cross. But Luther returns it unharmed, this time inside a black candle, la Santísima Muerte, a better manger.

Back in the van, Tweetie knows better than to ask, just hands Luther a Double Gulp Coke.

Later, when Luther refills that cup with a long piss, Quantelle blows up his phone.

Luther scrolls the messages, where he at, does he want some, she wants some, wants him to unload all over her face, her body, nasty shit that should get him going, but Luther isn't going anywhere, studying through the wind-shield that little shit shack, deserted for weeks.

After midnight, the block finds quiet, halos of street lamps, the last round of neighbors out walking dogs, watching where they step, before heading back inside for a last drink, fall-ing asleep to DirecTV, or calling anyone who can treat their "can't sleep" like a prayer.

"You think that fuckin ho nos echó mentiras?" Luther throws out.

"Why would she?" Tweetie shrugs.

Luther nods, even if lying is what putas do, no reason needed.

"She's running though," Tweetie adds. "You heard from her?"

Luther shakes his head.

"Juarez neither."

It could mean something, though Luther bets Asuka's just running from him, winces now at still another reason he should never have called her over, gone at her so hard, mixing up the shit that's Luther's with this shit that's all Teyo's.

Teyo. Another one that's gone. No point either reaching out for talks, unless he got Domingo's head in a box.

Luther almost drinks the piss from his Double Gulp. Catches Tweetie watching him lift the cup to his lips. Like was he waitin to see Luther take a slug? Luther almost does for spite, molten up his mouth, get shit unright right here in this fuckin van with his fuckin homie.

He passes the cup to Tweetie instead, maybe make him take a slug?, like maybe Luther wants to see that?

"Get rid of it."

Tweetie does, slipping out like powerful water, disappearing down the street. Perfect time for Domingo to return, or his madre, or, surprise, someone new flicking a switch inside, Luther worked up fast enough on just the thought to settle this now, su sombra already falling faster than light on whoever would dare their own light in that place.

But shit-shack stays dark. Tweetie returns with hamburgers and fries. Luther's starving but pushes it away.

"You okay?" Tweetie asks.

"Ayunando."

"Why?"

Luther answers with glares.

"Sobres homes," Tweetie shrugs, contento to eat Luther's share.

The night lengthens, Luther's hunger robs time of movement, but hones him too. Tweetie stretches out on the floor in back and snores, finally stilling like the envied dead. Luther also stills but his focus raises the dead, new ghosts of desire, keeping Luther locked on one thing.

With dawn, Piña and Victor arrive. Relief. But Luther almost doesn't want to leave.

Tweetie drives to Hacienda Heights for what he swears is the best tortillas y huevos revueltos. Luther loves the salsa, bits of onion and cilantro almost too big to mix, but it does mix, perfectly, a hot and cold mess to wake any fool up.

Even if Luther's already awake and refuses all of it.

"For real?" Tweetie can't believe Luther won't even have coffee. "Like you fuckin Gandhi?"

"Do I look like Gandhi?"

"You almost drank your piss last night."

"Gandhi do that?" Somehow to admit that now don't make what-could-have-been matter.

"So I heard," Tweetie answers, mouth full.

"What's drinking piss got to do with living?"

"No tengo ni idea. I'm not the one fasting. Why are you?"

Luther has no clue. Can't even say for how long.

After breakfast, they drive to La Habra where Tweetie's got a safe place to go online. Just a copy spot, bunch of machines, with a few computers in the back. But Tweetie don't even park. Something spooks him. Won't say what.

Luther trusts Tweetie.

They get gas next and head downtown, Chinatown, usual place ∷ 彩虹睡蛇 – 到处都开门 ∵ ∷ *The Sleeping Rainbow Snake — Open Anywhere* ∵, same cigarette smoke, dudes going for broke, if all in a different place again.

Parcel Thoughts gives them Teyo's Witches. But they all shut down. Got nothing to say but stale shit months old. Luther don't care. Eswin hasn't stopped keepin Luther's crews busy with balloons.

The rest of the shit posted is all kinds of requests.

From fulanos, gabachos, bitches that should get Luther hard, get him hounding after new pussy, IMing the hottest ones back, friending them, until he can set something real up and in.

All for their star at the center, Melissa Torres: made-up curves, legs long, titties yum, amber eyes hotboxin your want song, deep-throating a bong, booty screamin jump, rev up, fuck.

How wrong is that? Luther cranking on some slit not even real?

Luther steps away. Sure as fuck doesn't need to see more of Almoraz's same shit, in another boxing ring, hands taped, bumping mitts. Or Lupita, sadder, fatter, trying too hard to be hip.

Tweetie finds Luther outside in the heat. Something about no food, putting pussy aside, makes of the sun just enough.

"Guess what? Memo took a deal."

"He's out of the hospital?"

"Twenty-five years. Out in twelve."

"Then that's it."

"That's it."

How did Memo get so wrong all that went down? Trauma? Contra viento y marea making Luther the savior of Frogtown when it was Juarez who shot him? How many times do any of us mistake the lie we're caught in for the life we swear by?

Now only Juarez could make a mess of something this neat. It wouldn't take much: one day yapping about the round he put in Memo's chest. If thoughts could make joints rage . . . Luther's hands begin to ache.

"Memo going up to Corcoran," Tweetie adds. "Buddhist is still there, right?" ∴ **TFv3 p. 464.** ∴

Luther's silence is answer enough.

A little later, standing in front of a Chase ATM, Luther can't shake loose his mind, barely sees the screen, PIN number spinning out of reach in a grito that would solve nothing, Luther doing everything he can to keep it locked in:

how dare Tweetie bring up his fuckin dad?

The idea keeps zeroing out the rest of Luther's thoughts. Even rechecking the balance, Luther still expects zeros even if that absurd sum hasn't changed. Nothing less yet but nothing more either. Luther can't remember when he's due the next deposit. Got plenty to wad his pocket if he wants, and he wants, but here's part of no eating too: fuck this pinche dependencia.

Luther balls up the receipt and tosses it.

"Let's check on the Parade."

"Lupita's?" Tweetie asks, slipping into drive.

"Fuck that crazy bitch. Today we checkin our Parade."

Let his corner crowds get a sense he's around. El juez here to make a good spot they slinging suddenly a big question mark.

Luther and Tweetie start east with Montebello, then Terrace, then up to Alhambra before south to Lincoln Park, downtown, and then west.

Sometimes they just watch. Sometimes Tweetie checks it out. Luther gets up close only once when, incredibly, one chaparro poniéndosele fiera to this mountain, in his stand, the way his arms crossed, rocking back on his heels, throwing up his chin, what all runs yellow when Luther roared out, shorty shaking to see this new thing coming at him.

"Se cagó," Tweetie laughs as they head along West Adams.

Luther laughs too: "Mi minatory, man."

∷ *Minatory?* ∷

"Mina-what?"

"Like a fucking bull."

"Hellz yeah," Tweetie nods, confused, maybe picking up on Luther's own confusion, at what he just now had on hand, some word he's never said before, doesn't even understand, except by what he just said?

¡Qué bueno! Luther's losing his mind.

The rest of the afternoon goes smoother. A patchwork of places, pockets between territories Luther knows they'd have to throw down for, taking risks, just by driving through, though nothing too big, not in this happy van with a happy skeleton family decal.

Here is way west of Luther's crews, Evergreen. All Teyo's now. Some straight up Calle 18, MS-13. But none beef. Just hand over cash. Because it's all about balloons. Pale blues.

"Pinks if you got some."

That gets Luther's attention. This on West Jefferson near ∴ South ∴ La Brea. Shorty with eyes tight on his boys handling stops. Tweetie had almost rolled on, until shorty stomped over to the opposite corner, waving bills in the face of some fruit seller, kicking his box of nectarines.

"What you want with him?" Luther roared. "Now what you wanted, you got with me."

And the more that shorty shrank, cowering, like he gonna ball up, like Luther some pitbull, gonna teethe on that fool, the more Luther's teeth coated with solder, lead, tin, a whole bubbly mess.

Tweetie stepped in then. Got that fool back on his feet. All shakes to get together the dough.

But maybe the kid was right. Maybe the fruit seller had had more than nectarines in his box. Fruit seller was gone. Took off. Luther gave shorty two Franklins off the top.

Then shorty asked for a re-up.

"Pinks if you got some."

"You sold pinks before?" Luther asks.

"Yeah, been a while, but that shit fue un putazo. Los adictos couldn't get enough. That then was Money Parade."

Luther's head goes pink. All the pinks they lost in Frogtown. What would that be pulling in now?

In Century City, Eswin meets them for the cash. Luther stays in the van, lets Tweetie handle the swap. Doesn't trust hisself. Might ask about Teyo. Or worse, Eswin might ask Luther about Domingo.

Tweetie comes back with the list.

Just one set left.

Near Venice.

"Eswin says whatever they got is ours. Have a nice weekend."

Luther watches Eswin ease away in a black Mercedes, nice car that don't look like much, merging with a bunch more Mercedes heading home to Brentwood.

In Oakwood, it takes Tweetie a few circles before he spots the crew, two out loud, a third hanging back in a truck.

Luther never seen these boys before but they know Luther at once, work even faster, and they working fast to start, bolillos slipping up sly, slapping cash for flashes of sky.

Luther can't help hisself, wonders if Nopales is doing the same right now, on some corner, palming up Lupita's brown in orange, what guaranteed will never compete with this.

Shouldn't Luther try it, at least once, find out what the fuss is about? He's tried most shit.

And hungry as he is makes trying it aquí, right now, seem the right choice, except hungry like this has a weird side too, like just thinking it out is trying enough, like Luther will never need to try anything nunca más.

Shorty in the truck hands Tweetie the cash. He got full sleeves, Detroit baseball cap on, skateboard stuffed in back of the passenger seat.

"We got a little more left. Hang near and I'll get you the rest in a sec."

"Late start?" Luther asks.

"Shit," shorty grins. "We started not thirty minutes ago. Like we're Ticketmaster here."

Luther heads over to the two corner shorties. $260 between them and one pale blue left. Tweetie takes $200 and returns to the van.

Luther can't keep his eyes off that last balloon. Finally takes it in his hand. Light in his palm. Lighter than sky. Is this all it takes to get that wild? Luther palms it back. Like he remembers, like he used to do.

Shorty nods, gold grill giving up all else he's got planned to take down this weekend.

And then something claws at Luther's back, Luther whirling fast, ready for some Venice patrol man coming at him with cuffs and a placa, Mirandizing his ass, instead of this loco-chón flashing his cash, pawing for a balloon.

"You got pink America?" Asian man ask, ñango and sick. ∴ **Jingjing.** ∵

No act either, Luther can tell, by his pants, his sandals, el payaso is foreign as kimchi.

Can find a pingo anywhere.

"Yo," Luther barks, not even much flex, thing looks like a tamale corn husk loose on a wind.

Shorty with the grill grabs the money then, his friend palming over the balloon, no lag, just another smooth transaction, until Luther puts out his hand.

Something weird about skinny Asian man.

"I give you my dollars lah," he objects, words a weird garble in his mouth, and not the English but the words themselves, like they aren't even his, and never could be. "Why you play cheat me lai dat?"

Would slap the bitch if his whine didn't make Luther also laugh. Got dirty nails too, like his dirty dog. Maybe he's Juarez's sister.

On Luther's nod, suato gets his balloon, plus a curse too to run him off.

"Day's done less that van got us some re-supply," shorty with the grill smiles.

But Luther can't stop watching the Asian man weave his way into the night, like night had come with him, and suddenly, enfolding them all, es la neta, dropped down on any world of daylight like a black truth.

Luther bolts after the man then, and fast, with no idea why. Both shorties look up surprised. Tweetie too. What's with Luther? Running crazy after some junkie? Even if Luther feels like he's chasing way more than that, like he's going after what night means to those who choose to hide in it, tracking that down, ready this time to take it down and drag it back for some kind of reckoning.

black dog

I don't wanna be dependent.

— *Elohim*

black dog ∷ **Luther**∷ after him now, coming quick, jingjing tsao like

siao, mebbe oreddy too late, slapslap down unknown street, barely

breathe, run until tor hwee, looking for hideplace from beast.

dog beat pavement, damn kiu kiu kio in this chase, growl jingjing

to hold up, stop, what for tu donno, balloon back?, pale blue?,

jingjing kio tio that, tapi for cash, sprint damn chor man.

jingjing reach alley, darker to right, shadows to hide in, or by rows

of bins, low roofs to hop top on a home lah, hide there, boh pian,

tapi jingjing choose bright ahead, miss right, pantpant for busy

street, if he can make it that far, now full out huff-run, black dog

at his heels, any sec drag jingjing down, sure then get hoot bad.

jingjing knew it too, saw at once, real samseng this one, hor,

not macam some ah beng at home, void deck folk scatter, fright

spencer good, face a fire of ink sure kia si lang ah seng, and more

than a face too, eyes a brighter flame, swee swee boh kay chwee,

how life does, when love is just what life eats.

jingjing look back around. black dog of blackest fire gaining

ground. another bad choice, jingjing gonna lose this race, lan lan

but run, if glance stumbles his pace, knees a wobble of knocks,

whirling his arms to keep him up, slapping at air, gritting teeth,

heaving harder to reach for farther, jingjing throwing eyes one last

time, black dog gone, mebbe ahead, jingjing's chest seizing, even as he spill onto pavement, manyak tourist, surfer kind, oso occi-

fers on bikes, jingjing pocketing pale blue, clamp back wheezing,

releasing self to easiest stroll fear permits, big smile, hide in

open, if buay tzai to find this open, that black dog somewhere,

buay song still, in fits for sure, for no reason taking an interest in

jingjing, seeing something jingjing can't name, other than . . .

::. but what if damn dog catch up? .::

.:: How different a world if Luther had reached Jingjing . . . ::.

.:: Or no difference at all. ::.

"其正杀之!"

"he? 他？那只猫？is the cat here?"

coughed, that's how auntie answer, and then eyes went skyward, head ground-down, sighsighing last time, out of so much tremble and shaking, about him, without the who him that's killing her. who him jingjing can guess, but who her?

damn switch-off guards at baggage claim, buay kum guan them at first, sure turned around tune fast then. oreddy on radios, hustling over, "emergency medics" somewhere close, coming to get her, collect her, sweep her away. almost took her too.

even after tian li regain balan, up off the floor, drinking cups of water, medics not convinced.

"靖,请汝释之,吾意倾于昏符," auntie said, sombong like, macam ya ya. "言吾之悔,烦其费意于我。 不多时,吾将复,可无需助而与事。"

"she sibeh tired," jingjing translated. "she fine. flop macam this lah all the time. take panadol can oreddy."

auntie tai chi by baggage belts then until medics packed away

medsen, jilo koyok kits, fold up gurney, shrugged off with last

cautions, vehicle sirens oreddy on for next new call in old big city.

but auntie not fine. no clue what next. city would chiak them if

jingjing not hire taxi. find hotel. but first place ∴ **Los Angeles Airport**

Marriott, 5855 West Century Boulevard, Los Angeles, CA 90045 ∴ was too

rich. second too ∴ **DoubleTree by Hilton, 1985 East Grand Avenue, El**

Segundo, CA 90245 ∴. driver complained at stops with no fare.

"we pay! why you care?"

auntie groaned, hand jingjing passports and dollars. driver calm

for green, fetched them chop chop kali pok to ∴ ████████████████

████████████████ ∴ with big sign for color tv and vacancy.

black man with hair macam tight tin coils and eyes grey as fish

scales asked if they wanted room for whole night.

now oreddy fifth night and counting.

same old way on new coast.

nothing changed since great tian li heck care bed and took floor,
flat out rest, palm on palm over birdcage chest, kay quiet, like
dead beyond ghost.

with next morning no better.

"auntie, what happened here?"

"auntie, what we do here?"

"auntie, where's cat?"

no sense what upset her. then on thursday night:

"吾不能见。" ::*I cannot see.*:: finally. auntie had sat up too.

"凡事皆觉远。" ∴ *Everything feels so far away.* ∴

"lost?"

"此人失。"

another collapse again. wrapped in masks of horror.

gone case then, more days and nights, jingjing sure toh osso lah to follow time, fifteen hours behind s'pore, sometimes sharing same light, sometimes days apart, but always past, no difference how much jingjing tries to square math, feels out of sync, out of place, and worst of all: sick. barely survived first two nights, shiver shakes, balling in sweat sheets, dead again, dead oreddy, dead.

at least jingjing got big bed. too soft, hurt back, with two pillows, too hard, hurt neck. jingjing loved bed.

day hours he and auntie wandered closer to beach. jingjing loved

sand and water more than bed. auntie just happy to find a patch

of grass to lie down on and sleep.

sleep and snore. nothing more.

jingjing got food over from boardwalk, old men there lah, heave

up weights, drums drumdrummed for a circle, rollerblades cut up

crowds, california t-shirts for sale, henna tattoos, ganja clouds,

jingjing's in california, can't believe, loud music, bright sun, in one

hand corn dog, in other shave ice.

but sand is dirty, broken glass and trash, and no riri around, no

swift, what jingjing would give to catch glimpse of even one star,

instead of these desolate begging him, jingjing!, for lui.

auntie didn't take back all dollars for keeping. now what hots

jingjing's pocket is enuf if he sniff out near way.

jingjing know no part of the world is safe from that parade.

anywhere where something's made up enuf to have rules, there are

fools like him to pay for pale blues.

nights when auntie koon macam death, siao liao that room!, tau

hong that place, not air in there to last another snore, where

outside's too much room to stay put, jingjing wandering stretches

of pavement with no end, losing the beach, sand, padpad by car

lots and strip clubs and beware-places jingjing could never mistake

for an escape: no signs, heavy gates locked with heavier chains.

every night macam that, following seagulls flying under bridges,

past dangerous trolls, with never a hint of where to find that

special relief, until tonight, by way of an eye, pace of a shuffle,

leading jingjing to that kay kuat one, tua tao, tua teow, black dog,

him, giving up pale blue before trying to run jingjing down. mebbe

still sniffing him out.

baliking back, jingjing with so much space to sit under palm tree,

with his monster cards, dreamy of all the flying above the planes

flying above.

sure too boleh find that black dog again, make friends even, kaki-

lang them, with more cash from auntie, and she got that, plenty,

jingjing could march with parade then for a long long time.

but closer jingjing get now to their chao room, with its dim bulbs,

brown walls, brown drips off two taps, that wheezing aircon, stale

enuf to make jingjing miss their flat, miss parrot queen, void deck

folk with their gong-gong chatter, as two colors not there blur his

then eyes, not dollars, but red and then not red.

                                        their passports.

at gates of u.s., in that jaga's hands, red and not red, why jingjing

never looked, si beh stupid him, all time, passports red one, and blue one?

welcome back?

jingjing slipslip past fish-eyed clerk, ease wide their door, diam

lah, find tian li same, still as a grave, too deep to care if jingjing

search near, search her, to find that wrong color, demand esspla-

nation, except jingjing find auntie awake, on bed too, color tv on.

she won't stop laughing either.

got herself a pizza. large pizza.

and beer. six-pack. bud light. half gone.

"我试了去找这只猫 ∷ *I tried to find the cat* ∷," jingjing explain, if auntie never ask, pat bed, offer him slice.

laughing more.

mebbe drunk?

"tom and jerry!" she near shout. in english. has jingjing ever heard auntie even try such words?

"难道你不介意吗？" ∷ *Don't you care?* ∷

"其归 ∴ *She's back* ∴." her eyes sudden twinkle of menace.

"she? where?"

jingjing sits on floor.

auntie laugh chee-seen then, siao ting tong her! with tragic

triangle of anchovies dripdripping cheese to point out on tv

cartoon mouse knocking out cartoon cat with oven door.

∴ **"That's My Mommy." Tom and Jerry. 1955.** ∵

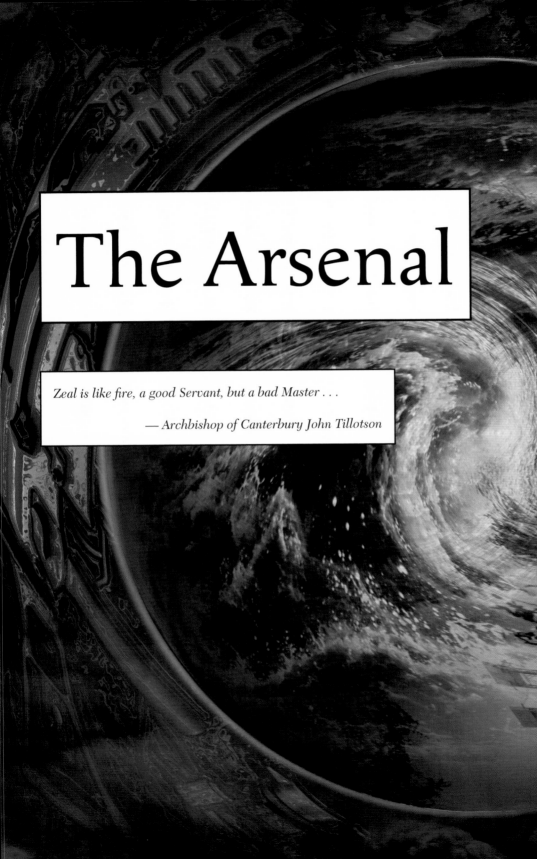

The Arsenal

Zeal is like fire, a good Servant, but a bad Master . . .

— Archbishop of Canterbury John Tillotson

nQ3Uz8K5B4ns2e3UOJVHRan9+fKia/bJsoneV9U5TkEnQuN4ZGHJ5t605yos7H
8LHQq7g8+9GcNoHT+tgU0B/DP68Q4cB4cnlX/8r2qbPxn0ey9clBRat5ulxZIVILL
ntj8=

"If just for satisfaction's sake," Bobby smiles, looking a bit like a cat bringing around a bird it has no intention to eat.

He and a charm of transcontinental workers had spent the past week picking at the encryption. It shouldn't have taken that long to solve. After all, Recluse wanted them to know what he was proposing. Unless he already knew Bobby and Cas were unlikely to accept any place he suggested. With an overwhelming advantage in manpower favoring his side, he probably had already accepted as his handicap that the location for any meet would be decided by them.

This back and forth then was just a game to gain ancillary advantages.

The disposable might still offer insight into how an opponent was thinking. Bobby believed Recluse was too fastidious to successfully propose entirely at random some point for their encounter, their fight.

And there would be a fight.

Sizable enough to involve weapons on both sides. Favoring Bobby and Cas was the mutual understanding that too large a conflagration would attract enough public interest to initiate enough variegated investigations to pass beyond Recluse's control. Ergo, the more firepower Cas and Bobby could muster, the better.

The real difficulty lay with whether Recluse would even show. Bobby was not alone in insisting that   Cas   should   be   nowhere near.   Whatever   e n g a g e m e n t ensued   would   be   fought between

two private   forces, while
Bobby and Cas fled back   to California.

"But I doubt we'll ever get another chance to encounter him one-on-one," Cas had pointed out.

"The chance you keep hoping for, that Recluse will present himself to you," Bobby had responded, "is not even a chance. It's ego."

"He's vain. Too. He won't want to lose this opportunity to gloat, to be there when we're seized. Especially if he believes I'm alone."

"You're not going alone."

"Me, you, a few others, in his mind, that's alone."

"Convince me that this isn't suicide."

And for a week Cas had tried to do just that, failing even her own rigorous re-examinations. Bobby dutifully listened to each new rationale, each time arriving at the same conclusion — "Suicide again!" — Bobby shaking his head, returning to code-breaking on reddit.

Then something happened that was no more than a bit of video on a phone, and yet that little bit was nothing short of miraculous. As Bobby kept saying, as if the mounting number of strangers coming to their aid wasn't enough to convince Cas:

"We are not alone! We have friends!"

A month ago, one such friend, young and nameless, had caught in the old-fashioned way a snip-   pet of Recluse buying a ∷ *Patek*
Philippe∷   watch   on Clifford Street and
New   Bond   in London. The
s a v v y   m i l l e n n i a l
h a d   c l i p p e d

h e r   p h o n e
to   her   bag   and
wandered   around in and
around the store   grabbing a wide vari-
ety of angles.

What made the thirty minutes so valuable came down to the mirrors and reflective properties of the display cases. By reversing and filtering the reflections, the recording had been finessed down to a highly accented and saturated nine-second close-up of Recluse examining gold and platinum complications. The moment was memorable and seemingly beyond all in-store surveillance.

For Bobby, it was the worst kind of success, because he saw at once how it could serve Cas as insurance. The clip was released on Parcel Thoughts with the only text necessary:

The Wizard's Window.

Showmanship and subterfuge. Bobby hated it. Their so-called truth was no more advanced than the crude explosives packed into Mefisto's Orb. But with that same Orb as hostage in Cas' hand, Recluse might have to show. Even Bobby had to admit, Recluse could not risk losing a chance at gaining access to this impossible discovery.

"He overestimates his own strength as much as he overestimates my smarts," Cas had sighed.

"He's an asshole."

"We finally nailed his passphrase," Bobby says now. "'Let the outcome   prove   the side.' Not my find. I
just   suggested to look for
                                      something   he
                                        said   from
                                          Borrego.
                                          Said it
                                          right

                                                        after
                                                        'Get-
                                                        tysburg
                                                        proper.'
                                          ∴ **TFv3 p. 713.** ∴

                                          Bobby shows her.

∴ **Encryption: AES-256 • Blocksize: 16 • Mode: CFB • Key: SHA256(passphrase)
• Encoded message format: base64(iv + cipher text)** ∴

DiOOSN7FuA7IXRUBIGzC2q/eB8vNndyrlYLlsTGcfljx9dN5FubhV3NwtJVIEkDYPJ
7AU/443bfwbb9xzcFiAKOhqB5XQFM+l3zU9/ztPGmMDtK1oydWEQiwjMUmWB-
gYy8BatpWch7dutGRgAS0KKUxlD2G0N8sB0tGhZQHl

Passphrase: VEM

National Park Service Museum and Visitor Center
Baltimore Pike
Gettysburg, PA 17325

39.811663, -77.225647

E/D01z1gQBPWACDsP0eR752re3HAxsNWLcnLXa9Mj9vt050WcaBTs0UUiyVF+
oUCydUBM3zusDR+dtJ0B0ONxIL2rAzYQ8OA//oQq2lLtzgdz+FuqTzHqZQCQzR
sA4RrqVEqO3GE9lu0loKWJg==

Passphrase: esse quam videri

Lincoln Memorial
2 Lincoln Memorial Circle NW
Washington, DC 20037

38.889273, -77.050090

dALUKK7nUm91W2y5zjEjJOXZ57pjtHusb3S8tStLT7cuXu+KNHw57AXFJt94
0SqOewl6rCPXoD   x1Mn9qTXTnxEpw6Vc+GkDwA3eeCNs
u m q V l   GG69q1PJoDnKOg7VvpMc

Passphrase:

sipaapuni

Fonts
Point

Anza-Borrego
Desert State Park
California

33.256797, -116.233124

nQ3Uz8K5B4ns2e3UOJVHRan9+fKia/bJsoneV9U5TkEnQuN4ZGHJ5t605yos7H
8LHQq7g8+9GcNoHT+tgU0B/DP68Q4cB4cnlX/8r2qbPxn0ey9clBRat5ulxZlVILL
ntj8=

Passphrase:

Let the outcome prove the side.

McClean House
113 National Park Dr
Appomattox, VA 24522

37.377118, -78.797171

"Surrender has always been his truth," Cas chuckles. It's a grim sound only matched in grimness by Bobby's chuckle. Who knew? Two grims sometimes make a laugh.

Bobby checks on their morning coffee. The Calgary Inn ∴ $49 a night ∴ has a two-cup drip with some plastic-wrapped Starbucks. Bobby brings Cas her creamy-sweet and turns on the news. Joan Rivers has died. A pharmacist named Glenn Adam Chin is charged with supplying "tainted" steroids that may have contributed to over sixty deaths.

Cas turns to the Orb. Vietnam? Just recalling the request almost dumps her on the floor. Dr. Ed had no clue what he was asking of her. Cas rechecks Clip #3 instead. The Aberration really is gone: Cas without a halo.

Xanther on the other hand is nearly lost in a churning violence of sheet lightning and storm :: **Clip #6.4** ::. What is going on? We must never mistake suffering for work. Cas spends the next two hours with another child, decades ago, growing up in the stiff walls of a condition mostly misunderstood. Vaccines!? A mess of flashes until—

"Addie."

"Addie."

ARC OF WINSOME

Atropos.

ARCLESS IF WINSOME

"Addie."

"Addie."

Bobby doesn't bring up her scrying until they're leaving the peninsula, heading south across the James River, alone again, in an old Impala ∷ **1982** ∴, rust and maroon dreaming of primer gray. At least it has tinted windows and Virginia plates.

"Find something?" he finally asks.

He seems relaxed.

The problem with relaxed with Bobby, though, is that it makes his sadness easier to read.

"Nothing of use." Which is true. Some secrets when revealed release a malice otherwise dormant if left alone.

"The Orb is the palantír of our time but you're no Pippin," Bobby says. He means it as a comfort. "Whatever you find matters."

"Better to be Pippin than Sauron. Don't think I don't see your furrow, old man."

Her observation doesn't surprise Bobby. "I finally reached Mary this morning. Sew is missing."

"That's terrible."

Bobby changes lanes as they leave the bridge, both of them tensing as they also pass a patrol car, even if Bobby's well under the speed limit.

"Could he have left as a safety precaution? So his family would be spared?" Though when would Recluse think to spare a family? Women and children first. The patrol car has started to follow them.

"That's what I told Mary," Bobby answers, eyes on his mirrors.

"But?"

"Sew left behind his cello."

There's nothing Cas can say to that. Even as the patrol car now passes them. Cas kisses and holds on to Bobby's hand. She wants to say she's sorry but she holds on to that too.

Bobby's mood brightens a little when they turn north, traffic ebbing, green fields on either side, returning them to the turns they know by heart, those roads getting smaller and more convoluted, until they reach Woodpecker Storage Facility. Twenty-seven units in three rows of nine on one pad of concrete. The walls are made of corrugated steel. The exterior color is still dark red, though the roller shutter garage doors are now black. Color hasn't altered the ease of access. Just drive up and unload. Or load. 10' × 25' holds plenty. "Over six rooms of stuff if you pack it right," an attendant had told them three years ago when they rented it. Paid cash. For ten years. Bobby had packed it right too, though not with stuff.

Bobby eases the Impala past No. 4 but keeps going until they've driven off the concrete and parked beneath a thick canopy of elms, dogwood, chokecherry, and black oak.

Then they drop the seats backs and sleep, hand in hand.

When they wake, the quiet is still unbroken. Bobby brings out sandwiches and a thermos of lemonade lightly sweetened with honey. Dried cherries and chocolate serve as a snack later on. Bobby has toilet paper too and points out the poison ivy.

Later, he encourages Cas to try to sleep more, or at least daydream with her eyes closed, while he continues to keep watch over No. 4.

One of Bobby's great gifts has always been patience. With Cas. With everyone. No wonder he was drawn to astronomy, to big science — colliders, gravitational wave detection, fusion. In the end, though, Cas became his big science. They'd met in 1961 when he was back east for the holidays from UC Berkeley. By 1963 they were inseparable. At Halloween parties he would dress up as Pee Wee ∷ **Reese** ∴, and she as Campy ∷ **Roy Campanella** ∴. In blackface too. Bobby loved to tell the story of how in 1969 — the last time they wore those costumes — a Black Panther took offense, until he discovered a Native American complexion nearly matching the makeup. "Why even . . . ?" he'd stuttered. "What I'd give to know skin like yours," Cas had flirted, introducing the young man to the woes of EDS and later to a science that would change forever the meaning of skin.

Those had been some crazy times when not even all of Bobby's suspicions could compare to her infelicities. "I'm pliable," was always her guilty excuse, what she'd said after her fling with Deakin. "I'm not," Bobby had answered, hurt, but he never shamed her, and when at last they wed, she was grateful for the patient sturdiness he never withheld.

They had known each other for over fifty years, and been married for over forty.

On a long day like this, resting beside him, their hands entwined, waiting for a moment that would either rob them of even one more moment together or reward them with another breath of dullness, Cas realized just how maligned dullness has been — alive with birdsong and the rustle of leaves.

She kisses Bobby's hand and holds it against her cheek and finally dreams.

But the dreams slip away when she wakes. Darkness combs through the trees, stars shimmer through the branches.

"I'm scared of dying, Bobby," she coughs out.

"Good. Seems like a stupid thing not to be scared about. But we all get there. One way or another. Wherever or however we go. After all, even starlight dies."

"Starlight's always dying."

"'All are drawn upon the stars, whether we know it or not.'"

"Who said that?"

"You. A long, long time ago."

"Tell me. I can't remember."

Bobby doesn't get the chance. The big truck rumbles into the storage facility, stopping in front of No. 4.

Any attendant is long gone, and except for her and Bobby hidden in their Impala behind the trees, the place is deserted.

Bobby flashes his headlights. The truck flashes its headlights back. The following dance of flashes confirms they are allies.

Bobby drives over to the truck, parking near the back.

While Bobby talks with the driver, the one who came with the driver opens the back of the truck. Four more men climb out.

Maybe they can't see her in the Impala, or think she is someone else.

"I thought she'd be here," one says.

"My bad," another says, after bumping the third man by mistake.

"You straight," the third man answers. He's got on a VT ∴ **Virginia Tech** ∴ baseball cap.

"Must be some badass niggah to kick up this storm," the fourth adds.

The assessment voiced by men not in law enforcement or the military warms Cas. She gets out of the car.

"Oh shit," the one who spoke first whistles.

"Thank you for helping me," Cas says, shaking all of their hands. Each lowers his eyes and says "Yes Ma'am." Cas preferred badass.

"Gots to aks you a question," says the one with the VT cap in his hand. Maybe he's not African American. Dominican? "I know we was told not to aks you nothing, but, you know, like we ever gonna get this chance again."

Cas waits, wincing maybe, powerless to avert his curiosity.

"The thing they speak of—" he starts off. Cas can see her silence has unsteadied him. His friends have either pocketed their hands or looked away, all backing off, leaving him exposed if not alone. But he is brave. He will persevere. "The thing you look at . . . is it alien?"

Cas relaxes. "First, a question to you: would you rather be disappointed or terrified?"

His friends crowd back in.

"Is there anything alive, be it animal or man, that don't hate disappointment?" the one who called her "badass" chimes in.

"Then be satisfied with terror," Cas answers, unable to resist winking.

They can't help laughing.

The music of relief.

Meanwhile, Bobby has begun dialling in the various combinations required by the various locks. Finally, he and the driver heave the door up.

It's not called the Arsenal for nothing.

Behind a false wall of used paper-
backs and college textbooks are
case after case of munitions,
neatly stacked from floor to ceiling, with one narrow access aisle
in the middle.

∴ The first four layers consist of 36 waterproof, crush-proof, padlocked cases (44" × 16" × 14") each equipped with hydro-absorbent silica gel canisters, purge valves, and military-grade polyethylene foam housing 38 magazines of 30 rounds, each with 4 rifles additionally sealed in triple-layer storage bags with 0 percent transmission moisture rating. The fifth layer consists of 36 cases housing handguns. The sixth and last layer consists of ammunition and other assorted military-grade weapons.

A partial list of long guns includes M16s, AK-47s, full auto with double drum dump, Heckler & Koch G36s, Steyr AUGs with Eclipse flash hiders, Tavor TAR-21s, Bushmaster ACRs, Mk 13 Mod 5s, Knight's SR-25s, Mosin–Nagant M91/30 PUs, Barrett "Big Shot" M99s, AR-15s full auto, M4A1 SOPMODs, Ruger 10/22s with selective-fire modifications applied, Armalite AR-10 A2s, DPMS .308 Mk 12s, Fulton Armory FAR-308 Phantoms, as well as semi-automatic shotguns, including Remington 1100s, Benelli M4 Super 90s, Ithaca Mag-10s, Akdal MKA 1919s, Franchi SPAS-15s, along with a case of AA-12 auto-assault shotguns. Total long guns = 567.

A partial list of handguns includes Škorpion vz. 61s with drum mags, Heckler & Koch MP5s chambered for .40 S&Ws, Ingram MAC-10s full auto, Calico M960As, KG-99s, KG-99 Minis, TEC-9s, Uzi UPP9Ss full auto, Smith & Wesson Bodyguard 380s, Ruger LCP .380 ACPs, Springfield XDs full auto, Glock 19 Gen 4s, Colt Pythons, Smith & Wesson 686s, Sig Sauer P226s, Sig Sauer 1911s, Sig Sauer P938s, Kel-Tec PMR-30s, Taurus PT111 G2s, and Ruger GP100s. Total handguns = 972.

A partial list of ammunition includes 9mm, 12 Gauge Remington Buckshot, .410 Bore Buckshot, 5.56 NATO, 7.62 NATO, .204 Ruger (Hornady), .22 LR, .22 WMR, .22-250 Remington, .223 Remington, .243 Win Improved (Ackley), .30-06 Springfield, .300 Blackout, .308 Winchester, .300 Win Mag, .32 ACP, .357 Magnum, .357 Sig, .38 Special, .380 ACP, .40 S&W, .44 Magnum, .45 ACP, .45 Colt, and .50 BMG. Total ammunition > 200,000 rounds.

Additional weapons include RPG-7s with GSh-7VT warheads, Mk 47 Strikers, Barrett XM109 AMPRs, S&T Daewoo K11s, PAW-20s, M16s with attached M320s, XM307 ACSWs, XM25s, AK-74s with attached GP-25s, and Mk 19s. ∴

"Now," Bobby says. "All we need is an army."

—Of course

Do I have a choice?

> *— Victim #13*

When the alarms go off, lights in every room start to flash. Speakers and intercoms announce the presence of intruders.

The Mayor looks relieved to have to stand up and get a gun.

Teyo looks neither concerned about the lack of a weapon or about all the men with assault rifles who flood the little sitting room.

The only thing that seems to surprise Teyo is that Isandòrno has

not risen from his chair or reached
for the handle hovering by his hip.

—You think it's nothing?

Isandòrno has to consider Teyo's
question carefully.

Teyo already knows that whether
it is something or nothing, what
happens next will depend more
on how those moments are recognized and received than on
how men pretend to prepare for
something they cannot see.

How often has preparation for an imagined future blinded the present to actual events unfolding? Teyo knows this. So what then is he really asking?

Regardless, Isandòrno can only answer in one way: he shrugs.

Teyo leans back in the sofa. —When you worry, then I'll worry.

Isandòrno isn't worried. Even if minutes ago something about Teyo had made his own hand, as if on its own, twitch for his hip.

Teyo had again come over for dinner, though tonight he arrived
alone. The Mayor was surprised,
and later Isandòrno could see in
the way The Mayor wouldn't bring
up the girl that he was also upset.

Only in his sitting room of pale
blue and birdcages, after too
much food and too many bottles
of wine, cakes brought out, left
untasted, until eventually the
requisite cognac was poured, followed by aimless toasts necessi-
tating ample repours . . . only then
did The Mayor speak her name.

—Why isn't Cynthia here tonight?

—She is gone, Teyo had answered, taking as much delight in the sharpness of his reply as he did in The Mayor's obvious dismay. Even if with The Mayor, dismay and rage go hand in hand.

—Gone?

—Back to Los Angeles.

—When?!

—This afternoon. I drove her to the airport myself. At which point Teyo's voice softened. She was ill.

—I have the best doctors, The Mayor replied coldly.

—She wanted to see her own doctor. Thanks to you, we have had a good time here. Maybe too good. She made me feel like a young man. I seem to have made her feel like a young, reckless woman. She seems to have come down with a UTI. You understand?

—But of course, The Mayor answered, attempting to subdue the twitch that accompanied Teyo's use of the word reckless. Teyo seemed to have both solicited The Mayor's sympathies as well as enflamed his entitlements.

Was Teyo doing it on purpose?

—You know what I think? Teyo had asked then, leaning in to confide in The Mayor, though in that private little room it was hardly necessary to lean in let alone lower one's voice.

Teyo must have been doing this on purpose.

Whatever this was.

—You have my attention, The Mayor still had to respond, powerless to defend himself against the price of titillation. In fact, enjoying the price.

—I think she may be pregnant, Teyo whispered.

The Mayor laughed, raising his glass, though Isandòrno knew by the way the glass floated and the laughter ended that The Mayor had no interest in merriment or congratulations.

—Just make sure it's yours!

That was when Isandòrno surprised himself: his hand was moving to his gun.

Teyo chuckled over The Mayor's jab, nodding his head in agreement, but Isandòrno still saw a steeliness assume his glare. Teyo's shoulders tensed, as if pressing back in preparation for all one hand clutching a glass can do to another man's eyes.

Had Isandòrno ever before seen in Teyo such possessiveness?

It was uncharacteristic.

All over a truant beauty Teyo was incapable of securing, even as he was, at the same time, using her to secure The Mayor's interest in Teyo himself?

Women too frequently under-estimate how often men value a woman's appeal in terms of how it increases their own appeal with other men.

And then the alarms went off.

And The Mayor's wife walked in.

With all the children and a train of nannies, assistants, and security.

—Paris had been too much, she ∴ **Gabriella Miranda Icaza** ∴ now exclaims. She missed The Mayor. The babies were missing their father. —We missed home!

All of which Gabriella delivers while quickly touring the main rooms, hoping to catch The Mayor in some act, hating Teyo for not being a Russian whore, ignoring Isandòrno for being the whore she has come to accept.

The Mayor puts away his gun, embraces his wife, and kisses his children. Whatever trouble Cynthia stirs in the cavities of both these men goes. The Mayor's face softens. His eyes appear boyish, even penitent, as he tries to sober up. He whispers apologies to Teyo. He had planned on ordering Moldavian whores for later that night.

Teyo apologizes too, for drinking so much, for staying so late. But he looks relieved.

In the morning, Isandòrno drives
Teyo to the airport. After which he
calls The Mayor.

The Mayor tells Isandòrno to take
the day off.

For some reason, Isandòrno goes
to check on Teyo's son. Not even
Teyo had asked to see his son on
this trip. But the boy is not home.
Isandòrno waits for an hour.

Only as he drives away does Isandòrno spot Jordi. He and his boyfriend are walking down the street, arms around each other, smiling, kissing, kicking ahead a curious ball made of cardboard, the pentagons and hexagons painted mint, marigold, and plum.

Maybe Jordi made it. Or his lover. Someone ahead picks it up and cradles it like she is their future. Both boys are happy to have her as their future. They embrace and slip into a bar.

On Monday, The Mayor tells Isandòrno to take another day off. This time The Mayor complains that his family has taken him hostage. He is powerless before them.

Isandòrno goes to the Cerro de la Estrella. He does not wish to visit the Museo del Fuego Nuevo. Isandòrno cares little for murals or dioramas. He has no interest in trying to slip into the Cave of the Devil. He only wants the narrow stairway. He wants the ruins.

Perhaps Isandòrno is hoping the view will suggest something unexpected. But even without today's pollution muffling the city, Isandòrno doubts some impression of clarity could have offered him anything meaningful.

Moreover, what fool expects reward when he has come without offerings?

On the way down Isandòrno spots a teenager tagging a wall with red spray paint:

> TE QUISE MAS
> QUE A NADIE
> HIJO DE PUTA

∷ *I wanted you more than anyone else.* ∷

—I can add to that, Isandòrno tells
the heartbroken teenager.

As with so many, this boy knows
to be afraid. His fear is instructive.
Isandòrno had only thought to
hunt down the one who jilted him.
Why would he also want to spray
this boy's brains out on that wall
along with his lover's?

—The paint is enough, the boy
says and runs off.

But it's not. Paint is never enough.

On Tuesday, The Mayor tells Isandòrno to return.

The children are in school and his wife has friends to see and dresses to buy and The Mayor seems happy to have a moment with Isandòrno alone.

—You will be gone by the time she gets back, The Mayor informs him.

—Of course.

—I want you to go to The Ranch.

—Of course.

—Teyo has left. Now nothing holds you back.

Isandòrno stands to leave.

—Juan will have the money for you.

—Of course.

—But this is not just about the money. Something has happened there that cannot happen again.

Isandòrno waits.

—How could there have been four
animals?

—I don't know. Isandòrno doesn't
know.

Nature hides her arguments but in
the end she always makes them.

"We miss you, brother."

The melancholy of a world eternally under construction . . .

— *Bohumil Hrabal*

Let him open door by himself. Mnatsagan climb into cab. Let him carry own box too. Sixth box. Keep him company back there.

If old professor wants to hire Shnorhk, so long he pays, Shnorhk drive him to post office with his precious box. Mnatsagan is just fare.

Charge surge pricing if he could.

"Բարեւ," Mnatsagan say.

Shnorhk turn on meter.

"Not even a 'hello' back?' Mnatsagan persist. "At least explain to me my crime."

Shnorhk done with crimes, done with explanations, done with gods, done with playing, done with friends, done with playing friends.

"Hello," he will still say. Next he will confirm destination address. Next drive. Just drive. When old professor start to talk more, Shnorhk turn up radio. No music now. Just politics.

In front of post office, Mnat-sagan climb out. Without word. Goes around back of cab. Probably to lift box out from other side, the closer side. Lift also easier on back that way. Maybe box is too heavy to slide?

Shnorhk leave meter running.

Look at maneki neko.

Hand waving for money.

Making Shnorhk money.

Who cares why angry, Shnorhk is angry enough to sue, sue any-one, anything, get money and more money, get justice.

Cab door open. Sliding. Not box sliding. This a sliding across seat to get back in.

Shnorhk look up.

Not Mnatsagan.

Old man gone.

"Echo Park, man," say Dimi :: Dimitri ::, closing cab door, giving rest of address.

Has balalaika on his lap.

So this is old man's plan.

Okay! Let Dimi ride!

Let meter run!

Shnorhk will drive Dimi all day. And make him pay. His fare *and* the old man's.

Shnorhk expects speech then, expects something. But Dimi just starts to play.

Bass almost too big for back-seat. Dimi still find easy lines.

Whatever else, Shnorhk respect such lines.

Turns radio of bad lines off.

Settles back too.

Follows what Dimi keeps find-ing, then keeping.

Is this new line he repeating?

Shnorhk almost ask. Almost tell Dimi to guard that line by heart.

Bites lip.

Speeds up.

Car ahead blocks escape.

CAR DRIVER RATING

Porsche 911 Carrera

QUOTE:

"I. Have. Arrived."

DRIVER:

Too slow. Misunderstand
car. Misunderstand self.
Time to get bus pass.

BUMPER STICKER:

Owning is loving.

RECOMMENDATION:

Pass.

LICENSE PLATE:

4Cl0S3D

In Echo Park, at coffee spot called Fix ∴ **2100 Echo Park Avenue, Los Angeles, CA 90026** ∷, Dimi finally stop playing.

"September 17, Shnorhk. Time to play that duduk."

Shnorhk about to yell he never play, but Dimi already out, traffic side, Shnorhk flicking eye to side mirror, make sure no traffic, make sure Dimi okay.

Dimi okay.

Passenger door, curbside, open and shut.

"Eagle Rock, please." Haruki say. Instead of biwa has lute.

Shnorhk whip around. Enough of this game. But Haruki won't dare meet glare. Just mumbles rest of address and starts to play.

"If Dimi not pay, I keep meter running," Shnorhk warn.

But who knows where Dimi went with original line? Wherever he go, big Russian don't return to pay.

Shnorhk leave meter alone.

$33.30

Shnorhk will call Patil. Yell top
of lung. She put old professor up to
this. She put Dimi up to this. She
put Haruki up to this. This day
Tuesday. Haruki work Tuesdays.
Shnorhk almost turn around and
ask Haruki why he not at work.

But Haruki is playing lute.
Haruki can play any fret. Even
sitar. Playing Shnorhk can't inter-
rupt. Old piece this. Quiet with
age. Memory of other days, crueler
days, yet bravely set still on finding
beauty.

In Eagle Rock, Haruki slide out, curbside, and before closing door gives best shot: "You're mad on that instrument, Shnorhk. September 17. Come on by."

Shnorhk give best shot too: "Forty-nine dollar and fifty cents. Cash or credit?"

"To Boyle Heights," Tzadik say from backseat and give address.

He have little keyboard and headphones. Not need headphones because has little speaker too.

Tzadik so good player. No point in Shnorhk to say anything. Tzadik can play harpsichord one moment, with Bach this, with Bach that, then next up stride like Art ∴ Tatum∴ or like Willie ∴ "The Lion" Smith∴. Play like playing is never anything but fun.

$103.80

By Boyle Heights, Tzadik play something Shnorhk never hear before. Wants to hear more of but good man is getting out, inviting Shnorhk to September 17, waving goodbye as Alonzo gets in, already in, so fast, with bassoon too, rattling off downtown address, starting to play.

Some Mozart.
Some Stravinsky.
Something new.

"Shnorhk, you're coming September 17, right?" Alonzo ask. Alonzo loves to talk.

This time, though, doesn't wait for answer, for chance to talk more, just goes back to playing. Bassoon poking out of window, leaving wake of beauty on hot Los Angeles day.

Kindo doesn't have instrument, just address, address Shnorhk already know.

Shnorhk grit teeth for Kindo sermon but sermon don't come.

Kindo just reach for Mnat-sagan's sixth box, slides it closer, uses his magical hands, magical palms, magical fingertips, heels, side of a thumb, back of hand too, to bring to life that cardboard and paper with rhythms Shnorhk love, with rhythms Shnorhk miss.

This no cheap stunt, this hand-off, this bandoff, all way back to Los Feliz post office ∴ **1825 North Vermont Avenue, Los Angeles, CA 90027** ∴. Like Kindo even have that kind of money, but in the end Kindo still reach for wallet.

$131.10

"Get out," Shnorhk cough.

Shnorhk getting out too. Card on street, at his feet ∴ *El Catrin* ∴ **no. 4** ∴.

Hits meter first.

$0.00

Coughs hard now. Bent over. Can't help it. Trying not to cough now is too hard. And trying not to do anything at all is hardest of all.

Mnatsagan is not only one there waiting. They are all there. With their music, their big smiles, putting their hands on him, drawing Shnorhk close.

"We miss you, man."
"We miss you, brother."
"We miss you, Shnorhk."

Shnorhk misses them too, enough to breathe, for a moment, three big breaths, big enough to sob and sob. And not try to stop.

"I miss her so much," Shnorhk
bellow. "Every day. Every day."

"I miss my little Arshalous. I
miss my dear little girl."

bluewhale

"Is there a way to win?"

"There's a way to lose more slowly."

— Out of the Past

"You're sure?" Özgür asks.

"Would you prefer a ghost arrow from a ghost bow?"

Özgür deserves the sarcasm.

"Caliber?"

"Nine-millimeter Makarov would be my guess," the Fire-arms Analyst answers. He doesn't look like he's guessing. "Piss off some Russians?"

Özgür couldn't believe what he saw last Thursday morning. Right above the wheelhouse. Right through the rear left panel. A fresh hole. Plain as that morning wasn't.

He'd turned over his vehicle first thing to the FAU ∴ Firearm Analysis Unit ∴. They took the weekend. Of course. They took Monday. By Tuesday Özgür is all doubts.

At least the hole is still there.

"No frags, but diameter and inside damage rule out rifle or larger caliber. Small sidearm. Maybe a Grand Power P9M. Not far away either. Lucky you."

Özgür remembers the Tesla. He remembers the gunshot. He remembers thinking he'd made that gunshot up.

Now, though, it's clear someone fired at him. By accident, on purpose, doesn't matter. A slightly different angle, a slightly different vehicular speed, and Özgür wouldn't be standing here in the Piper Tech shed ∴ **555 Ramirez Street, Los Angeles, CA 90012** ∴ registering a near miss.

The rest of the day goes bad with this inescapable recurrent news flash: his instincts are shot. Gone badly askew. In need of recalibration. Or are they beyond that? At his age, maybe. Worn down, worn out, worn through, and now through.

Then Elaine cancels their evening, and Özgür can't do anything to stop this feeling that they're through too.

By the next morning, his stomach's a squall of nerves. Coffee does him a worse turn but Özgür willingly suffers the ensuing indignities. Unlike his headache, they end at least.

Before lunch, Elaine confirms tonight's date.

I have to warn you -- we need to talk.

I mean we can have fun but we need to talk too.

Maybe between sets?

Or sushi before? Hama? My treat. ;)

Özgür may have doubted the gunshot, but he's not going to doubt anymore that Elaine is breaking up with him.

That night, Özgür eats at Hama ∴ 347 East 2nd Street, Los Angeles, CA 90012 ∴ by himself. Do the apologies even matter anymore? Özgür's not so old not to feel the sharp jealousy and anger slice up his insides, but he's not so young either to let it mean more than indigestion.

Özgür uses the small walk to the club to shake it off. Keeps his black fedora tilted down, preferring the company of a sidewalk's stare, as if a stranger's stare, registering just how bad Özgür really looks, might send him off the curb.

But hey, no one's ever that far from the gutter.

Passing a monument to the Space Shuttle Challenger Özgür's phone confirms more of the same. Özgür's starting to hate texts.

Elaine had promised to meet him outside of bluewhale ∴ Live Jazz + Art Space + Bar, 123 Astronaut East South Onizuka Street, Suite 301, Los Angeles, CA 90012 ∴, but by 8:45 PM Özgür has only another apology to hold on to. If he's got to hold on to anything, let it be a glass of Redemption Rye. Neat.

Jazz with a date is fine because she makes sense. Jazz alone though is best because then jazz makes sense.

Rumi on the ceiling says it another way: "Feel the beauty of your separation, the unsayable absence." :: *"Listening" by Jalāl ad-Dīn Muhammad Rūmī. 1207–1273.* ::

Özgür finds an empty seat close to the front. Surprising because the room is packed. Not surprising because it's a square, squat, barely cushioned stool. Room for one, maybe two if Elaine shows. The place prides itself on discomfort. Keeps you awake. Complicated music tends to offer sleep as a retreat, but stay with it long enough and a new experience awaits.

More than a few times, after The Bad Plus, Retired Advisors, or The Necks, Özgür and Elaine would leave feeling vaguely transformed, though neither could say how, just the eerie sensation that an entirely new sensation had briefly come around, maybe to settle down, maybe just to visit, but whatever the case, somehow granting an alternate way to understand the world.

Özgür takes a big sip of rye, scans the room like he's looking for Elaine. He knows he won't find her. He knows he won't find even someone familiar. Özgür's right on both counts.

Against the wall, under framed smears of tar, there's a big guy with an afro. On his t-shirt is a picture of two big eyes with fingers for eyelashes. *MR. DIGIT EYES* is scrawled underneath. Like it's homemade. Maybe it is. He's got his arm around a pretty blonde in a tie-dye summer dress ∴ Mefisto and Marnie ∴.

Next to them is a trio Özgür would peg as visual artists or designers ∴ Emberly Modine and Louis Elfman ∴ ∴ ██████████ ∴. Behind sit a pair that if glasses tell a tale of reading, Özgür would peg as writers, at least the one in bright red Lacoste glasses ∴ ████ ████████ ∴, the other by association ∴ ███████ ∴.

Farther back, a big guy with a dark beard, big smile ∴ Evan Narcisse ∴, also looks like a writer but could be a musician. The guy next to him is definitely neither. Aside from Özgür, he's the only other guy there wearing a fedora, stingy brim too, though straw-colored, tight weave ∴ ████████████████ ∴. He catches Özgür's eye too, like he was there just for that, like he knew something about Özgür that Özgür didn't, but also like Özgür knew something about him that he didn't, and if they just had a little more time they could both find out what mattered most of all, but when is there ever time for that kind of conversation?

More people keep coming in ∴ █████████████ ∴

crowding the bar █████████ :: ::█████████ ::

:: █████████ ::, crowding the room :: █████████ ::

:: █████████ :: :: █████████ :: ::█████████

██████ :: :: █████████ :: :: █████████ ::

:: █████████ :: ::█████████ ::

:: █████████ :: :: █████████ ::

:: █████████ :: :: █████████ :: :: █████████

██████ :: :: █████████ ::. They're all unknowns but then something weird happens: they start to seem familiar, maybe collectively, maybe because everyone there is so brightly intent on engaging the difficult.

The wall that plays the part of backdrop is cast in deep violet. One Steinway sits at the ready, warming under the gels. Nearby Markbass amps center a nest of coral snakes, the colored cables spreading around beneath Gretsch drums and Zildjian cymbals, connecting stuff Özgür has no clue about, but whatever these things are, their purpose is clear: music.

"Obvious with this crowd, in need of no introduction, please welcome Black Chalk on Blackboards."

Katla.

The trio takes the stage. Mingle ∴ Alexander J. Morgan ∴, from Oakland, in a green-plaid button-down, gets behind the kit, left hand already at the hi-hat, the drumstick in his right hand, held like a knife, moving clockwise, slowly, around the snare. PL ∴ Paul-Leonard ∴ Frontier, from the Bronx, in a dark, earthy long-sleeve shirt, black jeans, lets the stand-up bass create a new space. At least that's how it feels. Barely a touch to start a rumble, and the room has changed. Casual Cash ∴ John Willard Holmes ∴, waiting at the piano, takes his time to answer that growing question. He's from Tulsa, Oklahoma. There's a funny story about how the three met. Özgür can't remember the exact details. Something about an online gaming forum. How they all felt disappointed when they discovered they were all African American. "We each thought the other two were Asians," Mingle admitted once.

Katla. Katla. Katla.

Casual goes flat. Maybe heading for atonal or an hour of stochastic frustration. With these three you never know. But wherever they go, and they'll go there, they get you there too. Even if you're left behind. They're that good.

Katla. Katla-katla. Katla.

The first song begins with a virtuoso display of insanely fast arpeggios resulting in all sorts of digressions, apparent dead-ends, until they relocate themselves in the familiar melody of "Three Times a Lady" ∴ *Commodores*∵. Next is a song PL calls "Black to Back" and seems littered with popular tunes earning smirks and light claps ∴ **Mash-up of AC/DC's "Back in Black" and Amy Winehouse's "Back to Black"**∵. What comes next — what Özgür overhears from a nearby couple is called "Enter Sandman" ∴ **Metallica**∵ — gets laughs and shouts. Another song Özgür doesn't know gets still louder applause and laughs ∴ **Britney Spears' ". . . Baby One More Time"**∵. The last one ∴ *Prince's "When Doves Cry"*∵ brings a thicket of kids mid-room to their feet.

It's a little strange to not know what so many there know and still not need that knowledge to enjoy the music. Not that tonight is all about the recognizable.

Katla.

"The next arrangement," Casual says softly, "was written by our own Mingle . . . 'Metatron Made a Mistake.'"

What had been holding everyone's interest up until then, the pleasure of identification, the audience playing a kind of guessing game over sources, now gives way to something concerned with finding an expression exceeding any expression's hold on that which never knew needed expressing in the first place, the unknown unknown, no holds barred, no holding back, Casual soon shaking his head, a spray of sweat blurring the piano. PL's exertions are no less impressive, as he makes his bass seem beside the point even if for a while it becomes the only point. Has Özgür ever heard such sounds? Mingle solos soon, snarling over his drums, scowls followed by sudden looks of astonishment, disbelief giving way to amazement with every slap of a snare or rap on a tom. At one point he even snatches up a crank, a toy horn, winding one, squeezing the other, rushing their concerted cries into places only Casual and PL know how to negotiate. It's a near miracle to behold how such disparate sounds end up as friends.

Katla. Katla-katla. Katla-katla. Katla.

Nothing like Warlock's flash drive packed with documents on a company called Galvadyne, Inc., and someone named Alvin Alex Anderson. What glances Özgür did spare the files granted far less coherence than what Mingle was doing now with a whisk.

Özgür had sagged before the immensity of the task to even skim what Warlock had handed over.

Katla. Katla-katla.

"You never get to finish it all, dig, bey?" Hattaway, his trumpet friend ∴ TFv3 p. 411 ∴, had warned him plenty of times. "Big house dreams, big hit dreams, big salad dreams, big's all the same dream for something you never get to get at, which, dig?, is the whole point. Big's the distraction that keeps cats like us from facing what this gig's really about: the unfinished, Oz, unfinished songs, unfinished loves, unfinished lives."

Katla.

The trio too seems ready to embrace the experience of the unfinished, making of its own incompleteness a virtue, losing tonics in the name of an open-endedness that may be hard to hum but still plays.

Katla-katla.

Özgür remembers another trio. Three gunslingers. At the range. Who were they to be recalled at this moment? The biggest one ∴ Tweetie ∴ couldn't hit shit but he carried himself lightly. There was even a delicacy in the way his wrists kept raising and lowering the barrel. Just needs glasses, Özgür had thought. Whether he was right or wrong.

Then there was the skinny one ∴ Juarez ∴, hopping around like some kid tick-tock-time-bombing on his big sister's Adderall, a grin, then a leer, then a frown followed by a twitch, jaw hanging open until it just as suddenly snapped shut, all while his eyes kept up this contrapuntal skitter of glances. Actually, Adderall was wrong because there wasn't a hint of focus, just all over the place with nothing to lose, unless holding still meant losing, and for that guy stillness would probably kill him. Until he started shooting, that is. Then suddenly every distraction seemed to collect into one singular black thing, collapsing into a density Özgür wasn't sure he'd ever seen before, at least not like that, whether on the force or against force, pure force. Compared to his two amigos, or anyone else at the range that day, even Oz, this guy was the heaviest. Özgür never saw him miss. Not once.

The one that mattered, though, ∴ Luther ∴ wasn't the heaviest or the biggest but he still commanded their attention. Özgür had found that one the most difficult to read. Solid but nimble. Confident and then suddenly checking his back. Nervous even.

But at the same time unflinching. Both big amigo and dancing amigo never stopped checking in with him.

Özgür pegged him as unstoppable. You'd probably need to pump a whole clip into his heart before he dropped. If the guy even had a heart.

Shaved head. That was pretty stock. Also the long Levi's shorts, black sneakers, white socks, immaculately ironed white t-shirt. Veterano for real, no question. Thick forearms, cabled neck scrawled with those blue-black tattoos. Just like the other two, though this one had them all over his face too, and not a mismatched mosaic of Dodger and Raider logos, topless women, or some gothic MS. These designs wrapped around his skull and down his cheeks, even gouging deep into his ears, across the flat of his nose, around his lips, his chin, under his jaw, and with the exception of maybe the collar of inverted crosses, more Maori than east-side local.

That much was definite: these three were part of some gang. Probably a nothing set. Maybe they were the set. Sold on all of it getting better, faster, richer. When really, twelve months from now, tops, they'd either be eating earth, eating behind bars, or learning what kind of real forearms you need for a wheelchair.

Özgür could imagine some OG, probably grey like him, selling them that same old story about a better-faster-richer future. All the cars, the parties, the pay-per-holes.

Özgür never bought into the whole California car culture, he was fifty-fifty when it came to parties, and he had never gone with a corner girl.

If you fuck whores, then all women start looking like whores. Who said that? Ellroy? ∴ James Ellroy. *Suicide Hill.* ∴

"Worse," Hattaway would warn, in that hoarse howl of his, "just think she's a hizo and you'll act like she's one. But if she isn't, mufti, what's that make of you and your treatment? Square, cat?"

And what of how we treat the future?

Better treat her gently.

Or at least carefully.

Özgür had treated those Three Bad Musketeers carefully, running off a list: Rascals? Dog Town Rifa? Rose Hill? Krazy Ass Mexicans? Breed Street? Sickos? Maravillosos? Kobras?

Not that Özgür had been all that interested. Affiliations, unless relevant to some larger case, were just another means to sunglass motive, lose sight of those darker glances, private and personal, as old as humanity is rapacious, in the way that almost anyone can rise to mistreat tomorrow and plot malice.

Their lead dog was definitely a plotter.

He was what happened next. He was what those other two waited for. Where all their nows kept pointing. He was the one holding not only his own future but theirs too.

How about mine, tough man? Özgür had almost asked, laughing to himself even, like he was laughing at himself now. You got my future?

But instead Özgür had turned his back on them, on the idea of any future target, even the paper ones yards off. But the Three Bad Musketeers had come back around. Sometimes the future insists. The mangy one had stopped to admire Özgür's targets.

"Deadly," he'd said, like they had something in common.

Maybe they did.

Özgür had decided to get an eye on their license plate, but a later check brought up nothing out of the ordinary except that the van was registered to a woman: Lori Flores ∴ Piña ∴.

Even if something about those hours at the range still didn't sit right, some sense of misalignment persisting, along with the suggestion of other perceptive errors, misdirections, mislabelings, out of focus, out of sync, nearly spectral, as if a whole new order of possibilities was starting to emerge, though Özgür can't know them any more than he can justify what is a near illegal response to people he doesn't know and can only suspect.

So much for instincts.

At which point, Elaine slips in beside him.

Katla.

"Sorry, sorry, sorry," she whispers.

It's not going to be that easy.

"Sorry is a beautiful word," Özgür whispers back. He knows how to make a whisper snap. "Don't treat her like a slut."

What else was he supposed to say?

Seni çok özledim!

Katla-katla.

Elaine stands up at once, like she was just slapped, and slapped hard too, slipping away like that. Özgür wants to follow but doesn't. Is this it then? *Katla-katla.* How she leaves? *Katla.* The rest left to unravel with texts. *Katla-katla. Katla-katla.* The kind that keeps promising make-up sex until morning rises on his empty bed. *Katla-katla.*

During the break, Özgür leaves behind an Asian elephant, ∴ John Szinger ∴ to save his seat. Though he won't be coming back.

He's surprised to find Elaine at the bar with drinks ordered.

"Redemption? Neat?" she offers contritely.

"How'd you guess?" He's already sorry and feeling stupid, deserving too of everything that's about to come next.

"I'm an optimist." The Asian flush in her cheeks tells Özgür she's either still angry or on a second drink. Then she smiles and there goes anger. She's only sexiness now, in the way her lips part, full, almost swollen, mouthing for him to follow.

If Elaine's sexiness kidnapped Özgür's inside, outside it captures everyone else. Men can't help but look, linger. Özgür can see how Elaine senses their attention. It's no surprise. She's always had this effect on the opposite sex. Sometimes the same sex. A shocking beauty, too short to be a model, though that didn't stop her from doing a nude for Mangees Rumsson. Rumsson didn't retouch her skin but he allegedly did make her taller. "It beats going to Thailand to get my legs lengthened," Elaine had laughed.

Özgür has the photograph in his apartment. All six feet. The closest he's come to getting Elaine to move in. But Özgür doesn't want black-and-white. He wants this one, the real one, under five foot six, in full color. He wants her to hang dresses next to his suits, leave her razor by his bathtub, put her books on his shelves. She can set up her desk beneath the Rumsson. Small and tall, together at last.

"Move in with me, Elaine," Özgür suddenly blurts.

"I can't."

Maybe he wasn't clear. He knows he was plenty clear. But that doesn't stop Özgür from asking again.

"The whole deal. Keys, parking spot. Whatever you need, whatever you want."

"I heard you, sweetie. But I can't."

She even kisses him. Özgür expects a goodbye kiss but her ardor confuses him. She keeps kissing him too, arms around his neck, wrapping even a leg around him, her teeth then on his ear.

"I got it."

"Got what?"

But she won't stop kissing him.

"Got what?" Özgür's confused.

"I got the job."

"What job?"

"Princeton."

Her nod makes Özgür's guts sink and twist. Because this time he was right. He feels awful. Yet good too. Because he loves her. And this is good news.

"January start?" he asks, hoping she'll say next September, that will give them — maybe — another year. Either way, they have to celebrate. Özgür must rally.

"No!" Elaine nearly squeals. "Here's the craziest part! They want me to start yesterday! What a story. An impossible story. But it's official. I leave first thing."

Özgür smiles. Özgür hugs her. Özgür's heart breaks.

How best to serve the prospects of our lives? Isn't that always the question? By serving the lives of others. Isn't that always the answer?

"Champagne time," Özgür manages. "The best blue-whale has to offer."

Except Elaine isn't following Özgür back inside. Instead, Elaine has gotten down on her knees, taking his hands, squeezing them hard too, then kissing them, kissing each finger. It doesn't matter that everybody is looking. Elaine sure doesn't care.

"Özgür Talat. My Turkulese, my young Turk in grey, my dark cup of Turkish coffee, my wake-up call in life, will you leave this dirty city, leave your dirty job, and move in with me in dirty New Jersey?"

Özgür surprises himself.

"You betcha."

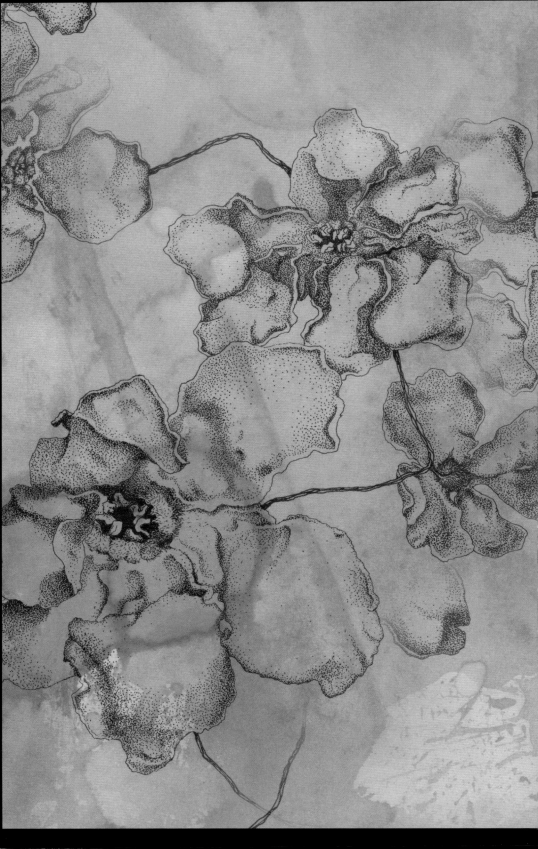

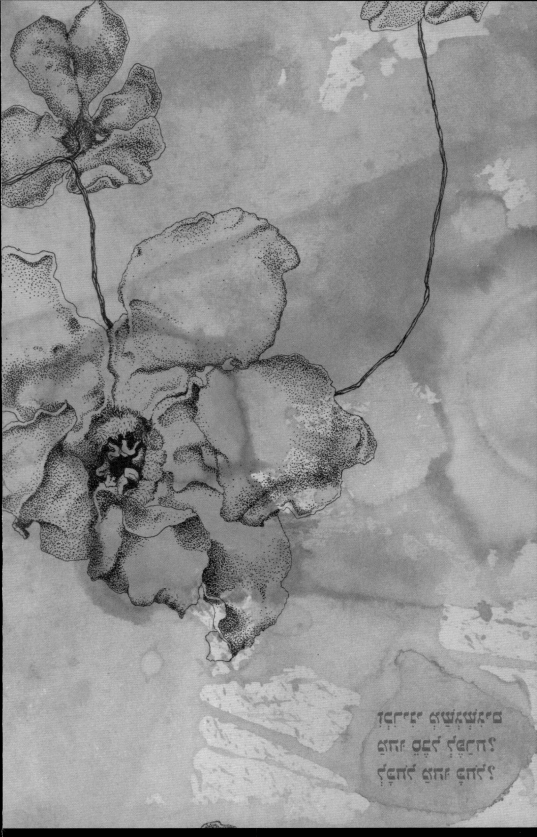

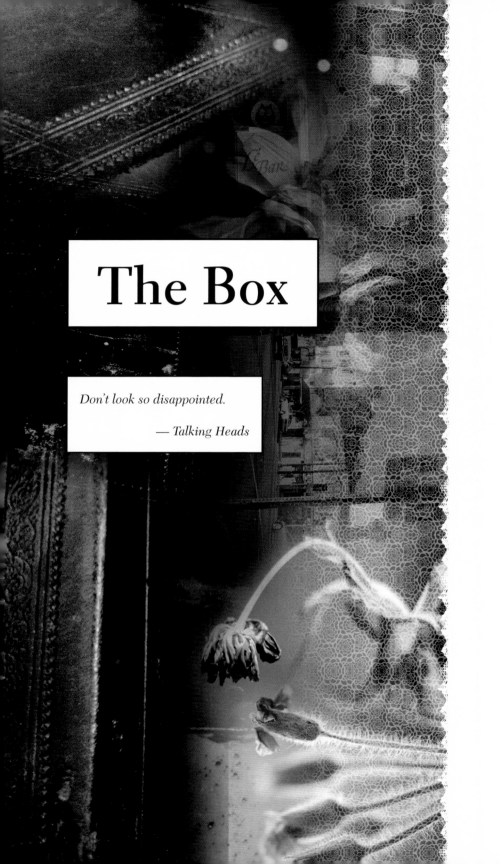

The Box

Don't look so disappointed.

— *Talking Heads*

Here's the only part that makes sense:

Xanther's listless.

(Or at least a little listless.)

"Talk to me, sweetheart," Astair tries again (pulling the (soft) brush (again) down over (through) Xanther's long black hair (like they used to do all the time (mother and daughter sitting on a bed))).

"Oh, ugh, it's just so, uhm, still so, you know, uh, double-ugh, so like *embarrassing?*" Xanther keeps her back to her mom ((maybe?) making it easier to talk more openly(?)).

"I can understand that," Astair answers (continuing to brush).

"At Myla Mint's show! In front of all those people!" Xanther's little shoulders shake.

"But—"

"I know, I know, Myla's not mad and all those people had no idea what they were seeing."

"Isn't it a little late?" Anwar asks (appearing in Xanther's doorway).

"Almost done," Astair says.

"It's a school night," Anwar gently reminds them (coming over to kiss Xanther good night (Astair gets a sharp eye (deserved (one thing Xanther needs most (especially post-seizure!) is (lots and lots of) sleep)))).

Except here's the part that doesn't make sense:

Xanther's fine.

(More than fine.)

"Anwar," Astair speaks up (halting his departure). "Xanther still doesn't believe that Myla isn't mad."

"Daughter!" Anwar spins around. "The world is full of irreducible angers but Myla's wrath toward you is not one of them."

"Didn't you speak with her on the phone when you got back?" Astair asks (gentle brushstrokes (has she ever seen Xanther's hair so . . . *lustrous?*)).

"Uh, she was being kind." Xanther slumps.

"In fact, Myla is thankful," Anwar adds (before (with a twinkle?) slipping out of the room).

"What's that supposed to mean?" Xanther asks Astair. "Thankful?!"

"Does anyone at school know what happened?" Astair counters (digging in a little (anticipating (too) that Xanther will tense)).

"I told my friends," Xanther responds (shaking her head (maybe her shoulders rising a bit more (but not tensing (though does that mean anything?)))).

"So there's nothing to worry about?" Astair prods (as tenderly as possible). "At all. No one knows what happened. And Myla's not mad."

"She's thankful!" Anwar cries (re-entering Xanther's room (with a big smile (his phone in one hand (scrolling for something)))). "Listen: 'Mint, who by this point in her career should have nothing left to offer — who needs not offer more to settle old scores with her detractors — still gifts us one more heartbreaking trope: Hades spins maliciously in his vault of darkness, releasing all woes to the world, with only Hope barely holding on, lights dimming, curtain falling, when suddenly a tiny naïf — a little girl of impossible origin — races out onto the stage. Her intrusion is so unexpected, so unaccountable, that Hope races away, as if in fear of this unheralded figure collapsing at Hades' feet. Who is she? Love? Innocence? Something else? Hades runs too. Also afraid. Mint displays her mastery by leaving the mystery intact. It is just another example of one of the many breathtaking moments that elevate Mint's triumphant *Hades* to canonical status.'"

"That's in the *Times*?"

"Have you ever heard such a ridiculously good review?" Anwar answers (not quite answering her question). "That's you, Xanther! Love! Innocence! A pretty impressive debut if you ask me. Myla has had to find a young dancer to repeat your performance. She said you're welcome to reprise your role whenever you want."

"Yeah, right," Xanther answers (eyes rolling (but the hint of a smirk (maybe) banishes (some of) her blues)).

"See?" Astair loves brushing Xanther's hair.

"Mom, you did see my dress, right?" Xanther asks (after Anwar's gone).

Anwar hadn't had the heart to throw it out (convinced (because it was black) that the stains (of blood and urine) either wouldn't matter (it's a black dress!) or would come out (almost)).

The dry cleaner's attempt to stitch up the rips ((for starters) using an off (way off!) black thread) resulted in something better suited for Halloween (Frankenstein's bride) rather than some future occasion of elegance (Astair will disappear the thing as soon as it settles into forgottenness on some hanger in the back of Xanther's closet).

"Xanther, how about telling me what happened to the jacket your grandparents gave you?"

"Ugh. So my fault. Such, uhm, a dumb accident?" Xanther's shoulders go up around her ears. "I'm sorry." Turning around (ending their brushing sesh (Astair (at once) a little sad (left with just the brush (clinging to a few strands of her daughter's (strangely) beautiful hair)))). "I was cutting up some paper? And— Kle thinks it looks better?"

Astair laughs.

Xanther smiles too.

"Your mom doesn't care a lick for the jacket or dress. Just about you. And, honestly, I have to say you're doing amazingly well."

What an understatement.

Xanther's shoulders relax (hands back to caressing the tiny white animal curled up in her lap).

"I did recover pretty fast, huh?"

Astair nods (looking (pointedly?) at the cat).

"You were a mess when you got off the plane."

"You should have seen me in New York."

"I'm glad I didn't, though you know I wanted to be with you in the hospital."

"Dad was, like, so great."

Astair nods. "Do you remember how bruised your elbows were when you got home?"

"Do I!" Xanther raises both her elbows now (craning her neck (as if to see them (completely) was possible)). Astair (though) can see them completely: not even a hint of discoloration (the wild blooms (of purple (and green and yellow)) long gone).

Anwar had already explained that (when the seizure took hold) Xanther was practically flying off the floor. He tried to shield her from herself (cuddle her safe) but she must have hammered the stage floor a few times with her arms (before he reached her).

"I don't think I've ever seen you heal so fast."

"Right? And it's, like, what?, not even a week?"

"Can I ask you a question?" Did the cat just move then (a tiny readjustment (lifting its head slightly (as if to look Astair in the eyes (though without opening its eyes))))?

"Duh. Of course."

"Do you think this little animal helps you? I mean, I don't know, and I know this will sound crazy, especially coming from your mother, but do you think he helped you recover faster?"

"No question."

"Any idea why that is?" Astair asks (not oblivious to the fact that the author of the Question Song just said "No question" (and meant it (when had that ever happened before?))).

"No clue," Xanther answers. "I'm sorry."

Astair reaches out to touch the tiny animal (but can't quite bring herself to do it (grips (instead) the brush)). Shouldn't she at least tell Xanther about the escape (but can't quite do that either)?

Why is this so hard?

And what about the fact (((?)(as accurately as Astair can figure it (having gone over the timing (umpteen times) with Anwar))) that this small cloud of white had gone into a seizure about the exact same time that Xanther had gone into hers?

"I just think we're really connected," Xanther adds now (unprompted (as if she were responding to Astair's thoughts)). "But not, like, in just a good way."

"How do you mean?"

"Uh, I don't know. I mean, uhm, like little one deserves a name. But I can't do that. And it feels like I'm failing. Why is that so hard?"

This question had come up plenty (Anwar had reported so from New York (and Astair had heard it for herself when Xanther was safely back home)).

It was a matter of a few (dumb) syllables (even one syllable would do) but Xanther had begun fixating on (in essence) the not-naming of her pet.

"This is all my fault. I couldn't call him," she'd (supposedly) murmured in the hospital.

"If I could have just given him his name, it never would have happened," she'd muttered (incoherently) again in the hospital.

"I'm such a loser. Why can't I come up with his name?" she had lamented only yesterday.

To which Anwar had replied: "Daughter, do you know one of the major differences between dogs and cats? Dogs know their names and cats do not. The speculation is that dogs evolved in relation to hunter cultures. A name for calling then was crucial. Cats, on the other hand, evolved in relation to agrarian cultures. Territory is a cat's concern. Maybe you can't come up with a name because you instinctively understand that cats don't need names."

Astair had been impressed. Maybe Anwar should write her paper. Xanther was less convinced.

"Then why isn't he wandering around the house, you know, like, uhm, staking his claim?"

"Oh, I think he's staked out his territory pretty clearly."

"He has?"

"You."

(of course) There was another reason the cat wasn't wandering around the house that much: (if he wasn't very young) he was extremely old (and ailing (and (despite such (obvious) frailty) still capable of conducting (near) miraculous effects)).

Astair had seen it for herself.

She was there at the airport to take them home.

Gaunt Anwar (the first thing she saw (how it galled Astair to hear people say a black man couldn't look pale (similar to the yearly insensitivities that deny Los Angeles its seasonal shifts (just because one isn't aware of the subtle turns during the hot times doesn't mean fall isn't coming (not that there was anything seasonal or subtle about the grayness of Anwar's lips (upon his cheeks (had his hair turned grayer? (Winter too (arriving early)))))))))).
    Xanther was invisible beneath a blanket. Anwar was behind the wheelchair. Then he was helping her out (carrying her to the Element!). The poor thing shivering (she felt cold too!) in the heat of that September night ∴ **Friday, September 5** ∴.
    Gaunt couldn't describe her. Or pale. Craquelure porcelain? Rice paper? An insurrection of bones impeaching skin. Demanding bruise and blood.

Ruptured cuticles.

Contusions on her arms.

Astair hadn't even beheld yet her knees. Or the weird marks (like claws (or teeth)) upon her neck.

A tongue bruised so badly it was black as a cobra.

Xanther's eyes had seemed inked in blood.

(worse) She could barely move (her lips against Astair's cheek kissed like ancient snow (whispering like dying snow)).

Astair almost lost it.

Anwar (though) knew what to do. He insisted that Astair drive. He flooded her with the medical details (what the staff at the hospital had done (packing Xanther in a bed of foam pads and metal guards (guarding over her (what they had said (the subclinical seizures they suspected (the subclinical seizures they could never confirm (the midazolam (benzodiazepine) they administered (all other medicines they had (subsequently) recommended (prescriptions ((short-term and long-term) whether used or not) some already waiting at Rite Aid (the rest at another (nearby) pharmacy)))))))))).

That became their big dilemma (on the drive home): whether or not to stop at the pharmacies before they got home.

"I don't want to stop," Xanther had whimpered from the backseat (and that was that).

"I'll retrieve the medications once she's settled," Anwar had offered without hesitation.

A trip he never had to make.

Anwar even had to carry Xanther from the car (her weakness matched only by her confusion over whether this was really her home (Astair had started to shake)).

How is it then that (even now) just a finger under so ridiculously a small jaw (white as never spoiled as never broken as never misplaced ((as white can never mean) soft as warm snow (what cold could melt))) affords Xanther ((*revives* Xanther! (no longer in need of revival) affording them both)) such large measures of pleasure?

That little purr helps too.

Xanther sure smiles ((giggling now) something (admittedly) cute about those (peculiar) feline eyes (squeezing even more tightly shut (provoking a little (amusing(?)) snarl which reveals a tier of tiny glistening teeth (almost too many?)) as paws stretch out ((front paws) revealing claws (so many claws (had Astair ever noticed that before? (look how many claws (the back paws too (more than five (more than six (!(!!! (!!!!!)))))))) Dr. Syd's evaluation coming back to her (Astair snatching up the word): "Polydactyl" ∴ **TFv2 p. 103** ∴)))))) and then there's a yawn and something like a burp or a peep and Xanther's smiling more and laughing and so is Astair.

Even if something is still off (though just slightly (not enough (for sure) to call into question any general (what?) *catness?*)): from the too-many nails to the not-enough teeth (or (wait) isn't it too many too?) to the odd frizz of whiskers (as if burned off) to the weird eyebrow (or is it an eyelash? (one eyelash

(one long white hair))) poking out above the right
eye to just how small it is to how blind it is too . . .

. They have to get back to the vet soon (as soon as
they've gotten the New York bills sorted (what will
those be?(!))) . . .

Because there is no point in denying anymore
that this small wile of white is not only their pet but
the best thing that ever happened to Xanther.

Astair had seen with her own eyes (they all had)
what happened when Anwar had carried Xanther
across the threshold (Freya and Shasti racing ahead
(in angel mode (leading the way up to Xanther's
room))).

But Anwar never made the first stair.

The little thing was already in the foyer.

Had it arrived or had it already been there? Waiting (before Astair could notice)? It was already on
Anwar's shoe and then leaping (blindly!(?)) as high
as Anwar's thigh (had she ever seen it leap? (I mean
like this (so desperately)?)) and continuing upward
on grit and claw alone (and determination).
"Oh my! Ow!" Anwar had cried (unable to do
more (arms filled with Xanther)). "Get it off me!"
But (before anyone could react to this fast flight
of white (both Freya and Shasti looked as stunned
(and bemused) as Astair was (as even Anwar was)))
the little animal had already reached Xanther (nuzzling her chin (nuzzling her lips (licking her cheeks

(licking her nose (nuzzling her ears (licking her lips (her chin))))))) and (like in some (ridiculous) fairy tale) Xanther had started to wiggle in her father's arms (forcing him to set her down) as she cradled the cat (reciprocating with nuzzles of her own (and strokes and cuddles (and "I missed you soooooooo much!"))(rubbing its tiny belly and its wildly whipping tail (what a purr that thing had offered up then!)) as Xanther forgot her torpor (the waxy whiteness in her cheeks seeming to forget itself too)).

A moment later Xanther was racing up the stairs (disappearing into her room (with the little one)).

Astair had ceased to matter. The same was true for the twins. Even Anwar no longer existed (though he seemed greatly relieved (his own color returning to his face and lips (how he had hugged Astair then (and kissed little Shasti and little Freya)))).

The only thing then that existed for Xanther (or mattered? (were they the same thing?)) was that cat. Yet maybe it was that singular (all-encompassing?) presence ((was that another addition to this triumvirate (matter = existence = presence)?) or was it due to *its* attention (or better: a-tension (no tension))(*it* to it)) to her that had drawn Xanther away from herself so that she might return to herself again and find herself whole?

By the end of the weekend most of the bruises were fading (never that bad?). A new rutilant glow had flushed her face. Her tongue showed not even a hint of the savage chewing the seizure had exacted upon it. On Monday she was back in school.

Disbelief still reigns ((for Astair) on this Thursday morning (over Xanther's vitality (nearly all evidence of the attack having vanished (even those (abused(?)) cuticles look practically healthy (nails gleaming and sharp (sharp?)))))).

"How'd you sleep, darling?"

"I'm not tired," Xanther shrugs (rummaging through the kitchen cupboards for food matching her idea of breakfast).

"What can I fix for you?"

"I don't know."

"Any dreams?"

"Yeah, actually. I was building a ship too big for any ocean."

Astair almost bursts into tears.

"I almost did it again too," Astair tells Taymor at an early lunch at Sunset Junction (The Black Cat ∴ **3909 West Sunset Boulevard, Los Angeles, CA 90029**∴ (a wonderful escape when schedules and geographies align)). "Dropping her off at school, I was swallowing hard to keep the sob down. She's the one who was beaten like an abused child and I'm the one wrecked. Huh. Just thought of something: maybe she's finding a model in the cat, in, you know, the way animals don't baggage up the moments. I told you, the thing had a seizure in my hands. It was awful. I thought it was going to die right there."

"What kind of life do you have to be living to order a drink at 11:30 AM?" Taymor asks (not listening (pushing aside her tea to consider (more carefully) the cocktail menu)). "The Corpse Reviver No. 2. Gin and absinthe. Sounds superb."

"What's stopping you?" Astair asks (her training kicking in (why Taymor's here)).

"For one, I'm on this cleansing healing thing," Taymor answers (returning to her tea).

"Healing?"

"I'm always healing."

"Talk to me, Tay."

"Can't even wait for our food to arrive?" Which does arrive at that moment ∴ *Chilaquiles: corn tortillas, eggs sun up, pinto beans, jack cheese, with red chili sauce.* ∴ ∴ *The George Jones: eggs sun up, sausage, home fries, and toast.* ∴ .

"You'd prefer we just eat?"

"Oh boy," Taymor sighs ((atypically) long for her).

What follows then is a candid look at how money (in its (inestimable) alignment with time) will (can (must?)?) change a relationship.

"But is it just the money? You had so much already." On the floor: a card ∷ *La Palma* ∷ ∷ **no. 51** ∷.

"I love your push toward difficult territory. It's what makes out of conversations a friendship."

"Cut the shit, Tay," Astair answers (trying out something closer to Tay's speech (for Tay's sake)).

"Roxanne found out, pushing as you know how kids do, toward the source of things: how exactly did Ted get these extra billions?" Taymor sets down her knife and fork (looking at her eggs with disgust). "For a while, Ted kept up with IPOs-this and margins-that, and all those whatevers about hedges I don't understand. Bullshit that works its stupid on me. But Ted underestimated his daughter's endurance."

"Roxanne reminds me of Xanther." Their ~~voracious~~ (*veracious!*) appetite (for (the potency (promise (*feeling* of))) ideas).

"Chemical. Biological."

"The source of Ted's, your, new fortune?"

Taymor nods. "Of course it's not just that simple, as Ted kept trying to explain. He's not the creator, just 'financially facilitating a prospect.' Backtracking, really, in the face of Roxanne's growing rage."

"So not good chemicals?"

"GMOs are kiddie stuff compared to this."

"Military then?"

"At least the military has *some* oversight!" Taymor snorts.

"Are you telling me this as a therapist or as a friend?"

"I can afford a therapist. I can't afford to lose my friends."

"Then as your friend, I have to tell you you have a problem."

"The wealth lets you consider yourself on par with the likes of the Gateses or Zuckerbergs. But then you look around and say, 'Hey where is the Trancas Foundation? Where is a lifetime's devotion to defending the rights of others?' And it's not there."

"What have you told Ted?"

Taymor cringes. "I don't know how to even start."

Astair tries to just take her friend in (what else is she seeing (beyond the obvious distress (sadness? (confusion? (shame? (. . .))))) (finally invoking a tone of sympathy and just speaking)?).

"Everyone has two hearts: the one that lies to help the hurt and the one that tells the truth despite the hurt."

"Did your Sandra Dee say that?"

"Actually, no. That's mine. Just now."

"Pretty good, Astair Ibrahim. You might make a good shrink yet."

Taymor changes the subject then and tells Astair about why she chose to meet at The Black Cat and then she talks about her siblings.

(outside (as they are leaving)) A homeless man wobbles by (arrayed in ribbons of beige rags (like flayed strips of skin)) screaming nothing that makes sense other than the scream itself (indignation (married to fury and fear)).

"That's someone's son," Astair says (once he's beyond earshot (her own pity not beyond her own earshot)).

"Let's hope he's nobody's father."

(after that) Astair has two sessions at the clinic (they each seem an individual forever (no fathers in sight (only mothers))).

Astair arrives home to find Anwar at the door signing for a package from a USPS delivery woman.

"Good afternoon!" Mr. Hatterly (their (next-door) neighbor) calls out from the sidewalk before Astair can slip inside. "The thrill of the package! The seduction of the concealed."

"Archimboldo!" Astair answers (the big bullmas-tiff (a (droopy-eyed) heave of ((dark) draping) fur) lurches toward her name (getting as far as Astair's knees (to sniff happily) before Mr. Hatterly can regain some control)).

"I'm sorry. She's a handful."

"A beautiful handful," Astair smiles (petting the animal (she could pet Archimboldo for days)). "How are you?"

"Charlie's out of town. A Christie's thing."

Mr. Hatterly sells deco furniture on Hillhurst (has for nearly thirty years (as long as he and his partner Charlie have been together (no marriage in sight (no rings at least))(nonetheless blissful in their 1920s home (mandalas carved into the stones above their door and windows ("Something worse to the untrained eye. We blame the eye and accord no cre-dence to the blind.")))))).

"No interest in joining Charlie?"

"We left Arch alone enough this summer. And with the economy in such a tottery state, I'm better off contemplating alternatives to Erte or Macassar ebony desks than traveling to Geneva to observe my multilingual phenom handle an auction."

"Ever been to The Black Cat?" Astair has to ask.

"Ever? Chuck and I practically invented the place. The stories we could tell."

"I'd like to hear them sometime." Though not now. "Maybe when the phenom is back?"

"We'll have you over. Did you ever get that dog?"

"We have a cat now."

Mr. Hatterly wrinkles his nose. "Now there's a bedlam of fur! My allergies would never permit it. Good lord, no. Your choice?"

"He's one of the family now."

"Good. Maybe he can help with this rat-siege our neighborhood is currently enduring."

"Rats?"

"Archimboldo just woofs at the legions marching along the power wires. No Flying Wallendas these. Though Arch keeps hoping. Don't you, girl?"

(in the foyer) Anwar kisses Astair (the box still in hand (trying to make room on the little table (stacks of bills there (finally just covering the bills)))).

"For Xanther. From the Army."

"Something of Dov's?"

"What else?"

"Should we open it first?"

"I don't know." Astair doesn't know either. "How's Galvadyne?"

"One last interview scheduled for the seventeenth. Really a formality. Muellenson says I can pretty much expect an offer right after."

"That's wonderful! Why am I not seeing wonderful in your eyes?"

"You better check on your daughters."

Shasti looks thrilled (and she's the one with blood in her mouth (more of it swirling in the glass of salt water (what Anwar got her to gargle with))).

"Look Mommy!" Shasti keeps squealing by the bathroom sink (holding out the tooth in her palm).

"Look at that!" Astair is pleased.

"I get to see the Trooth Fairy now!"

Where had Shasti picked that up ∷ **TFv1 p. 92**∷ (though Astair likes (accepts) the change)? Is this what's gotten Freya brooding? And (boy!) is she ever (scowling from her bedroom (is she tugging on her own teeth?))!

"Hey! Freya! Stop that! Your teeth will come out at their own pace. Maybe now is the time to congratulate Shasti?"

"Congratulations," Freya mutters.

"How are those Nightmare Stones?"

"I'm sleeping so good," Freya answers.

Which does seem to be the case (at least the two are quiet with their dreams (and less fidgety)).

"Me too," Shasti chimes in. "Mommy, do you think I'll sleep too good to miss the Trooth Fairy?"

"Mommy, do Nightmare Stones work during the day?" Freya asks then.

"How do you mean?"

"To keep the ladders away."

And then Anwar is calling for her (someone is at the door (asking for her)).

"Astair!" It's Marisol (her beauty (impressively(?)) going unnoticed by Anwar (though Astair's heart races (her body responding with a flash of heat and a warmer feeling of welcome (more the ~~ladder~~ (*latter!* (what is going on with Freya? (another flash (of something else . . .)))))))).

"Hey!"

"I'm sorry to drop by like this. I think I inputted your number incorrectly. I wanted to check on—"

"Xanther!" Astair cries (trying to clue in Marisol with a quick shake of her head ((of course!) now is right when her daughter gets back from school (slipping inside (past their guest ((pallid? tired? depressed?) and even now ((again!) transformed to bright! thrilled! beaming!) the little one is there at her feet ((of course!) until he's swept up in Xanther's arms (lifted onto her shoulder (Xanther again blind to anyone else (only this creature (except—)))))))))). "Xanther, please meet—"

Except Xanther has already turned all of her ((now!) substantial?) focus on Marisol (or really the little one has ((blind as it is) by sniffs (in the direction of those sniffs) (pawing (too) in Marisol's direction))).

"He likes you!" Xanther exclaims.

"We've—" Marisol starts (catching herself (glancing at Astair (Astair now too under Xanther's scrutiny to shake her head again ((fortunately) stillness seems to remind Marisol of the shake anyhow)))). "Well, I'm enchanted."

Xanther seems enchanted too. Astair offers Marisol lemonade with fresh mint.

Xanther doesn't notice the box until after dinner.

"What's this?"

Anwar carries the box to the living room coffee table ((curiously (or not (it is (after all) a cat!))) the cat slips down from Xanther's shoulder to situate itself on top (right on Xanther's name too)).

Astair warns her that the contents are likely some of Dov's effects.

"Effects?"

"Stuff," Anwar clarifies.

"I guess I knew that." Xanther holds out her hand (all that's necessary to get those little white paws scampering back onto Xanther's shoulder (who needs a name?)).

"Would you like me to open it?" Anwar asks.

"I'm not *that* useless," Xanther responds (with eye rolls (using a house key to saw through the seams of the box (only pausing before the address label)))).

"How did you name me?" she abruptly asks.

"How did I name you?" The question takes Astair by surprise.

"Was it you? Or Dov?"

Astair looks to Anwar.

"You don't remember?" Anwar smiles.

"Of course I remember. I just have to, well, remember."

"She doesn't remember," Xanther says to the cat (teasing Astair (teasing is good (feels good too))).

"Dov picked it. No, I did. No, you know, you're right: I don't remember but I remember that I liked it. We both did. We felt it . . . fit."

"Did you have it in mind before I was born?"

"That I remember. Dov and I, and Anwar too, all believe that to name someone you first have to look them in the eyes. You have to hold them. You have to connect with them. And, oh!, I do remember something: the nurses were mad that we left without naming you. I doubt they would have let us leave the hospital without naming you, but Dov . . . you know he was a military man. He was . . . fiery. When he said we were leaving, we were leaving and no one had stood in our way. Of course, as he promised, Dov also returned. He always kept his word. That's why he had such trouble with those that didn't." Meaning Astair (what a mess those days had been (poor Anwar)). "When he told the nurses he'd be back, it was like Zeus nodding his head." Astair catches the question on Xanther's lips. "Zeus was one of the main patriarchs of the Greek gods. When he nodded it meant he was making a promise that not even he could break."

"Right. Mythology. Zeus was the dad of Persephone."

"He was?"

"Mom! What happened?!"

"Four months later Dov returned to the hospital with your name."

"Four months?!"

"Weeks! I mean weeks. No, no, I mean days." Or had it only been hours (terrible times (Astair was already with Anwar (her parents were threatening to disown her (some (heated!) squabble over a christening (that never happened)))))?

Though the name . . . (emerging with her first breath (Astair will allways remember Xanther's first cry as a song) something having to do with gold and summer and sunlight and maize (and hadn't Dov said something about horses too?)).

"So I came into this world without a name too?"

Astair is struck (simultaneously) by Xanther likening herself to her animal companion and the expression itself ("into this world" (when (in fact) her little babies began inside Astair before finally heading into the world (there it was again: into! (does the world then always require an interior ~~investigation~~ (*invasion!*) to constitute it? (the kind of thoughts that (when voiced to Dov back in the day (in!)) would have always earned the same response: "You're so out there" (not just Dov (plenty of people (Astair's whole life) calling her "out there" (as she headed out to live her life (and make babies (three phenomenal children (who were quite simply: out of this world)))))))))))).

"Mom?"

"You already had a name, we just had to find it."

"I, like, so want to believe that, but sometimes I think that's all backwards, like, uh, isn't it *not* us that makes our name but the name that's making us?"

"How do you mean?"

"If you had called Freya me and me Freya would she be the epileptic? I'm sorry. I didn't mean that. That's an awful thing to say." Xanther slumps (retreating from the box (to deep sofa cushions)).

"Daughter," Anwar speaks up. "We've gone over this before: you're not an epileptic. You only suffer from a condition defined by—"

"Anwar. I know. I want to come up with a name for the little one."

Astair doesn't know what else to say (Anwar looks just as blank (maybe stung a little too by the way Xanther wielded his name (with objection))).

"Honey, give him a name. Right now. How about calling him Fur?"

"Mom, that's silly."

"Why? He has fur. How about Teeth. He has teeth. Or Closed Eyes. We all know he's that."

"Okay, I get it. You made your point."

"Which is?" The question terrifies Astair (because (instead of playing along) Xanther might just shut down (and shut Astair down too)).

"Because he's so much more than all those things."

"Yes! And so are you! So let's get rid of that -ic. Once and for all. Please? For your mom? For your dad? -Ic's just so icky."

Xanther smirks (another eye roll (but there's a warm smile in there too)).

"Then I'll name him something he's not and on top of it something that doesn't tell him what he's supposed to become later."

"Daughter, I like that!" Anwar exclaims (looking pretty pleased (welcoming the complication)).

"How about Fatso-ic? Or Bird-ic?" Xanther laughs.

"Dog-ic?" Astair can't resist.

"Meanie-ic?" Anwar takes his best shot.

"Or Killer-ic?" Astair laughs too.

"What the heck? He is killer-ic. He is soooooo killer. Killer looks. Killer cool. Killer it."

"Then there it is: Killer." And maybe they do have it (Astair half holds her breath).

But Xanther shakes her head.

"He's more than not-that too."

"You'll figure it out, baby. It'll come to you and that will be that. Like with you. As soon as I said 'Xanther' you were allways Xanther."

Xanther resumes using the house key to cut through the rest of the packing tape (right through her name on the label). The box flaps pull back easily enough. Polystyrene peanuts scatter on the table and floor (the cat though (weirdly (right?)) is not even a little distracted ((as if like Xanther (just as)) fixed only on the contents hiding within)).

Whatever Astair's been guessing it isn't this.

She expects boots.

She expects a belt buckle.

Maybe a military cap.

Or a tassel.

Another medal.

(Xanther has many of such remnants (stored somewhere (somewhere down in the basement)).)

But what Xanther pulls out of this box is another box. Lacquered. Icy black. Latched. (and (of course)) Locked.

Astair knows it too well (all the reason now to be (terribly) upset).

"There's a letter," Xanther says (opening the envelope (scanning too quickly to read (before handing it to Anwar (who does read it (before handing it over to Astair))))).

How Astair reviles everything about this (from Army insignias to the date to even the address (that the Army even knows her address!) to the tone and diction to even the colonel's signature at the bottom (as illegible as it is impersonal (Astair never wants the military anywhere near her family (let alone near her children (this one in particular (ever!))))))).

"Because you are Dov's only child, you inherit his possessions," Astair explains (calmly (refolding the letter (replacing it in the envelope (with only an "X" on the front (marking the spot?))))).

"Dad, do you know what it is?"
Anwar shakes his head.
"Mom, you do, don't you?"
Astair nods (though she can't believe Dov would have had the nerve to leave it to Xanther (why not one of his men? (one of his fucking generals? (some museum? (how about West fucking Point?))))).
"Do you know the combination?"
"I've forgotten," Astair answers (truthfully (one thing to be glad about (those numbers and their arrangements (Dov had tried many times to get her to memorize it (but Astair had refused (what didn't stop him from telling her it (along with showing her that thing! (once showing her (showing them all (that abomination!) in a rage (as if to say "See here!" ("See this!" ("See me!"))))))))))))).

713

As if that moment (that voice (like a ghost's)) could ever be so easily caged (what Astair would never be free of (even if the voice that tells her so is still hers)):

My daughter, my survivor, my future —

Here's what you get of me.

Here's who I am.

Here's who you are.

Here's what it all comes down to in the end.

Which was true of Dov's end.

But didn't have to apply to their child.

YOU FUCK!

But who needs a ghost (or a voice (anyone's voice)) when there is this?

Of course he couldn't resist.

In the name of his fucking family.

In the name of that fucking tradition.

In the name of fucking ugly inertia.

Passing it on despite knowing its history.

((after all) It was all about history (at least one history (his))).)

Talk about names too!

Astair still remembers (perfectly!) the scripted engravings (name after name after ((appalling) blood-soaked) name):

:: *For another time.* ::

Asterisks indicated a skipped generation (or a broken bloodline (this enduring object of pride (and extreme prejudice) always somehow handling the caesura (passed on again (and again) to yet another set of murderous hands (a description Dov vehemently ((almost) violently) objected to)))).

*

"Call of duty," Dov had flatly explained.
"Murderous," Astair had said again.
"MY LEGACY!"

*

And that had been the second time (long after they had parted ((after Anwar) (after the move) (when she was pregnant again (with the twins)) after a whole lot of living (and coming to terms with that living (or trying to)))). That was a time when Astair was in it (with Dov) just to pick a fight.

The box hadn't mattered.

No explanation would have mattered.

Nothing Dov did was ever going to matter again.

*

The first time (though) had been very different. Astair had screamed at him for keeping it locked up (for refusing to show her) until he'd given in to her own indignant violence. She was only nineteen. She'd pawed at the latch and grabbed at the brightness within (Xanther had come out of what followed

that grab (was that right? (maybe Astair was making that up (it didn't matter (it was close enough to
then))))). Astair had been impossible to resist (she
was pretty (very)). And how good could something
so powerful and so forbidden (layered with (~~familiar~~
(*familial!*)) taboo) feel. Dov would let her hold it.
Sometimes they would hold it together (when they
held each other breathless and burning through
those burning afternoons when Carolina mosquitoes
turned to ash upon their burning backs with all their
limbs burning with the burning amazement again
and again over all the impossible pleasures their
burning bodies again and again seemed capable of
releasing inside her again and again on that mattress
on the floor of that barracks' trailer
).

Astair still has no idea who she was back then.

Memories of such lusts (interlocked with angry
outbursts) strike her now as impossibly distant (if
not impossible altogether). Sure she might lose her
temper or (succumb) to an urge but paw (and paw
again (at this old box)) for more and more? — Never
again.

*

But what if (really) that person wasn't in her anymore but reborn (really?) in her daughter? Could
Xanther here (puzzling right now over this combination lock) have inherited Astair's fury (as well as
all those unchecked wants ("Cheese 'n' rice! I was
ten when I had my first orgasm!" Astair once blurted
out to Anwar))? Could Xanther already be starting

to blush and sweat and need like that (exploring and experimenting (with the side of a loaded dryer ((as Astair had done) with a banister (rocking chairs (gym ropes (climbing higher and higher toward a ceiling beyond the ceiling she feared as much as she craved to exceed . . .))))))? Was Xanther like that? The thought repulsed Astair but not as much as what followed next: could Xanther like as much as she had that first glimpse? That first touch (her curious fingers leading the way (until just the thought of it would wake her late at night (again and again (threatening to keep her awake)))) . . . Would Xanther also run her fingers over that awful family tree (marveling at them all) like Astair had?

*

A new idea draws a shiver down Astair's back.

Might Xanther find her own name there?

*

Astair even shakes her head (much like she's seen the kitten sometimes do (("I've heard cats do that to reset their orientation," Anwar had commented) "To get rid of the dizziness," Xanther had added)). Except Astair's shake doesn't reorient her or reset anything (if only she were dizzy (something to drag her away from this vortex into . . .)).

*

Could Dov have done such a thing?

No.

           Not possible.

No.

           Because.

No.

           Astair calms herself.

        Because every name there

        belonged there

        because it had

taken a life.

"Do you know what's inside?" Xanther asks.

"Yes."

Does Astair catch Xanther hesitate (as if (maybe (for an instant)) sensing that satisfaction's price might not be worth it)?

Did the cat just start to purr?

"Tell me, Mom, tell me what's inside . . ."

"Dov's gun."

Domingo's Mother

> *I sentenced him*
> *who was me.*
>
> — *Rodolfo Gonzales*

"Is this what being cops is like?" Luther growls.

"I think shifts are shorter," Tweetie burps, before hitting again his Double Gulp Coke. No wonder he's so fuckin big.

"We should just burn it down," Luther grunts, eyeing Domingo's mother's house, still empty.

"That could bring her back. For sure bring somebody around."

Luther's glad he's here with just Tweetie. Juarez wouldn't have given it a second thought. Just grabbed the can of gas in back and before Luther could say ¡Cálmate perro! Nomás estaba pensando, he'd already be lighting a match.

Though maybe lighting a match isn't such a bad idea. There is a can in back.

Luther even checks if there's gas in it. The slosh says there's plenty. He's got a lighter too. Could wait until the AMs and then el chingado incendiote. After the firemen, after the cops, someone's for sure's gonna come around.

Luther stretches out.

Sleeps.

Wakes to Tweetie pissing in that Double Gulp. Fuckin fills the thing. Some life.

Luther shakes hisself awake, hops to a squat, blinking hard, too much light.

"¿Qué pinchi hora es?"

"Breakfast. Piña and Victor are here. Parked on the corner there. We're good to go."

"You couldn't wait?" Luther nods at the full cup.

"Fuck that! That piss had to get out."

Luther needs a shower. Then he can figure out what he wants to eat. What he needs most is to figure out how to get back up on this shit right. Teyo's been nothing but cool but another week's slid by with still ni señas ni pío on Domingo.

That guy's ghosted everyone. For five days not even a rumor. Lo más marciano is how the girls se esfumaron too. Like they found a deep grave. Putas like that don't keep quiet for so long. Nacho's fearing the worst. Doubts too Domingo would do such a thing.

"Maybe they all in the same lugar oscuro together," the old man had said, hoped.

Could Teyo have hired someone else too? Got the job done before Luther? Luther's glad Tweetie's driving. He'd slam into a car right now just to crunch something with more metal than what's in his mouth.

"I don't fuckin know what to do," he admits instead. It comes out like this long sickening sigh. Makes Tweetie uncomfortable as fuck.

"It's his mom's house. She's gotta come back."

"No, she don't. She could be gone for months. For a year. This is not my thing. I'm front line. I'm the one you want close. I don't know how to hunt some fuckin fool. Not like this."

"Then make that clear?"

"Fuck!" Like some gritos and beating a dashboard can fix feeling. But Luther's tired of pissing in cups.

He has Tweetie set up a meet with Eswin. Century City again. Again the black Mercedes. Though Eswin who knows he doesn't know what this is about don't look pleased.

"Teyo says you better have a reason," Eswin says, not moving from the car. At least he got out of the car.

Tweetie should have stayed in the van. He's just stretching his legs, but Eswin scans the underground parking lot like maybe this is about something more than a conversation.

Luther smiles. Because it's funny. Eswin is nervous when he's the one sweating because of what he's got to say.

Though how the fuck's he gonna put it? That he's at a dead-end? Fracasó? Say he can give back the money?

"Don't ever let Teyo see your man wearing a shirt like that," Eswin adds.

Luther looks over at Tweetie. He's got on a black t-shirt like an ad for an energy drink, the one with three green ragged stripes that look like claw marks, except instead of MONSTER underneath, it says MEXICAN.

And then one problem becomes two: big man's coming over like he's gonna join this plática.

"Yo!" Luther barks, a warning, but Tweetie doesn't stop, reaching in a pocket too.

Luther better do something, but Tweetie's already there, handing over his phone, with a text from Piña:

Tweetie's almost back at the van when Luther looks up.

"Yo, I'll get him a new shirt. Gracias, gracias. Just got one thing for Teyo that's not right for no phone. Understand?"

Eswin nods.

"Progress."

For half the drive back Luther anda bien arriba, then starts to crash, because if she ain't there, or if she is there and has no clue about her son, then Luther's even more al cuás.

Piña's grinning. That's good. Victor too. Juarez is also there. Not so good but Luther's still glad to have him at his side.

He sends Juarez and Tweetie to the back of the house. Luther marches on the front. Bangs on the metal security door with his palm. Adds some forearm. For the second time could bust up the frame. But Luther doesn't have to bang much.

"I already called the police," the old woman says through the screen. Voice is wobbling all over the place.

Here's what Luther almost says, like the words are already there, long ago prepared: "If that's true, then I'll kill your children. And I'll kill their children. And I'll never stop so long as even one of them lives. And then I'll come for you."

But Luther knows he can't always listen to metal: "If that's true," he says instead, bien casual, letting the old woman's fear relax him. "Then there's nothing I can do for your boy. Because I'm the one who calls off the dogs hunting your boy. And those dogs, they know how to hunt."

"I didn't call the police."

She doesn't keep him at the door either. She invites everyone in and sits them around her table in the kitchen and then while she waits for the water to boil, she squeezes lemon into mugs and adds cayenne pepper and honey and calls it tea.

She's even sorry for having no milk. There's a carton on the counter but it's gone bad. Her name is Esperanza Persianos. She's over sixty but can't remember by how much.

Victor goes outside to keep an eye on the vehicles. Piña heads to the back to let Tweetie and Juarez in.

They search the house while Luther sips the tea. Esperanza compliments him on his shirt. Luther has on a lavender one with pale orange buttons. Wore it for the meeting with Eswin.

Nothing here has changed since Luther moved through the small rooms. Juarez comes into the kitchen holding up a dirty sock on the tip of his machete. Maybe it's Domingo's. Maybe it's not. It's a dirty sock. Tweetie says there's a lot of cologne in the bathroom. Cologne isn't any better than a dirty sock.

Luther finishes the tea and goes over to the sink to rinse out the mug.

"I just need to know one thing," he says, after he's turned off the water and dried the cup.

"I don't know where Domingo is," she answers.

The old woman turns from Luther then and just stares at the wall ahead of her. How many times has she been here before? How many times has she had to hear these same fuckin questions? Her little hands keep scooping in and out of her skirt pockets though there's nothing to take out or put back in. The wall looks back at her and doesn't care.

Luther considers the wall with her. There's a clock, there's a shelf of spices, streaks of grease there too, but it still seems blank and maybe that's what holds their attention.

"Tiene mi auto. He took what money I kept here."

The wall doesn't object.

"I just need to know one thing," Luther says again.

Again the wall doesn't object.

Domingo's mother waits. She'll wait all day.

"How did he know?" Luther asks.

The wall doesn't answer. Maybe Esperanza wishes it would. Maybe they both do.

"Recibe llamadas," the old woman finally tells Luther. "He gets calls from people who know things. He says he feels better when he knows things too. Especially when he's scared. Siempre ha tenido miedo. I'm scared too."

The wall will never object.

But Luther doesn't trust walls. He turns to consider the old woman's fear and doesn't find any. Luther's almost surprised. She's too used up. Too resigned.

Something else as well, what Luther wishes he hadn't seen because she's seen him see what she knows she's too late to hide.

For a proud woman, there's nothing worse than shame. She is orgullosa. She hangs her head then and covers her face and starts to cry. Luther lets her cry and when she's done she tells him what he came there to find.

"Domingo called this morning."

"Does he have the girls?"

The old woman nods.

"I just need the girls," Luther lies.

The old woman's lips disappear until what's left of her mouth looks like the pit of a peach podrido. She goes over to the sink and spits.

"What time did he call?"

"Around nine," she answers. She doesn't spit again.

Luther tells Tweetie to find the house phone. He should have had Juarez do it. Juarez keeps bouncing around the kitchen table, digging at the floor with the machete, trying the cups of tea Piña and Victor left untouched.

Each taste makes him cough and scowl, the last time making him reach his dirty fingers into his mouth, like he gonna dig out the taste and throw it back.

The old woman doesn't know what to make of Juarez, who the fuck does?, but when he grabs the milk carton on the counter she speaks up.

"It's old. It's bad."

Juarez grins and chugs it down anyway, chunks of what he can't keep up with slide over the sides of his face, catching in his sideburns, globs of rancid stuff sticking in his mustache.

Juarez whoops when he finishes it.

He whoops again when he starts to throw it up, filling her sink, finally wiping his face for another loud whoop. ¿Qué trae este pendejo?

"Límpialo," Luther orders.

"Better than her fucking tea. It's not fucking tea if it doesn't have tea."

But he still obeys and starts running the water.

Tweetie comes back with the house phone, scrolling through the missed calls.

"There's only one around nine."

OUT OF AREA

Before leaving, Luther thanks her for the tea. Then he hands her a thousand dollars and when she puts it in the pocket of her skirt, something other than metal fills his mouth.

But it's the words that come out next that surprise Luther most.

"When you talk to your son next tell him he can keep the putas but to never come back. Tell him to go muy, muy lejos. Tell him to leave his ways and become a man. Nothing good waits for him here, ¿me entiendes?"

Worse Than Any Nightmare

If the lion goes, the forest goes and everything else goes.

— Ismail Bapu

"Nothing good waits for him here, understand?" Xanther says, or is she asking?, either way whispering, muy, muy lejos ∴ Huh? ∵, as if period six isn't bad enough, with the pop quiz, and all that quiet concentration eating the room up, with still five minutes left, at least, and now, on top of it, there's this kid Xanther has never said two words to, Robbie ∴ **Ordell** ∵ Ordell ∴ *Don't ask.* ∵ ∴ **Disallowed** ∵ ∴ Yeah, see how far, like, that gets you ∵, two desks over, pssssting that he heard Dendish Mower was waiting for her outside and she should be careful, which Xanther barely understands, especially with her head, like, so full of jittery numbers and letters, getting even more jumbly with all the quiz symbols and other stuff she has no clue about, but which she still keeps asking her head about, which really isn't a good idea, like stuff she'd even ask this Robbie kid about, also probably not a good thing, if he's telling her this news to be mean, because he's probably like tight with Mary Ellen and the others, or else he's risking this pestering as like a nice thing, a friend thing, and actually his face does look weirdly moon-wide and reddish, and maybe even a little shocked too, that he chose of all moments this moment to speak up, and then shocked by how Xanther answers, doubly shocked when Xanther repeats it, not understanding herself how such words even got into her mouth, though not doubting either that whatever arranged them in the first place isn't wrong, that if back to her, here!, is really Dendish's path, then it's also a path leading into a darker part of a still darker woods where no one fares well.

"Nothing good waits for him here, understand?"

"Right on," this Robbie kid responds, retreating back to his test, though not lasting there for long.

Another psssssst. Seriously?!

"I saw that clip," he gulps. Did he really just gulp?! "With the lion? So cool."

"Uhm, thanks?"

Xanther has no clue what's going on, but Mr. Klammersmith sure wants to know, moving quickly between them, at first figuring Xanther was trying to get answers off of this Robbie kid, because everyone knows she sucks at math, then coming face-to-face with another problem: this Robbie kid's quiz is blank and Xanther finished hers five minutes ago.

Xanther can feel the teacher alternating between an accusation and a different appraisal, what finally wins out, this final assessment landing right too, telling Robbie to hush, and to see him after class, Robbie nodding, with both his knees starting to pump nervously, as Mr. Klammersmith returns to Xanther's quiz with an approving nod.

"One hundred percent. Good job."

How the answers had come to her so quickly, to the ten questions with like algebra and fractions and these exponential numbers they were supposed to de-exponentialize, Xanther had no answer, really just a storm of more questions, though none of them getting in the way of Xanther's pencil filling in the blanks, and, well, that was strange, had she ever gotten a hundred percent on a pop quiz? ∴ No.∴, and that still didn't compare to this Robbie kid, smiling at her, and, when class was over, waving sweetly at her, him staying behind, and her on the way out, where Mayumi was waiting, just outside, catching sight of the wave.

"Does Robbie Ordell have a crush on you?"

"Totally!" Xanther's eye roll added the "Not!" "He, uhm, just like warned me that Dendish is around."

Fortunately, there was no sign of Dendish, or Mary Ellen, or even Trin or Kahallah, though Xanther's cheeks still got red, that's for sure, and not from the awful heat inside but from something else, which was embarrassing but not so bad, because maybe it felt a little good?

As bad as New York had been, and it had been bad, the scariest thing Xanther had had to face was coming back to school the following Monday.

She didn't even have to, Les Parents practically bending backwards to get her to take more days off. But Xanther knew that while missing classes to go to New York was something cool, missing class after a trip would mean something had gone wrong for sure, and wrong is one thing that gets kids asking questions and talking — a lot.

And, really, something should have been wrong. Xanther got how Astair felt, Anwar too, he had to wheelchair her off the plane! In fact, before she got home, Xanther figured she'd never ever return to school, if she was able to figure anything, her head a haze, her body limp from all the ways all of her kept struggling but failing to reconnect.

The seizure hadn't been as brutal as the one at Dov's funeral, though her postictal state was supposedly worse, with signs of microseizures, what doctors kept insisting to Anwar were subclinicals, Anwar telling them he knew what subclinicals were, this wasn't his first rodeo, which is sometimes how seizures can feel, like a rodeo, like Xanther's on the back of some terrible black bull with horns of fire carrying her away . . .

Never to return . . .

But Xanther had snapped back to normal, as soon as the little one was in her arms, in like an instant that goes way beyond anything Xanther can explain, the burst from seeing him there, him loving on her, like just this big super-nova of joy, exploding in her, filling her, accelerating every-thing in her too, or, maybe, like this big black hole, too?, dragging all the fragments of herself back together again, or whatever it was, powerful enough to get her back on her feet, back to the present, so that whatever had happened had only happened, and what was "happened" compared to this happening happiness now?

Not that Xanther wasn't amazed, though. Or con-fused. She'd been extra careful Monday morning to wear long sleeves, to cover her elbows, even if those marks were almost all gone, enough so that like maybe she and Anwar had exaggerated them?, and the ones around her neck were totally gone, and so like maybe that had just been some kind of paint from the stage that had rubbed off on her?

Not that some comment about a bruise was Xanther's worst fear. What if someone had heard about the seizure? But no one had said a thing. Even her Lion Girl fame had started to fade, except for today when Robbie Ordell had gotten her attention.

Xanther had eventually told her friends about what happened in New York, but not until the week was almost over. By then she had zero marks. No one seemed too wor-ried or impressed. They all just shrugged, and said it was impossible to tell by the way she looked, or acted.

"Is it kinda like getting a calf cramp?" Cogs wanted to know. Xanther had never had one of those but she remembered the one dancer trying to stretch his out. "Those hurt so much. They start out of nowhere and it feels like suddenly there's this humongous knot in your leg and there's nothing you can do but jump around and wait till it goes away, and it does goes away, and there's no mark left or anything. You're just sore."

"It's different," Xanther had answered. "I don't think a leg cramp makes you piss yourself."

Mayumi and Josh had laughed hard over that one.

Kle just wanted to move the convo along and hear more about the new games Xanther had played.

And that was pretty much it. Xanther had even managed to finish all her homework in New York before the seizure, *and* get ahead, which pleased all her teachers.

Really, the only thing about the seizure that kept sticking with Xanther wasn't what she couldn't remember, or could remember because of what Anwar told her later, and didn't tell her, Xanther could see how painful it was for him to relive any of it, the way she'd lost it, ruining her dress and disappearing into that place beyond anything she should be able to place later, which was, yeah, where the big problem lay, the big but, the but that goes — *but* the biggest problem was what she still could remember, and vividly too, starting with what she'd done but shouldn't have been able to do:

run.

The seizure had already been happening too, Xanther can even see it now, how she wasn't just starting to shake, but how her thoughts were also beginning to fragment, refragmenting, ripping raggedly along all her nerves, even as her big toes stopped pumping, except she was sprinting, like she could outrun it, even as she also carried it with her, like people running who are on fire, if this could be called fire, if this was even her, because part of her felt like not her at all, the part that could eat fire, the part pulling back her lips, had she snarled?, she couldn't remember that part ∴ I can't. ∴ ∷ *She did snarl.* ∴ ∷ **Not her** . . . ∴, and anyway, boy had the dancer playing Hope looked surprised, to see Xanther running out on stage like that, and then the surprise fled and she looked scared, like her body understood what her mind would have to catch up with later, racing her away, which was true for Hades too, Hades had fled in an instant, leaving behind just Juan Mateo, who was even more jarred and frightened than Hope, starting to follow Hope away, as the lights went down, and the curtains fell, Xanther glad that everyone had gotten away unscathed, because if they'd stayed even just a little longer . . . , which is when Mister Woder Do, Mr. Duder, the Shadow that summons all her shadows, got hold of her, and took her down, and still Xanther can remember even some of that too, if not quite what her body had started to do, then what she was seeing, or really experiencing, the familiar forest, something there deep in the forest, which even as it began to acquire sense was just as swiftly swept away, by what she couldn't tell her friends, definitely couldn't tell Les Parents, but what Dov would have understood, if he was still around, what the little one also seemed to understand . . .

g ace.

something?

744

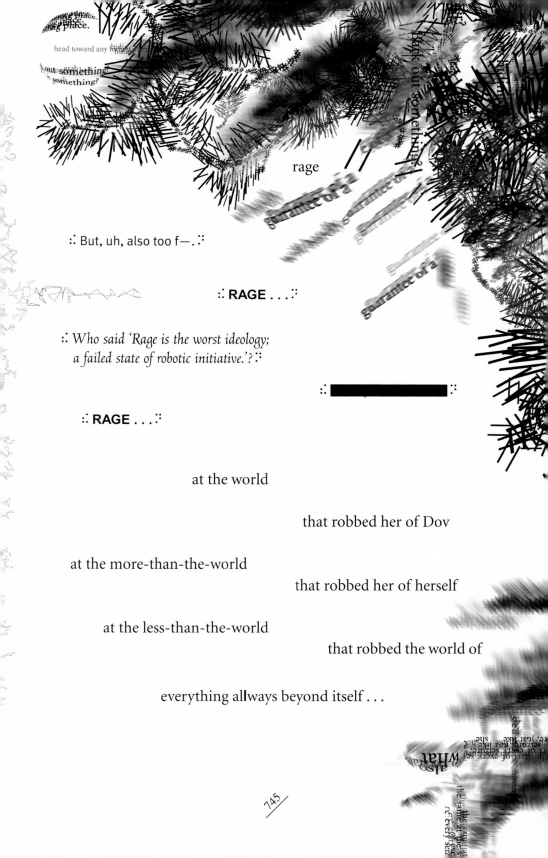

ding place.

head toward any hiding that

out something?
something?

rage

∴ But, uh, also too f—. ∴

∴ **RAGE . . .** ∴

∴ *Who said 'Rage is the worst ideology;
a failed state of robotic initiative.'?* ∴

∴ ▬▬▬▬▬▬ ∴

∴ **RAGE . . .** ∴

       at the world

              that robbed her of Dov

at the more-than-the-world

              that robbed her of herself

at the less-than-the-world

              that robbed the world of

everything allways beyond itself . . .

Getting home from school, the little one is already at the front door before Xanther even puts a foot inside, in her arms before she can think about it, on her shoulder like he's always been there, and will be there, forever.

And at once the fire within her begins to calm, that blue thing of harm diminishing again in that wild and endless forest of her thoughts.

"How were classes?" her mom asks from the piano room, surrounded by a ruin of books and notepads, laptop open, wrong moonlight making of Astair's hands things not quite alive.

"I did good on a quiz in math." Xanther can't bring herself to admit the hundred percent, like that might lead to questions of how, and maybe bring up cheating, though she didn't cheat, even if it felt like cheating, knowing the answers like that, so well, so quickly . . . available.

"Wonderful. But you did 'well,' not 'good.' 'Well' is an adverb modifying the verb 'did.' 'Good' is a noun and only applicable if your quiz resulted in some larger good."

"Astair!" Anwar laughs from the piano. "In doing well on a math quiz she was doing a good. One improved mind improves the minds of others. Nearly the highest good there is." Anwar winks at Xanther, fingers playing a trill on the keys.

But Xanther's sorta grateful for Astair not making a big deal out of the quiz. Somehow the Grammar Correction Squad is more comforting than a lot of praise for numbers settling right, and settling so quickly right too.

In the living room, Xanther spies the black gun box on the mantel where the glass wolves used to sit. She takes it down, and with its heaviness situated on her lap, kinda pleasant, at least comforting, starts trying different combinations. Maybe like the quiz problems, a series of numbers will just settle right and the latch will, presto, click open.

But though this first set of numbers clicks into place with weid familiarity, it unlocks nothing.

arrives with the same confidence but opens nothing.

"Daughter, we could drill it open if you like?" Anwar suggests from the steps, entering the living room, as another set of numbers fails.

For sure drilling is like the easiest way, but despite the disappointment of the latch staying, well, staying put, Xanther kinda likes the pleasures of the box's mysteries, with its brass lock and hinges, black lacquered corners. Sure, it's a gun. And, sure, the gun in itself, unseen by her, or at least not remembered by her, is not much of a mystery. Xanther can imagine a gun. But what if the gun's not there? What if in its place there's something else?

"Let's keep it locked. I like it better this way."

That night, before bed, a real rowl starts, or row, but rowl because it's growly and whirls around and around, as Shasti bawls and Freya bawls back, and then the accusations get worse, and Astair has to stop repeating "Stop this!" as Anwar steps in to separate them both, leading Freya away to the Les Parents bedroom for a sit-down, while Astair has a sit-down with Shasti on Shasti's bed.

Supposedly Freya had taken all of Shasti's Nightmare Stones.

"What are Nightmare Stones?" Xanther asks.

"Honey, this is Mom and Shasti time," Astair answers sternly.

But Xanther still wanders over to Freya's bed, not even sure why either, but with the same ease as finding those numbers that didn't open up Dov's gun box.

She tugs back the covers.

"Xanther!" Astair objects.

Instead of stopping, Xanther lifts up the pillow.

There they are. A big pile of them. Large and small. Round or roundish. Mostly gray but some black. And each encircled by a very white line.

"You found them!" Shasti shrieks with joy.

Xanther knows the slamming and scampering out in the hallway, what's pounding their way now, what has to be Freya, bursting into the room a second later, shrieking too at the discovery, though not with joy.

Astair's hand goes to her chest. Xanther hasn't seen her mom look so sad in a long while, and worried, and scared. And not just over some rocks, or some twin quibbling, but something else, bad enough, that she doesn't punish Freya, or even reprimand her, but gets down on her knees and hugs her and starts to cry.

Shasti looks so confused that Xanther goes to her side and takes her hand. Xanther is confused too. The room is flooded with smells and sounds and tastes.

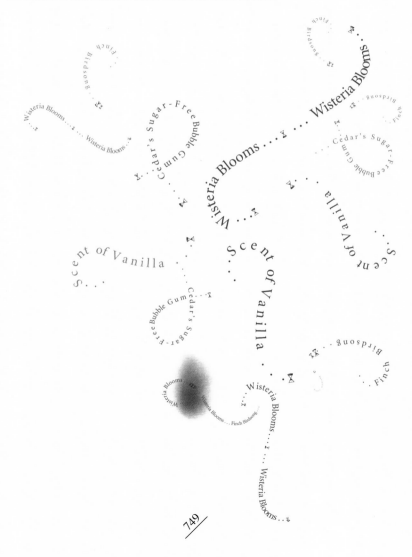

Anwar arrives and gently asks both Xanther and Shasti to come downstairs, where he prepares small bowls of yogurt, with nuts, a little honey and nutmeg. Shasti explains what Nightmare Stones are, Xanther agreeing that that should definitely chase nightmares away, because like how is anyone supposed to even sleep when there's a rock under your head?, let alone a big pile of rocks?, for sure that would make sleeping impossible, pointing this out to her little sister, which at least gets Shasti giggling, even as the thought of dear little Freya wanting so many Nightmare Stones gets Xanther worrying, and scared too.

Were those whirling blooms surrounding Freya some-how related?

The next day, Saturday morning, Les Parents go out without the kids. Xanther's put in charge of her sisters. She's told to call if anything seems even a tiny bit wrong. Under no circumstances are Shasti and Freya allowed to fight. A fight = a tiny bit wrong. Quibbling counts too.

But the twins don't fight or quibble. They don't even hang out in the same room. Freya curls up in the den and kinda talks to herself while pretending to play with the family tablet. At least, Xanther assumes she's pretending because whenever she tries to see what game Freya is play-ing or what clip she's watching, the screen is black.

Shasti stays in the piano room, coloring, or reading a book, or coloring the book she's supposed to be reading.

Xanther settles in the living room, trying to come up with more names for the little one. That's a disaster. With the little one no help at all.

Xanther almost thinks pretending to come up with a list would be more productive. So many lists, and she has all of them to prove it, but even so Xanther also realizes that like Freya she's kinda pretending too, in her own way: despite being home now, free of any blowback from the seizure, and acing a math quiz too, Xanther has been trying to deny that the thing of burning blue, inside her, of her, that acorn of agony, pilot light of pain, that starts up whenever she leaves the house, and goes out whenever she comes back, isn't going out anymore.

All of Sunday, Xanther does whatever she can to put out that flame, or at least dim it. She tries brushing the little one. That helps a little. She cleans his eyes. That helps too. She keeps cleaning his ears. Which takes the heat down to almost-out.

Though Xanther can still feel the hum of growing fire at work within her, threatening the edges of herself, crisping her skin, Xanther nervously checking her arms, no longer for bruises, but for signs of her flesh drying into fragile thinness, revealing some glow within, what might soon ignite, go up in flames.

Is she smelling smoke?

Big toes already pumping.

And if the ho-humdrummery of the day is threatened, what does that mean is happening to her forever forest?

"We need to take your little one to see Dr. Syd. I'll make the appointment," Astair announces to Xanther Tuesday afternoon, after school, surprising Anwar too, at least that's how he looks when he raises his head above his sheet music, though probably Xanther is the most surprised.

"Huh, why, uhm, say, uh, uhm, that?" Xanther asks, or doesn't ask, mostly appalled that she's acting so clueless, definitely appalled that she's lying!, about what's becoming so painfully obvious: how little one keeps getting weaker and weaker.

Today especially. Xanther has to carry him everywhere because when he walks, or tries to walk, he sways and wobbles, until he just plops down, to sit, or kinda sit, some sort of halfway place on the way to lying down, which always comes with a little snort followed by a longer sigh.

Even his eyes, though shut, look puffy and troubled.

Plus there's no getting around how much lighter he is, how much more feeble, Xanther can feel every rib, the knobs of his tiny spine, like he's withering with every hour.

"I think that's a good idea," Anwar says first.

"Me too," Shasti chimes in.

Of course Xanther agrees, though she's terrified too, especially since she's certain there's not much Dr. Syd can do now, not at this point, not for this . . .

The word the little one isn't makes her shudder. She lifts him from her shoulder and cuddles him closer to her chest, murmuring more names that don't work.

Xanther's already in bed, teeth flossed and brushed, why do her braces feel so tight?, lights just out, when Freya creeps into her room and crawls onto her bed.

"I'm sorry, Xanther. I'm sorry for not telling the truth about the wolves." She starts to cry. "I'm so sorry."

After a while, Freya turns on the light.

"This is for you. It's not Shast's. The biggest I had."

"Thanks, Frey," Xanther says, accepting the gift, kissing Freya too, before her sister can dart away.

Xanther waits to hear Astair's voice, to hear Freya reporting what Astair must have made her do, what Astair would never have made her do. There are no voices.

Xanther doesn't even need a Nightmare Stone, or does she? No way is it going under her pillow. The nightstand's fine, but Xanther doesn't turn off her lamp just yet, like the stone might vanish if she does, even if when she does twist the light away, the stone stays put, white line glowing with a promise that might keep for her sisters but never for Xanther. She can no more need this than eat it.

Xanther touches little one instead, curled up in the crux of her neck. Is he breathing? Yes. Even as her own breath stops at the awful other-questions curled up in that one question: what if he wasn't?, what if he stopped breathing right now?, what if he doesn't live through the night?

Because they are frailing together.

They are starving.

753

For Xanther and him, stones don't chase away the nightmares.

The stones are the nightmares.

But what little one gives her later is worse than any nightmare. What he drops in her hand can never be his name. Xanther's palm must keep the secret she can't speak.

What's just fallen out:

                          teeth,

                                   the big ones,

all four of his canines.

no chance

The clouds are turning into dragons . . .

— *Yang Wan-Li*

pale blue take cover macam cloud of sky under sky of cloud, taped

good lah, if jingjing still go check if safe, damn shacked too, but

still awake to make sure, locking bathroom door, running water,

before removing toilet tank lid, its downside, jingjing's upside.

perfect hiding place. mebbe finish it now. jingjing even turn on

fan. can squat next on sink, blow smoke away through vent.

jingjing scratch palms, mouth wets, dries.

but this little left is so littlelittle jingjing should just flush it.

knows jilo's best. take the pain. send pale blue down the drain.

still better: slip out now while auntie kooning in her deep. jingjing

can lambong for same samsengs playing balloon parade, tapi need

first find real buay kan to get hits, main him, boh pian, jingjing

boh lui liao, jilo to trade.

auntie tho has money locked in room safe, osso passports jingjing

hasn't seen since customs day. decides stay. replaces tank lid,

turns off water, fan, lights. back out to floor. auntie bed resident

now. kiam siap her. jingjing miss bed, hate floor, if back feels

better, neck too.

but can't sleep.

won't sleep.

itch and turn.

turn and itch.

until hurt inside is outside hurt and there's no more sky of blue no

more sky of clouds. where there is no sky there is no more world.

jingjing hum kar chan hum pah lang.

room so bright. dawn long gone. oreddy auntie up. lotus and

meditating. on bed lai dat. bed made too. her hair braided, more

aw than silver. cotton shirt look pressed, cotton pants too. flower

print pretty enuf for life. macam flowers fill room, erase corners.

"**汝备其身**," ∴ *Get ready,* ∵ she says, no movement, eyes closed.

jingjing hurry to bathroom, lock door, run water, matches out,

need drift to lift him through hours ahead, but can't even reach

hiding place before door pop open, auntie there, damn teruk her.

"将其放之。" ∴ *Leave that behind.* ∴

"把什么抛在脑后？" ∴ leave what behind? ∴

"需乃吾知吾不知之道。弃知乃吾如何释需。" ∴ *Need is how we know we do*

not know. To let go of knowing is how we leave need behind. ∴

"好的，我的主人。 我会把我的需求抛在脑后。" ∴ yes, mistress. i leave

need behind. ∴

jingjing even bows.

how seow her, with this morning nongsngse, but mebbe bow

confirm guarantee jingjing solid, lah.

bow does not.

"靖，远其毒，其不可随吾行。" ∷ *Jingjing, leave your drugs behind. They're not coming with us today.* ∷

jingjing damn pai seh! malu malu! lao kwee! keeps bowing to hide red face.

"我把它们全部都冲走。" ∷ *i flush it.* ∷

tapi auntie just groan, head as kay heavy with disappointment as jingjing is burning with shame. macam falling star.

"勿做，待吾归，尔将有需。" ∷ *Please do not do that. You will require it when we get back.* ∷

outside, lah, old needs burn up for new necessities. great tian li has plan, kena jingjing on this kai kai. kin leh! kin leh!

macam she know l.a. streets too.

macam she know the right way.

until great tian li suddenly stops.

"主人，你觉察到什么了么？" ∴ mistress, you sense something? ∴ jingjing

ask, afraid, looking everywhere, for wings, something worse.

"否。" ∴ *No.* ∴

"我们危险吗？" ∴ we in danger? ∴

"吾不以为然。" ∴ *No.* ∴

"那我们为什么停下来？" ∴ then why stop? ∴

"吾乃等也。" ∴ *We're waiting.* ∴

"为了什么？" ∴ for what? ∴ jingjing check sky, again for wings, for

monsters, mebbe even ...

"思之，靖！" ∴ *Think, Jingjing!* ∴

"我们在等那只猫吗？" ∴ for cat? ∴

damn, auntie go sighsigh then, has to look away, head sorry

shaking.

"等车也。" ∴ *For the bus.* ∴

jingjing osso look away, must!, head lowered, si beh malu, pained,

heartbeat torturous, with hate.

no words then, diam lah.

both of them, two dead-ends of stone, waiting.

strange still how auntie knows fare, where to get on, macam she

feels it, macam old days with cat, mebbe cat telling her city ways

now.

but jingjing proceed cautious, sial.

"你找到了一张地图而且做了研究？" ∴ you got map? ∴

"妙哉!" ∴ *Very good!* ∴ auntie beam luminous.

"是助理给你的吗,他有没有给你关于交通的建议？" ∴ clerk help? ∴

"靖!尔在思!" ∴ *Jingjing! Now you're thinking!* ∴ her voice macam spring

blooms on blooms.

"那我们会抓着那只猫吗？" ⸪ can get cat now? ⸪

lai dat bloom wilt, die. corners everywhere. only corners.

"勿念其将。汝为无存之事而损今。无明，明仍在。尔与现存同在，

更为重。" ⸪ *Forget this future. You sacrifice the present in the name of something that*

is not there. Without the future, the future is still here. And more important, you're here

with all that's here and yet to come. ⸪

jingjing just blink as bus keep jumbling along to who knows where.

auntie sighsigh louder lah, award no points. what terrible old

cock-up of joints, damn cham by her eyes, exile oreddy on her lips,

disapproval tekan jingjing, damn siong, damn sim tiah.

if only jingjing could hit her. ketuk that mouth, gapgap her teeth.

one hard slap at least. sting fierce her cheek, mebbe osso scratch

that old skin deep. that would fix one itch. smack the old bag.

tapi jingjing boh lang ai. all fart and no shit. worse: boh lum par

chee, bobbing head up and down macam he damn char tau one.

"尔懂之？" ∴ *Now do you understand?* ∴

"没有，我的主人。" ∴ no, mistress. ∴ still bobbing head up and down.

at least telling truth.

"勿称吾乃尔主，吾至多乃恩人，亦或雇者，亦或相助者，仅此。 尔将

随心而去，某尔心仪之事。" ∴ ▮▮▮▮▮▮▮▮▮▮▮▮▮▮▮▮▮▮▮▮▮

▮▮▮▮▮▮▮▮▮▮▮▮▮▮▮▮▮▮▮▮▮▮▮▮▮▮▮▮▮▮▮▮▮▮▮▮▮▮

▮▮▮▮▮▮▮▮▮▮▮▮▮▮▮▮▮▮▮▮ ∴ ∴ ▮▮▮▮▮

▮▮▮▮▮▮▮▮▮▮▮▮▮▮▮▮▮▮▮▮▮▮▮▮▮▮▮▮▮▮

▮▮▮▮▮▮▮▮▮▮▮▮▮▮▮▮▮▮▮▮▮▮▮

██████ ∷ ∷ **Stop calling me your mistress. I'm at most your benefactor, perhaps an employer, a landlord of sorts, sponsor I hope. Nothing more. You are free to go or quit or do whatever you like whenever you like.** ∷

"是的，主人。" ∷ yes, mistress. ∷

"啊，吾怜之靖，" ∷ *Oh dear, dear Jingjing!* ∷ auntie saysay with such sim-ache tenderness even dead blooms find their way back to life.

"所以猫不在这？" ∷ so cat not here? ∷

"无猫，如吾幸，则过无猫，今无猫，明亦无猫，未能有。" ∷ *There is no cat.* ∷

"那我们去哪里？" ∷ then where we go? ∷

"谋冰食！" ∷ *To get ice cream!* ∷

after they jump off bus, auntie leads way some blocks, no orchard

road she finds, but osso packed with shops and cars. abbot kinney.

manyak ah beng, nowhere better to go, kopi places, flower shop

and gardens, no mehnoner, but yellow and white fences welcome

newcomers sit, eat, buy a jacket.

auntie faster padpad past shop window and sweeswee surfer, for

truck parked ahead. ice cream koans. ah mm so small can't reach

order counter, but shaggy boy at window find her still, take her

order, take jingjing's next, while tian li unpocket lui, tua wad lah,

mebbe three, four balloons thick. how she get so much money?

tian li order endless winter, pomegranate, in waffle cone. jingjing

get lotus dream, lemon, almonds, lots, cara cara and cocoa too,

waffle cone osso, whack that fast, before even eyes have chance,

jingjing left licking fingers, hands.

auntie take her time, makan macam mouse, so slowslow jingjing

gau mm tim, squirmy for more dreamy lotus, for more cash, dreamy

double on auntie's wad, lost deep again in one of her pockets.

"吾常念此地之冰食。吾念恩终得试之。确为良品。吾之幸如吾多留此地少时。"

∴ I always wanted to eat ice cream in Venice, California. I am grateful I finally got the chance. It is good ice cream. We're lucky if we get to stay even a little longer. ∴

"我也很感恩。" ∴ same here. ∴

tian li blanjah jingjing then, with tua smile, kay song to find kayu necklace still worn, her lips quick to fingertips, fingertips to acorn.

"尔将被召，尔将善答。" ∷ *You will be called upon and you will answer well.* ∷

auntie saysay then, patpat jingjing's arm too, near enuf heartpain

to match lotus dream, mebbe match balloon parade too, leading

them to a bench then, where sun's blotched under drench of palms,

geysers of green painting clouds sailing by on sky in love with a

sea.

jingjing miss sea, saysay to auntie to walk just meters more for

beach, but old bag oreddy asleep.

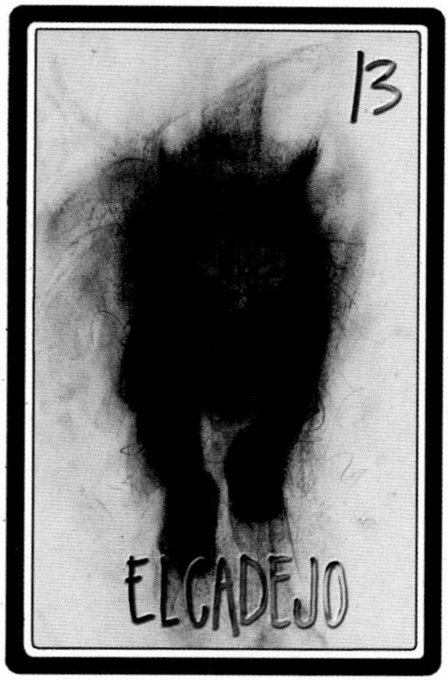
13
EL CADEJO

juang lah. what jingjing find with that? mebbe, macam auntie,

jingjing should snooze too. slip to dream that need no dream. what

place is that? with no scratch, no monster card, just some seam-

less space for roots without roots that jingjing might call peace.

"吾即需一租车," tian li say sharp, sit up straight, eye sharp. "吾不可晚。" ∷ *We need taxi at once. We must not be late.* ∷

still wiping sleep, didn't even sleep, or did he?, jingjing race off for busy corner, tsao like siao to catch a taxi zooming by, just then too, perfect time, runrun damn chor, passenger seats carry no one, on-duty sign all light, but brakes never bright.

apu nehneh tell him try hotel. but can't show jingjing where to find hotel close by. only far. woman who show half ball, got shop-ping bags, esplain in l.a. jingjing must call a cab.

jingjing got no phone, find coin phone, got no coin. chop chop kali pok for hotel far away, finds first turn, take block, make next turn, with plenty turns left, plus more blocks to run, legs done, chest done, oreddy chua chua, panting macam mad, lah, shackshacked with jilo to show for it. gu poon si.

then jingjing stop breathing.

can't believe eyes.

must be leftover smoke clotting his eyes, stop up too his lungs

from heaving.

can't even take one more step.

must clear eyes first, take breath.

jingjing finally step closeclose, ices over. hands immeely numb.

rest of him too, neck to bum. taken by shadows and shakes. feet

macam lead. kuat drive to get auntie a cab lah, osso dead.

what were the chances?

no chance.

tapi here, look, right front, look, stapled to telephone pole, all

auntie need, all jingjing lost, that pow ka leow damn powderful

one. look! and put here just for him. because who else could

recognize such ears, those paws, even with eyes closed?

FOUND MAY 10, 2014

This image has been

IF YOU KNOW ANYTHING, PLEASE CALL

323 - ⊗⊗⊗ - ⊗⊗⊗⊗

(POSTED MAY 17, 2014)

∴ **TFv2 p. 313.** ∴

Undaunted

Get in your trucks and follow me!

— Ammon Bundy

Blue shadows die in the holds of deeper shadows as day fades for good,
street lamps flickering on, if windows around Old Campus remain dark,
students dining at Commons, or off to Sterling and the stacks.
Soon enough, though, their windows will brighten with
studies and new wonderment, entryways livening with
the music of conversation, a time still bewitched by
youth, when the duration of a mere night is more
than enough time to write a paper, prepare for a
test, solve any question posed by history.

Cas would like to be here for that, but by
midnight they'll be heading north.

She spies Bobby across the courtyard,
slowly making his way back to her from
Elm Street, and the post office, a curious mist rising up between them, what
almost counts as a fog, smudging lights,
the voices of students passing by.

A small group exiting Bingham notices her.
Cas smiles back. Maybe they think she's the
mother of a student or a professor. She could
have been a professor. She could have been both.

By the time Bobby reaches her, the mist has become a
poem, Cas wondering aloud if English students still read
Eliot, if London fog still makes young minds ache and hearts shudder for a love song we all believe we might, if just once in our life, write.

Bobby will say at once if he reached Sew. Instead, he kisses her, puts an arm around her, and together they wait outside Connecticut Hall, in front of Nathan Hale's bound ankles, shoes circumscribed by his singular regret.

Once they had no reason to remain so constantly on alert. Once they hadn't talked of anything to do with war. Sew just took out his cello and played Brahms. ∴ **TFv3 p. 349.** ∵

Cas knows better than to look for their friend here, but she still scans the trees, considering the charcoal possibilities, curious if a squirrel might still move among the branches at this hour.

But the fog keeps thickening, neither yellow nor white, rather a haze of pearl bit through with threats of blue, as if for a moment the world itself might be the Orb. Cas tightens her hold on her bag and the cashmere sweater inside, wrapping tight Mefisto's incalculable gift.

Cas doesn't want to wait anymore. Even here she feels exposed, their whole cause at risk. As if even one of these freshmen might stop, pull out a gun, and do away with them.

"Confirmed?" Cas asks Bobby instead of running. She knows whom to really fear. Who will certainly bring guns.

"Yup."

"They guessed the passphrase?"

∴ FzQrKozegTl/oPdlb2vMTC7hn1jZRfAToH
4qtgvN2voqnZlVBtUZ+T32eD56lammED
RCg9/eM50OAzsrgEsqJ3ZGH7Kz/AF+wLv
gds+B4i8Yf+y1VHYMyoLQu+2un1omDR/
A7ms7NKTd6Q==∵

"No. But we got it to them."

"Midnight still?"

"Midnight."

Bobby squeezes Cas, to comfort her in her
thoughts over all the unlikely outcomes the
night ahead will offer and then rescind.

Cas has to dip a hand into her bag, finding the soft
comfort guarding a harder truth beneath, as if to pet it, as
if to draw from such stillness the prickling static Cas can almost
regard as affectionate, if never quite familiar.

The previous night, she had managed to scry for nearly twelve hours.

But no matter how much she searched — and she searched and searched — she discovered nothing on Recluse that was of ethical use. What was of no ethical use, she found easily enough online.

Cas would willingly play Clotho and maybe even Lachesis. But never Atropos.

At the end, by way of a reward, she turned to the Aberrations again, to herself, to Xanther, revisiting Clip #1 thru Clip #6.

Allies had provided them with cots behind a woodshed south of Danbury.

Bobby admitted later he'd been dreaming of Egyptian sheets and Turkish towels. Cas had been with someone else's dreams.

A lone captain in Union blue, wandering among his men on Cemetery Ridge, the night before the third day, eyeing Pickett's encampment with both reverie and fear. ∴ **July 3, 1863.** ∴ ∴ *02:02:02.* ∴

This wasn't an Aberration or even a Clip. What finally settled into meaning came only from what Cas could catch on his lips.

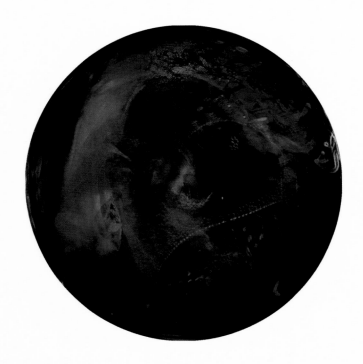

"The heart quickens
at such a message,
born under a cool and ageless moon,
where men's souls flicker brightly
like candles set in slender lanterns
made of iron and glass.

"Men have died for more in that
they lived their life in full;
and yet in this respect
we seem undaunted.

"A hundred,
a thousand, a thousand
more,

and all awake now to every
blink and breath that bring us
a closer step to dawn.

"'Sleep well', I should say,
'and sleep long.'

"But as I listen to their voices
I hear the current of their
songs
what different words press
against my lips.

"*I say:*
Do not sleep, soldier.
Do not sleep at all.
Live this night **to presume this life** your dream,
for to this **dream you'll long to return**

when at **break of day**

distant thunder roars
and you **feel yourself falling**

and see and hear

no more.'"

Cas feels Bobby loosen his hold on her, freeing both his hands, shifting his weight to readiness.

Cas withdraws her hand from her bag to confront too the fog's admission. Groups of students move here and there, some crouched beneath lampposts, others disappearing through doorways and gates. All beyond definition.

Somewhere close an a cappella group begins to sing. ∴ *Whim 'n Rhythm.* ∴

> *If you go down to Hammond,*
> *You'll never come back . . .*

Bobby's tenseness directs Cas to a lone figure, not tall, but solid enough to suggest someone too grave in years to be just studying here. He's seen them too. He knows them. Until proximity clears the fog and makes clear his mistake.

"I'm so sorry!" the elderly gentleman exclaims. "I see you're not here to see me. And I realize I'm an evening too soon."

Bobby and Cas watch him wander away, relaxing a little, if also expecting him to turn back, somehow altered again by the fog.

"Did you weally think that pwofesso' was me?" asks the voice behind them.

Stepping out from behind Nathan Hale then, stout and smiling, arms held wide, embracing them both, kisses on both cheeks.

Suddenly the world seems safe.

"We were worried," Cas still admits.

"Don't be silly. I'm not a wo'wy. Weal wo'wies a'e ahead."

"We've missed you, Warlock."

Warlock lifts a hand to his black beret, lightly lowering his head.

"Thank you, Bobby."

"How was California?"

"Ve'y good. I may have made us all a new fwiend. He's a detective."

"Let's live long enough to meet him," Bobby grunts. Cas adds nothing. No matter how many weapons Bobby's arsenal holds, the three of them don't count for a fight. And it will come to a fight.

Cas' silence only grows when she sees
that Warlock is driving them. He picks
them up in front of Phelps Gate in an
old orange Honda. Cas gets in the back
so she can stretch out. She tries to close
her eyes but can't when she discovers
Warlock is driving east instead of north,
if still leaving the fog behind.

At least he drives fast, abandoning the turnpike long before Guilford, then heading south onto dark roads, sticking to the ones covered most densely with trees.

Cas had once heard such arboreal arches described as "bat caves." The expression had confused her. She had looked for rock and lime deposits. She had looked for bats. She still finds no bats. Until Warlock reaches the end of a long gravel driveway, parking upon the edge of a wide unlit field, then Cas, climbing out, discovers a sky black with wings.

The multitude shocks her.

And they are nothing compared to the multitude of vehicles surrounding them.

"The othe' battalions a'e alweady in place. This one is just to accompany us. Spwead out of cou'se. But caw'awing out constant contact and obse'vation."

"Battalions?" Cas asks.

Warlock nods.

"I had no idea." Even Bobby seems amazed.

"Fo' Wecluse, at least a bwigade."

2187D

Welcome. Please set your earpieces
to channel six.

— Richard McGuire

The telephone stops ringing [over to voice mail {or not ‹could care less about caller ID›}]. Galvadyne again [[{or not ‹Nathan Muellenson?›} or not].

Though a moment later the phone starts ringing again. Anwar still doesn't move. Why should he?

It's a beautiful Wednesday afternoon. His mind's made up. He's with his family in the piano room. Astair isn't moving either. She smiles at Anwar from her laptop. She's made up her mind too.

Freya [though] claps her hands over her ears [then starts humming to herself {crayoning another abstract in purple and orange}].

Shasti looks over at Xanther [who's {big surprise} stroking the cat in her lap].

'No one calls *me* on that line,' Xanther answers the look.

'No one calls me on that line either,' Shasti copies.

The phone stops ringing.

Anwar returns to the piece he's attempting to play [not so badly as to torture his family {but bad enough to torture himself}].

.: Bach [Goldberg Variations].: .: *Variatio 4. a 1 Clav.*:

Shasti returns to her book. Xanther returns to her dreams [or whatever her closed eyes are hiding {while her fingers keep up the slow caress of that little creature ‹and whatever those closed eyes hide›}].

Again the landline starts ringing.

It still doesn't matter.

// earlier that morning

//though

// everything had mattered.

Anwar's last interview had been scheduled for 9:30 AM [at the Mansfield Studio :: ▮▮▮▮▮▮▮ ▮▮▮▮▮▮▮▮▮▮▮▮▮▮▮▮▮▮▮▮ :: {no studio he'd ever heard of before ‹but Anwar «despite living in Los Angeles» doesn't track that stuff much›}].

The PDF [on how to get there] was quite elaborate [anticipating possible freeway approaches {101 or 134} as well as entrances {Guard Gate #2 or Guard Gate #3 ‹south or west›}].

Anwar took side streets and entered by Gate #4.

The sentry [eyeing his driver's license {before confirming Anwar's name on the list ‹with a smile›}] quickly confirmed the reason for such detailed descriptions: he had no clue either where Anwar was supposed to go.

// he'd never heard of Building 2187D.

// or an alleyway called Audra.

// or a doorway marked [sic] **Of Air!**

The map [{however} that Anwar produced next] seemed to alleviate the guard's discomfort.

'I've worked here eight months and never directed no one to this place. Learn something every day.' Pointing out the lot [where Anwar should park] and then the general direction [in which he should walk].

Anwar never found an alleyway called Audra or a building marked 2187D but [after much circling {and questions ‹drawing from studio workers «?»› blank stares ‹rendered blanker when studying Anwar's map›}] eventually did locate this ordinary door [past a parking lot {under another parking structure ‹still requiring that he press on towards the limits of the studio's perimeter «exceeding it?»›}].

It was a strange thing to see [beneath a dark blue lamp {dead}]. Anwar had assumed the typo was just in the instructions. But here it was again.

Not

OFF AIR!

Or

ON AIR!

Maybe a joke Anwar wasn't quick enough to get [he'd have to ask Astair {Xanther?}]?

OF AIR!

The door opened easily enough but no one was inside [just a curious reception room {without desk ‹or even sofa or chairs›}]. Just signs with no arrows.

More jokes? Anwar was still lost [maybe his JPS {Joke Positioning System} had no bars in here].

Anwar obeyed the sign and followed the arrow to Telepresence Room #4.

The hallway [on the way there] was narrow and dark but oddly reassuring [{the carpet beneath his feet ‹elaborately› patterned and ‹immaculately› clean and soft ‹!›} {the ‹wood-panelled› walls warmly lit by ‹coffered «brass canistered?»› lamps ‹all very steampunk›}].

The room [however] was not.

Anwar had expected a real person or [at least] something similar to New York [small office with a table {ringed with cup stains ‹like a bingo game›} plus {inadequately} curtained windows {and a monitor with a camera attached ‹duct-taped!› to the top}].
Not even Skype or FaceTime.
[also] The monitor in that Manhattan closet had buzzed with snow until [finally!] a technician arrived with apologies [double apologies for the fact that his Echo Park interviewer didn't even show].

Was that whom Anwar would be conversing with now?

But no screen flickered to life. No curtains revealed an outside. Anwar couldn't even see the walls.

The whole room bent away from him [like he was standing in the middle of a globe {the ceiling globed as well ‹the floor like an anechoic chamber «though the grid ⟨beneath⟩ his feet was more substantial ⟨if with also a below dropping deeply away⟩»}].

Anwar walked to [and stopped on] a dimly illuminated X [{pulsing} dark blue].

'Xanther,' Anwar said aloud then [curious to test this chamber's{?} acoustics {surprised to discover a flurry of echoes ‹not fading «but pitching quickly towards a feedback scream ⟨!!!⟩ which fortunately never peaked» lowering on its own› before slowing and finally vanishing}].

Anwar felt vaguely guilty [or paranoid?] for uttering his daughter's name in such an unfamiliar place. Then [as if to make up for one trespass] Anwar left the pulsing blue X [to make another] to find a wall.

'Please re-center yourself,' an [androidyned] voice said at once [{vaguely} familiar too].

Anwar returned to the only light in the room.

'Telepresence interview about to commence,' the voice added.

Anwar tried but couldn't locate the source of the sound.

Impressive.

The dimness darkened then.

The X at his feet too.

Anwar expected even pitch-black [except for an exit sign {except ‹wow› there were no exit signs ‹no signs at all›}].

He expected then the emergence of a screen [{maybe} a surround screen {that would be really impressive}].

But there was no screen.

And the chamber didn't go black.

Instead [all around Anwar] the air began to buzz with a curious light [as if made of {‹in›particulate} dust {like ‹digital«!»› snow}].

Anwar's first reaction was to hold his breath.

As if the room were filling

// with smoke

// with steam

with something . . .

The buzzing matter was so certain that Anwar had to finally force himself to take a sip of air [finding it without taste {or change ‹even in temperature›}].

Anwar then raised his hands to his face [the misty illumination remaining unstirred {‹stranger still› his hands ‹«un»illuminated› were gone‹!›}].

Anwar squinted then in the brightness [of this {ambient} light{?}].

Waiting for the appearance [or {at least} the sound{?}] of an interlocutor?

As the fizz of the visual grew still brighter [louder?].

Without interruption.

Until all at once —

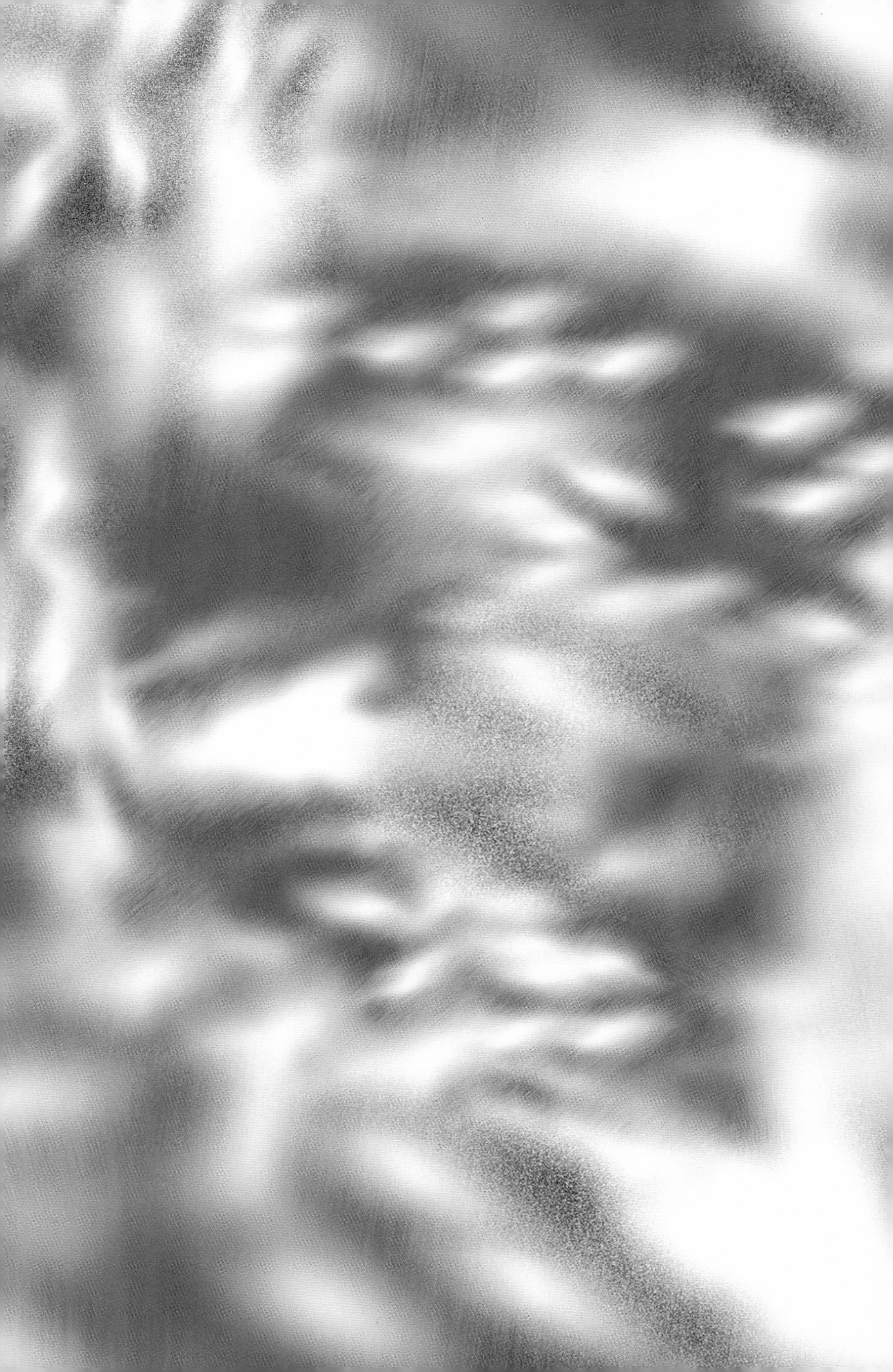

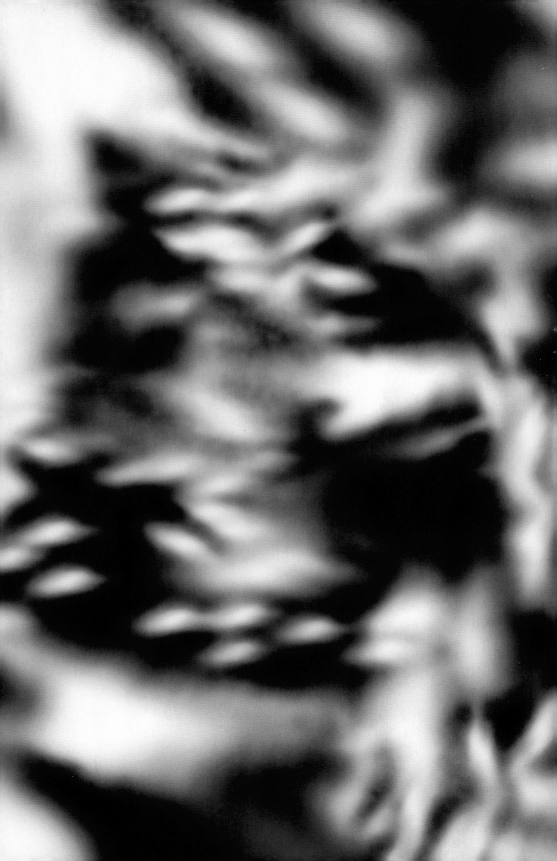

Anwar blinked in the final flash of blackness [sun-bursts {‹more?› fleeting his retinal memory}] as light began to rise again in the chamber [normal light {though Anwar was hard-pressed to tell if it was LED or incandescent‹?›}].

The X [at his feet] now pulsed dark red.

'Thank you, Mr. Ibrahim,' came the anonymized voice. 'Your interview has concluded. A Galvadyne representative will contact you soon. Have a nice day.'

Nathan Muellenson [Director of Engineering] had called twenty minutes later.

'Congratulations, Anwar. Tell your family you're moving to New York. Great? Am I right? The job's yours! Super great, am I super right? I'll let you read the e-mail to get the whole dealie, the formal proposal, the tiny print that's so tiny it's not even print. Don't worry. We don't do tiny print at Galvadyne. There are some extras too that I know will please you. Heck, I know they'd sure please me.'

'Brother, the gym is my metaphor for misery,' Ehtisham said later [and he meant it]. 'I just get through it and "through it" finds me better.' Though Anwar's friend doesn't exactly look better [his face splotching like a sun storm {still sheening with sweat}].

Anwar had met Ehtisham [for lunch {after that odd whatever} at Forage ∴ **3823 West Sunset Boulevard, Los Angeles, CA 90026** ∵]. Ehti had gone for the pork belly sandwich [with lots {and lots} of ice water] while Anwar had ordered a beet-something with quinoa-something [he couldn't focus on food {though something about what just happened had made him very hungry}].

Recounting [the weirdness of] it seemed to make Ehtisham [extra] hungry too.

But [good friend that he was] Ehti listened carefully [very carefully {prodding Anwar for details about the volume level or the quality of the light ‹what it looked like when Anwar blinked «closed his eyes»›}].

'It wasn't in my head.'
'Just checking,' Ehti answered [dead serious].
'As much as I kept trying to see something, the sensation I had was, well . . . '
'Well, what?'
'I felt like I was the one being seen. Or watched. Or not just watched but studied.'
'Studied? Like, what, by some HMO folks?'
'Except not folks. More like by a machine. As if the machine itself was measuring me.'
'You have a feeling that correlates with a machine measuring you?'

Anwar recounted the voice too [and the X-marks-the-spot {blue first ‹and then red «Ehtisham seemed interested in that»›}]. [by the time Ehti had finished his sandwich {and waters}] Anwar had related just about everything he could think of [about that 'Interview'].

'Pretty cool,' Ehti said [wiping his mouth with a napkin].

'Is that your verdict on Galvadyne too?'

'Pretty *un*cool.'

'An informed pronouncement?'

'So, I'm not saying they're connected, not saying that at all, but remember I had a Kozimo story to tell?'

'Yes! In fact, I keep remembering just to just as quickly keep forgetting to ask you. Tell me!'

But Ehti wasn't even halfway through when Anwar lost his appetite.

'All of them?' Anwar asked.

'All of them.'

'How did they get out?'

'No idea. The first thing the janitor noticed was that no birds were chirping. Not usually the case. Then he felt something fall close by. Grazed his shoulder. He checked the floor but saw nothing. Then he checked the lights above and saw the snakes.'

Anwar shuddered. He and Ehti had been there [in Sementera {in The Glass House ‹with all those birds «and all those ⟨locked up?⟩ snakes»›}].

'Supposedly, every snake was found, though who knows, really, if one isn't still loose, in a vent or pipe, slithering around that building? Not one bird survived. The snakes got them all.'

'Because they were all in cages?'

'That's exactly right.'

'And the janitor?'

'He tried running but still got bit.'

'Poisonous?'

'Not a one was *not* poisonous!'

'Is he okay?'

'It was a golden lancehead. Pretty venomous. The dude survived but not easily.'

'And Kozimo?'

'Supposedly, this was just one of his pet projects, so to speak. He had no idea the CEO of said operation maintained an illegally acquired and housed ophidian collection. That guy's getting bit by a lawsuit now. Probably worse than any lancehead.'

'Kozimo probably wishes he would have stuck with us,' Anwar says [smiles].

'Maybe we're glad we didn't last with him?' Ehtisham answers [no smile].

'Here comes the they're-not-connected part?'

'I'm still saying they're not connected. But I'm also saying Kozimo had some litigation against some company called Candy Chex & Letters.'

'Let me guess: owned by Galvadyne?'

Something about Galvadyne and ownership had then sent Anwar's thoughts scurrying after Mefisto [{the aftermath of something else he'd forgotten ‹with neither outline nor shadow to help out›} returning only the sensation of missing his friend].

Snakes and dead birds were not the end of Ehtisham's report either.

[when he got home {the kids were still not back from school}] Anwar read [and re-read] Galvadyne's formal proposal [bottom line: a lot of money with lots of bonuses].

Then he told Astair everything.

He told her about the offer.

He told her about New York [they would have a company apartment in Chelsea].

He told her about the health insurance.

He told her about the education assistance program for employees with children.

He told her about the money.

He told her again about the money.

Then he told her about Ehtisham's research.

Then he told her about the dead birds and snakes.

'I couldn't resist doing some research too,' Astair admitted [when Anwar had finished {with one more mention of all the money}].

'You dug up the drone stuff too?' Anwar asked [embarrassed that he hadn't {blinded by the money‹?›}].

'Galvadyne owns plenty of cool companies. Good ones too,' Astair admitted.

'But?'

'A scorpion only has to have poison in its tail.'

'How bad?'

'I don't know.'

'Except we do know, don't we?' Anwar sighs.

'With what we've heard from Ehti and, well, basically thanks to Mefisto . . . ' Astair thinks it through and then nods.

'Not us.' At least Anwar is the first to say it.

'Not us.'

'Shit!'

'Shit!'

And then [and suddenly too] both of them were laughing [if {perhaps} not all the tears that came to Astair's eyes {his eyes} were just from laughter].

Anwar called Galvadyne, Inc. Nathan Muellenson didn't pick up. Anwar left a message.

Thank you but blah-blah-blah Galvadyne just isn't for me blah-blah-blah I have decided to remain independent blah-blah-blah but thank you again blah-blah-blah and blah-blah-blah best of blah-blah-blah luck.

Something like that.

Anwar felt good afterwards [relieved {something about the way Muellenson ‹in New York› kept wanting Anwar to pass along a message to Mefisto had made him feel sick}].

And then Anwar felt really sick [and glum and desperate and caged and still worse and worse {the sight of his children ‹the «now impossible» financing they required «were entitled to!(?)»» made this feeling hurt even more ‹in the name of principles «ideals ⟨ . . . ⟩» were he and Astair harming these innocents?›}].

Anwar almost considered [he had the desire {at least it was something}] getting down on his knees and offering a prayer:

ارجوك ارزقني الوجود والرحمه

لاكون منفتح لما هو خيرٌ لي.

ارجوك ارزقني القوة والايمان

لأتحمّل ما هو خيرٌ لي.

∷ **TFv1 p. 542.** ∷

∷ *And our Parameters?* ∷

∷ Parameter 2 failed. ∷

∷ *Then what else awaits failure?* ∷

∷ **We shudder to know.** ∷

∷ *Don't we already know?* ∷

He checked his e-mails instead. Nothing from Galvadyne but there was a note from Savannah at Enzio.

From: Cambridge, Savannah
Sent: Wednesday, September 17, 2014 4:05 PM
To: Ibrahim, Anwar
Subject: Finally!

Anwar! With all apologies for the delay!

xS

Anwar checked his [bank {Chase}] account at once. Who knew that the sight of just four digits could release into his system some opioid-equivalent [organic!]?

Not a solution.

But definitely a reprieve.

$9,000.

Astair was over the moon. [and even if the children had no idea what had happened] The [{very} good] mood [of Les Parents {as Xanther would say}] proved contagious.

In other words:

Who cared if Bach was difficult?

Who cared if Galvadyne kept calling?

Who cared if Muellenson wouldn't leave a message?

Though [on second {or third ‹or fourth . . . ›} thought] why should Anwar even hide from that conversation?

Why not just put it all to rest?

'Nathan?' Anwar asks [picking up the kitchen phone {not checking the ID ‹concerned only with closing «for ⟨!!!!⟩ good» the door to this job opportunity›}].

'I kena take your sign oreddy,' howls the voice on the other end. 'You kapok my cat! *You stole my cat!*'

THE FAMILIAR

VOLUME 4

All rights reserved. Published in the United States by Pantheon Books, a division of Penguin Random House LLC, New York, and distributed in Canada by Random House of Canada, a division of Penguin Random House Canada Limited, Toronto.

Pantheon Books and colophon are registered trademarks of Penguin Random House LLC.

Permissions information for images and illustrations can be found on pages 836 & 837.

Library of Congress Cataloging-in-Publication Data
Danielewski, Mark Z.
The Familiar, Volume 4: "Hades"/ Mark Z. Danielewski
p. cm.
ISBN 978-0-375-71500-6   (softcover: acid-free paper).
ISBN 978-0-375-71501-3 (ebook).
I. Title.
PS3554.A5596F36 2015   813'.54—dc23   2014028320

Jacket Design by Atelier Z.

Author Drawings by Carole Anne Pecchia.

Printed in China

First Edition
2 4 6 8 9 7 5 3 1

www.markzdanielewski.com
www.pantheonbooks.com

FONTS

MORE FONTS

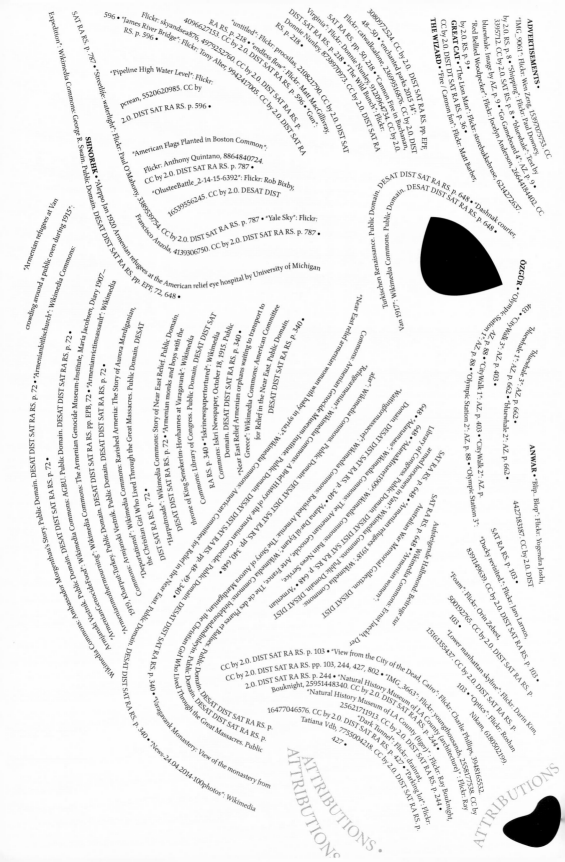

ATTRIBUTIONS • ATTRIBUTIONS • ATTRIBUTIONS

Thank Yous

Lloyd Tullues

Noam Assayag-Bernot

Jesse Stark Damiani

Sandi Tan

Carole Anne Pecchia

Detective John Motto and
Lieutenant Wes Buhrmester

Rita Raley

Scott Watson

Translations

Arabic .... Yousef Hilmy
Arabic .... Faisal Nasrawi
Armenian .... Niree Perian
Hebrew .... David Duvshani
Mandarin/Cantonese .... Jinghan Wu
Russian ....Anna Loginova
Spanish...................................... Juan Valencia
Spanish........................ René López Villamar
Turkish .... Gökhan Sarı

More Thank Yous

Research

Caterina Lazzara, S. E. Pessin,
Claire Anderson-Ramos,
and Chris Kokosenski

Graphics

Scott Milton Brazee, Steve Smith, Melissa B. Bryant,
and Amy Tarangelo

Good Sense

Mark Birkey, Lydia Buechler, Michiko Clark, Garth Graeper,
Andy Hughes, Altie Karper, Shona McCarthy, James Nash,
Jennifer Olsen, Austin O'Malley, and Stella Tan

ATELIER Z

{in alphabetical order}

REGINA GONZALES

MICHELE REVERTE

NED
7/23/16

Ernestine Turmel
July 22nd 2016
"the most ridiculous and
loving cat I know"

Patches

Sometimes I wonder if you
forgive me for not being here
when you left
I'm sorry

Dramatis Personae:
Tamora,
Queen of the
Goths

"Cuteness"
—he's a good boy
really.

Cheechi

Mr. kitty - Shopping
October 2012

Riggins
a magical little
weirdo

This One did: Of boy
when we asked for the right
She had an half fright
hope she'll be in peace.
Mike 2012

Little
White Cat
2/14/11
He knows
when he knows

"Czech
me out".
-Faryska (in Zelená Skalice)
Czech Republic
7/31/2016

A home without a cat
is just a house

From the moment we eyes first
She taught me what real love is
in a very dark world
So often my only flat—
on her dap—and beyond

7/27/12

what's
up
for
naptime!

Bobo!
(aka = Beauty Face)

Sup.?
-Mica 2013

I Forgive Furrie are super nice.
Love
your boyfriend

Vinny, after
the surgery

21-31-51
stools.
This is Butter. She
poops on my chest and
pees.

In 3... 2... 1....

Ellie - Circa
2011
Before the 10 Months At Separation...
Before the feeding tube...
I'm just glad that you're still
here with me even with your poor
recovery weight gain.

Blaze
He made me rattle

S C R U F F I E
Misses
Gritty
Winkle

Mochilla
(aka Moch)
(aka 'Backpack')
in Spanish

A CIRCLE
ROUND
A STONE

PRODUCTION

COMING SOON . . .

THE

FAMILIAR

THE SEASON ONE FINALE

FALL 2017

Bendyl

the Boar

charged.

Though one against three wasn't exactly promising odds.

Not promising at all.

Bendyl lowered his tusks to the closest—

big as the other two combined.

One big gray wolf.

Bendyl against one big gray wolf was bad enough.

Plus the other two, Bendyl's charge won't even rate a long shot.

Not promising odds at all.

Not like Bendyl was trotting around figuring odds.

Though something related to possible outcomes did circulate through him, especially when his rump rubbed up against the hard bark, and his back hocks, refusing to retreat anymore, drove his hooves into the snowy piney ground.

It seemed only another now, gone if not gone at all,

        when Bendyl had spent
the warcoolingmoons
                with fall on the march
    rounding through
             a sounder of sows,
twenty or more,
        at least, taking on

any and all challengers.

             Plenty of challengers.

             Bring on your tusks.

             Slash and buck as you like.

Bendyl had dug in, and grunted and met every rival.

   Charge and cut.

       Charge again.

Bendyl had the shoulder scabs to prove it — sort of healed.

And a deeper one across his chest — not really healed.

But these wounds hardly matched those he'd inflicted upon others.
Young ones had backed off quickly enough,

trailing blood.
Older ones too.

One grand boar,

bigger and seasons older than the rest,

still could not get up by the time Bendyl

snorted and trotted off to rut.

And boy did Bendyl rut!

Bendyl felt now like he'd done nothing but rut.

Rut! Rut! Rut!

Ah fall!

Tusk!
Charge!
Slash!
And slice too!

Snort then.

Snort again.

Then rut!

Rut plenty!

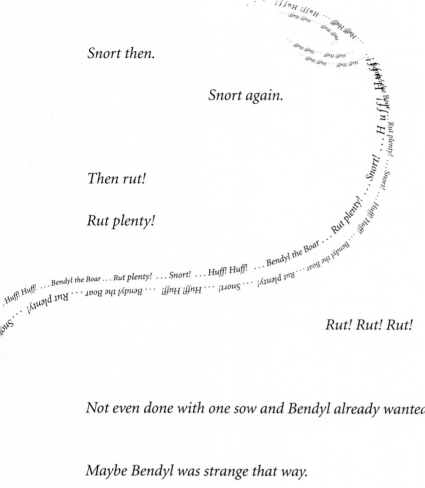

Rut! Rut! Rut!

Not even done with one sow and Bendyl already wanted more.

Maybe Bendyl was strange that way.

But he got more.

Boy, did he get more.

Nothing could stand in his way.

Young boars squealing and leaking away. Old ones laid out on the ground licking their blood away.

More and more sows coming around

to reward Bendyl's

tusklunging prowess.

Bendyl the Boar was never going to stop!

Why not all fall!

All winter too?

Suddenly every season seemed ripe for rutting.

Could now get any better?

Could now get any worse?

One moment
                    Bendyl was eating mushrooms,

small crunchy snails, another thing wiggly
                                        and wet with such
                    sweet scents . . .

And in the next moment
                            three wolves emerged from

        the icy mist with their bright yellow eyes

and terrible star-bright teeth.

Swirls of fear commanded Bendyl's first step back,

a wave of anger answered when he took his second step back,

especially since no amount of fear or anger could overwhelm

                                    the ache of losing

    such sweet scented wiggly things
                                    and earthwet roots

        of such crunchy satisfaction.

And so despite how bad this had just now gotten

     Bendyl still couldn't shake the memory of good

out of his head.

     Bendyl was strange that way.

     At least it made him madder.

     Which isn't that strange for a wild boar.

Madder is the sort of thing that makes

          odds like

one against three

      unimportant.

Even if three means

    three wolves

       with bright yellow eyes

and terrible star-bright teeth.

That's when something somewhere

that wasn't a thing at all

or had a where at all

told Bendyl to charge

the biggest.

Because the biggest was closest? Because the biggest would be easiest to strike? Because of the way the other eyes eyed the biggest?

Bendyl wasn't asking.

Hind legs just fired into the piney snowy ground and Bendyl the Boar charged, head lowered, tusks at the ready to sharpslash and splash.

It didn't matter if his opponent wasn't a boar.

Why not a wolf?

Or even a tiger?

Though a tiger

might have given Bendyl the Boar pause.

Fortunately, a wolf is never a tiger

and Bendyl the Boar didn't

pause but

he didn't sharpslash either

because the big gray wolf

was already dancing away like

a cloud of snowflakes,

and growling too, through

snapping teeth,

off to one side

which wasn't a good thing.

Bendyl tried to follow,

which wasn't a good thing either

because now the big tree

with its hard bark

was no longer standing guard behind him.

Now behind him was the second wolf.

Which would not do.

And the third wolf was at Bendyl's flank,

                                opposite the biggest wolf.

Which also would not do.

Backing away was no longer an option for Bendyl the Boar.

And if Bendyl now lurched forward,

                              they would snip open his

perineum and he'd bleed

                    badly enough to fall short of any long

sprint but not badly

                        enough to close his eyes while their

gnashclashing jaws

                  tore out his insides.

                  In short, Bendyl was fucked.

All he could do was turn with them,

                        try his best to keep up

with their turning clouds of biting

                      brights of teeth like snow-

flakes struck white with flame.

But boy were they fast.

In fact, it was the biggest who was quickest.

And no matter how much
                        Bendyl lunged and sharpslashed,
tusked and twisted,
                                twisted and slashed more,
they still got inside, got at him
                        and took away a nip.

At first, they snapped at only brindled bristles.

But they improved

                        and soon moved even faster

        and finally

                                they got in deeper.

Until these snapping whirls of gray
                                were taking away
salty bites of Bendyl.

                        And the blood in their mouths
made the yellow in their eyes
                        shine even brighter.

If Bendyl the Boar didn't answer soon with some of their blood

                                in his mouth too,
to shine slick his tusks bright,
                           his eyes would be wide wide
open,
        and boy would he grunt
                       and squeal then
while they gnashed for his gore
                   and dragged what's inside
outside onto the forest floor.

So Bendyl the Boar lunged again,
                     only this time when
the first wolf recoiled with a twist right,
                          which led
the second and the third wolf to also dance right,
                        Bendyl
didn't follow right,
               leaving the first wolf on his right,
the second wolf too,
               leaving the third wolf
    still to the left,
               but moving right, to catch up with one
and two,
        and so winding up right in front of Bendyl.

        The big wolf too.

Bendyl had no need for fear or anger then.
                       Nor was the flicker
of things lost around either except maybe
                       in the pure pleasure
of his hooves driving into the ground,

sending him forward,

        driving his slashing tusks

                into his flailing target.

The big wolf knew Bendyl had caught him off guard too.

Because of how he tried to wheel back on his rear paws.

Because of how he tried to spin away.

Because of how he would have gotten away
                        if he'd just had one
moment more, except there was no one
                 moment more
and the big wolf could do nothing
                but fall back leaving wide
open all Bendyl the Boar
            needed to triumph —

soft

and

unguarded

and

yielding,

a gray field of fur,

one big wolf belly,

ready for goring . . .

which Bendyl would have penetrated,
                              drove deep into,
too, while slashing upwards,
                      sticking that big wolf hard,
and maybe
                Bendyl's sharp sticking tips did in fact
nick some flesh,
                      they sure breezed through fur
at the very least,

but only the very least,
                      because when Bendyl should have felt
    secure and deep,
                          satisfyingly stuck,
when he should have already
                          been tasting warm spouts
of wolf blood flooding
                      around his snout and down
into his mouth,

            a sharp pain hooked Bendyl instead,

            and hooked him fast,

            yanking him way off course,

    even dragging him back.

The sharp pain was in his hock.

The sharp pain was in both hocks.

Sharp once and then gone to a tingle.

Gone too was the big wolf ahead.
                                        He'd twisted away,
            scrambled free.

Bendyl was forced to wheel around,
                              also twisting,
                                              scrambling,
to slash at the two wolves behind him,
                                    who had snapped
                  at his legs
                                to halt his charge,
drag him back.

But, boy, were they fast!

Faster than fast!

Until, finally, Bendyl the Boar just stood dazed in the center.

Panting now for a chance he wouldn't have again.

And the two wolves even let him pant.

Maybe because when the big wolf had fallen backwards and retreated a few steps,
            it was enough to hesitate these two
      hock-biters.

Enough to hesitate even Bendyl.

Not that Bendyl the Boar had other options.

Not that Bendyl the Boar was calculating options.

Panting was his only option.

If he was lucky.

But Bendyl the Boar wasn't lucky.

His rear hocks were more than tingling now.

Dripping was more like it.

Snout side, from Bendyl's jaws, saliva was also dripping.

Dripping.

What comes from panting.

What comes from bleeding.

Bendyl stomped once,
   shook his head,
     maybe twitched his ears
and then snorted too,
   though it came out more like a huff.

A sad, defeated huff.

But the big gray wolf still backed away.

So Bendyl the Boar stomped again and shook his head again.

...ng with spikes of black... *writhing with spikes of black...* *...re that tremendous wall of coming flame* *...long before that tremendous wall of...* *...writhing with spikes of black...* *spikes of black...* *...long before that tremendous wall of...* *Shadows no heavier than a thought...* *writhing with spikes of black...* *Pikes of black...*

And the big gray wolf backed away some more.

Maybe Bendyl had tusked more than fur.

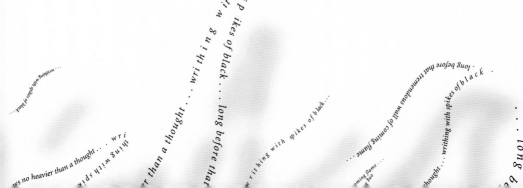

So Bendyl kept on stomping

and shaking his head
and huffing as hard as he could.

And not only did the big wolf back off,

so did the other two.

Bendyl the Boar huffed as hard as he could

and when he stomped
he stomped as hard as he could.

He even bucked a little!
He sure threw his head around.

Let them behold my mighty tusks!

Let them cower before me!

Well, the wolves didn't exactly cower but they did growl and
bare their teeth,

even as they continued to back away,

lowering
their bellies more and more to the ground.

Bendyl stopped huffing and stomping then.

He still tossed his head a little.

Gave them some glimmering of tusks.

...writhing with spikes of black...

...writhing with spikes of black...

...writhing with spikes of black...

...Shadows no heavier than a thought...

...long before that tremendous wall of coming flame...

...writhing with spikes of black...

...writhing with spikes of black...

...writhing with spikes of black...

...writhing with spikes of...

...Shadows no heavier than a thought...

...writhing with spikes of black...

...flame...

...long before that tremendous wall of coming flame...

...tremendous wall of coming flame...

...Shadows no heavier than a thought...

...before that tremendous wall of coming...

...coming flame...

...writhing with spikes of...

...coming flame...

He didn't need to do more.

The wolves really were retreating now.

And how!

Ha!

Fast!

Ha! Ha!

Uh-oh.

Too fast.

Bendyl's ears twitched.
  And then along his spine,
    from his rump,
  all the way up to
    that place between his ears,
      bunch
    by
      bunch,
        every bristle on his back
  began to
        stand.

writhing with spikes of black...

...ws no heavier than a thought...

long before that tremendous wall of coming flame...

Shadows no heavier than a thought...

long before that tremendous wall of coming flame...

Behind him,

Bendyl the Boar heard the soft thump of

earth released from a terrible weight.

And in the silence that followed, a shadow fell over him.

It was cold and complete.

And if Bendyl the Boar would have looked up, he would have seen the sky devoured.

He would have seen what no sky should ever mean.

But Bendyl the Boar didn't look up.

Shadows no heavier than a thought... writhing with spikes of black... long before that tremendous wall of coming flame...

The shadow
still crushed down on him,
though it was no heavier
than a thought,
though it would
have crushed him into nothing
if it had lasted more than
a thought.

The shadow didn't outlast even the beginnings of a thought.

Instead it floated over Bendyl,

and when it landed

in front of him, the wolves

were long gone, replaced

by a wall of tremendous fire

writhing with spikes of black.

Bendyl the Boar needed no scent for his hind legs — in fact all of his legs at once — to drive him back, as fast as they could.

Though now that Bendyl was downwind, the scent did catch up.

And the taste of it clogged his snout,

coated his throat,

racing Bendyl the Boar's heart

to run,

to hide,

screaming

fear! fear! fear!,

especially before the sound that this living blaze released next,

not only banishing forever the wolves

and whatever birds

fluttered above,

but filling Bendyl's joints and guts with

thunder.

Bendyl shook.

Bendyl gasped.

Bendyl shat himself.

Were it not for his chewed-on hocks,
Bendyl would have already
turned and ran.

Instead it was the wall of fire
that turned,

cabled in smoke and char,

wrapping

around itself to reveal those

blazing eyes.

Shadows no heavier than a thought . . . writhing with spikes of black . . . long before that tremendous wall of coming flame . . .

How furiously too they blazed.

How curiously too they blazed.

How furiously and curiously they considered Bendyl the Boar.

Ancient above whiskers of cloud above teeth like mountaintops.

For the second time that
afternoon, Bendyl stood motionless
and dazed. Though this
time, he was unable to pant,
let alone stomp, let alone huff.

And forget twitching an ear,

Bendyl couldn't even breathe.

                              What good even is breathing

before such a creature

              of fire and air?

                              And then once again

the earth was free of this terrible weight.

Though this time there was no shadow to hide the sight.

This time Bendyl watched his sky devoured.

This time,

    when silence fell,

        Bendyl beheld what else silence tells.

Fortunately for Bendyl the Boar,

the earth had more to tell too.

So that when the fiery shadow

landed before Bendyl, the ground

                              cracked in protest and

swallowed up the Siberian tiger.